2 5 AUG 2022

GW01561032

Please return this book on or before the date shown above. To renew go to www.essex.gov.uk/libraries, ring 0845 603 7628 or go to any Essex library.

Essex County Council

DS12 4005

30130505033101

DO YOU WANT TO SAVE THE CHANGES
BEFORE CLOSING?

SAVE CHANGES

A FACTUAL BASED FICTIONAL HISTORY

A NOVEL BY
LIAM J MADDEN
VOLUME ONE OF THE GYRO CHRONICLES

BASED ON THE RADIO PLAY
MR. BITTRE AND
THE DINER HOLISTIC

WRITTEN & DIRECTED BY
LIAM J MADDEN

BROADCAST IN SPAIN AUGUST 2002
PRODUCED BY
BRITT JOHANNES

authorHOUSE®

AuthorHouse™ UK Ltd.
500 Avebury Boulevard
Central Milton Keynes, MK9 2BE
www.authorhouse.co.uk
Phone: 08001974150

© 2010 Liam Joseph Madden. All rights reserved.

No part of this book may be reproduced, stored in a retrieval system, or transmitted by any means without the written permission of the author.

First published by AuthorHouse 5/10/2010

ISBN: 978-1-4520-1688-7 (sc)

All characters in this publication are fictitious and any resemblance to real persons, living or dead, is purely coincidental.

This book is printed on acid-free paper.

THE FUTURE IS MERELY A CASE
OF REMEMBERING

SAVE CHANGES

A FACTUAL BASED FICTIONAL HISTORY

A NOVEL BY
LIAM J MADDEN
VOLUME ONE OF THE GYRO CHRONICLES

BASED ON THE RADIO PLAY
MR. BITTRE AND
THE DINER HOLISTIC

WRITTEN & DIRECTED BY
LIAM J MADDEN

BROADCAST IN SPAIN AUGUST 2002
PRODUCED BY
BRITT JOHANNES

DEDICATED TO
NOREEN GALLAGHER
AND THE PEOPLE OF IRELAND

"Alelluah..."

*"...and Enya Angel for arriving just
as quickly as some people depart."*

Also dedicated to William and Molly for keeping life on the sunny side

Each time I listened to a patient, their life reminded me of one of the millions of lights in a vast sky that flares up for a brief moment only to disappear into the endless night. The lessons each individual taught us boiled down to the same message

Live so that you don't look back and regret that you've wasted your life

Live so that you don't regret the things that you've done or wish that you had acted differently

Live life honestly and full

Live

THE WHEEL OF LIFE
DR. ELISABETH KUBLER ROSS MD

CONTENTMENT

BOOK I - MORNING / UNCERTAINTY
CHECK-IN
YOU MUST WAKE UP/FRIDAY 7 SEPTEMBER 2001
THE HAIRSTYLE OF THE DEVIL/FRIDAY 7 SEPTEMBER 2001
THE HACKNEY GUIDE TO LIVING AND DYING/SATURDAY 8 SEPTEMBER 2001
VISITING TIME IS OVER/SUNDAY 9 SEPTEMBER 2001
SPIRITS IN THE MATERIAL WORLD/MONDAY 10 SEPTEMBER 2001
THE PLANET OF SOUND/TUESDAY 11 SEPTEMBER 2001
WHEN WILL I GROW OLD GRACEFULLY?/FRIDAY 7 SEPTEMBER 2001

BOOK II - AFTERNOON / SEPERATE ENTITIES
PASSPORT CONTROL
ORIGINAL MOTION PICTURE SOUNDTRACK/FRIDAY 7 SEPTEMBER 2001
NO ALARMS AND NO SURPRISES PLEASE/FRIDAY 7 SEPTEMBER 2001
SIMPLY EVERYONE IS ON COCAINE/FRIDAY 7 SEPTEMBER 2001
THE GENETICALLY CLONED SON OF GEORGE LUCAS/FRIDAY 7 SEPTEMBER 2001
STOP BY THE ULTRA-LOUNGE/SATURDAY 8 SEPTEMBER 2001
I LOVE EVERYBODY ESPECIALLY YOU/SUNDAY 9 SEPTEMBER 2001
CALLING OCCUPANTS OF INTERPLANETARY CRAFT/MONDAY 10 SEPTEMBER 2001
WHATEVER HAPPENED TO REAL LIFE?/TUESDAY 11 SEPTEMBER 2001
ANOTHER LOST WEEKEND/FRIDAY 7 SEPTEMBER 2001

BOOK III - EVENING / SINGULARITY
DEPARTURES
EXPLORING THE DEPTHS OF SPACE/FRIDAY 7 SEPTEMBER 2001
WELCOME TO THE OCCUPATION/FRIDAY 7 SEPTEMBER 2001
THAT WAS THE RIVER AND THIS IS THE SEA/FRIDAY 7 SEPTEMBER 2001
SAME TIME LATER LAST NIGHT/FRIDAY 7 SEPTEMBER 2001
THE LAST DAY OF OUR ACQUAINTANCE/SATURDAY 8 SEPTEMBER 2001
THE NEW FRONTIER/SUNDAY 9 SEPTEMBER 2001
FANFARE FOR THE COMMON MAN /MONDAY 10 SEPTEMBER 2001
A CHURCH NOT MADE BY HANDS/TUESDAY 11 SEPTEMBER 2001
THE REVOLUTION WILL NOT BE TELEVISED/TUESDAY 11 SEPTEMBER 2001
THE TEETH OF GLEN MILLER /FRIDAY 7 SEPTEMBER 2001

BOOK V - NIGHTS / CONSTANTS
DUTY FREE
DRUGS WON'T CHANGE YOU RELIGION WON'T CHANGE YOU/FRIDAY 7 SEPTEMBER 2001
THIS IS A PERSON TO PERSON MESSAGE/SATURDAY 8 SEPTEMBER 2001
AT HOME WITH RAY CONNIF/SATURDAY 8 SEPTEMBER 2001
THE PATH OF LEAST RESISTANCE/SUNDAY 9 SEPTEMBER 2001
THE DISTANCES OF THE STARS/MONDAY 10 SEPTEMBER 2001
BELIEVING THE STRANGEST THINGS LOVING THE ALIEN/TUESDAY 11 SEPTEMBER
I WAS LOOKING HANDSOME SHE WAS LOOKING LIKE AN EROTIC VULTURE/FRIDAY 7 SEPTEMBER 2001
NEVER UNDERESTIMATE THE IGNORANCE OF THE RICH/FRIDAY 7 SEPTEMBER
DEAD DADDY BADGER/FRIDAY 7 SEPTEMBER 2001
YOU KEEP COMING BACK UNTIL YOU GET IT RIGHT/FRIDAY 7 SEPTEMBER 2001
I CAN FEEL ONE OF MY TURNS COMING ON/SATURDAY 8 SEPTEMBER 2001
DON'T YOU POINT THAT RAY-GUN AT ME/SUNDAY 9 SEPTEMBER 2001
ANOTHER GREEN WORLD/MONDAY 10 SEPTEMBER 2001
TROMPE LE MONDE/TUESDAY 11 SEPTEMBER 2001
OUT OF MY MIND ON DOPE AND SPEED/FRIDAY 7 SEPTEMBER 2001

CUSTOMS
THINKING ABOUT SEX AGAIN/FRIDAY 7 SEPTEMBER 2001
ARTISTS ONLY/FRIDAY 7 SEPTEMBER 2001
HOW CAN THE ANGELS GET TO SLEEP WHEN THE DEVIL LEAVES THE PORCHLIGHT ON?
/FRIDAY 7 SEPTEMBER 2001

BOOK VI - TWILIGHT / PROBABILITY
ARRIVALS
FEELING YOURSELF DISENTIGRATE/SATURDAY 8 SEPTEMBER 2001
THE OTHER SIDE OF MIDNIGHT/SUNDAY 9 SEPTEMBER 2001
SCISSORS CUT PAPER BUT PAPER WRAPS ROCK/MONDAY 10 SEPTEMBER 2001
TOMORROW WILL BE LIKE TODAY/MONDAY 10 SEPTEMBER 2001
LISTEN TO THE VOICE OF BUDDHA/TUESDAY 11 SEPTEMBER 2001
SEND IN THE CLONES/TUESDAY 11 SEPTEMBER 2001
A BIG HAND FOR THE TIME DISCIPLES/WEDNESDAY 12 SEPTEMBER 2001
SIX GNOSSIENNES: No. 2 AVEC ETONNEMENT/FRIDAY 7 SEPTEMBER 2001
GODS PROVIDENCE/FRIDAY 7 SEPTEMBER 2001
MOVING THE RIVER/FRIDAY 7 SEPTEMBER 2001

BOOK VII - BEGINNINGS / DAWN
CHECK-IN
THE ROUGH DANCER & THE CYCLICAL NIGHT TANGO APASIONADO/
FRIDAY 7 SEPTEMBER 2001
THE SIZE OF THE UNIVERSE/SATURDAY 8 SEPTEMBER 2001
EINSTEIN A GO-GO/SUNDAY 9 SEPTEMBER 2001
THE LOVE FOR THREE ORANGES/MONDAY 10 SEPTEMBER 2001
WISH YOU WERE HERE/FRIDAY 7 SEPTEMBER 2001
YOU MUST WAKE UP/FRIDAY 7 SEPTEMBER 2001

Contents

CHECK-IN 1

BOOK I
MORNING / UNCERTAINTY

FRIDAY 7TH SEPTEMBER 2001 MORNING / CARISBROOKE
YOU MUST WAKE UP 4

FRIDAY 7TH SEPTEMBER 2001 MORNING / HACKNEY
THE HAIRSTYLE OF THE DEVIL 10

SATURDAY 8TH SEPTEMBER 2001 MORNING / HACKNEY
THE HACKNEY GUIDE TO LIVING AND DYING 22

SUNDAY 9TH SEPTEMBER 2001 MORNING / BRICK LANE
VISITING TIME IS OVER 29

MONDAY 10TH 1933 SEPTEMBER MORNING / TIME POCKET
SPIRITS IN THE MATERIAL WORLD 34

TUESDAY 11TH 2001 SEPTEMBER MORNING / HACKNEY
THE PLANET OF SOUND 37

FRIDAY 7TH SEPTEMBER 2001 AFTERNOON / SYDNEY
WHEN WILL I GROW OLD GRACEFULLY? 45

BOOK II
AFTERNOON / SEPERATE ENTITIES

PASSPORT CONTROL 54

FRIDAY 7TH SEPTEMBER 2001 AFTERNOON / ISLE OF WIGHT
ORIGINAL MOTION PICTURE SOUNDTRACK 56

FRIDAY 7TH SEPTEMBER 2001 MORNING / THE EAST END
NO ALARMS AND NO SURPRISES PLEASE 61

FRIDAY 7TH SEPTEMBER 2001 NIGHT / HACKNEY
SIMPLY EVERYONE IS ON COCAINE.................................64

FRIDAY 7TH SEPTEMBER 2001 EVENING / SPACE
THE GENETICALLY CLONED SON OF GEORGE LUCAS 68

SATURDAY 8th SEPTEMBER 2001 MORNING / HACKNEY
STOP BY THE ULTRA-LOUNGE 73

SUNDAY 9TH SEPTEMBER 2001 AFTERNOON / HACKNEY
I LOVE EVERYBODY ESPECIALLY YOU 82

MONDAY 10TH SEPTEMBER 2001 PROBABILITY / FIFTY-FIVE CANCRI
CALLING OCCUPANTS OF INTERPLANETARY CRAFT.88

TUESDAY 11TH 2001 SEPTEMBER MORNING / BIG NEW YORKER
WHATEVER HAPPENED TO REAL LIFE?.........................96

FRIDAY 7TH SEPTEMBER 2001 / 2002 TIME / FLIGHT 815Y
MUSIC IS JUST ORGANISED NOISE 101

BOOK III
EVENING / SINGULARITY

DEPARTURES 110

FRIDAY 7TH SEPTEMBER 2001 PROBABILITY / SPACE
EXPLORING THE DEPTHS OF SPACE............................. 113

FRIDAY 7TH SEPTEMBER 2001 AFTERNOON / THE WEST END
WELCOME TO THE OCCUPATION................................. 116

FRIDAY 7TH SEPTEMBER 2001 MORNING / HAMMERSMITH
THAT WAS THE RIVER AND THIS IS THE SEA.............. 124

FRIDAY 7TH SEPTEMBER 2001 NIGHT / HACKNEY
SCARY MONSTERS AND SUPER CREEPS 131

FRIDAY 7TH SEPTEMBER 2001 EVENING / SHEPHERDS BUSH
SAME TIME LATER LAST NIGHT 135

SATURDAY 8TH SEPTEMBER 2001 MORNING / SOHO
THE LAST DAY OF OUR ACQUAINTANCE 144

SUNDAY 9TH SEPTEMBER 2001 NIGHT / HACKNEY
THE NEW FRONTIER 150

MONDAY 10TH SEPTEMBER 2001 TIME / LONDON
FANFARE FOR THE COMMON MAN 155

TUESDAY 11TH SEPTEMBER 2001 MORNING / BIG NEW YORKER
A CHURCH NOT MADE BY HANDS 162

TUESDAY 11TH SEPTEMBER 2001 MORNING / JFK AIRPORT
THE REVOLUTION WILL NOT BE TELEVISED 165

FRIDAY 7TH SEPTEMBER 2001 TIME / THE PHILIPINES
THE TEETH OF GLEN MILLER 173

BOOK V
EVENING / CONSTANTS

DUTY FREE 178

FRIDAY 7TH SEPTEMBER 2001 AFTERNOON / HACKNEY
DRUGS WON'T CHANGE YOURELIGION WON'T CHANGE YOU 183

SATURDAY 8TH SEPTEMBER 2001 AFTERNOON / THE RITZ
THIS IS A PERSON TO PERSON MESSAGE 189

SATURDAY 8TH SEPTEMBER 2001 NIGHT / GERMANY
AT HOME WITH RAY CONNIF 193

SUNDAY 9TH SEPTEMBER 2001 EVENING / THE FIFTH DIMENSION
THE PATH OF LEAST RESISTANCE 197

MONDAY 10TH SEPTEMBER 2001 EVENING / NEWTOWN
THE DISTANCES OF THE STARS 203

TUESDAY 11TH SEPTEMBER 2001 AFTERNOON / MANHATTAN
BELIEVING THE STRANGEST THINGSLOVING THE ALIEN 218

FRIDAY 7TH SEPTEMBER 2001 TIME / HOLLAND
ANOTHER LOST WEEKEND 225

BOOK IV
NIGHT / SIMULATIONS

CUSTOMS 232

FRIDAY 7th SEPTEMBER 2001 MORNING / SOHO
I WAS LOOKING HANDSOMESHE WAS LOOKING LIKE AN EROTIC VULTURE 235

FRIDAY 7TH SEPTEMBER 2001 AFTERNOON / BRISTOL
THE ECSTASYOF DANCING FLEAS 243

FRIDAY 7TH SEPTEMBER 2001 NIGHT / THE FIFTH DIMENSION
DEAD DADDY BADGER 250

SATURDAY 8TH 2001 SEPTEMBER MORNING / THE MORGUE
I CAN FEEL ONE OF MY TURNS COMING ON 254

SUNDAY 9TH SEPTEMBER 2001 TIME / SPACE
DON'T YOU POINT THAT RAY-GUN AT ME 260

MONDAY 10TH SEPTEMBER 2001 NIGHT // NEWTOWN
ANOTHER GREEN WORLD 266

TUESDAY 11TH SEPTEMBER 2001 NIGHT / BRIXTON
TROMPE LE MONDE 272

FRIDAY 7TH SEPTEMBER 2002 EVENING / AMSTERDAM
OUT OF MY MIND ON DOPE AND SPEED 277

BOOK VI
TWILGHT / PROBABILITY

ARRIVALS 284

FRIDAY 7TH SEPTEMBER 2001 NIGHT / THE EAST END
THINKING ABOUT SEX AGAIN 286

FRIDAY 7TH SEPTEMBER 2001 TIME-TRAVEL / HACKNEY
ARTISTS ONLY 293

FRIDAY 7TH SEPTEMBER 2001 NIGHT / AMSTERDAM
HOW CAN THE ANGELS GET TO SLEEP WHEN THE DEVIL LEAVES THE PORCH LIGHT ON? 297

SATURDAY 8TH SEPTEMBER 2001 AFTERNOON / HOLBORN
FEELING YOURSELF DISENTIGRATE 306

SUNDAY 9TH SEPTEMBER 2001 AFTERNOON / ANTARTICA
THE OTHER SIDE OF MIDNIGHT 309

MONDAY 10TH SEPTEMBER 2001 NIGHT / NEWTOWN
SCISSORS CUT PAPER BUT PAPER WRAPS ROCK 312

FRIDAY 7TH SEPTEMBER 2001 TIME / AMSTERDAM
YOU KEEP COMING BACK UNTIL YOU GET IT RIGHT 321

MONDAY 10TH SEPTEMBER 2001 PROBABILITY / THE GARDEN
TOMORROW WILL BE LIKE TODAY 326

TUESDAY 11TH SEPTEMBER 2001 NIGHT / SOHO
LISTEN TO THE VOICE OF BUDDHA 331

TUESDAY 11TH SEPTEMBER 2001 EVENING / NOTTING HILL
SEND IN THE CLONES 335

WEDNESDAY 12TH SEPTEMBER 2001 PROBABILITY / IRELAND
A BIG HAND FOR THE TIME DISCIPLES 342

FRIDAY 7TH SEPTEMBER 2001 AFTERNOON / AMSTERDAM
SIX GNOSSIENNES: No.2 AVEC ETONNEMENT............ 350

BOOK VII
BEGINNINGS / DAWN

CHECK-IN.. 360

FRIDAY 7TH SEPTEMBER 2001 PROBABILITY / NEWPORT
GODS PROVIDENCE.. 362

FRIDAY 7TH SEPTEMBER 2001 PROBABILITY / TIBET
MOVING THE RIVER... 367

FRIDAY 7TH SEPTEMBER 2001 EVENING / TIME POCKET
**THE ROUGH DANCER & THE CYCLICAL NIGHT
TANGO APASIONADO**... 373

SATURDAY 8TH SEPTEMBER 2001 NIGHT / THE
WAREHOUSE
THE SIZE OF THE UNIVERSE... 381

SUNDAY 9TH SEPTEMBER 1933 PROBABILITY / TIME
POCKET
EINSTEIN A GO-GO... 384

MONDAY 10TH SEPTEMBER 2001 PROBABILITY / THE
HOUSE
THE LOVE FOR THREE ORANGES................................ 387

FRIDAY 7TH SEPTEMBER 2001 PROBABILITY / FIFTY-FIVE
CANCRI
WISH YOU WERE HERE.. 393

BOOK VII
YOU MUST WAKE UP...

FRIDAY 7TH SEPTEMBER 2001 PROBABILITY / CARISBROOKE
YOU MUST WAKE UP... 396

EMPEROR PENGUIN/1832... 402

PENGUIN BISCUITS/1960	403
KING PENGUIN/1833	404
ACKNOWLEDGEMENTS	405
CHAPTER TITLE / BAND	411
CHAPTER SUBTITLES / ARTISTS / TITLE / TRACK	412
NOBEL PEACE PRIZE ACCEPTANCE SPEECH	414
FROM THE AUTHOR	417

CHECK-IN

THE TICKLE OF leaf dancing on leave wisped out on a treacle of wind. And belief oh belief was an itching was a scratching and a creaking, all of a car door all of a Bohr on the car park linoleum floor of a crusty Americana Diner in Paradise a fifties style getting of age town near Chico California. Had ran the feelers out for the bitter mystery. Under fedora ran red and skin cell flaky. Plaque of nine ran the molars front and back. Glove red hands were the cane.

Rancid and puking his gut into the hedgerow announced the arrival of Mr. Bittre. Magnanimous and scare of large well capable and terror oh terror. Reborn again and a million light years from home. Cross of Quanti had nailed over meteor and dust-wusty. For all who looked with eye of Schodinger hard to believe he had a huge want to get off. A growing kidney of a need to leave and return to where his howling fitted snug and cosy around his shoulders and under his arms like a new born babe. Pack of case and of exchange. Mr. Bittre avec eyes and cranium of confusion had mission details to vexxen. Gee and gibbly Albert of white strands.

Mr. Bittre and horror gut evolved upward from the bush of leaves and sick. Burped out his arrival of truth on a carcass. Dabbed a hanky on the corner of mouth and chin drip and focused his little jiggy eyeballs at the neon across the way and vivied. The Diner Holistic read the hot sign of majestico magnifico. Buzzing and clicking with large vibe across the way from his car park distant relationship. Hawking ware zone. Lecker lecker thoughts sprang eternal. Woozy woo-woo and drippy fat fries dribbled down shirt. Once again the burps came flying out of his mouth and blended with the cool night particles everything with everything onward. Good cause to and inspired.

Mr. Bittre gogged up the long pole of metallic and travelled by iris and pupil toward the nighty-night sky. Signeo of majestico clunked with revolution of the time and televised backward. There will be flies of hope and lemons of love within, thought Mr. Bittre. Sewn-up fifties suit of the poorest boroughs bearable and black pinstriped and tight fitting. Textile of pin and houndstooth check of board came in the tie stylie. A not-too-shabby perspective on the humpety-hump night, with jewels and crystals of cotton and string to the sun keeping his intestines corseted. The incandescant play ball of gas bounced on beach of Compton alas and alive-oh. The longitude and latitude of plates of Mr. Bittre. Detestable plates of meet rocking on this pimple far from Sun. Looked around before entrance of grandness to the Diner of Holistic and mucho capery. Pondered oh so briefly on what the flippered one were to deal this time. Last reality but twice ballsed-up had he due to slight error of death and big metal smash. Time to sally. Time to Life and chokie-smokie. To hence forth and make it so. Through ripping and tearing. Gosh and gibbly.

Barked off to one side a last slice of vomit and with cane in fist glove of hand and red glove at that. Mr Bittre focused on the buzz and click Tesla reality of the neon 'D'. This time we egg ourselves on tongue and bread ourselves in mouth Mr. Bittre giggled to himself inward under his hat. Physics of feet on forward and march into reality. Across the car park marching drums sounded. The gospel choirs who sang joyous bumble. Mr. Bittre serpentined towards the front entrance of The Diner Holistic and all it stood for.

BOOK I
MORNING / UNCERTAINTY

WERNER HEISENBERG / 1901-1976
NOBEL PRIZE WINNER 1932

A Physicist born in Würzburg Germany on 5 December, Karl Werner Heisenberg became famous for studying the principles of the observer and the observed and developed this theory into a paper published in the year 1925 when he was only twenty-six years of age. Entitled the Uncertainty Principle. The title refers to the phenomenon of Uncertainty with regard to the position and momentum of a particle. **Karl showed that it was in effect impossible to know both momentum and location or energy and time to the same accuracy.**

The act of observation
affects that
which is being observed

Whenever, we analyse the location (momentum) of a particle we are in effect, altering it enough to disturb the accuracy of readings of its momentum (position). This is rather a unique situation, as it affects the accuracy of every measurement ever recorded to a certain extent.

In 1932 Heisenberg wrote a three part paper which describes the modern picture of the nucleus of an atom. He treated the structure of the various nuclear components discussing their binding energies and their stability. In 1937 Werner Heisenberg married Elisabeth Schumacher. They were married on 29 April 1937. He worked with Otto Hahn, one of the discoverers of nuclear fission, on the development of a nuclear reactor but failed to develop an effective program for nuclear weapons. He Died on 1st February 1976 in Munich, Germany.

FRIDAY 7TH SEPTEMBER 2001
MORNING / CARISBROOKE

YOU MUST WAKE UP

*I'm not aware of too many things
I know what I know if you know what I mean...*
EDIE BRICKELL

FLASHING PETROL BLUE digital numbers on black blinked on and off. Illuminating the lounge with a pale glow in the moderate semi-detached house in Carisbrooke. The video recorder had been unsettled since it had arrived in the house of the Grey family the previous week. Now it continued to flash a luminous pale blue light similar to an SOS signal across the green carpet, through tropical fish-tank and reflected off the school day colour photographs of the children pictured smiling on the lounge wall above the sofa. From the seventies era of love and hippies colour sounded out loudly with flares and braces.

The various portraits caught the light of the VCR and shone it back onto the face of snoring slumber that was Static. The sceptical face of youth that belonged to the Grey family. Photographs on the walls throughout the house on Kitbridge Road showed that his age in the Grey tree of life had transformed little over the years leaving some people wondering as to how old or young he really had been. The light caused Static to blink himself awake on the family sofa, disorientated. He found his body of astral returning and from the flashing of the digits on the video recorder at two o'clock in the morning on a warm night in September, also found that his physical body had somehow changed position during sleep until he was lying upside down on the couch fully clothed. He blinked again already searching the room for some clue as to his whereabouts on the planet and then stared with glazed eyes back at the VCR, head filled with much grogginess.

Information plodded a path to the brain but had been slow and learned and suggested he could be in a version of cartoon Australia. Everything in the room had appeared upside down. He gradually steered his blinking around the room in the dark and focused a glimpse at the walls of the interior. Sepia and pearl and naive seventies colours ricocheted through his eyeballs and onto his cranium. Then projected the correct way around. The words of brother, Mother, Father, sisters, family, forced their way into his mind and slowly he remembered. Static the Designer was back in Carisbrooke, on the Isle of Wight at the house of his parents.

As Static reached up to touch his mouth he could feel warm drool on his face. He wondered quietly to himself if this had been one of the reasons that humans had to drink so much water everyday simply because a lot of it spilled out of their bodies. Why most of it came out of his mouth at night leaving him dehydrated had to be a mystery as far as Static had been concerned and the Designer loved mysteries.

Sat upright on the cushions of the dark red couch in the lounge, Static began to recall almost everything that had happened before he had fallen asleep. He had been watching Eraserhead again. The dim electric light from the television informed the Designer that the film had since finished.

The film had been a splendid piece of opera scaled-down cinema on DVD. Static could only watch the black and white movie if he recorded it onto video-tape due to the lack of technology at the house of his parents. The video recorder had been *'Lynched'* his Mother had joked as it sat under the television set and refused to play any movies with the exception of the finest film maker in America. After Static had applied his limited knowledge of video repairs to the consumer durable no other videos seemed to be accepted. While his parents were away visiting friends in Lymington, Static had four weeks in which to repair the machine before his parents returned.

He recalled how he thought that he had fixed the problem until attempts to play any other movies other than Eraserhead had failed miserably. Static finally submitted. The machine had at this point decided to lock onto the film and refused to let go. Maybe the machine loved the film as much as Static did. What happened next had been a blur as Static had been hypnotised gently by the flashing of the digits on the video recorder and found himself falling asleep in front of the television screen. The curtains were still drawn in the lounge and Static realised that four hours had gone by since then. That had been over four hours ago.

In the dark interior of the room Static groped around on the carpet as he lay inert on the couch, until he finally discovered the remote control under the cushions. He pointed the gadget in the direction of the television set and pressed every button in an attempt to learn if the machine had been still working. The petrol-blue tints of electronic life continued to flash the time of zero hours back pulsing as the VCR lit the room like a strobe light. The sudden sight of London on the television blasted away any queries that Static might have had about which country he was currently in. The Designer adjusted the volume and wondered to himself just how much cocaine the presenters of Morning Television had taken to be so unnervingly perky at this time of the day. Suddenly colour images of London appeared on the screen interspersed with adverts for the new English Mini. A stark contrast to the classic black and white of the movie he had been watching earlier.

Static pondered briefly on watching the Lynch masterpiece again but felt somehow that in ten years time another viewing would be better received. His dream however had been pretty darn strange, he attempted to recall the images that swam up across his memory in random order. The words A NEW BEGINNING appeared in white type on a deep black background. Static had studied graphic design at art college for two years and now loved knowing the names of fonts in this way, it helped.

One scene in the dream revealed that he had been viewing the world as seen from the point of view as a baby in a cradle. The carrier had been left placed in a hotel lobby made entirely from dark maple wood. A series of qualm faces passed in front of him. He had been puzzled by the sudden appearance of one of them, a beautiful woman wearing an orange scarf wrapped tightly around her head. Her clothes suggested to Static that she had travelled from somewhere such as Cuba or South America. The rest of the faces merged into a blur simply because there were so many of them. The smile of his brother Shark seemed to have a filter of silent era black and white about it, crackling as if he had been forced through an old projector. Light music drifted from a mysterious source and lifted his whole body upward. Then Static had heard a soft and gentle German accent through the darkness announce with a slight cough. *"Oh and please be sure to remember your mission details this time Mr. Static, lovely to see you again. This is the twenty-third time however we've had to remind you. Seventy-seven more and you're due for a beautiful accident... Ciao bello!"*

Nothing much seemed to follow that last part and Static found himself uncertain and crash landing onto the carpet upside down. Mission details. Head in hand the designer recalled the voice in his head quite clearly. It had sounded so calm and relaxed. Outside the interior of the house on Kitbridge Road the North Atlantic Ocean continued its heavy descent from the sky downward onto the country roads and green fields across the island. Small floods were already beginning five miles away in the secluded village of Shorwell where Tony Webb lived with his daughter Ely. Most of the time the Isle of Wight was a serene place. Calmness and tranquillity were good friends. More recently the weather had become so bad in the south of England that Static had been stuck indoors with only Copper his dog and a film-script for company which the designer had finally finished recently and posted off to a company named Big New Yorker in London. In Soho an old confidant from school on the island had been employed as an assistant to a well known advertising executive.

However, from the whines scrapping and barking on the other side of the kitchen door, even Copper his brown and white Springer Spaniel sounded restless. Static looked over towards the kitchen where the Springer Spaniel had been sleeping waiting behind locked door to leap and pounce all over the house like Tiger from Winnie the Pooh. Then the islander remembered something. The German voice that had spoken in the dream had said something about a mission. Static Grey looked down at his watch and checked the time. Although the watch read nine o'clock, the sky was still pouring it down outside. It would be almost impossible to consider the journey he had to make later today without coffee. He decided to manouvre over towards the kitchen.

As Static stood up he recalled that he had promised a friend in London that he would perform as DJ at a party in some place called Hackney. He still had the music collection upstairs of his altar ego Gyro and had been wondering lately where his old friend had gotten to. A year spent travelling in Australia for Gyro was nearly up. The last thing Static needed was to drive up to London just as his comrade in music turned up on the doorstep from journeying around the world. Static had arranged a date to meet his ally at the airport and after stretching his various limbs he decided to check with the calendar.

As Static swung the door to the kitchen open the brown and white coated Springer Spaniel almost knocked him over with one swift leap of affection.

Copper then proceeded to clear a path around the lounge by bouncing and launching himself from every incalculable point until his body returned to his owner wagging with a medium unresolved wobble. His tongue hanging halfway out of his mouth.

Static half-expected for a moment that the body of Copper would explode with happiness at seeing his owner. He imagined the head and tail of the animal shooting in opposite directions. Apparently most Springer Spaniels were like this and the thought of a family of them all leaping around the house had been something that Static longed to see.

After the graphic designer had battled into the kitchen amidst the four-legged chaos and poured the dog food into the metal bowl Static cast a doubtful eye over the calendar above the washing machine and blinked twice hazily at what he had written there twelve months previously: COPPER TO NEIGHBOURS FOR 3 DAYS: WAREHOUSE PARTY! Then underneath in bright orange pen had been written GYRO RETURNS AT 8AM.

The designer looked down at his watch and quickly synchronised his watch with that on the wall. Sudden panic flooded through him. His watch had stopped and he was three hours out compared to the time on the clock. It had actually been twelve o'clock. No wonder the dog had been going spare while Copper merrily tucked into his late breakfast. Static quickly ran upstairs and grabbed the boxes of compact discs and tapes belonging to Gyro and brought them down the winding staircase into the dining room. He still had an hour or two to get to the ferry in Cowes and at least a couple of hours to drive up to London in his new green Mini.

Static checked the answer machine and froze standing still in the long hallway when he heard an unknown voice. The sound of loud music blasted ambivalently from the small plastic speaker, then a distant voice could be heard shouting *'Friday 7th September 2002. One Sigdon Passage. Warehouse. Hackney. London. Tonight. Nine. Party of the century. Be there!'* He speculated to himself as to whom it could have been. There seemed to be no message from Gyro however. Which was highly unlike his friend. The other half of the performing duo was often drunk or stoned but always managed to be punctual. Static figured that Gyro must still have been travelling from Australia somewhere. The designer rushed back upstairs and dressed in the only black suit that he had. Something about London made Static always feel as if he should wear a suit. He went and found the lead for the dog in the kitchen. Now for the arduous task of taking Copper to the neighbours across the road. Static quickly grabbed a travel alarm clock from the bedroom and then checked that everything electrical or electronic in the house had been switched off. He picked up the car keys and the house keys and then walked out in the cold September sunlight and began loading the black suitcases full of compact discs into the Mini outside on the driveway.

One hour after initially waking up, Static had begun to move with the speed and purpose of a man on a serious assignment. He often thought that music had always been one of the best things about life. He would have probably been unsure as to the reason it was so important on this planet called Earth to get people to hear good music and dance to it. He sometimes felt as if this had almost been his mission in life.

The theory had been demonstrated to Static many times just how not having good music at a party would quickly affect all the energy in the room to move in a precise direction out the door. Yet as he took Copper across to the opposite house of the neighbours to drop him off, even the tall friendly Irishman Mr. Madden had queried as to why Static had appeared so erratic. Standing outside in the cold rain Static thought for a precarious moment then answered. *"There's a party in London I've got to go to, hopefully things will make more sense when I get back. I'm trying to find out what happened to my film-script I sent to a company there. Is it okay to leave Copper here for a few days with you and Mrs. Madden?"* He asked pulling his long dark raincoat around him to keep out the ever-changing cold and wet weather.

"No problem Static." Said Mr. Madden. *"He's nothing but pure pleasure to walk!"*

"Yeah, he's the kind of dog who walks you, you don't walk him!" Laughed Static as the Springer Spaniel lived up to his name and bounced out of the rain and in through the front door of the house. Static turned and headed back towards his new Mini passing the front window of the house of his middle-aged neighbours and noticed through the curtains the cold glow of flashing petrol-blue digital numbers on black blinking on and off as another video-recorder needed setting, illuminating the lounge with a pale glow in the moderate semi-detached house in Carisbrooke.

FRIDAY 7TH SEPTEMBER 2001
MORNING / HACKNEY

THE HAIRSTYLE OF THE DEVIL

*What ever you want I've got it by the dozen
got it by the pound give me a call...I'll bring it round*
THE CRUEL SEA

THE HEADQUARTERS OF Winmau Diamond had been badly furnished deliberately. With over five years of drug dealing experience behind him, he had learnt over the years that one of the problems had always been getting customers to leave the house with as little of the product, for as much money, as quickly as possible. After living and dealing in the United States for ten years Winmau already had a tidy stake in a near global empire. The American differed from a lot of dealers in the business merely by the simple contradiction that he hated drugs of any kind. He even hated caffeine. Winmau hated smokers of any drug and he especially hated people that smoke and drank coffee with a passion that bordered on the criminal.

Winmau Diamond scratched at the folds of his fleshy fat neck as he brought a huge suitcase into what the English called *'the lounge'*. God, how he hated English words for things. They seemed to have no basis in logic. Even though, looking around the sparse conditions of the interior of the room, Winmau could not imagine any customers were that desperate enough to lounge around in it. He had been undecided therefore if it could still be called a lounge. Most of his clients would have not hesitated clearing this point up for him. Especially if they had seen the terrifying sight of Winmau grimacing in the room with them. He could call it whatever he liked.

The word lounge echoed around his huge American aircraft-hanger of a head and as he dropped the suitcase down with a heavy thud on the bare floorboards in front of him, Winmau made a chancy decision to ask

English people in the future, why they used the word *'lounge'* and not *'front room'* for this part of the house. Once he could stifle his hatred for them. There had been little in the world that Winmau did not hate. He even hated suitcases. He hated suitcases packed with drugs almost as much as he hated people that smoke and drank coffee. An indefinite image drifted across his mind of someone standing in the room who liked all the things he hated. The only person it would possibly be had to be O.D. Darren. Yet Winmau had reason to believe O.D. Darren had swiftly been promoted now to the number one spot in his list of most hated people, from the chart of hatred that the American kept filed in the dark recesses of the very small brain in his head.

If Winmau had been honest and that would have taken some serious effort, he knew he hated O.D. Darren simply because he had always been jealous of people who seemed to have such an easy going attitude to life. He hated reggae music because it had a relaxed beat to it. He hated any countries where the people smiled because when Winmau smiled it looked like the worst mistake his face could make. Winmau hated his body and he especially hated his hair as it clung to his head, greasy and lifeless.

Winmau had always been a big man. Not just in the criminal world, but also in the physical sense. He stood just over six foot in height with short brown hair. His general appearance had been that of a bodyguard assigned to protecting something bigger and more powerful than himself. If anyone had asked him what that had been though he would probably just have grimaced at them. He had always worn a black suit, red shirt and a black tie and gave most customers the impression of being a fascist, which was one of the few things he enjoyed in life, and the American had found this right-wing fashion to be highly useful for his business. The business of selling drugs. Which he also hated. His wardrobe contained three identical outfits and he hated each one of them equally.

The interior of the house if shown to anyone, would have given the impression that the builders were about to arrive and Winmau had just moved in. Or simply that he had broken into the house and eaten the builders himself. The interior had been specifically designed to be as unwelcoming as possible from the instructions given by his boss. The Madam. Most of the rooms had been stripped bare of any furniture or wallpaper. The only two uncomfortable chairs that remained were in the room he now occupied with his large hulk of a body and were placed directly opposite each other as if arranged for an interview. Winmau stared down at them with slightly less than the usual hatred that he held in reserve for furniture. In between them sat a black leather suitcase that contained enough drugs to kill a large rhino. Oddly enough The Madam had instructed him to hang up a faded colour picture of a large rhino on the wall above the collapsed fireplace which had been photographed yawning within the visible distance of a large lion sitting in the shade under a tree somewhere in the hot deserts of Africa.

Winmau hated the picture and had been unresolved about hanging it on the wall for the added effect until he noticed the way its impact had helped to unsettle customers buying drugs. They left quicker. This had pleased him immensely, simply because he hated all his customers as well.

Winmau walked over to the black leather case sat on the bare wooden floor and held the sides between both of his feet. He turned the combinations carefully until he heard a low click, then carefully he lifted the top of the case open by the handle which were had embossed with the initials P and G. Winmau had already searched carefully for any uncertain wires or other hidden surprises which had been placed strategically inside waiting for the inexperienced. Nothing he recognised. Only the petrol-blue cellophane wrapped packets of white powder compressed into the case as promised.

Winmau sighed with undetermined relief and momentarily thought of the number of people he had known who had died holding the handle of this one black case. Blood had stained the side of it and with a sponge from the kitchen, he wiped it off the black leather surface and grimaced thinking again of his only friend Challenge, who had been shot attempting to get the case and the contents into his car to him. One life in exchange for drugs and money. Winmau sighed again thinking of the tedious amount of time spent getting the container to Hackney from Notting Hill Gate. He had hated every second of it. Challenge had died during the journey and Winmau shuddered at the memory.

Suddenly the outside world contacted the inside as the blue mobile phone of Winmau Diamond began to vibrate on the cold metal chair opposite him. It rocked across the broken metallic seat until it fell to the floor with a thud. He leaned down and picked it up, then paused and mouthed the word *'brush'* in order to form a smile over the scowling features of his huge face. This would allow whoever was on the other end to get an impression of an extremely contented Winmau. He hated doing it but had to admit that it had worked many times in the past. The voice on the other end of the phone sounded as if it had learnt the same trick a long time ago. He groaned inwardly as he heard the voice of The Madam.

"Winmau Diamond? This is the police, we have you surrounded...hahaha. Mind you it would take a lot to surround you wouldn't it? Just kidding, just kidding." Barked the female voice down the phone. *"It's really the FBI! No no, it's not really. It's the RSPCA! We believe that you are holding badgers of a suspicious nature in your trousers. HAHAHAHA. No really...oh dear."*

Winmau held the mobile away from his ear and stared with intense fury at it. If there had been a human being that he hated more than O.D. Darren right now he decided he had direct contact with them. His boss. He quietly mouthed the word *'brush'* again to himself until his face held the broadest smile imaginable and spoke back into the mouthpiece. Forcing his hatred further into the back of his brain once again.

"Good day to you madam and how are you on this fine glorious day?" Winmau asked the blue mobile phone.

"So I guess you have the CD's yes? They have arrived?" Asked the well-spoken voice on the other end.

"Yes, maam'! They arrived exactly an hour ago and nothing got damaged in the post. They're all in perfect shape."

"How wonderful! I'll send the hippy round to see that they are indeed the imports that the kids want to hear..."

"No problem madam." Replied Wimau grimacing at the mere mention of O.D. Darren.

"Just make sure none of the cases are orange okay? You know how I hate orange cases. Ciao!" Said the voice.

Winmau pushed down on the disconnection button, terminating the call and slowly lowered the mobile phone back onto the opposite chair, his hand shaking slightly. The expression of absolute disgust returned to his face as his nostrils flared. Under his breath, he muttered to himself. *"My life... is good you old bat!"*

His anger was boiling up in his blood once again and Winmau decided that the hippy was going to receive more than the black suitcase when he turned up. O.D. Darren had been someone who brought his hatred out easily. The hippy embodied everything that Winmau hated about London. Drugged-up pompous slime who spoke in crawling slang about nothing of importance whatsoever. From all his years of experience in the business Winmau had been convinced that there had been little that he could trust about O.D. Darren. He had attempted to tell The Madam this several times but arrived at the understanding that she liked the fact O.D. Darren wound him up so much which is why she kept using him as a pick-up and delivery boy since Winmau had set-up the headquarters in Hackney.

Winmau walked into the stripped bare kitchen and decided to make a cup of horrible coffee. The expresso-machine with its two glass cups and a sponge were the only things in the kitchen that showed anybody had occupied the building. The Madam had donated them. The customers had a peculiar habit of thinking the place was a cafe and Winmau had been told by The Madam many times that an impression of friendliness had a lasting affect in London when dealing with people. The American had been doubtful.

He filled the bright red kettle with water and grimaced again as he plugged the kettle in and turned it on. God he hated the kettle. Another gift from his boss. The colour reminded Winmau of blood. Irresolute thoughts of Challenge his best friend of nine years from Florida coughing up blood and dying in a foreign country right in front of him elbowed their way into his mind. Challenge had been shot nine times and Winmau still winced at the memory.

He thought back to the phone call. Back to the voice of the girlfriend in Florida sobbing across the distance from hearing the news. Challenge had died. The remaining people who had known him refused to speak to him. Refused to return his phone calls ever again. That was the price of the business. Money became paper during such moments. Winmau thought about how he had been forced to bury Challenge in the forest. Anger flowed through the large American and he wanted revenge. Winmau wanted to shoot anyone just to make sure they understood how much Challenge had suffered. He wanted anyone to suffer in return. He could feel himself becoming jealous of anyone he saw still alive. As he returned to the empty house with the case he wondered not for the first time what would have stopped them. He decided there and then that something had to be done to make The Madam or someone pay for all this hate as the kettle boiled and filled the kitchen with steam, Winmau developed a scheme, spontaneous and highly devious. The doorbell rang. Winmau closed his eyes tightly and gripped the cup of coffee as the kettle boiled. He poured water into the expresso-machine and left it to stand.

Leaving the kitchen the large American walked back through the front room, grabbed the mobile from the red metallic chair and headed to the front door where he could see the unmistakable outlined silhouette of O.D. Darren through the red stained glass. He quietly mouthed the word *'brush'* to himself one more time and allowed the uncertain smile to break across his face. Then he opened the door.

"O.D. Darren my man! How's it hanging?" Asked Winmau. He stepped back slightly and invited the hippy into the hallway. *"You wanna' coffee. I'm just making it!"* If anything, Winmau had always been a great actor.

"Sure thing my man!" Beamed the lanky form of O.D. Darren as he followed the large American inside. O.D. Darren noted how Americans always seemed to be much friendlier in real life generally than when they were portrayed in the movies. O.D. Darren spoke hesitantly in his southern English accent. *"I brought you that video I've been talking about. It was filmed just down the road. Well, some of it was filmed down the road. I don't know where the rest was filmed... probably in a studio."* O.D. Darren continued babbling and followed the bulk of Winmau into the barren front room and noted the sparseness of the place immediately.

"Still waiting for the builders huh?" Asked O.D. Darren ambiguously.

"Sort of Darren. How do you want your coffee?" Smiled Winmau through gritted teeth.

"I like my coffee like my women. Milk and two sugars please... Hahaha." Replied O.D. Darren.

Winmau laughed back with a broad smile and headed to the kitchen to fetch the coffee from the kitchen. *"Have a seat man, I'll be just a second."* He said, already in two minds whether to shoot him or not. Then he remembered the scheme. The American became almost ecstatic as it circled around his mind.

"Sure thing man..." Called back O.D. Darren placing the video on the floor unsure as to when Winmau would ever get round to fixing the place up and making it a bit more comfortable. The hippy had been calling by the house for over six months and noticed it had always been this way.

He sat down in one of the two metal chairs and looked around the room amazed at the sparseness of the decor. The eyes of O.D. Darren widened slightly as he stared at the open case and its petrol-blue cellophane contents. The hippy leaned a little closer towards the containment in order to see if he had really been looking at what he thought he had or whether the case really contained compact discs. O.D. Darren pressed down on one of the packages hesitantly. The soft contents suggested they were filled with blocks of fine white powder of some sort. The sound of a large American male coughing politely by the door forced O.D. Darren to look up puzzled.

Winmau had been standing and watching him the entire time and now seemed to be a giant at full height framed in the adjoining doorway holding two small cups of coffee in his hands that looked like thimbles.

"Oh dear. Now, I don't think you should be looking at that..." Smiled Winmau back at the hippy.

"What's in the case Winmau?" Asked O.D. Darren as casually as possible.

"What do you think is in the case fucker?" Replied Winmau without the traditional wide smile.

"Er... sherbert?" Guessed Darren.

"What the fuck is sherbert?" Asked the American walking into the room. The cups of coffee seemed like small toys in his huge hands.

"It's like a sweet for children..." Explained the hippy. *"... made of white powder."*

"Well, do you smoke sherbert or put it into a syringe and inject it into yourself?" Replied Winmau the tone of anger now noticeable as his associate walked across the bare wooden floorboards of the lounge. O.D. Darren shrugged and looked back at the black case.

"I'm not sure. Some people might..." Answered O.D. Darren flippantly.

"Come on O.D. Darren, you're not that fucking dumb are you?" Asked the huge American as he brought over the coffee.

"It depends on the subject. I'm not too hot on geography." He answered sarcastically.

"How about chemistry? Can you spot class A drugs when you see them?" Asked Winmau.

A cold sweat quickly enveloped the body of O.D. Darren. *"Mmm... I'm just wondering about the other cases I've been delivering."* There had been twelve cases transported from this house to The Madam in Sheperds Bush and O.D. Darren had never thought to question what had been in each of them.

"Now you're thinking Darren." Said Winmau bitterly.

"What was in the other cases? The same?" Replied the hippy.

"Bingo!" Winmau smiled back at him through perfect teeth. O.D. Darren stood up quickly shaking slightly.

"You mean, each one of the cases I've..." O.D. Darren had no need to finish the sentence. An unforeseeable presence had begun to creep all over him.

"... Contained exactly the same amount. Here's your coffee!" The American beamed back at O.D. Darren with a big smile.

"Thankyou." Said the hippy, sitting back down unsteadily on the metal chair.

"There's about one and a half million pounds pure and uncut in the case. Once you mix it, each case has a street value of approximately three to four million. Multiply that by twelve Darren... " Winmau continued. *"Its around forty-eight million pounds worth..."*

"Maths is not a strong point with me either..." Answered the hippy with a vague smile.

O.D. Darren gulped. The numbers were reeling around his head. Along with the knowledge that he had transported forty-eight million pounds worth of hard drugs through London.

"I've been in this business for fifteen years Darren and the most I've ever seen has been one case...at a time. Congratulations man! You're officially one of the biggest drug-dealers in the Western world!" Winmau leaned across and slapped O.D. Darren hard on the shoulder.

O.D. Darren stood up bewildered by what he had just heard. *"Hang on a minute man, I THOUGHT IT WAS COMPACT DISCS. I'm a DJ! Not a bloody drug-pusher."*

Winmau adopted a tone of concern. *"I would seriously not recommend that you told anyone O.D. Darren. Mind you, whom would you tell? The* minute you go to the police and tell them you're not numero uno for the job of major dealer... I seriously doubt they'll believe you. Your prints are all over the cases!"

"All of them?" Asked the hippy stunned at the new turn of events. "This is the last one then... " He bit down on his bottom lip and frowned.

"Oh I doubt that as well really." Replied Winmau smugly. "They'll probably be about oooh I'd say another twelve at least." Answered Winmau smugly. "Happy Birthday." He beamed back a horrible smile.

"I won't do it. I refuse to have anything to do with delivering anymore drugs." Said the hippy as adrenaline began to flow through him. His looked down at the sponge and thought for a moment that the paint on it could be blood.

"O.D. Baby. I really think you don't understand the situation." Said Winmau. "I'll explain a little bit more. You see for each case that is transported there is a deposit on the case to cover any of them getting into the hands of the law. Which is $25,000 per case. Once the delivery is made the deposit has to be returned." He knew he had just been lying but was enjoying the expression of horror developing on the face of the hippy opposite.

"No one mentioned that before!" Replied O.D. Darren.

"Welcome to the business O.D.!" Yelled the American slapping him on the shoulder again and laughing.

"What's that got to do with me?" Asked the hippy. "Surely the Madam returns the cases. I never see them after she gets them!"

"That's because she keeps them and then calls her people and keeps mentioning to her people that you have all the cases and well after twelve cases have not been returned...that's twelve times..." The American scratched his head mockingly like a gorilla.

"Two hundred and fifty thousand dollars?! " O.D. Darren slapped a hand to his forehead.

"I thought you couldn't do maths?" Grinned Winmau.

"I'm a fast learner! " Replied the hippy suddenly feeling sick.

"Let's hope so my man. You have to learn a way of finding two hundred and fifty thousand dollars to return to The Madam's people before the next case reaches this house." Said Winmau.

Outside the house the echoes of distant cars driving around could be heard along with the far away sounds of children screaming and playing in the playground of the school nearby.

"...or the twelve cases? What about returning the cases?" Asked the twenty-six year old panicking.

"That's a possibility, but the chances are she'll tell you that she's sent them on to her people and you're back to the $250,000 debt." Smiled the American.

"This is fucking insane!" Yelled O.D. Darren, rage boiling out of him as he stood and paced the room. Winmau sat back in the opposite chair and closed his eyes in the manner of a true arrogant bastard as he relaxed his entire huge frame into the chair. This form of torture was so much more enjoyable than just shooting someone.

"O.D. its just knowledge. Ignorance leads to suffering and due to your ignorance, you are now suffering. You only had to ask at any point, but you didn't." Announced Winmau with a patronising tone.

"Thankyou Gandhi! I had no idea that you were so new-aged!" O.D. Darren spat sarcastically. "Fucking hell. I thought I was delivering CDs! Doesn't that count for anything? What about that?"

"This is the business Darren! If you want to be dealing with the truth you really should have stayed at college!"

"When does the next case arrive?" The hippy asked suddenly.

"That's the part you're not going to like much..." Replied Winmau smugly drinking his coffee as he opened his eyes again and looked upwards.

"Oh Please..." Said O.D. Darren.

"Tomorrow." Informed Winmau with another huge grin.

"...What?" The DJ dropped the coffee cup to the floor where the hot espresso began to leak over the wood and through the floorboards.

"At six hundred hours tomorrow morning. I'm supposed to pick-up the case from Notting Hill."

"Brilliant! So I have oooh, about twenty-four hours to get a quarter of million pounds together..." O.D. Darren stared at the wooden floorboards and wondered exactly how many mirrors he had broken in his life.

"No." Said the American.

"No?" Questioned Darren with a look of hope, suddenly standing still.

"You have to get a quarter of a million dollars together. It's not so much. It's around one hundred and twenty-five thousand pounds...actually." Announced the American casually.

"NOT SO MUCH? I'm on the bloody dole!" Yelled the DJ. *"I thought I was delivering CD's to a gentle old lady. You know, helping the aged and all that. Now it turns out she's a major drug-dealer who has fucked me over for more money than I'll ever see in a lifetime."*

"Hey. Take it easy. All problems can be solved!" Laughed the American.

"What's the deadline on getting the money to The Madam?" Quizzed O.D. Darren.

"No way! Don't even say any of this to The Madam. The money must go directly to my associate who deals with the cases and arranges the other work."

"Other work?" Something about the substance of the line caught his attention.

"The other work that I do..." Said Winmau licking his lips.

"You're being vague Winmau... what other work?"

"Shooting." Replied Winmau with a curious expression.

"You're telling me you're going to kill me if I don't give you all that money by six tomorrow morning?" Asked O.D. Darren with growing quiddity.

"Sorry Darren, it's the business..." Smiled the American.

"This is unbelievable." Said O.D. Darren shaking his head as he leaned onto the metal chair for support suddenly feeling a huge wave of sickness pass through him.

"How do you think I feel?" Asked Winmau unspoilt by the scenario.

"I don't think feeling is something you're capable of Winmau..." Said O.D. Darren bitterly and reached down to close the case, grabbed the handle

and headed for the front door. He was already running late for getting the delivery over to The Madam.

"O.D., I wouldn't have told you any of this if I didn't care..." Called the American after him.

"Fuck you yer sassanac!" Spat the hippy as he stood shaking and scared for the first time in the hallway then slammed the door.

"In your dreams!" Whispered Winmau to himself as his face returned to the former glory of a vague smile. He suddenly felt much happier.

The large American stood alone in the indistinct bare room and felt a sudden arrogant pride surge through his body across his shoulders and upward to his large head. Winmau congratulated himself over his part in the plan he had just formulated without any assistance from The Madam and decided to make another cup of horrible coffee to celebrate. He grinned to himself as he surveyed the cold ambivalent surroundings. Feeling secure in the knowledge that although he hated the uncertain situation he had passed onto O.D. Darren, at least the headquarters of Winmau Diamond had been badly furnished deliberately.

SATURDAY 8TH SEPTEMBER 2001
MORNING / HACKNEY

THE HACKNEY GUIDE TO LIVING AND DYING

Do I know where hell is? Hell is in hello
Heaven is goodbye forever it's time for me to go
LEE MARVIN

PULSING WEAKLY, PETROL blue lips of a body sitting in the centre of a room in an old Edwardian chair. O.D. Darren was about to die. Gradually his internal organs were melting one by one and although the feeling in his brain had become euphoric. O.D. Darren had been unable to move or say anything, profound or otherwise to the assortment of crumpled bodies lying scattered around on the floor of the Chill Out Room. O.D. Darren observed his part within the scene and compared it to a King surveying wounded and dying soldiers on a battlefield.

The DJ could hear wonderful music playing somewhere lifting his soul skyward. The party had been without doubt one of the best displays of gonzo hedonism he had seen in Hackney for nigh on five years. As well as for the hundreds who had gathered in the warehouse building. One death seemed a small sacrifice in comparison to most evenings out in the East End. Yet to Claire and Barnaby sharing a bottle of Vin de Rude in the corner of the Chill Out Room, the atmosphere had a rather rank feel about it. Death had been the last thing on both the mid-twenties mind of the couple. Yet death was anything other than boring to anyone who was dying.

Claire watched the hands of her boyfriend Barnaby fumble in the dark to locate the tape recorder somewhere in the twilight. He placed a tape inside and pressed the play button, allowing the sounds of graceful Brian Eno music to flow out of the big stereo speakers at the back of the room. Claire drank the red wine Barnaby had just poured out for her and thought of how O.D. Darren sitting still in the chair, looked detached from the whole setting somehow almost as if he had been a King.

O.D. Darren knew the situation too well. Throughout the evening the hippy had consumed enough drugs to halt a large rhino and had drunken everything but water whenever he had not been dancing. This had managed to raise his whole body temperature into the red and during the party he had felt as if he had been almost about to explode with happiness. The party had been his ticket out of a life that had been eventful, if not exactly what he had hoped for.

After the last week had passed, all the signs seemed to suggest that at the age of twenty-three, O.D. Darren had indeed given up all hope. O.D. Darren had not exactly given up on anything. He just had an idea that had been so rich in exuberance that if he attempted to explain any part of it to anyone, quite possibly, no one on Earth would have believed him. Soon enough the morning sunlight would reflect off a mirror the hippy had placed on the windowsill. Once the seven minute old reflection of white heat from the Sun hit the eyelids of O.D. Darren he knew it would be four o'clock in the morning.

The sensations occurring to him now of slow respiration and most of his body breaking down had not been as bad as O.D. Darren had previously expected. The lack of circulation around his arms and legs had spread throughout his body and the overdose of drugs had led the twenty-six year old to believe he had blended and become part of the chair at one point. The separation of himself from any other part of the room had been difficult to manage at first. O.D. Darren had set an alarm clock as a second back-up plan under the Edwardian chair ready for when the Chill Out Room would fall into relaxed mode, focusing on the light of warm sunshine seemed to him, to be a much safer bet. The battery powered travel clock currently read 3.54AM in petrol-blue coloured digits. However O.D. Darren could not see it as he recalled the feeling of warmth and security just knowing about its presence sitting under his crumpled form in the chair. O.D. Darren had discussed his plan with only one man that he had met at the early stages of the party. When drum and bass and bar of one pound a beer had opened the festivities. A person called Gyro.

The hippy had begun the night with two MDMA capsules at this point and had been cresting well, when he had started up a conversation between someone he had thought he recognised from distant school days on the

Isle of Wight. It had been Liz. He remembered now that they had been arguing. A horrible argument. She had left the party and had seemingly transformed into a teacher telling him off at school for taking drugs. He could see himself shouting at her somewhere in the region of France.

The talk with Gyro had been brief but O.D. Darren had enjoyed it immensely. Right now he could only recall passing a joint to the dude and laughed at the enthusiasm this man had shown for a country that meant little to him other than bad television programmes. O.D. Darren smiled slightly at the memory of this meeting. The digits of the clock glowed 3.56AM under the chair.

As O.D. Darren focused on the conversation and sketched in more details for a brief instant. Pure universal being shone out for all life from the mouth of the dude as he recalled the nail-on-the-head line that the suited figure had spoken to him as he had walked off to the bar shaking hands and seeming so tall. *"See you in the Dreaming..."* A voice announced in the Chill Out Room. That had been the line. O.D. Darren imagined himself gently kissing the hand of whoever had said it in the dimly lit room.

Claire turned around in the darkness of the Chill Out Room, spilling wine down the front of the shirt of Barnaby. She had heard a voice come from the other side of the room that sounded familiar. *"Barnaby. Did you just hear that voice?"* She whispered as the various bodies and dogs on string fell asleep or began to snore in the fallen twilight.

"What voice?" Asked Barnaby, a Time Out reader, he seemed to miss everything in life. *"I think I just heard someone say something about dreaming..."* The fashion-designer replied. She could feel the wine making her eyelids heavy and drifted into sleep. *"Alleluah..."* O.D. Darren spoke quietly in the room at 3.57AM. The alarm clock under the chair seemed to shine and illuminate the Chill Out Room with a ghostly pale petrol-blue glow along the high walls. Meekly the last pulse of O.D. Darren arrived. An overwhelming thirst had taken over his entire body now. He could see sand sweeping across the floorboards. Golden as it buried all the people underneath. As the DJ turned to look around the room one last time he could see dunes piling up against the walls of the Chill Out Room.

O.D. Darren knew well that this had been the final moment all along. He decided to give the troops one last look through tired and drug-fuelled eyes. At 3.58AM his right eyelid seemed easier to lift than his left, although it seemed to now weigh as heavy as a fridge. With tremendous effort he focused all his energy into moving his left eyelid up and wondered momentarily why an atomic bomb had been dropped on Hackney and yet everyone around him had decided to sleep through the spectacular sight. O.D. Darren wondered briefly why he had been watching someone who looked sort of similar in appearance to himself, look as if he had died in an Edwardian chair in the centre of the room that he had been inclined to call an ambulance. Then he noticed the long dark hair, blue jeans and white T-shirt with a yellow sunflower printed across the front and realised he had been looking at himself. He looked terrible.

The intense sounds of fire engines outside the warehouse did little to disturb the mass of bodies under bodies lying around him on the floor at his feet. Then O.D. Darren saw fire engulf the whole warehouse and everyone in the Chill Out Room. He pondered briefly why nobody in the room had bothered to wake up and get help. Whether the smoke of the room caused mass suffocation. As the heavy weight took hold of his brain and pulled him down O.D. Darren wondered idly how anyone could sleep through the disturbing noise around him.

He crouched down to look under the chair and came face to face with the travel alarm clock as the readout of the petrol-blue digits of the clock clearly displayed 4.00AM. Then as the hippy raised himself back up he found that he had been staring back at his own dead face. The pathetic beep of the travel alarm clock echoed out across the floor of the warehouse. The sound could probably bore through any material on Earth if it had wanted. O.D. Darren could feel it start to rain in the room. A torrential downpour had swept into the warehouse interior and washed across everyone sleeping. O.D. Darren continued to wonder as to why not a soul in the Chill Out Room had woken up.

The alarm seemed to reach its desired effect and Claire found herself naturally fumbling around on the warehouse floorboards in the dark as if she had been at home to turn the damn thing off. As she squinted her eyes and experienced the first thump of a hangover which would continue to get worse throughout the day. Disorientated, Claire looked around at the various crashed out bodies on the floor, then she steered her head over to the chair where she had seen O.D. Darren collapse earlier. The fashion-designer looked up at a thin translucent figure that looked like O.D. Darren standing by the window. When Claire abruptly saw something that scientists in the Western world had rarely had the opportunity to witness, simply because they did not believe in such things. The tall and lean form of O.D. Darren looked directly at her and blew a kiss, then waved and stepped into a mirror the size of her hand. Claire stared and blinked hard at what she just seen.

In the encompassing blue twilight lighting the room everything suddenly became still. Then a sudden breeze of cold swept across the floor of the room as Claire turned to Barnaby she could feel the terror and fear emanating from him as gradually every one of the hung-over and dishevelled people in the room began to slowly wake up. Disorientated by a mix of little sleep and massive dehydration. The smell of alcohol mingled with the smell of death.

Over the next few minutes around thirty people stood up silently and focused their attention towards O.D. Darren and the Edwardian chair in the centre of the room. Suddenly a sob broke out from someone behind Claire. It had been Barnaby. He had made eye contact with the hippy. Along with nose contact that seemed to suggest more than one window needed to be opened quickly.

"Holy shit!" Said Barnaby accurately. *"He's dead! O.D. Darren's dead...!"*.

Gradually a wave of disturbance swept around everyone in the room as the beeping from the alarm clock continued to echo out in the unnatural stillness. The new dawn crept into the room barely able to contain the excitement of what it had just witnessed as everyone had been sleeping. From the dance floor next door the faint distant sounds could be heard of classical music and Claire realised that Static had brought his DJ performance to a finish by playing his traditional closing music of Four Seasons by Vivaldi. He had told Claire many times that the best way to end a party had always been with Vivaldi. Static always claimed that it helped the dancers leave with their spirits lifted. Claire stepped over the various dishevelled bodies on the floor and walked over towards the still form of O.D. Darren sitting in the chair. A young girl quickly walked over to the body and touched one of the hands. *"He could have just gone into a coma..."* She said turning to Claire. *"There doesn't seem to be a pulse..."*

Pleased that this first stage of the plan had sprung into operation O.D. Darren had found himself surprisingly famished. He was already on the other side watching his own body from the small device he had placed earlier on the ledge above the sink. A hurrier.

Claire quickly moved towards the chair and looked into the pale drawn out face of O.D. Darren. She knew little about CPR but as the light appearing in the room seemed to be explaining to her as it fell across the lips of pale blue. O.D. Darren now had new make-up. She felt his hand and knew immediately by the feel of the unusual cold flesh that he had to be dead. She felt for a pulse at both points on his body. First at his wrist and then secondly on his neck. She looked back up at the girl standing with her and could tell immediately by the comparison to her face that O.D. Darren had died. The light in his eyes had faded. The girl standing next to her, with eyes full of tears was practically glowing with life. Her eyes were sparkling.

Claire estimated that O.D. Darren must have been dead for at least an hour. They quite simply had to let him go. There just had been no time to save him. Ever the responsible adult Claire knew the best thing to do had been to get everyone out of the room as quickly as possible. She crouched down and turned the alarm clock off. Claire had been raised religiously and after what she had just seen as she woke up something told her to take charge of the situation.

The fashion-designer watched as everyone in the room now stood up and stared at the body. She decided the best thing would be to not let anyone be frightened by the sight. They would then be terrified of death and would panic for the rest of their lives. She made a firm decision to announce what had happened carefully. In the timeless moment she heard her own voice begin to tremble slightly as she spoke and although she knew she had been the youngest person in the Chill Out Room. Everyone listened.

"Okay everyone listen up." She felt all the eyes around her looking directly at her as she stood next to the Edwardian chair. *" O.D. Darren has er... died. I guess, I don't know how many of you are religious but in my book he's still in the room and no one must speak badly of him. You must never speak badly of the dead."*

She closed her eyes calmly and opened them, then breathed out calmly.

"Can someone go next door and begin clearing out the dance floor? Tell Static and Gyro what's happened. We all have to go through this at some point so let's learn. Death is part of Life. I'm going to kneel here and pray. If you want

to join me you're welcome. If you're feeling any anger about what has just happened please leave now." She walked back over to her boyfriend Barnaby as they knelt down and began to pray.

The troops all stood silently around the King in shock as only the sound of Barnaby weeping echoed throughout the Chill Out Room. The tape in the stereo caused the machine to click off loudly and for O.D. Darren twenty-six years of pulsing stopped for the petrol blue lips of a body that was sitting in the centre of a room, in an old Edwardian chair.

SUNDAY 9TH SEPTEMBER 2001
MORNING / BRICK LANE

VISITING TIME IS OVER

I've been doing some thinking about the nature of The Universe
Found out that things are getting better its just people that are getting worse
MOSE ALLISON

BEN CYCLED ALONG the narrow stone path through Broadway Market with the purpose of a man possessed. The fresh Sunday morning air had a strange effect on some of the residents of Hackney as it caused them to emerge bright and early and go hunting for bargains from the boots of cars. The sensations created in the mind by heading to Brick Lane at seven o'clock in the morning every Sunday for the last five years was something that could rarely be explained to anyone outside of London. Ben now had his weekend routine securely mapped out to cover all the finer parts of Hackney bargain hunting within at least three hours.

First there had been Joseph at Hackney Wick where the artist had located four paperback books on the fascinating subject of the Illuminati by Robert Antoine Wilson. Each book had been sold to Ben for thirty-eight pence. He had also been forced into purchasing a plastic Italian hairdryer that had no intention of ever working but contained a name printed on the side of the retro style plastic body that Ben had thought hilarious. It had SMACK printed on the side in huge ornate letters. He had also found a replica of The Holy Grail which had been priced at five hundred pounds. Which Ben had managed to acquire through much haggling in order to get the bloke called Joseph who had been hawking from his car to drop the price to thirty-three pence after throwing in a dictionary. This had emerged as the reason he was now cycling at full tilt in the direction of Brick Lane market. The sole ambition of the artist had been in selling the tarnished Grail to American George a notorious lunatic who seemed to buy absolutely anything offered to him by Ben, within reason.

American George had been the only true mentally challenged and totally insane person in Hackney and Ben loved him dearly in much the same way cats love fire and milk loves cereal. Without the journeys across London Fields towards the stand of unfounded lunacy that the fifty-something George had set up on Brick Lane, Ben had sometimes felt as if his Sundays really would lack a great deal of appeal. Whatever the artist turned up with in his bag, whether it was old, damp and stained rolling papers or even electronic components from telephones which were beyond any true signs of ever working, American George would smile and hand over five pounds in exchange. Usually without even questioning what Ben had left him the previous week or asking much else. The enigmatic Ben had been one of hundreds of artists who squatted in Hackney and had currently been in-between planets. As well as being unemployed. Following his dreams.

So far his personal list of things sold to George had been endless. Melted candles without wicks were one of his favourite sales. There had also been a collection of Hoover bags, broken light bulbs, old hard-drives from personal computers, a stack of faded photographs of Queen Victoria, Athena posters, hair, even twigs and Toyah albums. Even the leaves he picked up that had fallen from the trees of London Fields had been purchased by George in the past once when Ben had slept late and missed the crucial opening times of Hackney Wick.

All George would ever say every Sunday morning as regular as clockwork whenever Ben handed him his bag had been, *'see you on television!'* Then George would hand over a five pound note and smile like a complete simpleton. However Ben had rarely watched television since arriving in Hackney. He could not see the point when real life had been so interesting. In the five years since this business relationship had begun, Ben had attempted to start a conversation with his client twice and both times it had ended with Ben smiling and nodding politely, putting his hands in his pockets and walking away from the old man as quickly as possible.

Whether George remembered anything about this the following week had been beyond the artist. Once he received the cash, he left. Whatever George had been doing with the junk had been his own business and if Ben missed a Sunday, the following week, the price would be doubled as George noted the amount in his little black book and would refuse to accept any disputes about it. Once over Christmas Ben had clearly forgotten to pay his usual visits to George due to the number of parties he had frequented and after a month he had found the American standing in the cold snow, holding a twenty-pound note in his cold pale blue hand.

As Ben rounded the corner hopped off his bike and wheeled it along next to him, the artist thought about the look of expectation on the chiselled features of the strange man once George would see the surprise that Ben had discovered for him this week. Simply for the fact that the replica Grail would help his blanket look a little bit worthy amidst the other various sellers on or around Brick Lane. George had always stood in the same spot with various pieces of sad rubbish scattered on a blanket in front of him, smiling his distant smile. Ben had learnt a lot over the last five years about patience from this tall simple Texan. He had guessed he was from Texas because of the accent and the white cowboy hat that George always wore which partly covered his grey hair. His skin was slightly dark and leathery as if the American had spent a great deal of time outside under the sun. George had always been a true artist to Ben. Whenever people had a free moment he would find himself encouraged to tell anyone he knew about the bloke. If people were curious enough and Ben was brilliant at provoking curiosity, then the artist would take them for a visit to George and persuade them to try and buy anything from the selection on his petrol-blue blanket. Usually the smile had been enough to scare them away. Even Chris T had tried at one time but had said the eyes were enough to force him back. George had just stood there clutching the traditional five-pound note in his right hand like a biscuit to the eyes of Chris T. His other hand fixed firmly in his pocket. Chris T had backed away gradually. *"See you on television!"* Said George eerily. He had even spoken with his Texas twang as Ben had promised.

By eight thirty Brick Lane had already been buzzing with crowds of people. Turkish and Slovakian immigrants attempted to sell packets of duty free cigarettes in their hundreds and cafe owners served up highly dubious fried breakfasts. The chilled morning air swept his thick black hair back across his film star features as Ben headed along past the hardened vendors who were selling everything from boxer-shorts that would shrink in the rain on the way home, to towels that refused to soak any moisture from your body whatsoever.

Then he saw it. The torn and used petrol-blue blanket of American George. The unusual array of hopeless and broken artefacts scattered across it. Something had been missing from the display though and after five years of repetitive appearances it took Ben all of five seconds to observe what had been missing from the picture. In the exact place American George had been solidly based for over five years like a cowboy statue, there had been only a Polaroid snap shot of faded colour perched on an old white biscuit tin. Exactly on the spot the life-size figure had stood. The square colour photographic image seemed to be the only evidence that he had ever been there at all.

Ben squatted down next to the picture left on the biscuit tin, crestfallen. He had finally found the ultimate bargain for the Texan and the Texan had vanished. Along with his weekly handouts. Then Ben noticed an orange envelope marked with the words FOR BEN THE ARTIST sticking out from under the tin. He looked around quickly and then grabbed the envelope, peeking inside. His jaw-dropped and his other hand released the handlebar of the bike as it fell to the ground with a clatter. Inside had been a neat stack of one-hundred pound notes. Without hesitating Ben placed the package and the Polaroid into his coat pocket. After some quick calculations, he realised the amount had been easily in access of five thousand pounds or more. Brick Lane was obviously not the best location to be counting such an amount of money in public. Ben quickly stood up and made some enquiries to the vendors standing either side of the blue blanket whether they had seen George anywhere. No one seemed to be forthcoming with much information as to the location of the tall Texan.

Walking hurriedly with the bike down Brick Lane in the direction of Spitalfields Market, Ben pulled out the orange packet and turned the envelope over in his hand searching for a number or clue to the whereabouts of George. On the back of the envelope read the words in black marker pen. SEE YOU ON TELEVISION BEN.

Ben continued to walk his bike down through the chilled morning streets of Brick Lane totally numb with shock yet apprehensive with excitement. He was still an artist but now he had been promoted to being a rich artist. More people were arriving now in the cold morning of Brick Lane on the street and he decided to head over to the squat of Derek and Clive. An abandoned pub just down from Columbia Market. A converted Pub. Ben needed a drink.

A Sunday in Hackney without meeting American George was just not the same somehow. Yet the shock of finding five thousand pounds in an orange envelope had been enough to leave this particular artist with something to think about. Derek and Clive were medical professionals and would always have some alcohol around the place. A Sunday in Hackney without beer was like Holland Park to Ben. He climbed back on the cycle and began to ride past Spitalfields Market and off in the direction of the two ambulance men.

Most of the crowd he cycled through barely noticed that within the space of an hour the long black hair of Ben had changed colour and now matched the colour of the new envelope in his pocket. However, a tall and slim woman wearing a matching orange scarf, not only noticed but also casually followed the artist on a white bicycle. At a discreet distance. A brightly coloured tartan shawl pulled tightly around her shoulders to keep out the cold, she observed and scanned all around her focusing intently on the speeding artist in front of her as Ben cycled along the path through Broadway Market with the purpose of a man possessed.

MONDAY 10TH 1933 SEPTEMBER
MORNING / TIME POCKET

SPIRITS IN THE MATERIAL WORLD

You just have to be crazy don't you?
You just have to eat chocolate cake. Truth or not.
GRANT LEE BUFFALO

HISTORY IS WRITTEN by the winners it is often said. The cold snow fell hard onto the rooftops of Berlin as Albert Einstein stepped into his favourite cafe and ordered his favourite drink, a cup of milch kaffee. Outside along the streets of Berlin crowds of people were gathering. The shoemaker looked down at his watch. Eight o'clock already. With the number of people gathering outside in the cold Winter streets, Albert knew there could be only one person who would generate this much interest in 1932 in Berlin. Red, white and black bunting and flags revealing the swastika draped heavily across every building. Albert had checked the date five times already and knew for a fact that eight years ago to this date, the shoemaker had made a bet in this very cafe with a young penniless Austrian gentleman as to how powerful a man could become in one lifetime. All for one deutschmark.

The waiter presented the milch kaffee to the shoemaker who moved towards the dark back of the dimly lit cafe holding the warm ceramic mug in both hands to warm himself from the morning cold. As the German sat at the back of the cafe he reached into his pocket and took out the one deutschmark note and rested it on the surface of the black table. The shoe shop had been doing reasonable business recently and he could at last relax with the knowledge that the relative luxury of a coffee would not cause any more financial hardship to himself or his wife. As Albert took off his hat and placed it on the hat stand inside, he stood still in surprise at the sudden appearance next to him of a young man with white blonde hair. Cautiously the shoemaker sat back down in his chair. He had been more than certain that as he had entered the cafe the waiter had been the only person in the room.

Outside the cafe the cheers rang out and Albert looked once again at his watch. A quarter past eight. In fifteen minutes the shoemaker knew that the Austrian would drive past and the bet would be complete. He would leave the money on the table as arranged. Sipping from his cup of milch kaffee Albert Einstein looked up and dropped the cup of warm coffee in surprise over a copy of his favourite book, which he had placed on the black tabletop. Paper Cranes by Origami Hiroshima. Shizer. The book had been stained all the way through. Albert sighed. He looked up again to watch the distracting sight of the blonde haired man next to him flickering and fading from colour to black and white as if he had been an image in a talking movie. Albert stared in fascination as the space around the figure became more distorted and then gasped as he saw the entity of Gyro turn and look at him then completely disappeared.

Albert blinked hard and rubbed his eyes. Bewildered he stood up and walked over to where the immediate form of Gyro had just been sitting. He touched the table and the wall, nothing appeared but solid matter. Albert looked down at the table in front of him and saw a copy of a colour magazine. On the cover read the word TIME and showed a photograph of a man with white hair poking his tongue out at the viewer. He picked the magazine up and looked at the date at the top, which read September 1955. Albert looked into the eyes of the old man and thought for a moment that there had been something familiar about them. English words ran across the face. Large white type asked the question DOES RELATIVITY DIE WITH EINSTEIN?

The cheering crowds gathered outside as Albert looked back again at the cover of the magazine. The colour image had faded to black and white and showed two huge dark towers exploding as a Boeing aircraft crashed into one of the towers. Albert looked up again and saw himself standing on a train track. He appeared to be in a huge outdoors prison. Huge concrete walls towered above him and as the cold snow fell from the dark still night he could recognise the forms of people so frail and thin around him wearing striped pyjamas. The cold winds of Germany howled all around him. He could see large gold stars sewn onto the front of their shirts. The eyes of each individual stared out at him. He could hear fire all around him. There was a terrible smell.

Albert looked down at the magazine again and saw an advertisement for a new drug called G-WIZ shining back at him. Words of German across the bottle announced a new form of Time-Travel. The announcement came with a warning that Time Pollution was causing problems. He looked back up and found himself standing exactly in the same spot in the cafe in 1933. He dropped TIME onto the floor and walked back over to his table where his milchkaffee was still warm as he picked it up. He knew what he had just experienced and knew that only his friend Max Born would understand what he had just seen. He quickly drank the rest of the coffee and hurried out onto the snow covered streets of Berlin rounding the corner at the end of the street just as a large cheer greeted the appearance of the most dangerous tyrant who ever paced the surface of the planet. Mr. Bittre waved to the crowds. Albert ignored the cheers. He knew something important was happening. History is written by the winners it is often said.

TUESDAY 11TH 2001 SEPTEMBER
MORNING / HACKNEY

THE PLANET OF SOUND

Daddy don't live in that New York City no more
He don't celebrate Saturday on a Friday night no more
STEELY DAN

BY NINE O'CLOCK that morning, deliberation and perseverance had finally paid off. The locks to the new relocated squat of Chris T and Ben had finally been put in place. Ben had been in the process of assembling one of their current pieces of art on the large wooden stage of the old theatre as part of an installation. The sunlight of a new day streaming through the skylight. The stage had taken on the appearance of a lounge that had been dropped onto the stage from a great height. Already two huge Edwardian chairs had been set either side of it by Chris T the day before, along with an Italian style standing lamp that had been connected amidst the various chords and wires leading from the extension socket. The orange cord ran along the floorboards and up to the fuse box where various wire were jammed into the pre-war electrical circuit through an ingenious system of matches and hot-wires assembled by Ben. An electrical wizard.

In the daylight the theatre held less of an intimidating air about it and had now slowly taken on the appearance of The Muppet Show. With only two Muppets present. As Chris T swept up some of the fallen debris in the aisles and filled up one of many black heavy-duty refuse sacks sitting around the interior Ben relayed the news of the sudden disappearance of American George the day before. He had yet to mention the envelope of money sitting snugly in his green boiler-suit pocket. Or even why he had dyed his hair blue.

"So you're saying you don't know where he's gone?" Asked Chris T working with broom and shovel to clear some of the mess left behind from World War II.

"No idea...he just vanished." Replied Ben cautiously. "I think he knew I would be there though...he, er... left a note.."

"What did it say?" Asked Chris T.

"See you on television!" Replied Ben.

"What?" Said Chris T, pouring the rubbish into the refuse sack from a dustpan.

"See you on television!" Ben repeated louder as he fiddled with the wires leading from the TV set and across the theatre to the extension lead which seemed to be spouting legs like a giant spider across the centre aisle.

Finally the current kicked into the television set bringing it to life with a crackling sound of static. A triumphant shout let out from Ben as he stepped back from the box. The sounds of an English chat show were now audible throughout the empty building as the blue-haired artist walked over to the stage and sat with his legs hanging over the edge taking on the appearance of a large Kermit The Frog in his green boiler suit. He took out a small black plastic box and some King Size rolling papers and proceeded to skin-up a joint with the contents. Using the floorboards of the stage as a table. *"Have you ever noticed something familiar about him?"* Enquired Ben, heating the lump of hash with a blue plastic lighter he had allocated from a nearby corner shop using a five-fingered discount.

"Who?" Asked his creative companion as he walked over to retrieve another refuse bag.

"American George. Something odd about a Yank being in Brick Lane." Ben scratched his head in a similar way to an actor called Robert De Niro he had seen the day before. *"I mean, now I come to think of it, he had an odd familiar quality about him. Like we had met at some point before but I'm hopeless with remembering faces..."*

"That's the hash Ben! Man, the bloke was a loony. How long did you know him?" Yelled back Chris T.

"He's been standing in front of that blue blanket every Sunday, since... oooh, possibly the Summer of ninety-seven. I think it was at O.D. Darren's opening of his new squat down on Sigdon Passage. Where they rebuilt the warehouse and where that peculiar girl lives, with the cute nose. What's her name?" Asked Ben clicking his fingers and losing track of the conversation.

"*What the Sasquatch?*" Asked Chris T, notorious for caricaturing people.

Ben suddenly appeared even more confused and looked up from his current mission. "*Sasquatch?*"

"*You know, that really tall hairy woman who has a ....*"

"*No! The German, the original German lady who moved there after O.D. Darren was evicted. She had that really strange party, the one where everyone wore personal stereos and she always dressed in a leotard.*"

"*Ben you've lost it...*" Laughed Chris T.

"*No, really! She was always carrying a camera. She was only wearing a leotard with a sunflower on it.*" Said Ben.

"*No idea!*" Replied his friend, shaking his head.

Ben stroked his chin and tried as hard as possible to force his memory into action so that he could remember the squat party. When suddenly, the thought occurred to him that it was the date of Darren's Birthday.

"*Here Chris T. When was O.D.'s Birthday?*" He asked, Chris T had known O.D. Darren since he had moved from the Isle of Wight, which had been at middle school. He shivered to himself. That had already been six years ago.

"*O.D. is... a Capricorn, so it would be... somewhere in September. No. Sorry, he's a Virgo. Yeah, it's September. Blimey, it's today! I'm sure it's today!*" Chris T suddenly stared down at his watch, which had stopped working for some reason since both artists had left the gallery in Bristol. After they had both met Britt, the curious German lady that Ben had fallen for big time.

"*Check on the TV. The news'll probably be on at some point. They seem to make a point of informing you of what date it is as if you're not allowed to forget!*" Said Chris T.

"*Good point.*" He walked over to the TV and turned up the volume.

Chris T walked down the centre aisle, sweat pouring off him and climbed up the front of the stage. "*Shall I finish rolling the joint?*" He asked eagerly.

"*Sure...*" Replied Ben.

Although Chris T had been anything but a heavy smoker, he knew the brain-numbing labour ahead of him could only be managed if was seriously stoned. As Chris T picked up the mix of hashish and tobacco, he finished rolling the cigarette paper into a near perfect cone-shape, pulled out a distinctly fashioned Zippo silver cigarette petrol-lighter from a pocket on his green boiler-suit, flipped the top back and placed the wide end of the joint over the naked flame, letting it burn the end until it caught alight. As he inhaled the smoke he glimpsed down again at his watch.

Since the German lady Britt had discovered both the artists in the Bristol art gallery, his watch had simply stopped working and any time he had wound the cog on the side, the hands of the clock had refused to budge.

Chris T looked around the theatre and pondered on the events that must have unfolded in the very spot he was currently sitting in. To Chris T the atmosphere of the building seemed suddenly to have revealed an electric history to him. Such a contrast to the Los Angeles style ghetto of Dalston outside. He wondered why it was that humans seemed to reveal themselves capable of such incredible dreams, as well as such terrifying nightmares.

During World War II, over fifty million people had been wiped off the face of the planet apparently. As he closed his eyes in the theatre and listened closely enough, Chris T felt certain he could hear the explosions of falling bombs onto the East End of London. He opened his eyes as he became aware of screams and shouts echoing around the disused building. The noises had been coming from the television, amidst bursts of static caused by the electrical endeavours of Ben. Chris T turned a stoned head over to his amigo, the joint sticking out of his mouth.

"Is that the news?" He asked dragging on the spliff. *"Ben...?"* No answer.

The artist stood up and turned to where Ben was standing frozen still as he stared at the television.

"Holy shit!" Exclaimed Ben. *"Look at this Chris T!"* He pointed at the monitor.

Immediately the artist ran across the stage to join Ben by the television set and watched in stunned silence at the sight of an airplane crashing into the World Trade Centre causing the entire structure to buckle and steadily collapse. They both watched in amazement at the sight of the two towers in New York, falling to the ground.

"Woah!" Announced Chris T passing the joint to Ben. *"I don't believe it!"* The image on the TV suddenly cut and changed to fill the screen with the sight of a podium and the distinct blue curtain behind it announced the arrival of The President of The United States of America who began to speak. Ben felt his legs suddenly weaken.

"Oh...my...God." Said Ben in stunned shock, seemingly missing the disaster they had just witnessed. *"That's American George! He's on television! "*

The image of the disaster repeated and the two artists looked in shock at not only the sight of huge bellows of thick smoke as it rose up from the skyline of New York but the sudden appearance of a lady dressed in bright contrasting colours walking calmly through the street with a distinct orange turban on her head. Chris T could feel his jaw falling open slightly causing the joint to fall from his mouth, onto the floor of the stage. They both looked at each other in unison and then back to the screen of the portable black and white television.

"Did you just see Britt walking down that street?" Asked Ben.

"Did you just see American George on television?" Asked Chris T.

Suddenly the sound of an electronic beeping echoed through the vast space of the theatre and Ben quickly walked over to where his coat had been left on the floor next to a copy of Empire magazine. He pulled out a mobile phone and pressed the answer button. It was Glenn Miller. Ben hurried back over to the television but the signal of the mobile phone created an interruption with the news coming through. Ben attempted to speak into it as calmly as possible. His stomach felt like Christmas.

"Glen...where the hell are you? Newtown? Where the hell's that?" Asked the artist, his hair turning red.

Chris T crouched down and turned the volume on the television up, lifting the joint from the floor. He had begun to view the day in a whole new light and was now only partly aware of the one-sided conversation coming from Ben.

"What? What do you mean it's Darren's funeral? I was just talking to him? Are you drunk?"

"Ask him if he's watching the news?" Asked Chris T over his shoulder still observing the images on the screen.

"Are you watching the news? A plane's just crashed into the World Trade Centre in New York. Britt's on TV! Yeah she was there walking down the street oh and I got some books at Hackney Wick for thirty-eight pence!" He called over to Chris T. "He's saying weird shit down the phone man. Speak to him."

Chris walked across the stage and exchanged the joint for the mobile.

"Glen Miller! What's up? You're in Newtown, yeah I heard Ben say! It's a really bad line Glen. You what? But you are speaking to me...no I'm er..in the new squat in Hackney...no. I am here! Why would I be lying? Are you drunk? Do I want to speak to myself? Sure!"

Chris T looked over to Ben and covered the speaker part of the phone with one hand.

"He says he's with Britt, you and me in the kitchen at a house and we're all celebrating Darren's funeral. There's loads of people and I'm chatting up with Juliet Binochet." Whispered Chris T to Ben. He returned to the conversation. "How am I doing with Juliet? Really? Wow!" Chris T whistled.

"Ask him where Newtown is?" Yelled Ben hypnotised by The News bulletin.

"Ben wants to know where Newtown is..." He turned around to Ben. "Glen says it's on the Isle of Wight!" Then he looked in towards the mobile phone feeling slightly confused by what he heard next. "Do I want to speak to myself? You asked me that already...okay if it's me, what am I wearing? Of course, it's a funeral, right...good answer yeah. Yeah." Glenn was notorious for winding-up people since the mobiles had become popular. "Look at the TV man! A plane's just flew into the World Trade Centre...There's no TV? Try the radio! It's a bit early for a party isn't it? It's around ten in the morning I thought. "

"Ask him..." Ben interrupted.

"You ask him Ben...the bloke's off his nut. He's saying something about Darren dying..." Chris T relayed the phone back to the original owner.

"Glen! Yeah...it's Ben. Calm down man...what about O.D. Darren? What do you mean? I'm standing right next to you?" Ben started laughing. "No...I'm here with Chris T in Hackney. Do I want to speak to myself? I do that anyway man. I just saw O.D. Darren at the shops five minutes ago man."

Suddenly his friend shouted out. *"BEN! Another plane has just hit the other tower!"*

"Glen! Look man, I've gotta go. Call me later. Watch The News. What do you mean? Right er...speak to you later! Ciao!" He disconnected the call.

Ben walked over to the television again with his coat and dropped the mobile into the pocket. He crouched down and sat cross-legged in front of the TV set where Chris T had become slowly hypnotised by the most startling images either had ever seen.

"What was Glen Campbell on man? " He asked distracted by the news.

"He says he's at Darren's funeral on the Isle of Wight with loads of people and us in a huge house...Jesus look at that. He also said that Britt's there and that they flew down via helicopter. Must have gotten hold of some acid again..."

Ben reached over and turned the volume up, the sound of noise and screaming could be heard coming live all the way from from New York.

"He did say something strange though.." Said Ben absentmindedly.

"What?" Asked Chris T.

"He said that this happened three days ago..." Said Ben pointing at the television.

"What? " Asked the artist again.

"He said go and read the papers!" Said Ben. *"It happened on September 11th"*

"Ben. It is September 11th." Said Chris T.

"I know..." Said Ben.

"What did he say about Britt?" Said Chris T still hypnotised.

"He said she was standing next to him at the party and that O.D. Darren's funeral was really good. Lots of famous people turned up apparently."

"I tell you man...this is it...I've got a strange feeling about this." Said Chris T.

Through all that had been happening so early on in the day the only thing that Chris T had been bewildered by was not the spectacular news bulletin which they had just witnessed or the most surreal conversation on a mobile that the young artist was likely to ever hear but that observation which a person subliminally picks up without truly accepting that they have. Like a painting by Escher that revealed the ease of the impossible. Chris T had been half certain that when Ben had arrived that morning at the squat, his hair had not been a dark red shade of Autumn.

Chris T reached over and turned down the volume on the panel and walked over to the edge of the stage. Resting a hand on the wooden floor, he leapt down into the aisle.

"Well...the only way to solve this mystery is to go and buy a newspaper... any requests?" Asked Chris T.

"Yeah...get The Observer." Said Ben as he stood still on the stage. He scanned the area around the new art installation and checked the time on his watch and wondered how long this new creation was going to take to build. He figured that by nine o'clock, deliberation and perseverance should have finally paid off.

FRIDAY 7TH SEPTEMBER 2001
AFTERNOON / SYDNEY

WHEN WILL I GROW OLD GRACEFULLY?

Did you do too many drugs? I did too many drugs
Did you do too many drugs... too?
VIOLENT FEMMES

GYRO EMERGED BLINKING and squinting from out of The Imperial bar and walked out into the rising sunlight of Erskinville, a suburb of Sydney in Australia. At five in the morning the heat of the sun had already begun piercing daggers of white light in through the shades of the bar. Through the venetian blinds. It had become once again time for the cockroaches to run scuttling for cover. Gyro staggered forward and stood at the entrance of the bar doors. Head and body full of Tooheys Old beer. He weaved over the bridge towards the direction of King Street and marvelled at how some people had decided the most important thing to do when they arrived on the planet had been to name nearly every street in the Western world either Queen or King Street. Even the pubs seemed to all be called the Kings Head or Queen Victoria. Since his arrival in Sydney he had thought that perhaps some changes of names might be a good idea if the new millennium would ever live up to its name.

He passed murals made of incredible colours, painted on the sides of houses. Houses with spectacular balconies. He had walked through the streets at night and sometimes thought he had been in New Orleans. The sun created an incredible colour scheme throughout Australia. Bright blues and oranges. Sydney and the people had been a wonderful home to him over the year spent away from London and he staggered on towards King Street, the main street which serpentined through Newtown as he wondered what had possessed him to journey so far from his home country of England. He had lost himself in the Newtown Bermuda Triangle for the last time. Beginning at The Oxford Pub on King street where his flatmates

Suzanne and Deb had convinced him easily, once again, to come drinking one last time.

He loved the relaxed way Australians spoke. *'Come drinking'* sounded almost essential to the day. Gyro had witnessed a number of things over the year spent in Sydney, one of them had been the inability anyone had to refuse an excuse to head for a beer. Maybe it had been the intense heat, continuing always without fail to pour down onto the Sydney streets. Gyro had found himself having to spend most of the time in the shade when in this country.

The choice of New or Old as names for beer helped a great deal when you were buying, especially after twelve hours of drinking. Compared to the variety of names you had to remember if you were buying beer in a pub in England. The Oxford had been a pub originated for serious drinking and either by destiny or blind luck Gyro had managed to find a place to live which had been directly above it. Spending one of the best years of his life with Deb and Suzanne, two of the easiest going flatmates in the world.

The outlay of the Oxford included the traditional jukebox, the obligatory New or Old on tap and the life force of Australian culture - pool. Over the three hundred and sixty-five days he had been in Sydney, Gyro had spent nearly every one of them walking past the pub on the way to work in Balmaine as a graphic designer for a magazine publishers. He had been stunned to see postal workers drinking from six o'clock in the morning. Which perhaps explained the reason he had only received five letters the entire time he had been in Sydney.

The heat and the seediness of the bars in Sydney had been a shock. Unbelievable yet somehow magical. Now on his last evening in Australia, he wondered if he could cope without being in such a relaxed environment. His fellow flatmates had found a pool table at the back and started shooting pool but Gyro had found it almost impossible to concentrate on the game after looking around the bar. The live characters around him were far too interesting and the atmosphere had been similar to a school common room run rampant. With half the cast of Mad Max vomiting or shooting-up drugs. To find one person in the bar that had not been on drugs, would be difficult. Since his arrival in Newtown he had begun to understand just how reserved the English were, after being informed of this nearly every time he entered a pub.

The Oxford had been a notorious establishment for many years, where a person felt naturally more at ease when they held a long piece of wood in their hands. For shooting pool with of course. Gyro played against Deb and Suzanne as one team and caused a commotion by pocketing five balls out of the diamond from the break, two of them a number five and an eight ball. Causing much mirth. He had lost the game to his flatmates as quickly as it had begun.

After several schooners and good luck wishes towards his return journey to Europe, Deb had decided that the infamous Sleepers Bar across King Street had been calling them even though neither Gyro nor Suzanne could hear it. While Deb had been chatting to Gyro, Suzanne the hippy decided that a farewell dose of speed would help the farewells along. A Newtown leaving gift.

The effect of the drug had been to gradually blackmail his brain into walking bringing along a whole new experience. Slamming the pool-cue down onto the table, Gyro crashed through the Wild West style doors and tagged after Deb and Suzanne into the sweet warm night air of Newtown. He stood out on the street as the stars in the sky took on a spectacular rush. Suddenly he understood that there had been a mission all along. Then he understood without a single doubt that he had completely forgotten what it had been. Yet the mission. The words had been in his memory somewhere and he had noted it down but had no idea what it was. As he ran through the line of cars heading through Newtown he felt a strong urge to explain everything he had ever learned about life but became to excited to begin.

At the cocktail bar of Sleepers incredible beer garden he had met up with Allanah, Chriss and Gregg. Three of the loveliest people Gyro had ever had the pleasure of meeting on the planet so far. Happy hour had arrived and somewhere amidst all the chaos of people in the back of the bar Gyro had lost them all as he stumbled to the bar, attempting to listen to and understand the words of a stranger he had unintentionally purchased a drink for.

"You seem to have no idea of the power that you possess do you?" Said the stranger with strong emphasis.

"How do you mean?" Replied Gyro as he drank from his schooner.

Suddenly, the crowd gathering at the bar forced him further back until he found himself sitting next to a mid-twenties version of a long-time hero named Noah Taylor. An Australian actor who he had long admired and had his appearance compared to many times. The speed mixed with the beer caused intimidation to pop by for a chat.

"Wow. Noah Taylor! I've seen as many of your films as I could possibly see. I have to say what a fine actor you are sir!" Slurred Gyro at the antipodean star.

"Thankyou. Are you speeding?" Asked the actor cautiously.

"You could say that. It wasn't my initial intention, but someone helped me along there." Gyro replied. He could feel his jaw nearly dislocating as both sets of his teeth had an overwhelming urge to grind down on each other.

"Are you feeling okay?" Asked Noah politely.

"Splendid!" Gyro beamed back. "I have to return to Europe though. I've been here a year and I've no idea what I'm doing so far from home."

"Where's home?" Asked the actor.

"I'm not sure." Replied Gyro. "It has something to do with England, but when I look at the stars, I get homesick. If home is where the heart is, I have no way of travelling that far!"

"Well maybe it's in The Dreaming..." Said Noah lighting a cigarette, giving the impression that he might always be acting but that was his job after all.

"Ahhh, the aboriginal doo-dah thingummy!" Replied Gyro as he drank some of beer of the actor by accident.

"Exactly." Smiled Noah knowingly. "Would you like to hear a joke before you head back? You can tell it to everyone in England that you meet. Okay, Sir Issac Newton and Albert Einstein are playing pool in the Oxford across the street and Sir Issac says; 'Every action causes a reaction so I bet I can strike the white ball off the side cushion and pot the first ball!' and he does the shot and it works.

Then Albert says; 'Okay I bet I can hit all the balls in with one shot if you want to place a bet on the table that will make the shot worth my while.'

Sir Issac says; 'Okay and puts 186,000 dollars on the bar.'

Just as Albert is about to take his shot he is put off by the arrival of a young American called Nick Bostrom who enters the bar and says; 'Everything is a computer simulation. When are you two going to play some real pool?'"

Suddenly Allanah appeared behind him yelling in her broad Australian accent out of the side of her mouth. "Gyro! We're heading to The Imperial. Come with us!"

Whether Noah had joined them, he had no recall at the moment.

All he knew had been travelling around Australia for a year. All because of a dream where a voice had suggested to him to visit Newtown and after eight months backpacking and travelling to the wide open cities of Melbourne and Adelaide he had been doing exactly as the figures in the dream had suggested. He had visited the Northern Territory, The Outback and hung out with aboriginals in the desert. All in an attempt to find an answer to the dream. Nothing seemed to have come out of it, except a strong urge to return to Europe as quickly as possible. Which if memory recalled he had to do tomorrow. Shit! No, it was today! Somewhere between Newtown and Erskinville he had completely forgotten in a rather relaxed fashion picked up from his flatmates that he had decided to return to London on a one o'clock flight in the afternoon. Gyro checked his watch as he walked past another incredible colourful mural painted on the side of a house, his watch read nine. Just enough time to get his belongings out of the flat that had been a makeshift home for over a year.

Gyro staggered hurriedly along King Street. Saying imaginary farewells to the buildings and cafes of Newtown, the road signs as the glorious and magnificent Sydney sky began the rise of another perfect day. This place had to be the closest thing to heaven on Earth that he had ever known. The speed had been still kicking around his bloodstream and he now had the arduous task of leaving Australia ahead. In less than ten hours he would be in Hong Kong. Once there, he could relax big time.

Whether it had been the drugs in his system or not or the lack of sleep, he had since forgotten. Yet he wished he had bought a ticket to New York instead. London had to be one the most depressing experiences to fly into on this planet. Especially after being in the sunlight of Sydney for a year. Perhaps he could change the ticket at the airport. His big mission now of course had been to stay awake until he reached the airport.

As he fished through his pockets for the first Winfield Blue of the day and fixed his sunglasses onto his tanned face, his fingers located a small petrol-blue cellophane packet inside the jacket pocket of his suit, which contained a white residue and a note within. He pushed the thin end of his house-key into the powder and lifted a small sample of the speed up to his nose. Blocked the left nostril and sniffed. As he read the note, written on bright orange paper.

'Gyro -God speed you, see you in The Dreaming. Love Allanah. Chriss and Gregg!' Read the note.

Heading across the park near Newtown Cemetery he thought of Ray Connif. A fellow European he had met on the first day of his arrival in Sydney, who seemed to be one of the most confused individuals Gyro had ever met. He had been from some place called Meissen. Which after investigating on a map, Gyro had understood had been somewhere in Germany. Ray seemed to be having some serious trouble adjusting to this part of the world. A lot of Europeans did. Yet, he had to admit that Australia had the same affect on him after a while. The longer you stayed, the more the urge came over you that something really interesting might be going on in the world somewhere else but that you were not included in whatever it was. Gyro hoped that wherever Ray had travelled onto he had become better able to handle things than when he had appeared in Sydney.

The traveller ran up the outside concrete steps and into the house, grabbed his rucksack from the room and his flight bag packed with anything that would assist in the long journey he was about to undertake. Fortunately he had remembered to pack the night before. He left the front-door key on the kitchen table for his flatmates and slammed the door shut. On King Street he felt the warmth of the rising golden sun on his face and tried not to think of this as goodbye to a country which had been everything he expected it to be and more and took another toot from the bag of speed. This time with the nail of his little finger. He loaded his bags into the Sydney taxi and gave instructions to the driver for the airport. As the taxi pulled away from the kerb, Gyro ogled out the back window. He watched as Newtown gracefully became smaller and smaller. Eventually fading into the distance. The lyrics of a record being sung on the radio seemed to summarise an entire year of searching with all the profoundness of a classical poem. Gyro felt himself being swept away from the wide streets of

Sydney as the intense Sun continued its steady rise over the lucky country. *"You travelled out in the world for a year, while I just stayed in my room... you saw the crescent. I saw the whole of the moon..."* Sang the voice on the radio.

Gyro looked out the side window and smiled. The side of a large white removal van momentarily swam along matching the speed of the taxi. The name of CRESCENT REMOVALS emblazoned on its side in large petrol-blue letters. The hypnotic expression of Gyro looked out through sunglasses and followed along with the vehicle to the front of the van where Allanah, Chris and Gregg sat frantically waving back and smiling. Gregg held a sheet of white paper pressed flat up against the window, which read in black felt tip the words A NEW BEGINNING.

The van turned off at a junction and Gyro watched as his entire life for one year disappeared down the main street and back to the city of Newtown in Sydney and suddenly he found in one minute an answer that fitted exactly with what he had been searching for an entire year. He turned in the back seat of the taxi and tried to imagine what it had been that he had thought when the sunlight had first broken in through the curtains that morning and the taste of Tooheys fizzy dark beer had swilled around his head as Gyro emerged blinking and squinting from out of The Imperial bar and walked out into the rising sunlight of Erskinville, a suburb of Sydney in Australia.

BOOK II

AFTERNOON / SEPERATE ENTITIES

ALBERT EINSTEIN / 1879-1955
NOBEL PRIZE WINNER 1921

A Physicist born in Ulm Germany on March 14th. Albert Einstein first proposed a theory of relativity in 1905 suggesting time is relative to the observer, which revolutionized scientific thought.

*When you are courting a nice girl
an hour seems like a second.
When you sit on a red-hot cinder
a second seems like an hour.
That's relativity.*

In 1901 he became a Swiss citizen and then became an American citizen thirty-nine years later in 1940. During the approach of World War II Albert Einstein wrote to President Roosevelt on 2nd August 1939 to warn him that scientists in Nazi Germany could be within reach of making an atomic bomb. After hearing the A-bomb had been dropped on Hiroshima he said. *"If I knew they were going to do this, I would have become a shoemaker!"* He won the Nobel Prize when aged 42 years, which he immediately passed onto his ex-wife Mileva whom he had two children with. A daughter who had to be adopted because both his wife and Albert were too poor to provide for the child and a son who spent most of his life in a mental hospital. Some years later after a divorce he married his cousin Elsa.

Einstein insisted that subatomic particles had to be thought of as discrete separate entities. He objected to the Quantum theory in which physical events can only be known in terms of probabilities.

He died at the age of 76 in The United States of America. When asked by reporters what his last words were, his nurse replied, *'I don't speak German'.*

PASSPORT CONTROL

INSIDE DINER, FIVE Buddhists Monks levitated in a line above counter. All in blue robes. Crunchy thoughts sprang eternal for Mr. Bittre. Here was style, harmony and levitation, unusual for California. He headed and bodied over to a pew near centre window and wrestled a pack of smokes from an Eskimo.

Seated at table he adopted a praying position. Feeling burgundy of pain which shot from his knees to his neck as he knelt. He looked down into the dark of linoleum table surface. Sick and mucus covered his face and blood dripped onto table slicked back top. Not too shabby.

"Wow! Is that really you Lunky? Lunky Fast bender?" A woman drinking an elephant waved and coo-coo kee chooed across from the eternal ends of the Diner interior. *"Donuts! Don't forget me now in the movies!"* She wailed and mailed over a kiss. Mr. Bittre burped loudly and offensive in her direction and smiled back. Burning menu and melting ketchup. Clicking his tongue at mystical shadow, which fell over table 23. Eye to eye met via one of Buddhist monk waiters who was experiencing tray to upright position after dive-bombing table. Buddhist waiter hovered over black linoleum calmly and revealed his order book.

"Welcome to The Diner Holistic Mr. Bittre. I am your waiter Baloo Balurmarr and I am appearing in triplicate throughout your dining experience." Announced the Monk politely. *"Once as physical, once as spiritual and once as part of The Dreaming. We specialise in Bardos and great coffee. What is nature of existence and what will be your order Mr. Bittre?"*

A match struck off nametag of Baloo Balurmarr and moved up to self-adjusting cigarette holder, which stuck out of festering gob of customer. Mr. Bittre attempted to light Diana protruding from end.

"Order from chaos. Give me egg on tongue and bread in mouth my levitating fellow!" Cried Mr. Bittre.

Soft mariachi trumpets formed in his ears and drums of knitting needles sounded from a sailor behind him. Knit one, pearl one, knit one pearl one. A rhythm of rowing struck up from jukebox. Much of pulsing and heart-pumpy took in night and fan turned and span sweet Diner air.

Mr. Bittre drank in atmosphere, surveyed his matchbook of clear perspective, caught between bony digits of his skeletal hands.

THE DINER HOLISTIC
Home to the Bardos and great coffee

Read the cover of gold type on black. Shiny and matt-free.

"Are the Bardos worth trying?" Asked Mr. Bittre through broken teeth and blood to nobody in particular. As he surveyed his imminent surroundings he noticed a huge wave of joy emanating from all customers of Diner. All nodded merrily with approval and laughed. The Diner glowed with enthusiasm and levitating Monks began chanting through their tripled nosed faces as they span around with delight.

FRIDAY 7TH SEPTEMBER 2001
AFTERNOON / ISLE OF WIGHT

ORIGINAL MOTION PICTURE SOUNDTRACK

It's my life yes it's my life and though
I can't be sure if I want any more
It will come to me later
THE SUNDAYS

THERE HAD BEEN a long-running argument between Static and his good friend Gyro as to which view of the Isle of Wight held the most fascination. Gyro had always maintained the opinion that the view from the ferry leaving the island had always been the superior one while Static held on firmly to the ideal that arriving always held more potential for him. His DJ accomplice had left three years previously for Australia and had since seemingly vanished into thin air, not only from the Empire base of Queen Victoria but also from the planet Earth entirely. Static had been determined at least that the two of them would meet at some point in the future and discuss their opposing views on the ferry once again. Static still had not received details as to where his friend had vanished to. The DJ had already met him twice in dreams but anything revealing the location of Gyro had been difficult to decipher. Gyro had mentioned some sketchy details about being with a Chinese woman and seemed his usual bizarre self.

The current emergence of someone who fitted the description of an older and wiser Gyro appearing somewhere in Heathrow Aiport had forced Static out of his usual hibernation in Shorwell where he had spent the remaining years since they last parted company attempting to put together a personal project to understand every dream he had ever had in his life. He had been developing his talent as a writer by working on a project that he hoped would earn him an allotted place amidst the local hidden celebrities of the island elite. Researching the process of dreaming and forcing some answers onto the world about what really happened between the ears of people when they were usually asleep. One problem of the century had been trying to find his friend Tony Webb in Carisbrooke in time to drop off his pet penguin Mr. Eco so he could head on to the party in Hackney.

Keeping track of dreams had not been as easy as it sounded. Static had developed a great insight into his own experiences that would give another and more noted island writer if not notoriety then at least some severe name checks. However, the lyrics of a band called The Waterboys were now playing loudly in his head and on the car stereo as he headed towards the direction of West Cowes to catch the ferry to Southampton and onward to London. Wondering briefly about his friend Gyro. For some reason, much like the students at school who could pass any exam by simply revising the night before, Gyro could simply travel around the world a number of times and return without so much as an interruption in his manor of speaking. Or a drop in his number of girlfriends.

The lyrics of 'Whole of The Moon' blasted out of the rolled down windows of the blue Vauxhall and Static felt that the line *"I wandered out in the world for a year, while you just stayed in your room..."* could not be more appropriate to his life at the moment. By any great shakes Static had little desire to travel any further than Newport, the island capital, a mere five miles away. The last letter Static had received from his friend Gyro had mentioned that the designer had travelled a staggering 10,567 miles from America to Australia and that had been about two years ago.

However the chances were slim that when Gyro had been spotted by O.D. Darren in an airport running along the runway and screaming *"Hold that plane! I wanna' get on...,"* to anyone who would listen, Static thought the description fitted his old companion a little too accurately. The blonde hair had been the clincher. Along with the kilt.

Static had received a call from O.D. Darren a mutual friend from college claiming that the sunglasses and insane hair could belong to none other than Mr. Scope. Yet whatever O.D. Darren had been doing at Heathrow Airport he could not say. He sounded stressed and Static thanked his maker that he had decided never to attempt a life in London. Static enjoyed life and London had been far too much hassle to be involved in any part of it.

His old blue second hand Vauxhall hugged the tarmac streets of Newport as he drove into the garage at the top of Honey Hill. He parked the vehicle and tanked up with petrol, quickly checking through the numbers in his pocket book for the one that O.D. Darren suggested trying. It had belonged to a lady called Liz and O.D. Darren had been convinced this was the very same Liz that Gyro had attended school with fifteen years ago. Static shot off down the road in the direction of Cowes on the West side of the island and fumbled for his mobile in the glove compartment, dialling the number as he attempted at break neck speed to dock with the one o'clock ferry heading across The Solent to Southampton. The phone rang twice before a professional sounding Australian accent picked it up.

"Big New Yorker?" Said the female voice as if any other statement in the Universe would be simply ridiculous.

"Awl right. Is that Liz?" Asked Static in his island country drawl.

"I'm sorry, everyone is in a meeting at the moment. Can I take a message?" Chimed the perky voice.

"Yeah, can you get Liz to call Static. When she's free? Thanks love!" Chimed Static in return.

"Certainly sir. She'll be out of the meeting in about one hour if you'd care to hold?" Asked the receptionist.

"You must be joking!" Replied Static cringing at being called sir.

"Well I'll give her the message and get her to return your call then sir, goodbye!" The line clicked off. Static briefly stared at the phone and wondered how much cocaine the reception had shoved up her nose that morning. The speed at which people in London spoke caused the DJ to thank whoever had created this planet that he had never moved to the capital. Static parked the Vauxhall near the ferry terminal in West Cowes and looked down at his mobile as it beeped loudly notifying him he had a message waiting. He then stared in disbelief as he read the message. [O.D. FANTASTIC. GO GO. LET'S MEET IN SOHO AT CAFE NERO. ONE MILLION FOR THE SCRIPT IS OKAY?]

Reading over the message Static realised he had no idea how to reply. Technology of mobile phones was something he had no understanding of whatsoever. Maybe it had been a wrong number. The DJ positioned his vehicle to board the ramp of the ferry from East Cowes. A sudden flash of the dream last night swam to the front of his mind as he steadily steered the Vauxhall up the ramp. He could see his own face reflected in the rear-view mirror as he mumbled the words aloud to himself in the warm interior of the car. *"What on Earth was that dream about then Static?"* He asked his reflection staring back at him. The reflection tried its best to recall it for him.

There had been some kind of explosion and Static had been on a train moving along a disused track with lots of American and Mexican people behind him. There had been dark grey clouds in the sky over a darkly sketched landscape and another explosion had forced him out of the train and onto the tracks. Out of sheer common sense the dream had forced him to stand still and check his bearings. He had been standing right at the edge of a huge cliff drop where the train tracks had buckled and stopped. There had been nowhere to move to. Behind him the train had locked still with all the people trapped between him and the front of the huge metal vehicle. The iron girders of the train were bent and twisted and yet no one had been hurt.

In a second dream Static had seen a group of airplane passengers following him across an iceberg. There had been a rucksack on a bed. The music of Laurie Anderson played and Static felt himself floating upward towards a countryside setting of absolute beauty. It looked as if he had been on the Isle of Wight. There had been an incredible party and the supplies of wine never seemed to end. Tony Webb had been talking to Charles Darwin and the Dalai Lama about building an extension onto his house, then Static had seen a terrifying figure dressed in a black suit, wearing red gloves and carrying a cane. A soft German accent had warned him that something terrible was about to happen. Then the DJ woke up. As Static parked the car in the lower deck of the docked ferry and stepped out onto the cold metal surface he wondered if the party in Hackney was going to be anything worthwhile to write about. He had been searching for ideas for writing a film-script but since he had begun his own personal 'dream project' little had forced him to get out of Shorwell and off the island. Or even out of bed.

Static walked up the outside metal steps to the upper top deck and looked out over the calm waters of The Solent, thinking of how great writers such as Tennyson, Charles Darwin and even David Icke had made this very same journey over the years from the island towards Southampton.

Then the DJ thought about Mr. Eco his pet King Penguin eating fish and flapping his little flippers with excitement as Static had dropped him off at Kitbridge Road into the warm comforting arms of his good friend Tony Webb. He hoped the King Penguin had enough fish to last the three days that he would be in London. What incredible mammals they were. Each one of the males could ejaculate sperm for over thirty seconds. Tony Webb had smiled and waved to Static as he had left the moderate semi-detached house on Kitbridge Road. Static decided to walk into the lower decks of the petrol-blue ferry and buy a latte.

As the DJ took a seat and looked out through the cabin windows of the ancient ferry, watching the boats and yachts as they weaved out of the way for the Red Funnel vessel to pass he pondered on what had happened to Gyro after he had lost contact with him and headed towards New York. That had been nearly a year ago. Nothing had emerged from that point onward. Static watched as the coastline of the island became smaller and merged slowly into the distance. The large tankers and cruisers of oil companies began to appear on the distant horizon. He was already missing Shorwell and Mr. Eco. Static promised himself that this visit to London would be the last for a while and that he would definitely attempt to track down Gyro once the return journey had been made. Static decided again that arriving back on the island always held more potential for him. There had been a long-running argument between Static and his good friend Gyro as to which view of the Isle of Wight held the most fascination.

FRIDAY 7TH SEPTEMBER 2001
MORNING / THE EAST END

NO ALARMS AND NO SURPRISES PLEASE

Instant Karma's gonna' get you gonna' knock you right on the head
You better get yourself together pretty soon you're gonna' be dead
JOHN LENNON

O.D. DARREN HURRIED along the streets of Hackney with the cargo of drugs in the black leather suitcase. Moving fast towards Victoria Park and the tube station. It had just started to rain and although he had been only dressed in his Haight/Ashbury T-Shirt and jeans, something about the imminent threat of being assassinated the following morning had caused him to develop a slightly relaxed approach to life. The hippy felt a strange uncertain elation forming in his mind. As he walked past the various houses along the wet streets towards the park he felt close to irresolute about the entire turn of events that had just occurred in a house that until recently he had thought simply as merely another building in London without a video-recorder.

The dealer had become convinced the house of Winmau had somehow been infiltrated by demonic possession. Nothing else could explain what he had just witnessed. As O.D. Darren strolled through the entrance of Victoria Park he could still not believe that a person he had been helping for around six months had turned around and not only threatened him with execution but had also placed him into such a situation that seemed highly unlikely to get out of. The wall of problems built around him had become so high that there simply seemed to be no solution to them all. Not within the allotted time. Less than twenty-four hours judging by the readings of his watch.

"You have to get a quarter of a million dollars together. It's not so much. It's around one hundred and twenty-five thousand pounds...actually." The smug voice of what O.D. Darren had thought before as being a reasonable intelligent male in his mid-forties had transformed into a monster from hell in the space of the time that it takes to make a cup of the worst coffee O.D. Darren had ever tasted, bitter. He walked under the trees and looked across at the statues of wild grey wolves that someone had decided would give the park in Bethnal Green a nice disturbing look of horror and wondered what it had been about London that caused nearly everyone he ever knew to either have a complete breakdown, commit suicide or have their anger raging away inside them until it exploded.

Somehow the whole of Hackney looked different today. Five years of living in the poorest borough in Europe had undoubtedly reached a peak and in much the same way that animals know they are becoming extinct. O.D. Darren knew that his number had finally come up. This looked as if it really would be his last day on Earth. He had fifty pounds a week from the dole and a large suitcase of narcotics worth over a million pounds. Once the hippy delivered the case to The Madam then O.D. Darren might receive his usual ten pound Darwin. The Madam would be fine and at eighty-two years-old he wondered briefly how on Earth she had survived this length of time in the business. O.D. Darren had reached twenty-six years of age and it looked as if the plan he had originated on his two year trip out to China and Tibet would finally have to begin. Just thinking about his plan filled him with new hope.

The streets seemed to reflect happiness and joy from every window. O.D. Darren felt as if he had just been dropped into a cartoon. All the shades of colour shining through the leaves of the trees looked more vibrant than he had ever seen and he found himself almost ecstatic with love for all that was around him. Life.

The sounds of children laughing echoed from a playground nearby and O.D. Darren thought briefly of the children that he was never going to have and the wife he would never have time to meet and not have them with. He tried to console himself with the thought that most people had no idea when they were going to die and yet here he was with not just the knowledge of when he was going to be killed, but also by whom and why. Along with the details of how it would happen. O.D. Darren sighed. He had never thought about being shot before but he knew somehow that deep down in his heart, it would have been the last way he would have chosen to die. He stood holding the case and breathed in the cold September morning air. Commuters were rushing past from the red London buses and the hippy now had the understanding as he looked around at the morning rush hour that one day, each person he saw would also die. However, the chances were that they were not going to die at precisely six o'clock tomorrow morning. Saturday. Then again what did he know? He avoided the oncoming rain by walking down the steps and into the underground. Purchased a single ticket and ran down the escalator.

It had only been when he boarded the train on the Central Line that the situation truly manifested itself. Time for him felt as if it had finally stood still. Winmau had given him an opportunity to be vaguely thankful for. O.D. Darren decided to keep his usual cool perspective about the situation. The Madam would be expecting him in two hours and he had at least twenty hours left to live. Enough time to get off at Tottenham Court Road and get a latte. After the quickest tube journey to the West End that he had ever experienced he arrived at Tottenham Court Road underground station. O.D. Darren hurried along the streets of London with the cargo of drugs in the black leather suitcase.

FRIDAY 7TH SEPTEMBER 2001 NIGHT / HACKNEY

SIMPLY EVERYONE IS ON COCAINE

I guess we agree the party's over now
It's plain to see, broken hearts for you and me
TRIO

LIZ UNWRAPPED THE paper fold and placed it on the lid of the toilet seat. She squatted down and pulled out a Darwin from behind her left ear and positioned it under her nose, temporarily surveying the white powder in front of her. She sectioned off a small line on the wrapper and sniffed. The buzz shot up the inside of her nasal passages and caused her brain to feel as if it had become twice the normal size for her head. Her teeth almost immediately began to grind together and she could taste the strange bitterness of the cocoa plant of South America slipping down the back of her throat. The lower part of her face felt numb. This was definitely the real thing.

The knocking on the wooden bathroom door caused her to quickly and carefully fold up the paper wrap and slip the Darwin back behind her ear, before exiting the bathroom and returning to the main dance area of the warehouse party. The music had sounded terrible before she had visited the toilet, now she wanted to own every song that she heard playing and her enthusiasm for all things loud had begun. Liz wobbled over to where the dealer had been standing, next to the speakers and waited as arranged. Within seconds he approached her obviously having watched her like a hawk and began grinning like a fox eating shit out of a wire brush.

"So, sixty as arranged?" Winmau asked as he placed a not unwelcome hand around her waist.

"Blimey, that's like a week's rent!" Liz guffawed as she handed over the six Darwins to the American.

"*Where do you live then?*" Asked the dealer surprised at the idea of cheap rent in London.

"*Hackney!*" Yelled back Liz over the music.

"*Ahh, fair enough. I'm a South London boy myself. Drive a Cortina. Later babe...*" Winmau mooched off in the direction of three teenagers dancing on the other side of the warehouse floor, leaving Liz to survey the party looking for her friend O.D. Darren.

The evening was still early for a party in London and people were still arriving from all over Hackney. The word had gotten around that the Summer solstice would continue after Glastonbury and the drum and bass party of a century was about to begin in Sigdon Passage.

Yelps seemed to be coming from a man in the corner of the dance floor who had just rinsed his eye out with beer. It was Glen Miller the cycle-courier. Cocaine prices had dropped across London again along with ecstasy, the drug of a generation. The price had intrigued a number of first timers into experiencing what the inventors of the most popular soft drink in the world had used as part of a secret recipe. Liz welcomed Glen Miller into the small crowd of dancers.

"*Glen Miller you old scroat. How's it hangin'?*" She shouted even though Glen was standing right next to her.

"*Interesting Liz, interesting. Did you hear about your boss?*" Yelled back the cycle-courier.

"*Hey! It's Friday. I just left the bloke four hours ago. What do you mean... Ray?*" Her buzz immediately deflated just hearing anyone mention the name of Ray Connif.

"*I just heard this from a mutual friend...*" Glen always knew best to be on guard if Liz was snowed-up. "*Apparently he's gone to Germany?*"

"*Duuhhh...Who do you think drove him to the airport?*" Asked Liz.

Glen Miller also knew that cheap racial jokes were his speciality. "*I'm not sure, did Jew?*"

Liz shot back a look that seemed to suggest that her Jewish ness was not an issue tonight this was a party and after shooting adverts all week, the production company she worked for was not appearing on the horizon until Monday.

"Why did you pour beer into your eye?" She asked in a manner which made Glen feel as if he was five years old instead of twenty-five.

Glen looked down at his feet slightly embarrassed. *"I would seriously not recommend it. I needed to rinse my eye out after getting something stuck in it. I couldn't get into the bathroom quick enough."* The comment was enough to get Liz off the subject.

"What was it you were saying about Ray?" Asked Liz.

"Why's he gone to Germany?" Yelled Glen.

"Oh, something about reading over the film scripts. He wants to move into film production and he keeps raving about this script he's gotten hold of called O.D."

A momentary pocket of recognition arrived between the two conversationalists. A mid-twenties blonde stranger, walking past them turned hearing the end of the sentence and interrupted the flow.

"Hello? I don't think we've met. What were you saying?" Asked Static.

The interruption was not unwelcome but was enough for Liz to be thrown off her train of thought. Something she hated about parties.

Glen Miller on the other hand welcomed anyone who drank beer and judging by the bag of clinking Biere D'alsace that the stranger was carrying, did not hesitate with introductions.

"Pleased to make your acquaintance, care to join us? The name's Glen Miller!" Said the cycle-courier eagerly.

"Static!" Announced Static over the drum and bass.

Completely missing the introduction Glen misunderstood all that the new arrival had said until the music suddenly broke. A pregnant pause arrived between all three of them, until Glen realised that he had been given a new name to deal with. He laughed out loud. *"Oh...I get it, your name's Static!"*

"Bingo!" Shot back Static.

A huge wave of embarrassment swam over Liz, who copied the body language of Glen Miller subliminally.

"Oh...sorry. I thought you were... oh never mind!" Continued Liz. "Would you two like to go somewhere quieter and talk?" She shouted.

"Granted!" Replied Static.

The three moved in the direction of the back staircase towards a room that had the words BINGO in huge orange letters painted on a door. A sign had been printed on a white sheet of paper and glued to the floor which read the words Chill Out Room in strong black type. An arrow pointed in the direction of a smaller room at the back of the warehouse and with Static leading the way, Glen and Liz followed.

"Do you have any chewing-gum?" Asked Liz as they found themselves being enveloped by the soft sounds of Brian Eno, a haze of thick smoke hung over the room full of bodies as the sounds of the dance floor became muffled behind a large green door. A small side door had been built into the bottom of the wall and as the group of three sat down in front of it. Liz turned to Glen Miller and Static with a look on her face that suggested she could hardly contain herself from opening the tiny door.

"Do you think there's anything behind it?" She asked Static.

"There's always something behind a door..." Smiled Static. "...when one door is shut, don't you know another is open." He winked.

Liz raised her eyes to heaven realising the chances were slim of getting a straight answer from someone who loved idioms more than chocolate. She leaned over and tweaked the door handle between two well-manicured fingers and opened it. On the other side of the ornately carved white door was a miniature scale toilet. Perfectly built into the wall. There was even a tiny pink toilet roll and a chain. Liz could hardly believe her luck as she looked over her shoulder at the other two. "Hey check this out, it's a perfect replica of the other bathroom." She said as she grabbed her bag and pulled out the small parcel of cocaine from inside.

Liz unwrapped the paper fold and placed it on the lid of the toilet seat.

FRIDAY 7TH SEPTEMBER 2001 EVENING / SPACE

THE GENETICALLY CLONED SON OF GEORGE LUCAS

A junkie's song a dancer's knees the laws of chance strange as it seems take us exactly where we most likely need to be
DAVID BYRNE

ONE OF THE biggest problems with being an alien had to be the learning. Most aliens were bilingual, not only in over several hundred languages and dialects but also in customs, ethics, morals, religions, styles, sciences and engineering to name just a few thousand of the encompassing umbrella subjects needed, even before a pilot had been given permission to enter the five-year training programme that this particular alien had decided to undertake. The Irrigation Project. The purpose of which had been to hold an intergalactic piloting licence which would allow a pilot to fly one of the white transport Zoa-pods that operated within a Techtonic-Freighter. These were the new highly mobilised and fluid vehicles that transported the operators and pilots around inside the Freighter in much the same way that blood cells carry oxygen around a human body. The number of transport vessels had to be at a constant balance in ratio to the size of the freighter.

The advertisements that appeared on monitors around the Freighters were popular with most pilots. They explained in brief how high the levels of training were that a qualified doctor needed to reach in order to pilot their first freighter. Dr. Bostrom had been fortunate enough to have not only learnt the initial requirements but to also have been offered an apprenticeship as a navigator under the guidance of the grandest pilot of the North quadrant known as Max Born.

Max had been piloting freighters for five years and had worked extensively at transporting the most precious of all cargos and fuels in the Multiverse.

The chemical basis for all life. Hydrogen and Oxygen. Known on Earth as water. Working consistently on the mammoth cargo ships which carried water for irrigation to any parts of the Universe that would pay the duty. Without the work that Max oversaw, a great portion of the surface of the Moon would have been left unfertile for many centuries to come.

Max was a true protégé of his Father before him. Most people needed a degree just to sit next to the alien. The skillful pilot had helped Dr. Bostrom over many difficult nights of study aboard the Tectonic-Freighter with understanding the initial fundamentals of the light years of time required along with the patience and skill which held most of the crew captivated. With elegance, poise and style Max taught which quantum periodic episodes required by pilots to avoid when approaching levels of deep acceleration between planets. Along with the five light years learning aboard the freighter which steadily passed as each five thousand million tons of irrigation cargo journeyed from planet Earth to the Moon. The time had finally arrived for the good doctor to take the controls and steer the Tectonic-Freighter for the first time. Dr. Bostrom had been waiting an entire four-year period aboard the gigantic Three Breakfasts Corporation ship, learning, learning and learning. Fortunately Max Born had been a patient teacher and more eager than most to explain how to steer and dock the bulkheads after leaving the Moon.

Great excitement had arrived on the evening of his first solo flight which Doctor Bostrom had to learn in order to control and pilot the vessel out of danger as part of his final examination. First day nerves were constantly rising up but if anything, slight quiet confidence was allowing him to take the controls and proceed cautiously into the atmosphere of Earth towards the hauling of the cargo from The Banda Sea. Steadily lowering the great ship down through the clouds over The Indian Ocean. The good doctor operated the required balance aboard the ship and gracefully hovered above a Boeing 747 carrier being extremely careful not fly to close. The vast size of the Tectonic-Freighter had been spotted a number of times over the five years of his training and the good doctor winced as he recalled the severe reprimands and punishments dealt to other Chromo-Pilots which had resulted from the previous errors. Dr. Bostrom became aware that one mistake would result in his expulsion to a place that most pilots dreaded with fear. Just the word had been enough to fill the good doctor with fear. Hackney.

He knew that rebirth was included as part of the court-martial should he fail. A severe punishment. Although practical the pilots in the past were forced through something called a womb to travel down to Earth and clear up the mess caused by any in-flight meanderings and were then sometimes punished again by seeking something called a Job. The doctor shuddered to himself as he recalled stories told of the rebirth procedure, which had occurred to Michelle - the finest pilot this side of the Moon. It all sounded quite ghastly. The doctor also recalled some of the horror stories he had heard regarding the barren wastelands of Hackney on Earth and he carefully practised his breathing exercises to calm himself down as he hovered above the Jumbo Jet which appeared on the front screen monitor weaving towards a huge lightning storm.

With a sickening sensation which forced his ears to sweat and his hair to slowly change colour to grey with fright. The good doctor flew immediately into the history data logs by accidentally causing the most colossal UFO spectacular ever to be witnessed by the passengers aboard flight 815Y. Along with twelve late night airport staff based around the Intertropical Convergence Zone of The Philippines on planet Earth. He forgot to turn on the radar-cloaking device.

By the time the colossal space vehicle had reached the outer rim near Jupiter, for refuelling, the news had been broadcast all over the sub-ether net and his career had been crushed with mighty humiliation before he had even left the docking bay on the return to the Moon. A board meeting had been scheduled as of immediately and the good doctor was heading there with possibly the reddest hair allowed in deep space. Dr. Bostrom climbed onto the back of the Zoa launcher and programmed a course for the boardroom of The Moon E-Wing Department of The Great Divide. He prayed that Max Born had a sense of humour at least as he steadfastly refused to bare most of the burden.

The good doctor arrived at the docking principle. Max greeted him with a loud angry shout across the floating elliptical table as various members of staff surrounding him operated computer scanners to maintain how many people on Earth had actually witnessed the craft and how the emergency services could resolve the entire debacle. So far the estimation had been at around seven hundred and fifty aboard the plane and one lone Englishman who had been motioned through time until some decision could be made about his future. The ground staff of the airport and the remains of the flight could be easily rectified with an exchange.

"Wowee! That was a fantastic display after five years of training Doctor. What the fuck?" Max exclaimed with a deep growling. *"Were we hung over? Too much Oxygen the time before?"* Everyone in the room laughed. Intimidation was still popular on The Moon.

"Er...thank you..." The Doctor stammered, bowing slightly to everyone at the table. His hair once again majestically changed to dark red. Max checked a screen in front of him and ran over some figures aloud in case the point had been missed.

"The population of Earth who witnessed the ABSCENCE of a cloaking device on the freighter has reached seven-hundred and fifty-two..." He paused for added effect. *"...and might steadily rise...you know what this means?"* He said menacingly. Dr. Bostrom stammered again. *"Er...yes I'm sorry about that."*

"You are now responsible, personally for the Earth discovering what we at the Three Breakfasts Corporation have been successfully concealing from the masses for over...two thousand Earth years. As you know, the punishment is affective as of now. We demand your licence and your Ray-gun and will send you to Earth. Where you will be transported to The Diner Holistic at an unspecified time. Do you have anything to say before you are reborn?"

"Er...gee-whiz, just that it won't happen again. Where is the location of my rebirth?" Enquired Dr. Bostrom.

"Darn right." Replied the doctor meekly. *"You will be dropped in a place called Hackney. Where you will attempt to verify the mess you've made on Earth in...one year after birth. We will generate a time-slip in order for you to dock into a womb."* Announced The Captain officially.

Max pressed a button on the screen as the tall form of Dr. Bostrom found himself transported into a white interior of a small UFO transport vehicle. Where the upside down floating body of Ray Connif greeted him in zero gravity.

"Gutten Tag! You're not Darth Vader are you?" Asked Ray jokingly, more than a little confused by the new arrival. The alien felt more than a little apprehensive at the idea of being re born in Hackney.

"Who?" Asked Dr. Bostrom before he dematerialised down the dark red cavern.

One of the biggest problems with being an alien had to be the constant learning.

SATURDAY 8th SEPTEMBER 2001
MORNING / HACKNEY

STOP BY THE ULTRA-LOUNGE

Getting married having babies...? But you haven't been to Paris!
THE WAITRESSES

MICHELLE HAD ENJOYED the party at Sigdon Passage more than most things in London. After rebirth he had moved to Hackney in the mid-nineties and had hardly been able to speak a word of English. Partly because he had spent most of his previous life travelling across deserts in the outback regions of Fifty-Five Cancri. Which by Hackney standards had been further than zone three by about forty-one light years. Michelle had once been one of the longest lasting pilots of the colossal Tectonic-Freighters and had achieved the cleanest runs of the Irrigation Project to the Moon under the guidance of Max Born that anyone had ever witnessed in space.

Everyone had admired Max as a teacher and storyteller on board the ship. His classic tales of adventure about Michelle had been passed around all the cities of the vast blue planet which had been his home until the time of the troubles. The moment the rebirth of Michelle had reached the outer limits of the planets most aliens had been shocked. Yet when the details of the error had been sent out most aliens had discovered the punishment of being sent to the barren wastelands of Hackney wherever that had been seemed to far outweigh the mistakes Michelle had carried out. However they are all agreed that accidents did happen.

Since rebirth the Frenchman had attempted to explain to various people at parties that the four years he had flown with Max had been fraught with danger. The system of balance had later been introduced through the work of his Father on Fifty-Five Cancri. This had been part of a huge plan to help the people of Earth. People would usually nod and smile at the stories Michelle told. The guests at the party had found themselves being hypnotised by the deep colours held within his eyes as he described in his broken French accent the missions and adventures he had enjoyed with his old comrade Max Born.

However when Michelle drank wine he became suddenly passionate about crop-circles, his memory files began to require attention regarding the party of the previous night and the conversations he had heard in The Chill Out Room. The pilot had been talking with a group of artists. One of them had been named O.D. Darren. He had been comparing the appearances of a crop-circle he had seen in Wiltshire to looking like that of the landing impressions from a large aircraft. O.D. Darren enjoyed conspiring with Static that the craft required for such a vast pattern would have to be alien. Michelle had interrupted at this stage in the conversation, spilling wine over both of them deliberately. He had decided that such an idea had been close to insanity and over a bottle of Oxford Landing told O.D. Darren this with such a determined conviction he had to be calmed down by one of the artists seated nearby.

"*Hey Michelle! One for all and all for one remember?*" Interrupted Ben. "*People are allowed an opinion.*"

"*But he's suggesting that UFOs and aliens are landing all over the country!*" Said the alien raising his voice.

"*So what? It's a party. He's allowed to say whatever he likes.*" Whispered Ben hard across at him. Well aware of the reason someone might be disputing such a fact.

"*Ben. If Max Born hears about this we'll be rushing around the entire planet having to do this job of disinformation!*" Replied Michelle already overworked.

"*But it's an interesting planet isn't it? I love it. They've discovered art here. They haven't got that on most planets.*"

"*But it's my job to convince people crop-circles are not from UFO's.*" Whispered the Frenchman looking around anxiously.

"*I understand that but you have to do it gently. Not shout!*" Said Ben. "*This is England...*"

"*Okay. Pardon.*" Replied Michelle tired from yet learning another piece of Earth culture.

"Okay." Said Ben as he returned to his wine.

During the old days Max Born had been a lot more relaxed as a pilot. Both Michelle and Max had a good companionship and understanding of the various Tectonic-Freighters and the journeys from the Earth to the Moon which had allowed them to experiment without being observed by the Three Breakfasts Corporation security cameras because the ships were out of range. Michelle had discovered that for twenty-three hours a pilot could land on Earth with a white Zoa-pod and simply park it on the surface and create huge beautiful markings in the landscapes. The first had been made purely by accident when Max had given permission for Michelle and a few hundred of the crew to take one of the Zoa-pods down to Earth to abduct some humans and bring them back to the ship for a party in the hope of trying to get some feedback on the work that the Three Breakfasts Corporation were currently undertaking.

Max had always been a stickler for publicity and he knew that if the initial plan being carried out for 2011 had a chance to work then people on Earth had to be on the side of the aliens. If only a little bit. Considering how creative and artistic Michelle could be there had been a fair chance that his plan would work. Anything the alien did had been creative. He could even steer the Tectonic-Freighter with style and would sometimes make drinks for the immediate crew with such panache that even Max had thought that rebirth would allow this star pilot to shine for the good of the future plan. The problem for Max had been that no one really wanted to go to Earth in a hurry. Even Mars or Jupiter had seemed more appealing. The only way to get the best pilots down there had been to rebirth them. The Three Breakfasts Corporation were becoming adamant about how punishments were carried out. The only way round the beaurocracy of the Universe had been to get the pilots to make mistakes in spectacular fashion and therefore punish them. Max hated doing it but he knew that if the plan had been carried out correctly the future would be far safer for just about every living thing in the Universe.

Michelle had taken off as ordered and landed the transport vehicle without a hitch. After landing he had abducted a few humans who claimed to be something called *'famous'*. As they arrived on the Zoa-Pod without a hitch he had taken off and returned to the Tectonic-Freighter on the Moon. Except one thing had ruined the entire expedition. Max Born had entered the cabin of the transport vehicle and had pointed to the reading of the magnetic field which held the vehicle in the air just above the surface and stopped any heat from damaging the facade of the planet or anything else on the surface of the Earth during re-entry.

When Michelle looked at the bank of controls he had been stunned to discover the magnetic field switch had been disabled. The Frenchman had quickly called up the viewing screen which had recorded everything the white vessel had done. A small digital read out had explained to the viewer the exact locations to the decimal point and as he looked at the monitor in horror Michelle watched the landing and take-off carefully. The Zoa-pod had left behind a huge patterned impression in the green area. Created by the weight of its time on the surface of the Earth. He could not believe he had been so stupid and looked over at Max with an expression which if they were on Earth, Michelle would have called guilt. He knew at that precise moment what the punishment for such a mistake had been.

Yet the Chromo-Pilot had never made such a blunder in his entire career. He simply could not believe that his career as the finest pilot in this part of the Universe had unravelled in a place called Wiltshire as they both headed for the Rebirth Room, Max could not help laughing at the error. The pattern left behind on the planet had been huge. How any alien could explain that one away had been even beyond him for the moment. As they both entered the room and Max began pressing co-ordinates into the computer, he had started to explain something he had never told any of the other Pilots he had sent to be reborn on Earth.

"This process you know well but I will tell you Michelle there is a plan in operation to help this planet at the moment. I cannot tell you anymore. When you are on Earth think very very carefully before you do or say anything until we meet again. All I will say is that we are scheduled to meet again in a year or so in the wastelands of Hackney. When you get details from Dr. Bostrom you will know of my arrival. Look into the eyes for the answers. You will not be alone down there. " Said Max calmly as he set the co-ordinates.

"Thank you Max. It's been a rare pleasure flying with you." Michelle had said as he stood waiting on the soft platform. The last part of the conversation had been interrupted by his arrival in the holding room awaiting the docking procedure of a Zoa-Pod for the journey of rebirth. Which for Michelle seemed unusually fast. He had even been surprised to see Mr. Bittre of all entities from the Diner Holistic interrogating an abductee from Earth before the room had glowed dark red and he had found himself

born inside the tiny body of a human life form in a place on Earth called France.

After his year of growing, Michelle had been searching for a sign to locate Dr. Bostrom and had been excited by witnessing him on a television documentary about a place called New York, walking out of an airport. Michelle had spent the frequently hectic years from that point heading to England and attempting to disperse the rumours that had already developed from witnesses around a field in Alton Barnes, Wiltshire. Nothing had prepared the X-Chromo Pilot for the shock of what he had discovered over the months since as he had arrived in England. There seemed to be an entire fleet making similar mistakes and leaving patterns all over the country. Which had possibly been the sign that his old boss had spoken of when they last saw each other.

As time had passed on the planet Michelle had found that he was already missing his old comrade more and more. Emotions on Earth were stronger than in space. Some days he felt that even getting out of bed and talking to people became quite difficult. With the increased weight of gravity around him.

Now as he sat down in the lounge of his house on Earth in Hackney, the X-Chromo-Pilot found himself staring in wonder at the birds sitting in the tree outside as the Sun began the wake-up call to another thrilling day on planet London. The punishment had been severe for Michelle. He had been allocated without any technological tools for communication and had been one of the few X-Chromo-Pilots that had to rely completely on his senses. He had also had to learn a language called English which had not been easy. His educational training in France had been impressive. The speed which he had worked as he learned the language and adaptation skills had been highly extraordinary. This had helped in the development of his understanding about life since arriving on Earth.

The X-Chromo Pilot had naturally been an incredible philosopher and welcomed the subject of questioning with such heart and nobility that a number of people had discovered life to be miraculous again in Hackney merely by the simple task of visiting Michelle. The alien had a way of doing things that seemed to reflect the idea that there was indeed a Universal plan to life and each character had an assignment. Even if this had not always been understood by everyone at the same time.

Since Michelle had arrived in England the Frenchman had fallen in love with words of English such as *'molecule'* and *'packed'* and would spend many happy days walking around his bed-sit near Sigdon Passage saying such words over and over and laughing to himself. After having learnt French, the language of his rebirth, the alien had thought that the differences between England and his own port of arrival were interesting rather than problematic.

However there were words that gave Michelle goose bumps all over his body whenever he heard them. The word Venetian had such an effect.

One such Venetian named Winmau Diamond lived next door and Michelle could barely contain his disgust at the sight of a Venetian living so close to him. Back on Fifty-Five Cancri, the Venetians had started a terrible war The Comma War. The determination to join and fight in this war had killed two members of the original alien family Michelle had been born into many centuries ago when he had been young. The result had been that Michelle had been forced out and off his own planet. When he had run into Max Born. Another refugee from Fifty-Five Cancri.

The chance that Michelle could travel the distance of forty-one light years and then be reborn in Paris, then travel to London whereby he could move next door to the very enemy he had been travelling from had been something the X-Chromo-Pilot spent most of the time in his house pondering. Michelle had attempted several times to move from the house in Hackney but had decided that this might just be one of the signs that Max Born had told him about before rebirth. His mind had since become divided on the subject.

However the Venetian had not presented itself as a problem to Michelle over the years of growing. Since he had been living next door they had only met twice. When Michelle moved in and then had invited him over for a meal, he had been impressed at first by the size of Winmau and then by his smile. Yet Michelle knew that you had to keep busy whenever near a Venetian and had found their first meeting exhausting. If not entirely uninspiring.

The second encounter had been more enjoyable. Once again Winmau had joined the X-Chromo-Pilot for an evening of curry and conversation with another great philosopher that lived in the area called Wittgenstein. The philosopher had called by and explained that he had just broken-up with his girlfriend and had been feeling depressed. Michelle attempted to show him his Bonzai Trees in an attempt to cheer him and Winmau up. Then in a rare moment of calmness the Venetian had been able to place one of the trees on the open palm of his hand and for the first time Michelle had been shocked by the tenderness that came from his enemy. He had seemed like a huge creature called a bear that Michelle had been watching on television on something named a programme.

Wittgenstein had listened to Winmau talking in the lounge while the food had been prepared in the kitchen. The large alien explained how he had played a classic Venetian joke on someone by telling them he had been a drug-dealer. He had gotten hold of a friend who pretended she was a chemist just to add some realism to the joke. They had a script all written out and he had asked her to convince the bloke that the white powder in the case was actually drugs when in fact some of it was sherbet from a sweet shop. The rest had been given to him by a lady called The Madam. As Michelle overheard the tale from the kitchen he could hear Wittgenstein attempt to calm the laughing Venetian down by explaining the story of the boy who cried wolf back to him.

When the X-Chromo-Pilot entered with the food he had been surprised to discover that Winmau had an expression on his face that Michelle had never seen before on such an alien. Michelle even had to look in an English Language Dictionary after his dinner guests had left just to search for the word that described the expression on the huge ugly visage of the Venetian.

As he thought about that evening Michelle heard a knock at the front-door and attempted to adopt his best French expression of bewilderment. He had been still dressed in the attire of his Musketeer costume for the warehouse party and had been cautious of opening the door in such an outfit, he pulled back the mahogany wood of the door and allowed the first warm light of the sunshine to enter the dark interior of his hallway. The sunlight on Earth was almost unbearable at times to the alien and Michelle had left his atmospheric eye-protectors upstairs. His experience so far living in Hackney had taught him that whoever it had been calling this early would be either suicidal or confused. The best thing to do would be to act with caution.

As Michelle opened the front door he could see a tall man wearing sunglasses, dressed in an outfit that suggested he had been at the party the night before dressed as an ambulance man. Michelle figured it must be someone from the party in Sigdon Passage, although when the figure removed the glasses Michelle found himself staring into the familiar eyes of another older X-Chromo-Pilot.

"Excuse me sir, sorry to bother you, but we received a call in this area from a pregnant lady who was having a baby. You wouldn't know of anyone would you fitting that description?" Asked the ambulance man as officially as possible.

"Er... pardon?" Replied the Michelle unable to contain his excitement of seeing an old comrade at his door.

The figure outside the door obviously had little understanding of French as a first language but Michelle could sense warmth exuding from the alien. Yet there seemed to be little recognition received back.

"Oh, tu Francais?" Replied Derek, stepping back a little from the door.

"Oui. Oui!" Exclaimed the Frenchman hopefully. *"Tu parlez Francais?"*

"Un peut! J'ai er...regardez la enfant?" Asked Derek.

The neighbour looked slightly bewildered back at the ambulance man. Michelle felt his heart soar suddenly at the thought that this might be another sign. Maybe he knew where Dr. Bostrom could be found.

"Er... Madame est avec un enfant?" Said the alien.

The Frenchman suddenly realised that a plan had to be carried out immediately if this particular X-Chromo Pilot would return to his house. After studying human behaviour with his teacher in France the only solution Michelle decided had to be the one of action/reaction. Michelle decided with lightning reflexes to copy the expression he had seen on the face of Winmau, he slammed the door shut quickly knowing well that in time the X-Chromo Pilot would have to return to his house due to something on Earth he had studied called *'curiosity'*. The alien had learnt in France that the only way to trigger off memories of rebirth had been to make an action completely out of place with the situation. Michelle returned to his lounge and decided to wait for the return of the old comrade. Intense training had taught him in space that it had been useless to approach another pilot after rebirth with any previous knowledge of their identity simply because the number of humans being born on various planets in the Universe left an infinite number of possibilities as to who it was you were actually talking to. The eyes had been a giveaway though.

The only guidance Michelle could rely on had been some of the experiences he had accumulated on Earth. Should anyone discover the vast means in operation to save Earth however through the Irrigation Project then Max Born would most definitely hear about it. Which would mean even more work for the X-Chromo-Pilots. Michelle laughed with joy as all the feelings of isolation slipped away. He had spotted the good doctor and now an X-Chromo-Pilot. The signs were emerging after a long year of questioning. Michelle sat down and looked under his Bonsai Tree for his English Dictionary and for the translation of the expression he had just practised for the first time.

The alien thought about the party the night before, of a man who had been dressed in the costume of a hippy in flared blue jeans. He had a huge sunflower on his T-shirt which read Haight/Ashbury and seemed to have stepped out of the year 1975 untainted by time. The X-Chromo-Pilot felt a huge wave of fondness for that particular human out of all the people who were dancing in the warehouse last night. Since he had left France Michelle had been surprised constantly that he had arrived in a place so similar to his home planet of Fifty-Five Cancri.

Flicking through the pages of the book he smiled to himself as he discovered the verb that described the look perfectly. DISMAY. He practised it again in the mirror where two photographs were attached to the reflective surface with sello-tape. The first had been a faded sepia photograph of his wife Kubler-Ross who had been killed during The Comma War and a new colour photograph next to it had been the only image of his Father. The great Egor Makeon who died in one of the many battles for the independence of his home planet of Fifty-Five Cancri. However on Earth they had both changed their names to Charles and Dalai. The X-Chromo Pilot sat on the blue beanbag in the lounge and remembered them with fondness and smiled. There was little that the alien understood or enjoyed such a vast distance from home. Yet Michelle had enjoyed the party at Sigdon Passage more than most things in London.

SUNDAY 9TH SEPTEMBER 2001
AFTERNOON / HACKNEY

I LOVE EVERYBODY ESPECIALLY YOU

I am tired I am weary I could sleep for a thousand years
A thousand dreams that would awake me
Different colours made of tears
THE VELVET UNDERGROUND

DEREK STEPPED OUT from the kitchen of The Marion Arms half asleep and stepped his bare left foot into something brown, soft and squishy which seemed to have the same impact in odour and consistency as nuclear waste. With the exception that nuclear waste had been easier to transport and left more of a positive impression with people who regarded cats as wastes of fur. Clive, his live in partner was one such person and therefore refused to assist in the area of little kitty surprises which littered the pub interior like soft mines. This one particular kitty surprise now covered the bare soles of both his feet. Derek quickly scoured the area around the antique bar for a mop and bucket and decided today was excrement clean-up day.

Both the ambulance men had squatted the disused pub for nearly eleven years and in a legendary tale of wonder had never once had an eviction notice or hassle from the police about entering the building on a daily basis. Their first year in Hackney had gone by relatively smoothly. As far back as 1993 Derek had travelled accidentally to the North of London after catching the wrong bus and had then stumbled into The Marion Arms to order a Snowball and lemonade, his favourite drink, only to discover that the landlord of the pub had long since left, along with the cash register and most of the customers.

Although extremely down to Earth, Derek had been anything but a fast thinker and had taken over two hours to realise that there had been no one working in the pub. Derek decided to sleep there that night and as time moved on, it became obvious that nobody was particularly bothered about him being there. He was forty-years-old by appearance, had an amazingly calm expression and was nearly seven foot tall, with a terrible memory. Most people thought of him as a lanky English student. He had short dark hair and one rare quality about his manor that had carried him through his life securely so far. Mostly without his knowing, his eyes. The eyes of Derek were the envy of most people he met and yet most people never seemed to understand how difficult it was for him to see properly. Impaired by having eyes like the singer David Bowie.

As he gradually found the mop surrounded by the assorted junk of old furniture and beer bottles which had gone uncollected for years. Derek cleaned up the excrement off the floorboards of the pub. He squinted into the dark wooden interior searching for his glasses which he had left on the bar after an unusually heavy session of drinking brought on by the previous day transporting bodies across London to morgues. Nothing uncommon when you are an ambulance man but deeply disturbing when the call you receive is for a corpse you recognise.

Derek had been unfortunate enough to have had such an experience by receiving the call to move the body of O.D. Darren to a morgue in High Holborn the day before with Clive his companion in tow, his trusty sidekick. The day had started promisingly enough when he had been told that a woman had given birth in a warehouse in Sigdon Passage. Births were a speciality to Derek. He loved delivering babies so much that the call had caused him to become as excited as a Springer Spaniel being shown a lead before going for a walk.

The expectations had quickly turned to disappointment when instead of a birth he had witnessed the dead body of O.D. Darren sitting in the warehouse of Sigdon Passage who he had not seen since he had been a teacher at a school on the Isle of Wight. Darren had been twelve at the time Derek had been teaching him chemistry and had been more than shocked at the untimely reunion. Especially when the conversation had been a little one sided on the way to the morgue. The various friends that O.D. Darren had made had stunned Derek. At least more than one mutual friend of O.D. Darren had seen Derek walking around Hackney but had been jolted by surprise to discover not only that he had since become an ambulance man but also that he used to be his old teacher from the island.

The atmosphere at the squatted pub however had been strange to say the least. A girl called Claire seemed to hold everything together brilliantly by telling funny stories about her friend as if he had merely gone on holiday somewhere. Yet Derek had become familiar with many of the signs of grief from working as an ambulanceman. Out of all the calls received what could have been the chances that one would be for an ex-pupil. Derek felt a wave of goose bumps appear on his arms and legs for the first time since leaving teaching and entering the hardcore work of hospital assistance. He smiled to himself remembering the twelve year-old Darren in class explaining to the other pupils how much money a drug-dealer made and why it had seemed to him just as honourable a profession as teaching because he had watched Scarface with Al Pacino the night before on television.

Suddenly a huge wave of sadness came over Derek. He had always loved reunions and yet this one had to be the only one so far in his life that he wished had never happened. A knock on the frosted glass entrance of the pub snapped him out of his trance as he recognised the form of Ben peering back at him through the front window. Although still dressed in pyjamas, Derek wiped a palm over his face and walked over to the entrance. Sliding the heavy metal bolts back and pulling one of the doors open with a loud creak, Ben had always been a pleasure to see on a Sunday.

"Morning Derek..." He announced, stepping inside the gloomy interior. "Do you have anything to drink?"

"Duuuh...it is a pub Ben!" Replied Derek with his reassuring smile.

"Oh yeah...I saw the sign outside. Are you Mr. Marion?" Bounced back the artist blowing into his hands to warm them. He parked his bike over by a broken piano at the antique bar. "What on earth is that smell?"

"That smell," continued Derek walking over to the bar and pulling two glasses out from under the bar and pushing them both up to the optic of Jameson. "...is the smell of napalm in the morning which has been left by General Kitty!" Derek had two cats which lived in the squat with him and his partner Clive. One of them leapt up from behind Ben and paraded up and down the bar at the mention of her name as if to say, *'Yep and whatcha' gonna' do about it?'*

"Woah! What have you been feeding them? Manure?" Asked Ben holding a hand over his nose.

"Nuclear waste actually!" Replied Derek.

"Even cat-shit is like gold to an angel I guess." Said Ben sitting on a red bar stool.

Ben sat at the bar and grabbed the whisky glass, draining it in one gulp.

"Could I have another please sir? I've just had an odd morning..." He winced as the drink hit the spot.

"You and me both..." Sighed Derek.

Ben had been a regular of the The Marion Arms secret drinking elite before the pub had become abandoned. Derek had decided at the time to maintain the illusion that The Marion Arms was open as usual. Maintaining it until Ben had quizzed him one night ten years ago as to the whereabouts of all the other customers. When he explained the truth Ben had laughed so much that they became firm friends, introducing Derek to the various members of the Hackney artistic elite with fond and detached admiration. With a profound majestical move, Ben reached into his bag and pulled out the tarnished metallic goblet found at Hackney Wick.

"My landlord! I bring you the Grail as requested!" Claimed the artist.

"Wow! Where did you find it my good knight?" Asked Derek fascinated.

"Of course, it was in Hackney the whole time!" Answered Ben reaching for the second drink of many.

"Hang about!" Yelled Derek and rushed around the bar to where a stack of old library books were piled up against the piano. He grabbed one of the larger ones, causing the rest to fall crashing to the wooden floor of the pub, then ran unperturbed back to the bar and leafed through the pages of the large dusted hardback. With relentless concentration he rifled through the pages back and forth, scanning the contents. His upper teeth bit down hard on his bottom lip with tight focus until he found what he had been looking for. Suddenly he yelled out with excitement spinning the book around to where Ben was sitting already on his third whisky.

"Check it out Benny boy!" He slammed an index finger down in the direction of the page he had found. Ben squinted at the page and looked back up at Derek who was beaming back insanely. Then he looked again at the tarnished silver goblet sitting politely on the polished surface of the bar. Then returned a transfixed eye to the book.

"Okay...er...it looks slightly like the picture..." Replied the alien doubtfully.

"Looks slightly like it? It's a dead ringer!" Exclaimed Derek. "That painting is around seven hundred years old."

Ben looked carefully at the caption underneath. Which read [1523 - Ireland.]

"Er...it says it's twenty-three minutes past three o'clock in Ire-land. Where's that?" Asked the alien with a strange expression. Derek span the open spread of the book back to face him surprised.

"What do you mean man? It's Ireland. It's the year - 1523. That's the date that the Doomsday Book was written or around that time was known as the Dark Ages." He reached for the glass of whisky. "Arthur was supposedly the rightful King of England and also...he was Irish." Smiled Derek.

Ben felt a sudden chill on the back of his neck. He turned to see the Pub door being opened by Clive who entered with The Sunday Papers and an even larger bottle of Jameson.

"Good morning Mr. Ben!" Said Clive walking over to join the two history students.

"Morning Clive you old rascal." Spoke the alien.

"Ben's just found the Holy Grail." Said Derek reaching for the new bottle.

"No way!" Said Clive joining them at the bar. His beard and grey coloured tunic seemed to bring another angle to the current situation. "Where was it then?" He asked pulling up a stool.

"Down Hackney Wick. Thirty-eight pence!" Said Ben presenting the bowl.

"You're kidding? I always thought it would turn up in Ireland." He studied the antique carefully.

"The bloke who sold it to me was Irish come to think of it. He said his name was Joseph and he would be drinking in a pub called The Arimithea Arms over in Notting Hill...if I wanted to give it back." Said Ben coyly.

"You bought it? Oh man that, by tradition is not a good thing to have done. The Grail has to be found without..."

"Uh-oh". Said Ben as the cup suddenly began to glow.

Derek stepped out of into the kitchen of The Marion Arms half asleep and stepped his bare left foot into something brown, soft and squishy which seemed to have the same impact in odour and consistency as nuclear waste.

MONDAY 10TH SEPTEMBER 2001
PROBABILITY / FIFTY-FIVE CANCRI

CALLING OCCUPANTS OF INTERPLANETARY CRAFT

*The Universe it is so big I feel dizzy when I think about it
My head swims I get giddy still I realise that long ago
It was so small I could have kept it underneath my little skirt*
THE SUGARCUBES

THE INTERIOR OF the vessel Static had just stepped into reminded him somehow of a gigantic pink sponge. He was instantly reminded of the problem he once had describing what it might be like to slip into the head of a stranger when the person was dreaming. Accidentally forgetting to return to their own physical body before they opened their eyes in the morning. *"Imagine what a major problem that would be."* Static had once mentioned to his friend Gyro, who had managed to swiftly deflect the question by asking him in return what he was doing with his life.

As the vessel lifted effortlessly off the surface of the Earth and began to ascend gracefully up into the heavens Static thought he had finally understood what all the nuns at the convent he had been taught at had been constantly getting excited about over his past ten long years of education. The sensations created in his stomach from the shock of being lifted at such an incredible speed out of the atmosphere of the Earth, pushed his whole physique almost through the floor of the vessel with such a force that for a brief moment Static thought he was about to suffocate. The floor of the interior seemed to be not only transparent and made of some sort of soft material but Static realised he was already sinking into the material and had already become trapped and motionless. The floor of the craft seemed like jelly cooling and setting around him. Then his body sunk down into it. He could only move his eyes.

The strain of craning his neck down to look at the pilots of the craft allowed him to momentarily view only pure white in all directions and then as if by magic, Static found himself sitting back in the huge manor house of his friend Tony Webb with two aliens. Procta and Gamble. Every person at the party posed still as mannequins, frozen in time. Beautiful music came from somewhere and Static noticed that he was now able to sit up and move around freely.

The DJ looked around the kitchen and noticed a small Galaxy hovering above the sideboard next to some fresh vegetables and a cutting knife. He peered into it. A soft female German voice spoke to him from somewhere far off in the distance and then reverberated close right next to his eardrum. The voice sounded so familiar that Static felt an overwhelming urge to hold onto whomever it had been that was speaking to him.

"That's Centaurus and Scorpio and those are the Star Clouds of Sagittarius. Gaseous nebulae and obscuring clouds near Ophiuchi. Globular Cluster M13 in Hercules. Spiral Nebula M31. Which appeared briefly in the classic movie A Matter of Life and Death by Michael Powell and Spiral Nebula M31. On your right is Nebula NGC 4365."

Static felt his whole body falling at incredible speed towards the Nebula as if he had jumped from a plane and took on the appearance of Superman in flight. Arms outstretched. As he looked down below him, his Father could see the distant surrounding stars and galaxies growing and expanding in the dark brown carpet of the house of his parents in Kitbridge Road in Carisbrooke. He could see his family gathered in the dining room having dinner as the warm sunlight poured in through the kitchen window. His Father was making everyone seated at the table laugh by talking about potatoes. The newspaper on the table read 1976.

"Your Mother's asking if you would you like some more potatoes Static..." Said his Father smiling.

When he looked up from the table to see the face of his Father, Static found himself staring into an incredible view of mountains, topped by clouds and waterfalls. Fresh water cascaded down through the rocks and lush green land of the surrounding hills. Static recognised the scenery of the Irish countryside. He saw himself walking across a bridge to the tall trees of a forest nearby. The trees were fantastic. They stretched up and up towards the sky which seemed to be changing from blue into light yellow and then warm orange. The voice continued.

"Greater Magellanic Cloud. Lesser Magellanic Cloud. Nebula of Normal Spiral type NGC 5236. Perhaps Bosch had seen the oncoming traffic and wrote the greatest painting persuading The Beatles to release their first probe into deep space and look there's Dario, a warm welcome for the one of the classic stars of..."

Static walked out of the doorway of a large flat building and into the bright blue sunlight of an incredible place named America. The heat was intense as he looked down to his feet he noticed his shoes were missing. One shoe floated past on the shoulders of jostling people crammed into the hot stifled tiny dance floor at the front of a packed audience. An incredible band called The Pixies were playing live on stage. The energy of the music caused the audience to smile in every direction. Moving and dancing to the music then Static was floating above the audience as the sound carried him further up and he had a perfect aerial view over the band and the audience. Now the whole perspective of the building grew further away into the distance and Static found himself staring in wonder as the image became covered by a pure glass dome reflecting in the sunlight. Bright light glimmered on the surface of the dome and then several others appeared next to it then another, until there were several multiplying and swirling images, spinning faster until they revolved around. From his perspective they became like bubbles, then brown. Static looked up. The coffee cup arrived and he could feel the warmth on his palms as he cupped the ceramic mug tightly, a penguin smiled and chirped opposite him. Playing cards were dealt out by the flippers.

"Statico baby! Me be Benedicto Perky Eco. Charmed and met previous. Tu aime jazz?" Asked the penguin.

As Static surveyed the contents of the quiet and empty Diner he watched the various colours swirl around him and listened to the soft accent of the bird.

"Welcome to Fifty-Five Cancri. Apologiseo for inconveenienceish!" Spoke an Italian sounding voice.

Static had often wondered what the sky must be like on other planets. Were there clouds? Or even people? Or did the sky change as much in colour as the incredible variations of Earth. He heard a distant whistle of microphone feedback and then thought he could hear the voice of a calm deep nasal voice speaking to him. Yet the physical form was nowhere to be seen. *"How do you feel?"* Asked the voice. Static stood still and looked around, searching for the voice.

"Okay I guess but I..." Static tried to reply but found it difficult to move his mouth. Speaking seemed almost impossible. His mouth became untrustworthy.

* *"You know how it is when you're reading a book and falling asleep, you're reading, reading... and all of a sudden you notice your eyes are closed?"* Asked the voice. Static nodded sadly agreeing. That was exactly how he felt. *"I'm like that all the time."* Said the voice.

"I feel kind of detached from everything. I guess it's like this in space." Said Static.

* *"Last night, I walked up to this beautiful woman in a bar and asked her, "Do you live around here often?" She said, "You're wearing two different coloured socks." I said, "Yes, but to me they're the same because I go by thickness." Then she asked, "How do you feel?" and I said, "Well, you know when you're sitting on a chair and you lean back so you're just on two legs then you lean too far and you almost fall over but at the last second you catch yourself? I feel like that all the time."* Said the deep slow voice.

"Who are you? Are you God?" Static asked peering into the light of the vessel.

"My agent would like to think so! Did you know people are God when they're together?" Came the reply. *"I have the world's largest collection of seashells. I keep it on all the beaches of the world... Perhaps you've seen it."*

The thin line of a stage could be seen in the distance and Static could feel himself floating towards it either that or the stage was moving slowly towards him. There seemed no way of telling these things.

**"A friend of mine once sent me a post card with a picture of the entire planet Earth taken from space. On the back it said, "Wish you were here."*

Static could feel all the hairs on his body being coated in a warm heat. He looked down at his body and noticed that he was wearing pyjamas that had a pattern of paisley on them. He felt very pleased with his new pyjamas.

**"Right now I'm having amnesia and deja vu at the same time. I think I've forgotten this before."* Said the voice. *"I like to reminisce with people I don't know."*

He continued to look off into the distance and could see the tiniest spec of a black dot slowly growing in the infinite reaches. The perspective of the view showed something like a tiny fish wiggling towards the dot from his left side.

"I was once walking through the forest alone. A tree fell right in front of me and I didn't hear it." Continued the voice. The dot was now meeting with the fish. He thought it looked more like a tadpole and he remembered how he had been shown the chart on the classroom wall of a school when he was young.

"He asked me if I knew what time it was. I said, "Yes, but not right now."

As Static looked up to the right he could see a tiny perfect scene of the classroom he had been in with his classmates they were being told by one of the nuns that they were going to study botany at the local pond down the road and all the pupils had become excited by the news. He felt worried by going outside with the class.

"I wrote a song, but I can't read music so I don't know what it is. Every once in a while I'll be listening to the radio and I say, "I think I might have written that."

Then they were all walking along the pavement to the pond as the teacher led them through a field of tall green grass towards a small stream with surrounding trees.

"I got up one morning and couldn't find my socks, so I called Information. She said, "Hello, Information." I said, "I can't find my socks." She said, "They're behind the couch." And they were!" Said the voice.

The sensations of Summer were all around him. Static could smell freshly cut grass and he could hear the distant shouts from the middle school opposite. They were all too young and small to play with the older children. Static could feel how much smaller he was and he started to cry. He was frustrated. Would he ever be tall?

"Put on your seat belt. I want to try something. I saw it once in a cartoon, but I think I can do it." Said the voice.

As they all gathered around the pond and looked into the water they could see frogs and insects balancing on the water. He was amazed and had never seen a frog before. Then he could see the eggs under a lily pad. Frogspawn.

The teacher was explaining how the eggs were transparent and Static liked that. He liked penguins as well. The chocolate biscuits that his Mother placed in his lunchbox had the name penguin written across it.

"I was going to tape some records onto a cassette, but I got the wires backwards. I erased all of the records. When I returned them to my friend, he said, "Hey, these records are all blank."

He wrote the word transparent down with his pencil on a sheet of orange paper and thought about what it meant. Static could feel the material of his school uniform and it made him itch. The word was too big to spell correctly so Static had spelt it phonetically. *Tranzzparint.*

"My watch is three hours fast, and I can't fix it. So I'm going to move to New York." Said the voice.

A girl sitting on the grass of the bank in the sunshine laughed when she saw how Static had spelt transparent and he had smiled when he saw her. He loved the way she giggled.

"I went into a clothes store the other day and a salesman walked up to me and said, "Can I help you?" and I said "Yeah, do you got anything I like?" He said, "What do you mean do we have anything you like?" I said, "You started this." Said the voice.

Static was now looking at the frogspawn and the teacher was explaining something about the cycle of life and thought she meant bicycles. He wished he had one. Then he could cycle up to the pond after school.

"When I die, I'm leaving my body to science fiction." Said the voice.

The sun was very hot and now Static was taller he had cycled to the pond and was looking for the eggs again. The dot in the distance was surrounded by white space all around him and he could make out the form and shape of a man standing on a stage.

"I was reading the dictionary. I thought it was a poem about everything." Said the voice.

Static looked down at himself and realised he was dressed in a white suit he almost blended in with the surroundings.

*"In my house there's this light switch that doesn't do anything. Every so often I would flick it on and off just to check. Yesterday, I got a call from a woman in Germany. She said, "Cut it out." Said the voice.

Static could see that the man on the stage was the only person around. Yet he was walking around the stage and talking into a microphone as if the whole world was listening. Static and the two aliens were the only people in the audience.

*"I've never seen electricity, so I don't pay for it. I write right on the bill, "I'm sorry, I haven't seen it all month." Said the voice.

Gyro was now sitting down in front of the stage cross-legged and he could see himself enjoying the jokes from the perspective of the comedian on the stage.

"If toast always lands butter-side down, and cats always land on their feet, what happen if you strap toast on the back of a cat and drop it?" Said the comedian.

Gyro strained his neck suddenly and he could see the two aliens sitting around the blue ball in the middle of the craft. He tried to speak but nothing came out of his mouth when he opened it. The aliens were laughing. One of them looked up at him. "Sorry about that - turbulence!" Suddenly the aliens had joined him in the audience, standing next to them and looking at the stage again.

*"I didn't get a toy train like the other kids. I got a toy subway instead. You couldn't see anything, but every now and then you'd hear this rumbling noise go by." Said the voice.

One of the aliens held onto a script and walked over to join Static and sat down in the audience. The other alien seemed to be holding onto a blue ball and was bouncing it on the white floor up and down. "We love your script." Said the comedian suddenly looking at Static. He pointed at part of the pile of paper, which was orange, sitting on a desk nearby.

Static looked back at him as they sat in the interior of a cinema. The seats were dark petrol-blue and Static felt as if both their bodies were outside somewhere in the cold. The temperature of the room had turned cold. He shivered. *"It doesn't matter what temperature the room is, it's always room temperature." Said the voice.

The appearance of all this suddenly forced Static to look down at the aliens who were looking more like the comedian on the stage. The comedian was wearing a brown suit and smartly dressed but seemed to be false in his sincerity. Static suddenly thought he was going to be sick.

"I think I'm going to be sick. Where's your bathroom?" Static asked as he looked down to his feet feeling the onset of a severe case of travel sickness. He felt as if he had become as small as a chromosome in a sperm heading towards the fertilisation of a new egg.

The interior of the vessel Static had just stepped into reminded him somehow of a gigantic pink sponge.

* **Courtesy of Steven Wright**

TUESDAY 11TH 2001 SEPTEMBER
MORNING / BIG NEW YORKER

WHATEVER HAPPENED TO REAL LIFE?

Oh my life is changing every day in every possible way
Though my dream is never quite as it seems
Your a dream to me dream to me
DOLORES O'RIORDAN / NOEL HOGAN

BRITT CONTINUED TO stare up at the black and white television set in the American offices of Big New Yorker, amidst the bursts of static that interrupted the impossible images that were being relayed directly into the interior of the room. A lukewarm cup of coffee held directly under her mouth had met once with her lips as she clasped tightly onto the latte in her right hand it showed no immediate signs of moving. Something important had just happened. Britt had felt it as she had entered the building that morning. She also knew this because the television announcer kept informing her over and over that something impossible and important had just happened in the centre of Manhattan. The same image had been being repeated over and over in an uncanny parody of an Andy Warhol film.

The image of two of the most recognised symbols of Western supreme power were shown collapsing as if they were built from bolser wood. The height of the buildings towering over the skyline of Manhattan had slowly diminished. Somehow the very buildings which represented the near impossible but incredible strength of the United States were collapsing in front of her very eyes immediately after another occurrence. The image came up again. One passenger plane had flown directly into each central point of both towers of The World Trade Centre as they fell to the ground in the most spectacular way imaginable and all anyone in television land had done was comment on how impossible this whole incident had been. Even though it had happened right in front of their very eyes.

Britt continued to gawp at the television screen but found herself crouching into a squatting position mimicking what she had just observed as her eyes were transfixed by the whole scene. The television commentary of the anchorman seemed to be missing a few pointers, which Britt felt she could put them straight on. However this did not seem like the correct time to be so picky about how many people were about to die.

The phone in her office suddenly started ringing. At the same time her mobile phone started beeping loudly. Britt guessed that who ever it had been calling would probably tell her to turn on the television, the German quickly leaned forward and turned the tuner dial of the set clockwise and discovered that the images of the disaster were being shown on every channel across the network. Surprisingly she found she had been able to travel a la virtual reality around the whole scene. People ran in every direction to avoid the collapse of the twin towers. Britt made a very Britt decision at eight o'clock that morning, it seemed highly necessary after seeing such an incident. She began to roll a joint.

As she moved to her desk and placed her coffee down on the table, Britt adjusted her orange head scarf as she picked up her rolling papers from her desk drawer and noticed her hands were shaking. She glanced up occasionally from the operation of making the spliff but remained focused on the job at hand in a similar way that the pilots of both the planes seemed to have been in their determination to park bang in the middle of what had been one of the tallest skyscrapers in the Western world. She exhaled and felt a little bit calmer by the second toke, her hands gradually stopped shaking. The aroma and hazy smoke filled the office until she became sure she could view the images on the TV set with a cool detachment. The only way Britt could concentrate on this news of all news had been to be nearly anaesitised. Stoned had been the next best thing.

Thank heavens she had not smoked the lot last night on the return from Amsterdam. She closed her eyes as she inhaled deeply for the third time and giggled slightly recalling what a great time she had in the place with Gyro. Now that Britt felt relatively normal she could easily pass off the news as ludicrously as possible. She could allow the experience of waking-up in America on the plane to wash over her as she looked once again at the massive pile of rubble which had been the twin towers only hours before. Meanwhile the two telephones continued to ring.

Sometimes reality had a funny way of catching her out and she freewheeled somewhere between the understanding of physics and the fact that she had been unable to understand everything on the planet. There simply had not been the time. She was only twenty-three years old and yet right at this moment she had to say that what she had been trying to understand had been a real chicken and egg scenario. She shivered with the cold of the current situation.

The news on the television seemed to be explaining accurately enough that The World Trade Centre had collapsed literally. This she could see and hear. The only problem she had been having right at this exact moment was going to be difficult to explain to anyone on the other end of a telephone. Britt was actually in the office of Big New Yorker on the forty-second floor of The World Trade Centre. Outside the bright blue sky and rising sun were both pulling the curtain back revealing another perfect day over the Manhattan skyline. She looked out the window down at the tiny cars and people pictured below. Maybe it had been time to roll another joint. Then again if Britt answered one of the telephones she could at least prove she had been safe to somebody. People did worry when they saw News like this. Maybe there were four World Trade Centres. She had only been in New York two days and this had been one of the three possibilities that she was desperately holding saneness together with. Britt decided to quickly lie down on the floor of the office, keeping her eyes fixed on the television screen she watched as both buildings completely collapsed. That would include the forty-second floor at least. The phones continued to ring. She stood up again and reached for the volume dial on the TV and turned it down to minimum. She decided that the best thing to do had been to answer one of the phones. Hesitantly Britt moved over to her desk and grabbed the handle of the receiver and picked it up. Holding the receiver to her ear cautiously.

"Er,...yar? Britt Johannes speaking...Big New Yorker?" She asked hesitantly.

There was a short burst of static. Then the unmistakable hollow windy far away sound of a long distance connection. The reassuring sound of her mother came on the line.

"Guyer Britt. It's Muter. Gutten Tag Britt, are you watching the news dear?" Asked the calm voice from Germany.

"Er...yar...I'm watching it! Mutter. How are you?"

The telephone line became noisier. *"WHERE ARE YOU DEAR? ARE YOU ALRIGHT?"*

" Yar Muter, I've just gotten in about an hour..." Answered Britt.

"Where are you? You're not in the building obviously!" The sound of relief was obvious down the line from Germany.

"Well, that's the funny thing...I'm at work...er, in the World Trade Centre!"

There had been a long awkward silence for the first time from her Mother who usually could not stop talking.

"Okay, well sorry to bother you at work dear, but your father thought we should call and see if you were okay. It's all over the television here in Berlin. I'll put your Father on..." The deep voice of Mr. Johannes came on the line.

"Haloo Britt! Good to hear you're okay, thank God. Where are you leibling?" Asked her Father. A slight twist of hysteria in his voice.

"I just told Muter. I'm at work, er... in the World Trade Centre...." Huge pause.

"Right, I see... well obviously it's not good to interrupt your work...when do you get lunch and we'll call you back later...? It's strange but we just saw someone who looked like you on the television..." The time delay caused her to answer a question as she heard another from her Father.

"Oh, around two...in about six hours time...call me back, I'll speak to you then..." She had been amazed at how calm she was sounding considering the situation she had just experienced.

"Okay dear. I'll talk to your Mother and we'll call you back around two... okay." Replied Mr. Johannes.

"Okay I'll speak to you then...Auf weidersen." Said Britt as a short burst of static ended the conversation.

Britt placed the receiver back in the cradle of the landline and looked back over at the television set, amazed to see her own calm face staring up at the camera as she walked with a group of people through the rubble, she recognised some people from the office next door. The tall German had been wearing exactly the same outfit as when she had been in Amsterdam. The orange scarf wrapped tightly around her hair. She laughed nervously at the discerning sight of watching herself on television during the worst disaster she had ever seen, yet it seemed as if she was looking into a mirror from another dimension. The building had already collapsed on television and yet from where she was observing the scene right now everything seemed fine.

Thankfully the announcer had been in the CNN studio already talking to a man who seemed to have filmed the entire incident whilst making a documentary about the New York Fire Department. The filmmaker explained the impossible scenario once again and how he had filmed everything that morning. Britt moved in a stoned haze towards the door of her office, the joint still smoking in her hand and grasped the handle of the door, surprised by the heat from the metal. She bit her bottom lip and turned the knob slowly pulling the door open. She could hear the sounds of typing on computer keyboards from the office opposite and the murmur of daily activity from the various office workers on the forty-second floor.

Britt poked her head around the edge of the doorframe. Everything seemed to be as active as any normal workday. She stepped back into the office of Big New Yorker and looked at the news on the screen, she winced slightly as she saw the image once again of herself walking with the people from the office across the hall. The tall German found herself being hypnotised by the shouts of New Yorkers running with dismay and shouting as clouds of commuters and fireman rushed through the streets injured and confused. She could not believe what she was watching. On television her hair looked a mess. Embarrassed, Britt continued to stare up at the black and white television set in the American offices of Big New Yorker.

FRIDAY 7TH SEPTEMBER 2001 /
2002 TIME / FLIGHT 815Y

MUSIC IS JUST ORGANISED NOISE

And if the cloud bursts thunder in your ear you shout
and no one seems to hear
And if the band you're in starts singing different tunes
I'll see you on the dark side of the Moon
PINK FLOYD

THE CAPTAIN FLYING the plane was either on crack or had the driest sense of humour Gyro had ever come across. He wondered if the noticeable tension aboard the airborne craft would have been the same if the procedure of boarding airplanes were arranged in the same way as buses and a person paid as they entered the vehicle.

Storm clouds were raging around the plain outside and turbulence was causing anyone on the plane to attempt a counter-balance of praying mixed with quantum physics. A beautiful Chinese girl was seated next to him crying near the cabin door and as he looked out at the forks of yellow lightning flashing between the clouds giving the impression of a large cloud-built four-poster bed Gyro put his arm around the girl in an attempt to comfort her.

The concoction in his veins of alcohol and speed mixed together, seemed to help more than praying right now and when he looked around at the passengers asleep, he wondered if anyone else had been awake to hear what the Captain had been saying. The plane seemed to be banking left across to the intense lightning storm and a calm Asian voice came over the intercom speaker above the two passengers. *"Let's see if we can get a closer look at that storm shall we?"* Spoke the voice of Captain Li quietly.

Gyro held his breath as the plane continued to bank to the left and in a moment of crystal clear clarity listened to the sound of lightning and thunder growing closer. The Chinese girl sitting on his right whimpered slightly. They both seemed to be the only people onboard that were about to witness a 747 passenger plane divorce itself in mid-air.

The plane returned to the original steady course. Gyro felt a surge of relief rush over him as he understood a pilot with a sense of humour was something he would appreciate from the ground in the future. Although he could only speak a small amount of Chinese there had been only one phrase he thought would be well appreciated. *"Nee how mar?"* Gyro asked. The girl frantically nodded her head in the affirmative. Letting him know that she was fine.

The rain lashed against the window outside of the rocking plane and he was reminded of a song by an American artist called Laurie Anderson about an airplane flight from the songwriter perspective whereby the Captain reveals himself to be a masochist with a unique sense of humour. The plane suddenly hit another huge air pocket of turbulence and dropped through the dark thunderous clouds like a stone. Then caught itself again after a few seconds.

Out of the window in the dark, looking down over The Banda Sea, a white light with the brightness of a star shone out from the darkness and began to match the speed of the plane, growing in size, moving closer. A sensation of familiarity grew into recognition, as Gyro noticed the face of the Chinese girl reflected back at him from the passenger window. Her face layered over the distinct shape of a cylindrical craft. She seemed to be smiling with him in wonder at the weaving object outside, he looked back at her quickly checking that she was witnessing the bright light that he was already convinced had to be the definite shape of a UFO.

Although the lightning over and around the plane continued unabated so did the speed of the vessel. One of the Korean Air stewardesses carrying out a check on the condition of the passengers, slowly walked down the aisle and noticed the light outside illuminating Gyro and his new friend, Hong Jin Wu. They both glimpsed over towards her but it had become obvious that they were both looking intensely at something through the clouds. The Chinese girl quickly waved over the stewardess urgently and babbled something in Korean causing the stewardess to join them, by peering out of the round cabin window.

At the front of the plane in the cockpit of Flight 815Y from Sydney, Captain Li had begun suddenly receiving hysterical calls from as far as Papau New Guinea and Indonesia. He switched to the controls of the autopilot and listened in to some of the nervous reports which were flooding his headphones amidst bursts of static.

His eyes searched the cabin quickly in the dim light for the plane codebook and his eyes fell across his family smiling back at him through the miracle of colour photography. His wife, daughter and son were waving happily in the sunshine from the back garden of his house in Sydney two years previously. They seemed oblivious to his current surroundings of rain and electricity that were raging outside. Caught in another time. Suddenly, a strong light caught the corner of his left eye and for a moment, he thought his worst nightmare had come true. That of the left engine catching fire. His heart skipped a beat as an object to the left of his view seemed to grow in size and a pale-blue light filled the cockpit.

Below him and the Boeing 747, The Banda Sea, Indonesia and the Lesser Sunda Islands were now starting to appear on the horizon. The airplane had been scheduled to pass over the South China Sea and refuel then move on to Hong Kong. The original hometown of the Captain. None of his pilot training however, prepared him for what was coming next as the cockpit interior became illuminated by the light, which spread over the dials and controls, Captain Li looked at the flight panel in shock as he watched the succession of red lights and dials lighting up and notifying him that the steering mechanisms of the plane were now under the control of a higher force, causing the aircraft to bank once again to the left, this time heading directly for the large electrical storm.

Captain Li knew something was over-riding the controls and quickly struggled to bring them back to manual by flicking numerous switches above his head to no avail, then the reports in his earpiece became more urgent. Although the intonation had become anything but negative. Words such as *incredible* and *fantastic* were coming down the wire. One voice had begun speaking in English amidst all the chatter of Asian voices from traffic control.

"It's huge! Can you see it? Wow. Look at that thing, it's fucking huge. It's the size of a country, how could that get through the radar? What the fuck is it?"
The various voices sounded as excited as an Australian seeing snow for the first time and Captain Li felt the hairs on his neck charged.

In the cabin, Gyro, Hong Jin Wu and the stewardess watched in awe as the vehicle continued to increase in size, the pale-blue brightness began to manoeuvre towards the lightning storm following the airliner. The light shining in through the one cabin window was waking some of the passengers into mistakenly thinking it was daylight. *"Are we there yet?"* Asked a young voice sitting behind him.

Whatever the object flying parallel outside was, Gyro noticed that the plane seemed to be angled as if it was banking to the left and moving underneath them, directly towards the lightning storm. Then he saw the lightning brightly illuminate the underside of the UFO. In three successive long flashes for the first time in his thirty years, Gyro felt a familiar thrilling sensation that his friend Static, on the Isle of Wight had once mentioned when they were discussing in a pub, the presence of aliens.

The lightning revealed briefly that the UFO was merely part of something bigger and the size of it seemed to stretch into the distance as the three pairs of eyes watched in wonder discovering that they were flying under something that was far bigger than the area of Australia, even. He heard the stewardess next to him gasp as the plane began to shake. The sheer scale of the vehicle outside was immense and took on the appearance of a vast landscape made up of ravines, lakes and mountains, stretching off into the distance. How something this size had been capable to hold weight and move so elegantly through the air seemed impossible. The petrol-blue light illuminated the interior cabin of Flight 815Y as the plane arched down to the left and underneath it.

All three of the alien craft audience craned their view upwards and it seemed as if a country was cruising over them slowly and steadily. Gyro suddenly felt as if the Boeing had been reduced to the scale of a tiny fish. A guppy swimming under the belly of a descending whale. The underneath of the vast object was shaped out of rock but it was just impossible to fit the size of it into his head. The silence on board suddenly broke when the air stewardess turned and shouted to the rest of the crew. She ran over to the other side of the cabin and quickly pulled up one of the opposite plastic cabin window covers. The right side of the airliner was also packed with the image of the UFO. The interior of the cabin took on the appearance of an aquarium at night. Slowly and silently the 747 began descending away from the UFO and the current generated by this immense vessel.

In the cockpit Captain Li looked on in wonder as the control panel readings displayed his own vehicle steadily and safely avoiding whatever was above them. Suddenly the breaking light of the dawn over the South China Sea could be seen on the horizon and a slight relief swept over him. He knew that if the plane held a steady course for the next four minutes they would be within reach of Philippine airspace and could then land. He began to relay a message as calmly as possible hoping someone would hear it, reading aloud from the codebook. *"Flight 815Y. This is Captain Li of Korea Airlines flight 815Y calling the Philippines over. I wish to report Santa Claus is real! Repeat Santa Claus does exist. We wish to report landing procedures, urgently."* He announced over the radio held in his shaking hand.

"Hello Captain Li. This is Philippines Airport, receiving you over." Came a calm reply.

"Thank God! This is Captain Li announcing the arrival of 815Y. We are already in descent formation. Experiencing turbulence and ready to land." Spoke the Asian as calmly as possible.

"I guess you've seen our visitor friends!" Chuckled the voice over the intercom from Air Traffic Control. *"We've been following your arrival with great interest. Are you okay? Can you see it?"*

"Affirmative. Can you see it? How come no one warned us? I'm not even flying this plane!" Exclaimed the Captain.

Static interrupted the conversation and the plane positioned itself ready for descent. Captain Li made the sign of the cross over himself and switched to the in-flight tanoy. Out of habit he nervously announced the standard flight arrival, hoping and praying that anyone on board the plane would still be asleep.

"Good morning everyone. This is your Captain speaking. Flight crew to positions. Please make note of the fasten seatbelt signs. Please place your tray-tables to an upright position as we are making the descent into Philippines Airport. On behalf of Korean Airlines I would like to thank you for flying with us and hope you have an enjoyable visit to The Philippines. The temperature outside is a fine 38 degrees. This is Captain Li signing off."

As the Boeing passenger plane broke through thin white scattered cloud and continued down towards the runway Captain Li checked the readings on the panel of the controls in front of him, even though the landing gear began to open and the plane began one of the smoothest descents he had ever been witness to he understood that right up until the plane stopped, he had, along with the autopilot controlled absolutely nothing aboard the plane.

The plane finally drew to a halt on the warm tarmac of The Philippines runway. Captain Li asked politely that all passengers remain seated until the plane had stopped, anticipating the usual sounds of excitement, which usually poured out from the cabin once the plane had landed. The Boeing 747 lurched slightly as the hydraulic mechanisms pushed down releasing brake-fluid into the pistons under the plane fuselage. Sweat ran down the side of his face as Flight 815Y halted on the tarmac runway of The Philippines Airport. The voice of traffic control broke the silence and he recognised the relief in the words of his Philipino colleague. *"Welcome back to earth Captain Li. We'll get emergency service vehicles over to you immediately..."*

As Captain Li pulled back the orange curtain to check on his passengers the wire from his headpiece pulled taught, the headphones snapped off from around his neck. He calmly stood up waiting to check with his crew that they were all in one piece. Captain Li suddenly experienced a blend of embarrassment and horror as he stood in the electrically charged cabin doorway, he found himself looking dumbly out at something new in his twenty-year career as an airline pilot. The sirens of the emergency services screamed across the runway outside. The pilot stared dumbfounded at the aisles full of empty petrol-blue airplane seats and felt his body shake as he began to cry, collapsing onto the carpet in the aisle of Flight 851Y shaking from the rush of adrenaline. The Korean Airlines logo seemed to stare back at him from each of the headrests of each abandoned seat on the plane. A fire-fighter peered into the cabin through one of the airliner windows and after hearing the reports from Air Traffic Control and observing the empty seats, he wondered briefly to himself whether the Captain flying the plane was either on crack or had the driest sense of humour he had ever come across.

BOOK III
EVENING / SINGULARITY

PROFESSOR STEPHEN HAWKING
PROFESSOR OF COSMOLOGY AT OXFORD UNIVERSITY

1942

Hawking, who was born in Oxford, graduated from the university there and obtained his PhD from Cambridge University. Hawking has worked mainly in the field of cosmology, in particular the theory of black holes..

No government agency could afford to be seen to be spending public money on anything as way out as time travel. Instead, one has to use technical terms, like closed time, like curves, which are code for time-travel

In 1965 Roger Penrose had shown that a star collapsing to form a black hole would ultimately form a singularity - a point at which the density of matter is infinite and at which there is an infinite curvature of space-time. Hawking realized that by reversing the time in Penrose's theory he could show that the big bang originating the Universe must also have come from a singularity.

BOOK III
EVENING / SINGULARITY

SIR ROGER PENROSE

PROFESSOR OF MATHEMATICS AT OXFORD UNIVERSITY
WINNER OF THE WOLF PRIZE FOR PHYSICS IN 1988
SHARED WITH
PROFESSOR STEPHEN HAWKING

1931

Penrose, the son of the geneticist Lionel Penrose was born at Colchester in Essex. At Oxford University with Stephen Hawking, Penrose proved a theorem of Einstein's general relativity asserting that at the centre of a black hole there must evolve a *'space-time singularity'* of zero volume and infinite density where the present laws of physics break down. He continues to teach Mathematics at Oxford University.

When we see the validity of a theorem,
in seeing it we reveal the very nonalgorithmic nature
of the 'seeing' process itself.

DEPARTURES

"YIP-YIP TO the Bardos! You should try the coffee..." Chirped in a voice somewhere near the back of the knee. Mr. Bittre looked down to picture a tubby penguin smiling back. His appearance was dapper and yet sunglasses covered the eyes of glass which held the soul of a window captive within.

Fluffy thoughts filled the hat of Monsieur Bittre. He offered a hand to the penguin D Van D style.

"Care to join me? I'm having eggs!" Crooned Mr. Bittre

"Tu che, if I may? The name's Benedicto, Benedicto Perky Eco. May I join you if I may join you yes?" He asked.

The cold-blooded mammal hopped up onto the seat opposite and assumed a relaxed lotus position, tenderly opposite Mr. Bittre. He discovered a strong desire to hunt for fish come over his waist coat and blew triangular smoke rings out of his orange beak. He giggled and chirped, tapping out a smooth steady strong beat of Africa on the tabletop.

"Your name is Bittre, yet I do not recall seeing you in The Diner Holistic before?" Quizzed Benedicto amidst the attempts to fire up his doobie.

"Well, I was only reborn one hour ago you know." He replied. "It took me a while to focus on the D and while I may be here, I may have been here before. There really is no way of knowing these things."

A clap of thunder sounded outside and a bolt of orange-blue exploded through the window and ignited the gumball machine by the door. Cascading luminous balls of Americana brand chewy across diner tabletop and chequered tile. Each bouncing atom of gum from linoleum floor landed neatly on the tongue of each client in the Holistic Diner.

"FRREE GUM!" Yelled a baseball player causing much mirth and jest.

"I enjoyed, yes, enjoyed looking at your hat Mr. Bittre. The suit of threads of black fits well upon your reborn bones, but what is this smile I see through blood and mucus, dripping like gutted fish?" Queried the flightless marine bird.

Cold-blooded animal or mammal thought Mr. Bittre waiting for the man with the eggs and waiting was its own reward but making conversation with a cold-blooded mammal? Damn the maker which of the West was it? He was certain to say something rudey woo-woo now! Black and white and orange and chirping. Mammal or bird. Fruit or mineral. Mental note to self, be polite with a penguin. Always be polite!

"That takes the bird, er, biscuit, biscuit bird..." Fumbled Mr. Bittre in time to the music. Russian picking cake on a rumble. *"The smile sir, the bitter smile."* Toked Benedicto casually, grinning under his sunglasses, across to Mr. Bittre. The mammal had produced a new set of playing cards from his waistcoat and was shuffling them idly as he tangled with the plastic wrap. He slowly dealt out the cards neatly in a row, holding the intense manic street gaze of his new audience. *"The first of the many laws of order is chaos Monsieur Bittre, you just have to focus and your focus becomes your reality."* The sensations of spirals and jacknack sandwiches brought in cotton tunnel vision for Mr. Bittre. Muffled toners grew in size and for all and sundry there seemed to be a want to tone it at the back you men and keep it low and Tuesday morning. A crunchier number two of static hit the backroom and all pinball machines were made of felt. Primary upturned card reflected in the jiggy-wiggy eyeballs of the suited Mr. Bittre and he noted the same logo of The Diner Holistic on the underside of the cards. How about them apples? A warm ripple of applause drifted in and out on perfect speakers of woof and tweet as the smallest of small dewdrop sparkled. Reflected in the chirpy beak of politeness and calm of a Benedict tear.

"Advice is mere nonsense you do understand." Spoke the penguin. *"There are, this is said, many reasons for wearing a smile in this world Mr. Bittre but many of them involve happiness. Your smile will remain the same but you will change Mr. Bittre, you will change. As you saturate the pores of your undersuit. Think and you will trap a fine clue."*

"As eggs is eggs!" Interrupted the Buddhist Monk with the order of egg on tongue and bread in mouth.

The order of chaos come hen package hit the table in three little pink shells. Square and cubotic, neatly wrapped in silver paprika. Tight collar concentration looked in from starboard at the eggs.

"Excuse me Benedict, but the gut is calling and the chaos has arrived!" With polite non-shallots Mr. Bittre extended a bone towards the first of the

Father, Son and Holy Ghost and popped it into his mouth. Ahh, crunchie is as crunchie does. His teeth broke down hard on the pink shell. Benedicto continued to turn over the second card, also an ace and this time a red glinting Diamond. Bird looked up and winked and eye flirtatiously at his egg munching audience. Three cards to go. A relaxed black flipper fondling the corner of new ace.

"Noticed the first ace as noir, the second as rouge, Mr. Bittre..."

His audience nodded ecstatically, the shells distinct taste cut into his gums and blood spilled onto the black surface of the table. Lecker thoughts filled his hat. Canned laughter filled his ears. A couple of pigs were fighting next to the jukebox for the collection of prime cuts. Slapping down Lakme for Swan Lake, the tunes of sweetness filled the air.

"Birds, birds and birds!" Cried the Monks above the counter and where the cards were turning cards, the flippers found a neatly packed joint avec a gold tip. Hidden in the waistcoat of darling Benedicto.

"Do the eggs taste good?" Antarctic breathing caressed. A Mary Jane flipper tapping idly on the black linoleum top. Little ash fumble of hot coals bringing on home the scent of sweet Lennie-Lee and April rain on window pain. *"Eggs that are cubotic in shape and taste...make haste."*

Best part of a four-wind shuffle broke now sounds of opera and all kings horses crowded around the booth. For unveiling of card number three and although The Diner held no pause in its moving and no rthymn in its monkey-bumping, the squeaking was a creaking was a moving, was ate at eight and five by five.

FRIDAY 7TH SEPTEMBER 2001
PROBABILITY / SPACE

EXPLORING THE DEPTHS OF SPACE

*I could stand here for days or I could stand here for hours
I could stand here for a lifetime watching you and waiting always*
GARY NUMAN

RAY CONNIF LOOKED around the metallic reflective interior of the vessel. Nothing but white light shone out from every direction. There seemed to be no discernible shape to any of it. Any area the German looked bright white returned and if he had been offered words to point at and compare it with something on Earth, Ray would have possibly chosen the word Art and Gallery. He might have offered a polite cough and pointed towards the words of zero and gravity also.

With the exception of a large black suitcase that floated slowly and gracefully throughout the ship interior and a mobile that seemed to be doing pretty much the same thing the only passenger seemed to be the Advertising Executive with sights set on a future in movies. The aliens Procta and Gamble had already left. The mobile phone would occasionally bounce off a wall of the interior as if in slow motion showing the vast size and depth of the room that Ray Connif was trapped down one end of. The German reached out his hands and touched a transparent rubber that seemed to be keeping him cocooned in what he could only guess had been, looking at the sparse but tight fitting surroundings, not a garden.

Suddenly a sharp pain dug into the right of his neck and Ray clasped his hand over it. The cause of the pain seemed to be a pink beam of light emitted by a metal-looking wand held by a three-fingered talon. As his gaze followed to where the talon led, he became surprised to discover that he was now in an open field at the base of a mountain. The sky held his gaze transfixed in horror at the deep purple of the atmosphere above and the two towering figures who were looking down on him and firing pink lasers sharper than the sarcasm of an Australian into his neck.

"WHAT DID YOU DO WITH THE TALENT WE GAVE YOU?" Boomed a deep voice directed at Ray, who had never felt so small and hopelessly inadequate in his life. *"What do you mean it's not the right one?"* Said the voice to another form behind it. Ray looked down at his feet and now discovered that he was on the other side of the cellophane barrier, back inside the white room just as the black case floated across and banged him on the side of the head. The mobile phone bobbed past and the German reached out in an attempt to grab it several times as if it was an insect in-flight. On tiptoe Ray Connif stretched his entire frame up until he held the plastic handset in his right palm and floated up to what must have been the ceiling. Ray brought the phone towards the front of his face as he tumbled over. The mobile beeped merrily back at him and showed a computer read out with the words YOU HAVE ONE NEW TEXT MESSAGE scrolling across it. He clicked to receive the message and heard the distinct English accent of a woman he knew all too well.

"Hi..., er, Ray? Oh God Ray! Where are you? " Liz sounded as if she had been a thousand light years away, which was as accurate a guess as possible, given the circumstances. *"We're all watching the news and well, obviously we don't know what's happened but we're watching the news and obviously... hang on! You're phone must be working or we wouldn't get a message on your line. Please call the London office IMMEDIATELY! You hear me! Don't be dead Ray! I'll keep calling!"* Yelled the newly promoted Executive from the tiny mobile.

Ray floated across the room to what looked like a small circular window which held the view only a fortunate few on Earth had seen up until now, the planet Earth from the distance of at least twenty-three million miles away. As he looked out at the view the disorientation and constant spinning caused him to vomit and the mobile phone began to beep urgently. He clicked the answer button on the handset whilst attempting to vomit the last remains of his airplane meal off to one side.

"Ray? Ray is that you?" Screamed Liz into the telephone.

"Urghhh I've gotta blech..." Vomited Ray as his lunch continued to careen around the interior.

"OHMYGODYOU'REOKAY! It's Liz. You're alright?" Asked Liz.

"Liz I bleeeuuuchhhhggghh...the view is...beautifu..blllarrr." More vomit.

"...Possibly the worst news we've ever seen. I can't believe it...we all thought..." The hysterical voice faded again.

Static ripped through the mobile signal causing the line to go dead and floating blobs of vomit hit Ray in the face and body as he span. The smell caused him to be sick again and the mobile slipped from his hand. Suddenly he found himself in a dark red room with the two masked figures again. He suddenly dropped to the floor like a sack of wet spaghetti. Zero gravity returned.

"Er... are you okay there?" Enquired the first alien looking down at Ray. *"Did you hurt yourself?"*

Ray Connif looked around the metallic reflective interior of the vessel. Nothing but white light shone out from every direction.

FRIDAY 7TH SEPTEMBER 2001
AFTERNOON / THE WEST END

WELCOME TO THE OCCUPATION

*Remember what you told me make your own moves
and don't wait for the other man*
ONE THE HADDOCK

THE RED DOUBLE-decker bus lurched along The Balls Bond Road with a triumphant early Friday morning acceleration of almost six feet. It halted immediately behind one of the new designed Mini cars that had appeared in an advertisement made by the production company of Big New Yorker. Liz looked up through the dirty lower level front window with eyes of cobalt blue and stared at the line of traffic ahead. She sighed to herself. Fumbling in her bag she retrieved her new mobile phone, pushing at a button and scrolling for the number of the office in Soho. The phone made a happy beep and informed her that the number she had dialled did not exist, even though she had called it several times that morning already. She then somehow managed to switch the device to a newer more expensive network instead. She sighed and pressed down on the off button, then read the message that had just arrived.

PLEASE CALL RAY AT THE OFFICE. RAY. Accidentally Liz deleted the message. Then preceded to wipe half the numbers out of her electronic phone book which she had spent programming in the previous week. She then made another attempt at calling the office but instead got her own answer-machine that she had switched on half an hour ago and suddenly felt that the day was already moving in an unusual direction. Liz sighed again and threw the mobile back into her shoulder bag. At the speed the bus was currently moving she would have to get out at The Angel and catch the tube instead. The Mini in front of her bus suddenly turned right and drove speedily up a side street into the distance. This allowed the bus to increase its speed. She opted for a third attempt at calling the office.

The result this time began with the phone telling her that she was only three seconds from a cheaper rate. She had just decided on throwing the phone back into the darker recesses of her bag when another friendly beep informed her that yet another message had been sent. This time her mobile enquired DO YOU HAVE THE BRIEFCASE? MAX BORN. Obviously the day was already unwrapping spectacularly. Liz had been receiving an alarming amount of text messages for the attention of Max Born recently and had only bought the mobile last week after dropping her last one in the toilet at work. Most of the messages seemed to be directed for the attention of Dr. Bostrom and yet she had never heard of either of these names before. Maybe they were new clients of Big New Yorker.

She threw the phone back into the bag and stared out the bus window as the traffic began to move along the Balls Pond Road at a slightly slower pace than stationary. Her hand felt reassuringly for the black suitcase under her seat and suddenly she had the bright idea to check the contents. Maybe she could get it into a cab instead and get the advertising company Big New Yorker to foot the bill.

Liz loved advertising. She had been working for two production companies for over five years and although the money had been incredible and had allowed her to buy a flat in Hackney, there seemed to be something far beyond normal about the industry. She loved the way people rushed around and seemed to be constantly shouting for no reason at all. She had been constantly hassled at parties by drunken people telling her that compared to nursing or teaching, advertising was *'a crock of shit'*. To which she would often find herself agreeing. This usually caused a bad reaction with people in London who preferred a good fight to agreeing any day of the week. Whenever Liz disagreed though they seemed to get upset as well and so she had opted for her clinch move which had been to offer them some cocaine in an attempt to get them on her side which usually worked.

Last night however had been a strange exception as a young man had offered her a drink in the local pub. She had liked the bloke straight away which had been a new experience for her and after three pints of London Pride, she had been stunned when he had offered her a line of charlie in the toilet. It turned out to be the best cocaine Liz had ever come across. She had returned to her flat dyed her hair bright orange that night as a result and was now amazed by how electric and bright it looked in the grey of the London morning, compared to the grey cold of September outside.

The clouds were refusing to let any of the promised sunshine through in much the same way the traffic seemed to be refusing to let her number thirty-eight bus through to the West End on time. Liz searched frantically through her bag for the keys to the black suitcase that Ray had requested her to bring into the office without fail or face the consequences. The words were enough to remind her of who she had been working for and so she had dyed her hair in a rebellious attempt to show just how much she would not be spoken down to, especially by someone German.

Most of the women in the production company would get the message even if Ray refused to acknowledge the fact. However, Liz being the young assistant had managed to lose the briefcase in the pub after panicking slightly on the detour to the toilet. Luckily the barman had seen it and had handed it back after her enquiries. Liz had always been a regular at the local pub and the barman had sometimes witnessed her bawling out people in the pub when pushed on certain matters.

Liz thought back to the hippy looking bloke in the pub. She wondered why he had to rush off quite so quickly. She had just begun to relax after about four pints of ale and the cocaine had put her in fine form to talk about herself until the pub shut or the sun came up, which in Hackney had been quite often since she had moved into the realm of advertising. Unfortunately the hippy had to leave and see his mother or something so Liz had continued to sit in the pub drinking and talking at anyone who would listen until the barman had begged her to leave.

She had made a list of points to talk to Ray Connif, the creative head of Big New Yorker regarding the film project that had become his new obsession. He had mentioned in passing that in the black case he had left in the office there sat an incredible film-script called 'O.D.' Whereby Liz had the idea of how good a production assistant she could really be. Her plan had sprung into action after a quick toot in the toilet. She had decided that the best help delivered would be if she took the scripts back to Hackney. Showing her passionate dedication to Big New Yorker by reading through all of them she would then inform Ray of her opinion on the following day. Luckily she had not left the case in the pub. Otherwise today would be a day searching for new employment.

The tube station at The Angel had been the only option left to get into Soho before Ray turned up around nine looking for his case. The clock near The Angel tube read 8:15AM, in effect Liz could get to the West End via the Northern Line and still have time to walk to Denmark Street in Soho. Enough time to get a latte as long as someone had not decided to attempt suicide again by jumping under the train. As her little legs worked speedily away to get down the highest escalator in the Western world she thought for a brief moment what it seemed to be about the Northern Line that made people want to kill themselves so much.

After she arrived behind the dark heaving masses on the platform, another option presented itself with a more logical reason. Accidents did happen. Liz found herself squashed into a compact area and suddenly had a glimpse of her commute into work being similar to the old arcade games that show copper coins about to tip off from the ledge when more coins are added. She had played the game when she used to live in Shanklin on the Isle of Wight but had never won anything from it. She stood on the crowded platform and wondered for a moment if anyone had.

She grimaced her face a little as she swallowed some of the bitter taste of cocaine and mucus back down her throat and sneaked through the throng of commuters, managing to sneak aboard a carriage at the front. Her blue eyes sparkled from the impact of the drug as she held tightly onto the black suitcase. The change from bus to tube with suitcase in tow had worked smoothly and as Liz surfaced from the Underground she serpentined passed the bustle and throng of various commuters that marched up Oxford Street. This part of London on a Friday morning reminded her every time she docked at Tottenham Court Road of how London could sometimes make a person feel as if they were starring in their own personal movie. The excitement and buzz created by so many different cultures moving around in the chilled September air suggested the word cosmopolitan. Liz had used the word cosmopolitan frequently in the pub last night, to describe where she worked, inaccurately it turned out.

The hippy who had arrived in a sunflower T-shirt and denim jeans at the pub had corrected her almost immediately. The hippy had explained that Denmark Street could hardly be cosmopolitan due to the fact that the verb referred to people who were free of national prejudices and he had become more than certain after having attempted to get a job as a runner at a company called Big New Yorker, that the fact a man called Ray Connif had not only laughed smugly in his face when he had mentioned that he had been from the South of England but had then said *'Not another bloody Englander,'* that prejudices were fresh in abundance in that part of Soho.

Liz had become defensive the second she heard the mention of the name Ray Connif in the pub and after explaining that her boss merely had an unusual sense of humour she felt an urge developing somewhere in her beer to jump all over the hippy and kiss him. As Liz marched along with the frontline of London in the bright sunshine she felt a deep nagging confusion about meeting the hippy. There had been something about his eyes that had forced her to forget what she had been hearing when he spoke. She had missed the coincidence immediately. Liz suddenly stopped walking. A loud gong had sounded in her head.

The hippy said that he had already been to the office of Big New Yorker. Now that she had not been looking into his amazing eyes she could actually think straight. Yet the thought had been lost. Liz checked her digital watch. It had stopped again. First the mobile, now this. She knew from living in London for five years that the chance of spotting a clock that worked anywhere in the big smoke was low and decided to ask someone in the Prêt a Manger instead what the time was. She ducked into the side opening of the cafe and as sometimes happens in a city of over twelve million people walked straight into O.D. Darren ordering his latte, the hippy from the night before. The two of them stared at each other in reasonable disbelief. This thing happened all the time after all.

"Wow! Hi. How are you? Hey, great minds think alike!" She said wishing she could rewind and say something profound about his eyes instead. They were smiling back at him already.

"Hello youngster! Look, I'm really sorry about dashing off last night but I had to be in two places at once and I tried calling you this morning. Did you get my message?" Asked O.D. Darren as he paid the Brazilian lady behind the counter with some circular pieces of metal called coins.

"About the briefcase or being at the office?" Quizzed Liz. *"Your nick-name isn't Max Born is it?"*

O.D. Darren looked at her cautiously. *"No...No, I meant about meeting here in the cafe? I sent a message to you about eleven minutes ago."* He looked at his watch and cursed lightly.

"What's the matter?" She said swinging her case idly and completely forgetting where she was.

"Oh my watch has stopped again." He looked back at her and smiled again. *"Yeah, so you usually come by here at this time then, do you? My phone is playing up all the time as well."*

"Well, if my phone allows me to have the message then I'll get it. Usually it doesn't!" Said Liz hoping for profoundness.

"Oh yeah, I've got a phone like that." Said the hippy. *"Doesn't allow me to make calls but let's everyone call me!"*

"Bingo!" Profoundness came at last.

The hippy steered her out of the way of the oncoming hoards of commuters who were rushing past for their first caffeine fix of the day and spotted a rarity in the cafe. Two seats were free by the window. He seized the moment.

"Liz have you got time to sit down, for just five minutes, I need a latte. I just want to quickly ask you something..."

"Sure." She said.

Liz sat by the front window with anticipation and stared out onto Oxford Street in wonder at how many people were already rushing along at this time of the morning. She placed the precious suitcase down next to the stool she was sitting on and waited for O.D. Darren to bring over her coffee. After he joined her she noticed that he was holding an identical black leather suitcase.

"I don't believe it! I meet you twice in twenty-four hours and now you've got exactly the same case as me!" She pointed at the receptacle by her feet. *"What a coincidence!"* She beamed.

O.D. Darren looked down and noticed that nearly everything about the cases was identical accept the combination locks. The ones built into the case he had taken from Winmau were silver. The locks on the leather case which Liz had were gold metallic. Yet the initials embossed at the top near the handle were the same. P and G.

O.D. Darren took heed of the correlation and looked at Liz anxiously.

"Do you know who those initials stand for Liz?" He asked suddenly. Liz sipped at her latte and looked down at both the tops of the black handles.

"Woah..." She looked up at O.D. Darren. "Ray Connif. Wow! Are you working at Big New Yorker as well then?"

"Ray Connif?" Asked Darren returning the question. "P and G?"

"Yeah, you told me last night, in the pub that you'd been to the offices." Said Liz ignoring his questioning expression. "Oh sorry, I thought you meant..." She bit her lip suddenly.

"No worries." Asked the hippy distracted. *What did you want to ask me by the way? I've got a busy day ahead of me."*

"Well, there's this party that I've been invited to in Hackney and I need a chaperone to escort me there and I wondered if you would like to join me?" Liz asked her coffee.

"I would be honoured Liz." He replied without hesitating.

Liz suddenly felt ecstatic and could hardly keep the expression of cheerfulness off her baby-like oval face. Out of embarrassment she looked down at her watch and realised the time was already 8.30AM. Her watch had started working again. The colour of London had been turned up to eleven on the great controls.

"Oh my Gawd! I have to go!" She barked." I'll meet you in the pub we were in last night at nine okay?"

Suddenly she found herself kissing O.D. Darren goodbye as if he had been her long-lost husband. Such a strong feeling for this man had developed since she had met him twenty-four hours before. Their lips met and when she next looked up at the time she noticed eleven minutes had gone by. Red-faced with embarrassment Liz walked back towards him smiling. Both their expressions seemed to hold a new fascination with each other. Liz rushed towards the traffic lights of Oxford Street, then heard the gong in her head once again. The suitcase. She halted and ran back to O.D. Darren who sat with it on his lap expectantly grinning. *"Gee-whiz, thanks, I thought I'd forget it!"* Said Liz with her infamous barking laugh.

O.D. Darren handed it over and watched as a petite brightly coloured orange-haired lady neatly skipped across Oxford Street and disappeared into Soho with his heart. All of a sudden O.D. Darren experienced for the first time in his twenty-six years on planet Earth a feeling that caused his entire body to soar like an eagle, he could have scaled a mountain and cut it down with the side of his hand. He understood why Tibet had never started a war and why Italy had joined with every single one in history.

As the feeling grew within him O.D. Darren understood the answers to many questions that had caused him to ponder the same way that poets, priests, astronauts and chefs on television had for many decades, even eons. Images of the Cisteen Chapel and knights fighting battles for their King and Queens passed through his mind. He wanted to dance. His heart flew over the tops of the buildings and parks of London, up into the far reaches of the sky and beyond to the planets. The light and warmth of the morning sun split the clouds and shone its seven-minute-old rays down onto his hippy appearance through the glass of Prêt A Manger and the entire planet smiled with him. Love had finally found O.D. Darren and it had come directly from a woman he had not seen since he was at school fifteen years ago. She had not recognised him yet and it would perhaps ruin the moment of transcendence if he had told her that they were once at the same school together, yet he doubted that it would somehow. The feeling just grew stronger.

He wanted to write about this woman. He wanted to paint a portrait of her. He would even perform live on Top of The Pops with a backing track gladly for her. He adored her. He realised he cherished the coffee in his cardboard Prêt A Manger cup just thinking about her. He treasured the moment he laid eyes on her and he would not rest for a moment until they met later in the pub in Hackney. He grabbed the briefcase in one hand and with his latte in the other felt strength of such magnitude as he skipped out the door of the cafe that if a policeman on Oxford Street had attempted to warn him that he was looking too happy for someone who lived in London he would have kissed him.

The feeling grew and O.D. Darren understood that everything in life would be fine and dandy from now on. There was indeed a plan and this feeling was strongly linked to it somehow. The feeling was exactly the same as when a person rewound a tape, left it running and then hit the stop button only to discover the song needed was lined-up perfectly. He beamed with pride and joy.

He was indeed a brand new bright and shiny London bus of love. Then O.D. Darren turned as he saw the red double-decker bus lurch along Oxford Street with a triumphant early Friday morning acceleration of almost six feet.

FRIDAY 7TH SEPTEMBER 2001
MORNING / HAMMERSMITH

THAT WAS THE RIVER AND THIS IS THE SEA

If you are lonely I will call
If you are calling I will send poetry
I love you I am the milkman of human kindness I will leave an extra pint
BILLY BRAGG

AS O.D. DARREN RAN down the escalator of Tottenham Court Road tube station, he passed an Eskimo holding a sheet of light blue writing paper wrapped in cellophane and held at arms length as if he had been photographed for a criminal record. Nothing had been said using words of speech, yet enough had been communicated through the eyes of the unambiguous expression of the Eskimo that all the hippy had been able to do as he sped passed the weathered figure had been to throw a fifty-pence coin into the box that had been strategically placed between the feet of the Inuit and continue moving down the second escalator.

A thought crossed the mind of O.D. Darren as to how an Inuit had managed to get to the West End of London from as far as Eastern Siberia and what kind of life he had been having to arrive in such a place as England. Most people begging on the underground had a story or explained why they were begging, however the Eskimo seemed to turn the whole maze of tube tunnels into a museum. Maybe that had been the motive. Maybe he was looking for South Kensington tube. To be honest, O.D. Darren had been too happy to care. He had still been thinking about the kiss he had just received from Liz and had been too busy looking out for the correct tube line to enable him to continue onward to the house of a rather special old lady known as The Madam. As he dashed past various advertisements towards the underground platform he considered how ludicrous the idea of having to deliver over a million pounds worth of drugs to a sweet grey-haired old lady had been considering that she would possibly be the cause of his immediate demise, he realised that he would still be killed tomorrow. No doubt Winmau Diamond had been arranging that the moment he left the house in Hackney.

On the dark grey platform the hippy sat down on one of the bright colour co-coordinated plastic seats next to a machine that had been specifically designed to never operate properly. O.D. Darren had discovered this after he had attempted to retrieve the change from three separate attempts at purchasing chocolate from the metal machine to no avail. The strange familiar sensation of being mugged by a machine reminded him of Winmau. Once O.D. Darren had travelled to Germany and had been amazed at the constant devotion to machines that the country seemed determined to follow. Now London seemed to be closely following their example. That was comforting.

O.D. Darren placed the black case next to his feet and looked up. He had sat directly opposite an advertisement for the new Mini. Which looked to the hippy somehow worse than the original Mini. The huge bold expanded type written across the colour advert read GREAT MINDS THINK ALIKE in bold petrol-blue type. O.D. Darren felt an uncertain sensation creep over him as the hairs on the back of his neck stood up to attention.

He double-checked the case by his feet and felt a cold unambiguous sweat develop across his palms as he noticed the top of the black suitcase had the letters P and G embossed under the handle. The hippy blinked twice to be sure that he had not been hallucinating. He was positively certain the P and G had not been there before. Terror suddenly gripped his entire body. He grabbed the case and checked the combination locks and noticed that they had also changed magically from gold to silver. Just as the tube to hell arrived.

As O.D. Darren stood up and watched the sliding doors of the newly arrived tube carriage open he realised that it had been too late to go back and explain to Liz that she had the wrong case. He stood in the entrance of the train quietly panicking to death. Liz was about to discover that O.D. Darren was one of the biggest drug-dealers in the Western world. He attempted to find a section of the tube that was empty and tried to sit down and think calmly.

At the front of the tube was one carriage with a couple and a man asleep. The couple seemed to be discussing something intimate. O.D. Darren quickly placed the case on his lap trying not to make eye contact with anyone. Instead he had a whole new set of problems to deal with. As the tube doors closed and his journey to The Madam began he was beginning to see that this day was going to be one to write home about if he lived to see the end.

The case did have a combination but considering Liz probably knew the code, there was little time before arriving at the location of The Madam to get hold of her, then he noticed the locks were not set and the case had simply been closed. Pushing down on the silver tabs he heard a distinct clicking sound that announced the case opening. He slowly opened the lid oblivious to the distant rumbling noise of the train. The contents inside brought forth an indefinite sensation that in his twenty-five years on Earth O.D. Darren became convinced he had never experienced before. His expectations conflicted wildly with what he had been staring at in the case.

He looked down at the contents that were almost identical in appearance to those he had previously been looking at in the house of Winmau with the vague exception that the packets of drugs if they were drugs contained within were now wrapped in orange instead of petrol-blue cellophane. He prodded the packets and half expected Winmau to walk onto the tube and tell him which drug it had been. O.D. Darren lowered the black lid of the case only to see a blonde haired policewoman sitting opposite him in full uniform. The hippy was unsure as to where the officer had appeared from so suddenly. The officer seemed to be instructing him to be quiet by holding an index finger up to her lips. Making a sign of silence. She then nodded her head slightly towards the opposite end of the carriage where the couple sat who he had thought were talking intimately. As O.D. Darren followed the gesture he now realised that the couple were both crying. O.D. Darren looked back in silence at the police officer with a questionable expression on his face. All four of them sat in silence as the train rumbled along its journey. In the long carriage only one other body sat in a crumpled heap at the end disconnected from the others.

The tube came into Hammersmith Underground station and stopped. The police officer continued the charade of silence whilst standing up and gently gestured towards the doors of the carriage as they separated. O.D. Darren stood up to disembark from the train he let his eyes quickly follow further down past the couple until he caught sight of a small pool of red blood collecting at the feet of the man asleep. A small sword held in his pale limp hand.

O.D. Darren stepped off the train and made eye contact with the lady officer as he followed him off the train. Along the platform stood a line of policemen and women. The hydraulics caused a low hissing sound to come from the train as it lurched to a halt and the officer moved to the door and whispered at O.D. Darren as he stood sundered from what he had just witnessed. The sight of yet more police lined up along the platform caused him to wonder what else this particular day had instore.

"Sorry sir, you'll have to get off here." Said the lady officer with a parting smile." *There's been an incident. I hope it doesn't inconvenience your journey."* Two ambulance men arrived wearing dark glasses and moved onto the train as O.D. Darren stepped out of their way. As the rest of the train carriages were evacuated Officer Stitch stood up on the carriage and briefly explained how an argument had developed between the couple and the other passenger O.D. Darren had thought had fallen asleep when the hippy had boarded the train. The female officer explained that he had been stabbed and the couple had actually been a man being taken hostage by the woman who had carried out the stabbing. The policewoman had gotten on the train at the previous station. Due to his staring into the case, O.D. Darren managed to miss the entire incident.

"You're a lucky man there sir," said the police officer. *"Do you need any counselling sir?"*

The shock had caused O.D. Darren to ponder on how unlucky someone could be. He forgot for a moment that he had most of the Metropolitan police force standing next to him as he held a suitcase containing what appeared to be enough white powder of a dubious nature to divide the situation into a paranoid schizophrenic jackpot.

The thought crossed the mind of the hippy briefly that he could pass on the number of Winmau to the police and refer him as someone who could seriously do with some counselling. Instead he declined and took the business card of the officer instead as he smiled politely. Urgent business was at hand. O.D. Darren broke from the scene and bounded up the stairs of the tube station, he glimpsed at the name on the card which read Officer Samantha Stitch. He placed the card in the front pocket of his chequered shirt and ran through the ticket-barriers. Outside into the subway tunnel until he reached Hammersmith Hospital.

O.D. Darren walked quickly along the pavement towards the hospital. Checked his watch and noticed that he still had an hour before reaching the front door of The Madam. Now would be a good opportunity to find out what the contents of this case were before moving on to Shepherds Bush and the house of The Madam. The hippy walked casually into the front of the hospital and headed for the nearest toilet. The only place he could think to go to in London in such an emergency. Most of the churches were run down. He headed straight for the toilets. In one of the cubicles he placed the suitcase down on the top of the porcelain seat and opened the black lid of the case once again. Still shaking from the incident on the tube.

The orange tightly packed wrappers appeared as they had before. O.D. Darren grabbed one and opened the small part of a flap on the side then scrapped a little of the powder off onto his thumbnail. He suddenly remembered what someone had once said about the way a person would never really taste drugs this way in real life, the way they do in the movies, simply because you never knew if you were dealing with poison or not. Considering this had been the first time he had looked in the cases, O.D. Darren had forgotten how many times in his career as a dealer people he knew had done this all the time. He decided to file the advice away for another day. He looked again at the contents.

First petrol-blue and now orange. There could be some kind of code system going on but it seemed impossible to work out what it meant. O.D. Darren had no idea which colour The Madam had been expecting.

Considering he would be killed tomorrow O.D. Darren half prayed that the white powder had been poison. At least dying in a hospital would be easier than dying in Hackney. The irony of this last thought seemed determined to echo around his cranium for a while. The hippy held the nail under his nose, closed his eyes tightly and sniffed hard at the miniscule amount of white powder. A strange but not unpleasant sensation worked its way up his nose and O.D. Darren felt suddenly euphoric. If this was poison then dying had been not as unpleasant as he had been led to believe. He quickly sealed the packet back up and shut the case. Then O.D. Darren headed back out the front of the hospital and returned to the direction of the Underground station in the rain.

An odd fortuity raised itself as he almost slipped on the damp surface of the subway entrance that stretched under the large concrete motorway flyover. So many thoughts disassociated themselves from him as he bought a ticket at the terminal and swiftly moved through the ticket barrier. The hippy headed down towards the hard grey platform, thinking about the moving staircase of the escalator and wondered if the person who had invented the folding metal steps had them in their house and if they ever worked.

Then he remembered a toy he had seen in Hamleys on Regent Street the previous week that had been made of white plastic and depicted a curious setting of little plastic penguins being carried up a smaller scale escalator only to slide back down to the bottom again as if they were on a permanent loop. O.D. Darren scanned the underground map to check he had been heading in the right direction for any trains going to Shepherds Bush and ran towards the Metropolitan Line just as he turned one of the corners of the underground. He considered walking in the rain but then remembered how upset The Madam became the last time he had been late visiting her and opted for the tube instead. A sensation of a slight warm fuzziness crept into the back of his head, as he checked his watch for the deadline he was amazed to see that it had not only stopped but that it also seemed to have changed its design from the usual dark blue to a slightly lighter shade. O.D. Darren had not noticed before but there seemed to be a tiny image of a penguin on the strap, it must have been hidden under the leather toggle.

With the black suitcase swinging in his hand he passed yet more commuters on their way to work and then saw the sign announcing that the escalator had been stopped due to repairs, he sighed wondering if at any point in history London had actually ever worked properly. O.D. Darren put any negative thoughts asunder and decided to run for it, whatever he had just taken had given him enough energy to physically leap the entire flight of steps. O.D. Darren climbed the steps two at a time with renewed vigour and then discovered as he arrived halfway up the broken down staircase that he had not even been out of breath.

He checked that the case had been still intact and proceeded up the remaining flight moving fast. He could see the bright colours in the appearance of small advertisements for the new Mini pasted on the wall up the entire flight of stairs. It seemed as if the green of the car had been turned up and he could feel his eyes widening as his pupils began to dilate.

He turned to see the words GREAT MINDS... printed on each one just as his brain flipped slightly from the appearance of what next took him by surprise.

As O.D. Darren ran up the metal staircase, his hand holding onto the banister of the escalator of Hammersmith tube station he looked across the metal separation as he passed an Eskimo holding a sheet of light blue writing paper wrapped in cellophane at arms length as if he was being photographed for a criminal record.

FRIDAY 7TH SEPTEMBER 2001 NIGHT / HACKNEY

SCARY MONSTERS AND SUPER CREEPS

Teach me all the things I need to know it, turn all the pages I need to show it
I need the laughter and I need the pain,
won't you show me how to do it all again
MONIE MARKE

THE CHILL OUT room interior had been dimly lit with candles scattered across the warehouse oak floorboards. Ambient haunting music played through huge speakers at the back, with the exception of two lights hidden in the corner which lit-up the back wall with eerie petrol-blue and deepest red colours that slowly shifted and mixed thanks to the mechanics of Ben an alien X-Chromo Pilot who had already become one of the notorious artists of Hackney. An Edwardian chair sat in the centre of the room unoccupied. Ben stood at the edge of the room chain-smoking, dressed in a tuxedo and tails, while he explained with great patience to a group of impressionable guests who had newly arrived at the party dressed as genetically modified aliens how the lights were controlled by an amplifier and a computer, that had been rigged up on the opposite wall. The group nodded politely at the description of technicalities that he came out with but really had no more of an understanding about these sorts of things than a badger.

Tonight he was performing as host and DJ in the smaller extension of the warehouse. Ben left and walked over to join Static in one of the darker corners. Static had been using one of the hundreds of candles around the warehouse to assist in the lighting and construction of a large joint on a large round wooden coffee table.

"Alright there young Static?" Asked Ben placing his hands in his pockets and adopting a North Yorkshire accent. *"Ehh, I've just spent the day at the Tate Modern. There's been a bizarre exhibition on from this Yank artist. He's been doing stuff with pipes and sound. Got any skins?"* Asked the alien.

Static had managed to meet Ben a year previously in Hackney off Mare Street, getting out of a skip. The alien had already become a legend in the area. A mix of ye old English and gentlemen artist, Ben had developed since his rebirth into a real charmer. Max Born had sent him to Earth with the intention of using a disinformation technique known as flattery. The only social abnormality he had developed since living in Hackney had been that he had become a kleptomaniac and had already stolen three cigarette lighters and a watch from the group of artists he had been talking to. For this reason alone Static felt it necessary to ignore about fifty percent of whatever Ben said. Static could never understand whether a person should believe anything that came out of the mouth of a thief, yet in Hackney Ben had been in his element. Instead, Static decided that he had only arrived in London for this one party, then it would be back to the Isle of Wight and relative sanity. Being polite as always, Static introduced Ben to O.D. Darren and could already see the questioning look on his face as he passed him the joint he had just manufactured.

"So what does the O.D. stand for?" Quizzed Static, missing the fact that he seemed to have answered one possibility simply by asking the question. However due to the strength and effect of the hash Static had already begun to forget whom it had been that he was talking to. Or even why he was bothering to talk at all.

"Take a wild guess!" Replied O.D. Darren toking on the spliff his new associate had just passed him.

"Okay, err... let me see... it must have some Scottish connotation...um... I know, how about 'Oh Dear'!" Guessed Ben with wild stoned logic.

O.D. Darren coughed and exhaled some of the inhaled joint in surprise.

"Unbelievable! In over fifteen? years I've never heard of anyone getting it correct. You are without doubt a true original sir! You deserve a prize." With control on the inhaling he returned the joint to Static and reached out for one of the beers in the brown paper bag by his feet, slightly curious about the accuracy of the intellect of this new fellow.

"What on Earth is Scottish about 'oh dear' exactly?" Asked Static bemused.

"I have no idea how to express it in words of English. My parents are from a background of Gaelic heritage though and I'm unsure if it's the hash, but for me, it makes perfect sense." Replied O.D. Darren swaying steadily.

There seemed to be an incredible sparkle in the eyes of O.D. Darren. Maybe it had been the lights of the strobe, then again it could be just visiting Hackney, Static had never seen anyone with eyes so full of life before. *"Wow! I had no idea that ecstasy could be this enjoyable."* O.D. Darren said to nobody in particular loudly. *"I've been selling the junk for this long, it never occurred to me that it was great fun. Could I possibly interest you in a bean or two?"* The hippy offered to Ben as he adopted a similar tone of voice to that of a waiter from The Ritz.

"A bean?" Enquired Static bemused by the style of conversational technique his new friend had begun using.

"Excuse me, it's my own code-name for tablet. This stuff seems to fill your whole body with complete honesty. Would you care for a tablet?" He asked as he attempted not to chew the inside of his cheeks off. With a quick dive into one of the pockets of his combat trousers O.D. Darren pulled out a small sealable bank-bag of what seemed to be paracetamol tablets, held them up to Static eye-level and shook it.

"Magic beans!" He announced triumphantly, grinning like a lunatic. Still smoking the joint Static became transfixed by the amount of 'beans' crammed into one bag.

"Well, if you're sure you could spare one or two..." He laughed out loud.

"I would be honoured to give you a couple as a gift. Any more after that however and I'm afraid the price jumps to the excess of five pounds a bean which is refundable as of immediately, should you die whilst in the process of taking the aforementioned 'magic bean'." After O.D. Darren had announced this he felt a huge wave of honesty rush up to his head from his stomach. Now he was beginning to crest well.

"Many thanks young O.D." Replied Static as he took one of the tablets and popped it into his mouth. He swilled it down with the water in the bottle by his feet, wrapping the other pill in a Rizla paper and hiding it in his shirt pocket.

Liz came over and joined them on the floor, sweat dripping from her forehead. She nodded at the boys on the floor.

"Wow! The music in the other room is fantastic." Beamed Liz with chemical induced enthusiasm. *"Alright there Ben! They've been playing that wild Roni Size track and mixing it with something that sounds like the theme from The

Two Ronnies! Could I borrow some of your water Mr. Static?" She asked politely.

"Of course Liz." Static chimed, thrilled that not only was the woman back but had remembered his name as well. This had been a first for Static in about three years. He made a polite gesture to indicate the presence of O.D. Darren and thought he had introduced the two of them for the first time. *"O.D. Darren, Liz."* Said Static. *"Liz, O.D. Darren."*

"Hello O.D. Darren. What to do you do then?" Asked Liz jokingly, still in West End London mode and crouching down to meet him. The others were oblivious that Liz and O.D. Darren were already more than well acquainted.

"What do I do? Mmm. That's a good question! Well whatever I'm about to do Liz, it's going to be all the easier now that I've met you, you beautiful young lady!" Replied O.D. Darren offering a hand to shake.

The moment had been perfectly timed to allow Static to make a play for Liz. Which he attempted much to the amusement of Liz and O.D. Darren. Ben had begun to catch on to the situation at hand.

"Hang on a minute you young rogue. She's mine!" Joked Static.

"Says who?" Replied Liz, allowing O.D. Darren a chance to kiss her hand in true gentleman style.

Ben passed over a newly rolled joint to the hippy as all four continued to discuss topics as diverse as the potential of the Tate Modern to be turned back into whatever it had been before it was an art gallery and the subject of leeches.

The Chill Out Room interior had been dimly lit with candles scattered across the warehouse oak floorboards.

FRIDAY 7TH SEPTEMBER 2001
EVENING / SHEPHERDS BUSH

SAME TIME LATER LAST NIGHT

I'm not numbed out anymore no longer filled with hate and pain
No longer drenched in shame I'm not numbed out anymore
Now I have the key to the door
JAH WOBBLE / SINEAD O'CONNOR

THE MADAM WATERED her peottie cacti in the back garden. She peered from the garden to where the plastic orange clock on the kitchen wall reached her own invariable deadline of three in the afternoon. She wondered to herself where on Earth the hipppy O.D. Darren had gotten. The clock made a low sound like a gong and the big hand struck twelve. Instantly a firm knock at the front door answered her question. The Madam darted into the shed and stared at the black and white monitor installed over the blue wooden workbench. Even though her cobalt blue eyes still sparkled The Madam could barely see the outline of O.D. Darren as he made himself known to the security camera fixed above the front door by waving frantically as if he had been on national television. The Madam was impressed. She always appreciated punctuality and she still carried a torch for O.D. Darren.

The hippy stepped across the thresh-hold of the door into the front room of the house. He carried the case and felt an odd sensation of familiarity sweep across him. A neighbour passing by at any moment might have considered the possibility that a grandson had come to visit the old Victorian split-level apartment with a suitcase of laundry. There had been something about being close to The Madam since his first meeting which automatically caused him to reach for a cigarette and drain all the nicotine from it in one swoop. Now the sensation was returning as the old age pensioner shuffled into the kitchen to make coffee, reminding him of the character Yoda from The Empire Strikes Back. The Madam held a cane in one hand for support and O.D. Darren was reminded of the warning words of Winmau. He still knew that any anger he had experienced in Hackney over the situation was disadvantageous to him within these new surroundings. He had to remain polite in order to survive.

O.D. Darren lifted the case as requested and placed it carefully on a desk which had been carefully covered with large sheets of white drawing paper containing detailed sketches made in fine black pen of different jars and packets. He recognised some of the glossy advertisements from colour magazines. Above the desk were two long shelves crammed with textbooks. O.D.Darren studied the spines, reading titles such as Presentation Techniques In Advertising and The Graphic Language of Neville Brody, then one caught his attention as he reached up and pulled it down from the shelf. Blowing the dust from it, he looked at the title and blinked hard, twice. If there had been a camera in the room also he would have acknowledged the audience on the other side looking back with a concerned expression. O.D.Darren saw the words on the bright orange cover that read: G-WIZ THE MARKETING WORK OF LIZ GOLDBERG in huge petrol-blue letters.

The hippy sat on one of the green Edwardian chairs next to a drawing board and proceeded to make a joint using the textbook as a rolling table. Whatever the powder contained in the case had been, the sensation in his brain was eliminating any possible sociable normalities. As he sat staring at the case he gradually became aware that his teeth were grinding together giving him the appearance of a ferocious horse. He could see his long face grinning back at him from tarnished glasses and trophies displayed along the fireplace. This was the room of a winner. He could sense a tremendous atmosphere of competition all around him.

The meeting with Winmau Diamond that morning had been expected long ago. O.D. Darren gave an impression of being a lost hippy student but that was only the surface of the character. Underneath the epidermis he was still angry once he had comprehended the situation he had gotten himself into with Winmau Diamond. He had pictured himself as a Samaritan helping The Madam but that was to merely disguise his deeper incentives. Paper. Moola. Big cases equalled money and although he had made enough in the five years of drug dealing, O.D. Darren was certain from the weight of the cases that The Madam, who judging by her appearance, had been in the business for at least three times as long as he had, seemed to have bigger fish to fry.

The hippy had spent time in China and Tibet in order to learn. To learn about controlling situations in life. After living in Hackney for five years he had seen many times the consequences of the actions from people who had not used control. He had lived on 'the Murder Mile' for a year at least. Even Harlem paled in comparison with the number of shootings and killings that sprouted there every minute. The place was a war zone.

As The Madam shuffled back into the room, O.D. Darren was still holding the large book in his lap. The Madam passed the photographs of various memories on the wall showing a petite orange-haired lady shaking hands with men in dark suits and sunglasses, displayed with certificates for various awards given in advertising around the room. Some were used as paperweights on tall stacks of paper. He made a decision to be as polite and calm about the situation as he could possibly muster. Whatever the outcome was of this visit. O.D. Darren had been determined that it would most definitely be his last for whatever darkened schemes The Madam had planned for him, one way or another. *"Here's your latte O.D. Darren..."* She said as he carefully watched her place the cup down onto a round coaster which O.D. Darren considered for a moment had been stolen from a local pub. *"Thankyou for not being late... this time."* Much like Yoda, The Madam shuffled slowly around the room laughing occasionally with a slight bark. O.D. Darren had never heard her laugh before and noticed immediately how the sound had been so similar to Liz when she had been drunk or excited on their brief encounters. He noticed something familiar also about the huge orange logo which spelt the letters G-WIZ on the white mug that sat next to him.

The powder he had sniffed in the hospital toilet was having a serious effect on his vision and a warm relaxing sensation spread across his neck. He felt strangely confident and thought of the kiss that Liz had given him in the cafe. Then the question of the initials near the handle sprang up in his mind. No time like the present he thought, but be polite. *"Excuse me if I'm being rude,"* Continued O.D. Darren as he ran his tongue over his teeth. *"But whose name fits the initials P and G?"* He asked.

The blue cobalt eyes of The Madam twinkled as the golden sunlight outside attempted to shine through the petrol-blue curtains like a chunk of twisting laser catching the million flecks of dust in its rays.

The Madam rested on her cane and adjusted the orange shawl around her shoulders as her heavy petite figure sank into the folds of the Edwardian chair opposite him. O.D. Darren noted that she seemed to have the figure of a woman of fifty-five at least. Hardly eighty-two as she claimed to him before in Hackney.

"Thanks for the coffee." Said O.D. Darren as he grabbed the cup with a free hand. He blew the smoke out from the joint he had rolled. The dense smoke drifted above the two of them and hung in the air. The sweet smell of hash seemed to transform the setting of the lounge from Shepherds Bush to Morocco in one puff.

"May I have a go on that?" Said The Madam nodding at his spliff. O.D. Darren became amused momentarily at the sight of an eighty-year-old smoking a joint. Then he remembered the case on the table and the conversation at the house of Winmau and resolved himself to question everything about the room.

"What does your lodger do for a living here?" He asked surveying the reading material in his lap.

"What lodger?" Asked The Madam exhaling smoke from the joint like a professional gambler.

The hippy faked an expression of surprise. *"Oh, I was under the impression that this room was for a tenant?"*

"Good Lord no. This is my work room!" Chuckled The Madam her blue eyes sparkled towards him.

"Your work room?" Asked the hippy. *"I had thought you'd be retired years ago!"*

"Well I did but I ran my own studio from home after my old business partner died." A distant look seemed to appear in her eyes. *"He was a copywriter. One of the legends of the time! I was fortunate enough to have his business passed onto me after he died and eventually I passed it onto my son...Darren."* She said and passed the joint back to him with an odd smile.

"Darren?" Quizzed the namesake feeling small eggs appear over his face.

"Yep... " The Madam pushed her glasses up a little and looked directly across at him. *"...you! Don't you remember?"*

Even though he had seated himself into the large surroundings of the comfortable chair O.D. Darren suddenly felt himself almost falling back into it further as the words of The Madam floated over to him and echoed vaguely around the room. He managed to move his eyes up to face her but felt his whole body freeze suddenly as he reached a hand out for the joint. Even his eyelids refused to move.

O.D. Darren watched carefully as one entire front of the room shifted and stretched away from him seemingly made of elastic. He could hear The Madam clearly speaking yet the scene seemed suddenly two dimensional and made of layers. His perspective had been altered and the depth of three dimensions had transformed to two. The walls looked as if they were stretching. Elasticised. The lounge and its contents appeared to be made of rubber. He could see Liz sitting next to him in the chair. The Madam had gone.

"Its me Darren. Liz...you must have taken the powder. Don't worry. It'll wear off in a minute. You won't remember any of this. So I'll try and be brief. You'll remember my words..."

The Madam sat in the chair looking lovingly over at the frozen form of O.D. Darren and chuckled to herself.

"You still look as handsome as ever. For you it's been only hours since we met on Oxford Street, but for me it's been forty or fifty years. Just trying to find you. You have to stop me. Something terrible will happen if you don't." She looked sadly into the eyes of her young lover and sighed, then inhaled on the joint.

"Time-travel is unique. Yet I had no idea what Ray Connif had gotten hold of. I was young and had so much in life to be distracted by. Naivety and money beyond belief was offered and I took it all. Yet if I had only known what was coming..." She began to weep. *"I could never look at myself again. Something is wrong with time Darren..."* She banged her cane loudly down on the floor with anger. *"All that is needed for you to know is that you must stop me. Tell me that G-WIZ is dangerous. I'll listen to you. Tell me in the pub tonight...please Darren. You have no idea how important this is. Sorry about the inconvenience by the way."* Liz banged the long black cane down hard again on the floor and O.D. Darren found himself able to move freely. She watched him carefully. The sound of the cane knocking loudly on the

wooden floor still hung in the air of the lounge and the walls returned to their usual solid consistency.

"Did you get the message?" She asked politely.

O.D. Darren leapt out of the chair and collapsed onto a blue rug on the floor gasping. He breathed a huge lung full of air in deeply as if he had just been held underwater. Panic swept over his entire body forcing him to shake. Adrenaline rushed through every vein in his body and for a moment the hippy truly believed he would explode. Then the feeling passed and calmness reigned again. *"Yes Liz..."* He whispered as he knelt on all fours crouched in front of The Madam. Tears were welling up in his eyes and he slowly massaged his jaw, feeling as if he had been punched. He pushed his whole body back onto the comfort of the chair as she handed him back the joint.

"This will help calm you down O.D. Darren from the shock. But don't drink the coffee. I'll make you some tea..."

O.D. Darren looked over at the case on the table and considered how much of the drug he had sniffed. He had ingested grains in comparison to what lay dormant next to him. He was still shaking.

"You have done everything that was required and I'm so proud of you." Liz said then laughed. *"Don't try and understand anymore of it. I've been attempting that for around fifty years."* She barked.

"But...I took..." He replied still numb from the experience, *"...such a small amount...wow!"* He sat up suddenly. *"What the fuck is that stuff?"* Asked the hippy. He had sampled just about every drug imaginable in the last five years. Even some illegal ones.

"That..." Said Liz pointing with her cane at the case with an expression of absolute disgust. *"Is hopefully the last of it. From what Ray Connif told me. Although...you can never trust anyone in advertising."* She said with a wink. *"I called it 'G-WIZ' and thought I would market it as an energy drink or sweet... like sherbet fountains. What a discovery!"* She barked a laugh and O.D. Darren watched as the lines on her face slowly returned her appearance to that of The Madam. He kept blinking at her and shaking his head attempting to adjust his vision.

"It turned out to be a powder that allows humans to travel in time. Instead of space. If you take enough of the stuff! And boy did the kids go mad for it!

In the last Summer of love in 2011 my personal fortune had become so great I had to move to Switzerland. Ray and myself became multi-millionaires but it took me twenty years just to discover the research papers on it after you told me what it did to your insides."

"This is all in the future?" Asked O.D. Darren incredulous.

"Yep!" She barked another laugh and leaned her full weight down onto the black cane. *"You have to stop me Darren and I promise I'll listen. I was so in love with you and love does win over death. Tonight I leave for The Diner Holistic with that case."* She said as her whole persona returned to its eighty-two years in minutes.

O.D. Darren tried standing as he suddenly remembered the warning of Winmau Diamond but collapsed back into the confines of the chair.

"What about Winmau? He's going to kill me tomorrow!" He exclaimed suddenly.

"He...doesn't kill you. He can't! It's not part of the plan." She explained. *"He goes to New York with all his anger, sadly and with Mr. Bittre."* She tutted to herself and chuckled. *"Due to a severe time pollution problem...er...he is...a pilot, or X-Chromo-Pilot I should say. There are thousands of them on Earth. Here, apparently clearing up mistakes. They all operate for one man called Max Born."* She smiled back at him and O.D. Darren suddenly saw that the blue in her eyes had not changed.

"G-WIZ does help to explain a great deal of lose ends but if you see Max Born, keep away from him. Along with a bloke called Mr. Bittre...he's bad news." Liz sighed suddenly seeming very tired.

"You must leave now...with a present which might help...someone." She reached under the Edwardian chair and pulled out a smaller compact case. *"In this are the details I kept of the last forty years. I've done my research and if I don't believe anything you say in the pub tonight, give me this. There's also account details and stuff to help you along for the inconvenience..."* The Madam smiled.

"What inconvenience?" He asked as she led him to the door.

"You"ll find out at the party...anymore I can't say!" She stood up and leaned forward to meet his face as O.D. Darren looked down into the blue cobalt

eyes of The Madam. He realised that it was indeed Liz, older but still her.

"I always thought that love meant people stayed together...not that they parted so much." He said feeling himself begin to cry. Liz was already opening the front door for him to leave.

"Don't be angry Darren. We will meet again. Hopefully I'll be looking a little younger next time. Don't worry about Winmau. He just has no idea about the plan, that's the way it should be for some people..."

"How do I know we'll meet again Liz?" O.D. Darren asked as he felt all the hate towards The Madam mysteriously vanishing.

"Have faith Darren. You'll have to excuse me now, I have a meeting with my last client... a warm blooded mammal." She handed him the small case and winked again.

"Don't be sad...I'll see you tonight and then quite soon after in The Diner Holistic...for lattes. Now hurry up. I'm dying to meet you in the pub!" She smiled at him excitedly. *"Remember life is crunchy and goes like a bunny... enjoy it!"*

As O.D. Darren walked away from the house in Shepherds Bush he felt for the second time that day that each time he could predict an outcome of an event something caused him to question everything around him that he was seeing as he walked down towards the tube station. He cast his mind back to the cases he had delivered and remembered that each had the same letters embossed near the handle. The problem with meeting two versions of the same person at different times in their life presented him with a new situation.

In theory she had made quite a convincing argument for Winmau and O.D. Darren felt as if a great weight had been lifted from his shoulders or he had resigned himself to being killed. Either way he had to check the contents of the case as soon as possible. The Madam had given him some new possibilities to work with. As the hippy walked passed the hospital he had tested the G-WIZ in. He stopped and thought for a second in a way that astronauts sometimes do before they enter the bomb that everybody else has been calling a space shuttle all year. He still had no idea what the initials P and G on the leather case meant. As he started to hurry down the road towards the underground station as the rain began to fall from the sky, he checked the smaller case he had been carrying and saw the same initials again. Then he realised he would only have to ask Liz in three hours for an answer.

As O.D. Darren left Shepherds Bush The Madam watered her peottie cacti in the back garden.

SATURDAY 8TH SEPTEMBER
2001 MORNING / SOHO

THE LAST DAY OF OUR ACQUAINTANCE

Love is stronger than death
MATT JOHNSON

AS FAR AS Liz had been concerned there were only two points on Earth that she believed secretly were the centres of the Universe. She paused for a moment from sketching some rough ideas for the client brief and scratched her chin, thinking. She had never been certain how a Universe could have more than one centre but she could only explain that if anyone had asked her about such thoughts, Liz would proudly announce that she had been to both of them. The first Universe concerned geography and time. Friday from 12PM on the corner of Old Compton Street and Frith Street in Soho to her had always been the centre of the Universe until 10PM. Like most centres this one seemed to have a habit of moving. However, much akin to a person chasing his or her own shadow on a Summer day across Hyde Park, she could follow this central pivotal point until the following night if she wanted, without much consideration for her own physical well-being, most of the population on planet London did the same every Friday night. Consuming enough alcohol in the process to sink the Titanic twice over and leave room for the cast and crew of the movie.

The second centre of the Universe that Liz had experienced could be found on Sunday morning as early as 7AM in the bastard-driven streets of the East End past Broadway Market and down into the dank, donkey-dark narrow roads until reaching an area known as Brick Lane near Shoreditch. Along that long surface until the hours of 11AM a person would be hard-pressed to find a more frequently centred Universal melange. Considering how quickly the time moved when a person was in love, a second could be an hour relatively speaking. Liz had already decided to plan the movements of the next day and was already thinking about walking along Brick Lane to Columbia Market arm in arm with O.D. Darren and drinking latte.

However for now she had to make do with sitting in the office of Big New Yorker on Denmark Street and thinking up the advertising campaign of all campaigns in order to launch onto the world an energy sweet for children. Despite the thought occurring to her perhaps for the first time that children were notoriously full of energy already. Yet had her Mini campaign required any thoughts on the direction of mass pollution for the planet or computers taking over the world thanks to her brilliant schemes for Apple. Heavens no. This would be a breeze once she could get the image of the naked posterior of O.D. Darren in the local toilet of her local pub out of her mind. She decided to exorcise all images of what she thought had been a true catch from her cranium for at least two hours. This would require some of her known professional concentration to come through, which Ray Connif had convinced her could already be discovered in her bank account. Somewhere in the recesses of Creative Review many dashing young journalists had attempted to drive her over in the direction of the same idea.

Since she had met O.D. Darren in the pub the night before, she had to admit that her life had finally come together spectacularly well. The ability to receive a contract where you were actually encouraged to take as many drugs as you were already taking but then be paid to do so had surprised her to say the least. When Liz considered her first successful launch five years previously where she had assisted in the fabulous Bacardi campaign which had been voted unanimously as the single most infuriating advertisement of the twentieth century, she found that something had been blocking her usual line of thought. It felt like guilt.

Members of the public had been forced to write in their thousands to newspapers all over the country requesting that the advert be taken off the repeated appearances at the cinemas, creating a depth of free publicity for Bacardi and Big New Yorker in the process. Even Time Out magazine began a weekly feature of people reporting how disturbing the constant repeating of this advert had become. Nothing had prepared the offices of Big New Yorker for the barrage of hate mail which had arrived on the desk she was now sitting at. Controversy and yet more free publicity, her boss Ray Connif had realised her potential immediately and employed her on a permanent basis from then on. Her idea had been simple yet without doubt the public had helped her to continue the rest effectively. *'It should be as annoying as possible, like the drink. It should be like a drunken sixteen year-old schoolgirl at a disco. Really annoying and repetitive. Just keep showing it!'* This had been her suggestion one night after work as she drank the product and barked her infamous laugh. Ray had taken time to query her on the budget but she had been convinced that they could earn it back ten times over at least.

The launch had been a success unless you were one of the several million who had been driven to the brink of alcoholic destruction by the sight of a smug and grinning Aerosmith look-alike DJ telling listeners about his friend 'Ray on reef radio' who had left the tropical paradise where the miniature movie had been set only to return perhaps due to the promise of yet more Bacardi. Those had been happy days thought Liz to herself smugly and she laughed loud with her notorious bark of a laugh, with the natural confidence of a true professional she looked down and out from the office window at the various hung over passers by on Denmark Street. The ideas for the children market would be a doddle now that she had considered some of the names for the product and selected the title of G-WIZ as a potential winner.

Just after two o'clock, Liz took a break for lunch and whistled out the door of the empty offices to go and meet O.D. Darren for lunch after having to leave him at the party of the century at the warehouse the night before in order to start work on the national launch of *Phenylalainemontovia Dymulsive Cronoconiff* which had already become G-WIZ in her mind. She hoped the hippy would have managed to grab some sleep before heading into Soho for their first official date, or had at least remembered to turn up at Cafe Nero as arranged. She had her orange mobile phone with her in case he called but recently she had decided to keep focused on the job in hand so she had it switched off. The latte experience seemed to be just as much research as anything else.

Outside on the corner of Old Compton street Liz gazed in fixed astonishment at the majority of men walking around and suddenly realised the connection that Gyro had been explaining at the party regarding the name of the street. He had been explaining how a certain beech on the Isle of Wight had been named Compton and also how his hometown of Newport had reappeared as Great Newport Street on one of the traditional white metal corner signs.

"You have no idea of the connections between the Isle of Wight and the Western world!" He had ranted at the party. *"There's a road near my parent's house named Hinton Road and Hinton was a bloke linked with Jack The Ripper. The island never appeared on maps due to Queen Victoria ruling her Empire."* Gyro drained his glass as he continued his rant victoriously. *The best way to protect your Queen, was to hide her. If the actual island she lived on wasn't on the maps, then nobody would try and kill her! Therefore how can you believe any maps? Have you seen the size of Africa compared to the United States on a map? It's insane!"*

Liz had been fascinated by how much Gyro knew about an island that was only thirty miles by sixty miles, yet she had never heard him mention anything that had not been proven later by someone else. The talk of the maps had given her an idea straight away for a direction to take the *'G-WIZ'* campaign and so she had to start immediately on the work. Yet she understood now that she had left O.D. Darren at a crucial point in the beginning of a relationship. Just after sex. They had made love at three separate moments throughout the night and each time she had found herself becoming enriched by this man so much that she had met exactly three days before.

Thinking of which, where the hell had he gotten to. Liz reached the last lukewarm third of the latte and had only twenty-three minutes left of her break before she had to get back to the G-WIZ campaign. She looked again at her watch and realised the thing had stopped. Looking up again through her new Ray-Ban sunglasses at the drifting throng developing along Old Compton Street she wondered briefly how anyone could compare this area of London with its pornographic video cabins and insanely strong coffee shops to one of the more serene and beautiful stretches of the England southern coastline perhaps there was a bigger picture.

Maybe there had been a connection she had not worked out yet. Knowing Liz, it had probably been staring her directly in the face. Then she saw the worn out figure of O.D. Darren through her reflection in the large front window staring back at her, she hopped down from her stool to go and tell him off for being late. He looked terrible. Almost as if he had seen a ghost, as if he had not slept a wink since she had last seen him ten hours previously. Most people would not have considered O.D. Darren good-looking in the classical sense but then most people seemed to think Robbie Williams had talent.

As she stepped out of the cafe to greet him Liz looked across at the hippy and wondered if the pills they had taken the night before were kick-started off again by the coffee she had just been drinking. She suddenly felt as if everyone walking through this part of Soho was not observing her directly but somehow had a heightened sense of awareness. She felt as if she and O.D. Darren were the only heterosexual couple meeting in the whole of London. They both sat down at one of the silver tables which had been chained to the wall of the cafe in order to avoid one of the many coffee-table robberies that were so common in London. O.D. Darren stood on the opposite corner waiting to cross the street. *"I've got some bad news dear."* He shouted across at her grinning bashfully.

"Well I've been kept waiting before for a date so don't worry..." Replied Liz, wondering why it seemed so many of the cafes customers were staring at her, maybe it had been the new orange hair colouring.

"No. I mean, you're not really going to like this too much." He called.

"What's the matter?" She asked as he finally crossed over the road towards her.

"Um...I don't know how to say this. I've never had to say this to someone I loved before." Said Darren keeping a distance and stepping nervously from one foot to the other as if he needed to use the toilet.

Liz closed her eyes for a moment prepared for the inevitable dumping line.

"Let me guess, you want us to be friends?" Asked Liz.

"NO! It's not that...it's worse than that...you're really not going to like this..." Said O.D. Darren.

"Look. Just say it, whatever it is!" Now she was really getting worried.

"Okay... I'm dead!" Said the hippy.

Flicking her orange hair back from her head, Liz quickly checked her reflection in the dark window of the cafe and was unclear as to why so many people were now staring back at her as she stood on the corner of Old Compton Street. Then something odd about the reflection caught her attention. At the exact location and in the area where the form of O.D. Darren was supposed to be standing there seemed to be nothing reflected back from the large smoke-glassed window of the cafe. Even his loud chequered shirt and the sunflower T-Shirt and denims, the unmistakable signs of hippy-ness were nowhere to be seen. There seemed to be a distinct lack of physical presence anywhere near her on the street. Liz looked back at him as he smiled at her sheepishly. In essence, she closed her eyes for a moment and realised that when O.D. Darren spoke she could hear him clearly and yet when she opened her eyes then calmly closed them again and looked back at the window, all she could see was herself and the staring faces of the customers in the cafe looking out at her, she smiled back at them and barked a short nervous laugh. She looked down at the spot on the ground she was standing on and felt her reality shift slightly around her as she wobbled. As far as Liz had been concerned there were only two points on Earth that she believed secretly were the centres of the Universe.

SUNDAY 9TH SEPTEMBER 2001
NIGHT / HACKNEY

THE NEW FRONTIER

Take a train or steal a car, ride a bus not making no fuss
I just got to get there, just got to get myself to you
YARGO

THE CREAKING OF the wooden beams which had been situated fifty feet above the seats of the theatre might well have been capable of holding more weight than one twenty-year-old male body. There really was no way of telling such things. The sound currently being forced from them made Chris T ask himself if now was indeed the moment he would experience one of the first laws of physics in all its glory. Each action has an equal reaction, there had been only one way to find out. He crouched on the roof as the sound of police sirens echoed across the Hackney night and carefully opened the largest of the three skylights of the theatre, wide enough to slip his legs through. Then, with gloved hands, the artist reached out and grabbed hold of a slanting wooden crossbeam of the attic, lowering himself gently onto it.

The distance from the seats to the roof of the theatre was over fifty feet and a fall at this moment could easily break a number of bones in his muscular body. Slowly and with great patience of strength, he lowered himself down the hatchway until his feet found one of the beams in the dark. The beam was wide enough to manoeuvre onto and sit balancing calmly until he had worked out a way of tying the rope around it to support his weight.

The artist peered down into the darkness and could just make out how part of the attic had fallen away revealing the ornate music hall of the theatre beneath him. Chris T loved theatres, especially old disused ones that could be used as squats. His theory had been that if a person were going to start squatting, they might as well aim for quality and from certain enquiries made in the area it seemed that this particular building had remained empty since World War II.

Sitting on the beam, he tied one end of the rope around it securely and let the length fall down into the darkness until he heard it land on the floor below him. He wiped a gloved hand over his shaven head and face and prepared to slide down the rope when the distinct sound of footsteps below forced him to freeze exactly where he had been sitting. He cocked his head to one side like a bird sensing danger and listened with complete concentration. There it was again. The definite sound of feet walking around echoed across the abandoned theatre. The envelope of silence was so intense that all he could hear now was his own heart as it pumped adrenaline around his body.

Who on Earth could be in here? Both Chris T and Ben had even double-checked yesterday when they arrived back from Bristol. They had discovered the eviction notice nailed to the front of the disused Synagogue that Ben had squatted for a year. Nobody had taken this building yet, it had to be a sure thing. Chris T exhaled quietly to himself and waited for more sounds to clue him up on who the people below were. Then he saw something that made him almost fall off the beam in shock.

The only light in the whole building was coming directly from the sun as it reflected from the Moon outside and shone down through the skylight, which luckily Chris T had closed behind on his rather creative entrance. The same beam of light now fell down across two blue uniformed members of established law enforcers who were discussing over bursts of static on their radios, their own location. As Chris T listened in the dark without attempting to breath or even move, something highly unusual was being discussed by the two officers. He sat still and prayed that they had not noticed the rope which was now secured.

"Did you hear about Stitch?" The first voice asked.

"You're joking aren't you? The whole branch was talking about her today. Mind you, they're always talking about her." Replied the second officer.

"They're always talking about her because she's good at her job Judas." Replied Officer Lazar, a touch defensively. *"Did you hear about the body she found?"* He asked as he inspected the theatre by shinning a torch around the inside.

"What? The hippy?" Asked Officer Judas.

"Not a hippy man. Clovelly over in Holborn...do you know what she said?"

"What?" Asked Officer Judas.

"She was in the morgue when they did the autopsy on him. She said there was something highly irregular going on with the body..." Officer Lazar broke off for a moment as he thought he had heard something.

"How do you mean?" Asked his colleague.

Suddenly static interrupted the conversation and Chris T breathed out as carefully and quietly as he could. The amount of bad luck he had experienced in one week had become slightly ominous. First homeless in Portishead, now he was about to get arrested for breaking and entering in London. He pulled his legs slowly back up onto the beam and sat in a mock-meditation pose, praying that the beam would hold his weight. Instinct told him however, that whatever the police were looking for was not in the theatre.

"Er, Yeah, this is Officers Lazar and Judas, over. We're both at the abandoned theatre in Dalston over. Signs of a disturbance? No, there doesn't seem to be anything going on here. Must have been just some kids messing about. Over and out." The first officer clicked his radio off and continued his conversation as Chris T continued to listen from above.

"Yeah, so she radioed in about this body found at some warehouse party by these kids and when she gets to the morgue with it, Government officials swarm all over the place telling her she didn't find it!. Then they take her into a side room, where these two Yanks begin to have a bit of an interrogation with her and explain that if she mentions a word of it to anyone else, they'll have her job!" Continued Officer Lazar opening the front doors of the theatre.

"I tell you Judas, there really isn't any need to go to America, just wait in England a few more years, you'll be there already!" Laughed Officer Judas as he walked out of the building.

Chris T listened as the doors of the theatre slammed shut. The echo of wood and metal sounding throughout the empty building as he once again was left alone sitting on the cross-beam of the buildings dark attic. Suddenly the loud sound of an electronic beeping followed the exit of the two policemen, as a pager attached to the belt of Chris T began to suddenly emit its distinct presence from under his leather jacket. He frantically fumbled for the pager to switch it off, forgetting his present location on the rafters and lost his balance in the dark.

He felt an overwhelming sensation of panic sweeping over his whole body as he rocked first forward and then backward on the single beam, his arms spread outwards either side of him. Then his entire body moved backwards off the beam, catching the back of his knees, leaving him hanging free upside down. His leather jacket falling down over his chest. He scrabbled blindly to remove it as it slipped off him and disappeared down into the darkness, landing with a dank thud, with all his strength, the artist reached out with his left hand and caught the rope, just as the wooden beam he was hanging from split in two from the weight. With both hands, he held onto the rope and began to swing. Knowing the top wooden beam had snapped, it would only be a matter of seconds before the top beam the rope was tied around would snap also. Then he looked down in horror as the sound of the theatre door creaking back open reached him. He resigned himself to having to explain why a twenty-year-old artist dressed in black leather was swinging from a rope in an old abandoned theatre at one o'clock in the morning. At least the gloves would allow him to slide down the fifty feet to the buildings wooden floor without the friction burning his hands.

As he sailed down the rope, Chris T speedily decided that perhaps he could convince the police he was a performance artist who worked mostly with rope and would attempt ignorance on the knowledge of breaking and entering. Looking down to his point of landing, he caught a glimpse of the distinct form of a man standing by the theatre entrance. He slid down in perfect abseiling style towards the floor, crashing onto the rubbish and chairs below painfully as dust blew up in all directions. Chris T lay groaning in the dark as the silhouetted figure moved over to him, having watched the entire aerobatic display and stretched out a hand to help him to his feet.

As he stood up on his feet, expecting the officer to announce his right to remain silent and slip on the handcuffs he suddenly realised the figure was without a uniform and watched in stunned silence as the face of Ben was lit eloquently via the moonlight through the skylight.

"Wow man, that was fantastic. Can you do it again?" Asked Ben laughing, impressed by the stunt. Chris T had never been happier to see someone who was not a policeman in his life. He stood panting and tried to catch his breath from the winding he had just received from the fall. Ben was standing with a mobile in his right hand.

"I just tried paging you!" Said Ben looking slightly concerned. *"Are you alright?"* Asked Ben.

Chris T nodded in the affirmative, more surprised than hurt.

"Why didn't you use the front door like a normal person?" Asked Ben smiling.

"Nah... too easy!" Replied Chris T.

The thick rope continued to swing and Ben looked up and briefly wondered if the creaking of the wooden beams which had been situated fifty feet above the seats of the theatre might have been capable of holding more weight than one twenty-year-old male body. There really was no way of telling such things.

MONDAY 10TH SEPTEMBER 2001 TIME / LONDON

FANFARE FOR THE COMMON MAN

Last night I had a dream about you my friend
Had a dream that I wanted to sleep next to plastic
CAMPER VAN BEETHOVEN

MAX BORN WAS pondering on the idea of having another accident. He had already written off two cars since arriving on Earth. The first had been a blue Vauxhall which the Captain had purchased at a second hand garage in Detroit in exchange for the green and white paper that Dr. Bostrom had telexed him about called 'money', when he had been aboard the Three Breakfasts Tectonic-Freighter. In America Max had driven the first vehicle in the direction of Lake Michigan with the intention of reaching Chicago. As he stepped out of the warm Diner and onto the sidewalk of the busy street in Manhattan Max reflected forlornly on the incident. Opposite the TIME/LIFE building in Manhattan he paused and thought about the first accident that he had.

Max had forgotten about the gravity on Earth and had not even considered that the vehicle would be drawn downward into the water of the lake rather than above it. The car had simply sunk down into the cold liquid and the alien had nearly drowned inside it as a result. Since his first day on this new planet Max had learnt two important things. One had been that every action has an immediate and definite reaction and the other had been that humiliation, the powerful force which he had always believed strongly was the building blocks of life in The Universe was possibly the most emotionally harmful and damaging thing on this planet. Max had also discovered language and had used a great deal of it to express his fury at the sight of the Vauxhall vanishing as it had sunk into the lake.

However, something had changed the emotions of the alien from fury to exhilaration after he had splashed and scrambled to the surrounding edge of the lake. He had experienced new water. Everywhere. In his eyes, up his breathing apparatus, covering his clothing and making him feel heavy, forcing his whole reborn body to shake as he had stood watching the vehicle sink in the cold of America. Max had tasted the water and there seemed to be no salt in it. He had never considered such miracles possible before rebirth as landing in hidden water. He was rich. None of the entire area had been marked on any of the Bio-maps he had studied and as he watched his car slowly sink under the new treasure, Max discovered a new sensation. Attachment.

As the alien walked across a street in Manhattan he understood that he was already missing the blue vehicle. It was made of metal and he was missing it. On the Moon Max had always hated metal. It was all he ever saw. Metal and glass everywhere, all night. Twenty-four hours a night. His eyes were so dazzled by the colours and tones on Earth he had thought he would be driven insane at first by them, or blind. Thankfully some of the aliens had been able to send him a device to protect his eyes while on Earth which they had named after a new arbitrate who had been abducted from a place called Germany. Ray-Bans.

The second vehicle had survived for even less time than the first when he now thought about it. As he walked along the sidewalks of the city known as New York, Max had encountered weapons via a group of Venetians who he had avoided once they had fired metal at him through short instruments that made a ridiculous noise. Max had laughed at the sound until he had suddenly fallen asleep in the car and woken up amongst some trees. Accident number two.

The second car had once again smashed beyond repair and Max had decided to walk along the road after his second day journeying across planet Earth. He had been unsure as to why he had been so tired until a truck-driver had informed him that he had damaged his genetic space suit. His skin. Something called blood began pouring out of his red stained arm and he had begun to understand that the colour red had used all over the planet to describe warning. The prior level to danger. It seemed that every time he attempted to move forwards some action caused him to fall behind schedule. He recalled the second law of thermodynamics on planet Earth which states that entropy and disorder increases as time moves forward.

As Max had fallen asleep for the thirteenth time he recalled how the truck-driver had said to him, *"You need to get to a hospital..."* The truck-driver had suggested over and over until he drove him to one and he had woken up in a white room similar to the Zoa-Pods on the Freighter ships, whereby he had slowly recovered. Max had needed to study humans as quickly as possible and America seemed to be at first, a good location to start the search. He had spent a good year growing his human form after rebirth in the town of Superior in the State of Wisconsin near yet another lake. He had spent an eventful year explaining the physics and dynamics of the Universe to his Mother at the age of four months after she had been attempting to explain to him how to make a poo in a plastic container called a potty. Max had thanked her for the advice and left after one year. Still carrying the potty. The alien had been fortunate with the rebirth yet now he was behind schedule so much that the only option had been to head for the Airport called JFK and fold to a place called London in order to meet up with Dr. Bostrom who had the unique tools to fix his suit.

The process of rebirth was frustrating once you knew what was coming next and after surveying the locations and reading the reports from Dr. Bostrom he had been convinced that the good doctor had become slightly deranged from the affects of the intense colours of the sky and the land of this planet.

Max felt that he was probably the only life form on the planet at the moment who had less of an idea as to what was happening in the Universe than anyone else. Even the truck-driver who had acted in such a disgusting fashion on the way to Ohio by trying to kiss him had given Max the idea that one Earth expression in particular made more sense by his third day on the planet. Bad things always come in threes. The third shock had been the discovery that some joker in the rebirth room had sent him to Earth as a female instead of a male human. Hence the unrequited advances from the truck-driver. When the X-Chromo-Pilot finally managed to get to New York after accidentally boarding something called a train in Cincinnati. Most of the passengers on the train had advised him again to get to a hospital quickly. When he finally arrived at the destination of a big apple, he did so. The language he had been using since rebirth was named English and Max had become amazed to discover on arrival at New York that not only could he speak English easily but also that he had been reborn as something called a woman.

As Max reached JFK Airport he staggered towards the closet at the back of the building which had been explained to him once again by the good doctor via text messages before the rebirth. He fumbled around the underside of the white porcelain toilet until he located the orange envelope the good doctor had left hidden for him when visiting Hong Jin Wu. Inside was a tablet of G-WIZ which Max swallowed quickly, relieved that the initial part of his journey had finished. He counted to sixty Earth seconds and then opened a smaller door in the cubicle that contained various long poles and brushes then fell in. A tremendous noise caused him to experience the sudden rush of time folding and then another door opened. He finally tumbled out onto the carpet of the bedroom of Dr. Bostrom just as the Mother of the good doctor was vacuuming the carpet.

The sudden appearance of a young woman bleeding from an arm wound in the bedroom caused the Mother of Dr. Bostrom to scream. The good doctor had then come running up the stairs and almost fainted with shock when he had seen his old employee lying on the floor of his room panting and anaemic with blood coming from his suit. Luckily Dr. Bostrom had managed to fabricate the story of his friend being a film make-up artist who had become interested in trying out some new visual ideas for a movie he was currently making. After his Mother had calmed down and made Max some tea she continued to vacuum outside the room.

The good doctor looked down at the reformed figure of his employee as he sat on the bed and proceeded to repair the hole in his suit. The hair of the alien changed gradually from pale translucent yellow to a more appealing shade.

"There you go Max. As good as new. Why didn't you call from New York?" He asked placing the medical tools back into his black briefcase.

"Don't ask! Thank you for repairing the puncture." Said the alien. *"Good to see you Doctor. How have you been?"* Asked Max.

"There are easier questions to answer than that sir! Welcome to Earth by the way." Dr. Bostrom looked up at him eagerly. *"What do you think?"*

"This place is insane! My eyes are aching. Do you have any protection?" Replied Max rather loudly.

Outside the bedroom the hoovering seemed to stop.

"Why are you here?" Asked the X-Chromo Pilot cautiously.

"First, let me apologise for sending you here. I made the same mistake one week after you arrived, due to the strict laws of the Three Breakfasts Corporation...

er... I had to rebirth myself to clear up the mess!" He looked around the small bedroom, his eyes darting here and there.

"Its safe to talk here sir." Whispered the good doctor.

"Believe it or not, it's part of a plan to save the Earth. There's a war coming. The Comma War. The scale of it is unsurpassable and incomparable. Terrible in its scale and just plain ugly in its intention. Like all wars really." He walked over to the window and looked down at the chilling streets of Hackney below. The cold rain had just begun to fall. Max stood for a moment and stared in awe."This place is like discovering a secret treasure. There's water everywhere!" He turned and smiled at the doctor.

"Only in some parts." Said the doctor drinking his tea. "Other parts are as dry as Fifty-Five Cancri. I guess there is a way of accessing the lakes you spoke of but there's something else..."

"Something Historic I hope?" Asked Max looking at his friend fondly.

"I think there's some startling evidence that none of this is really happening!" Said the good doctor as calmly as possible. "I've been studying some research made by a previous doctor of Earth and some of them are quite convincing for building a case that we are currently in a computer simulation which has been playing since our rebirth." Max shook his head with a tired expression. "I had a strange feeling the colours down here would have an effect on you." He said.

"No really sir. I'm aware that time-travel broadens the mind but some of the X-Chromo Pilots here are thinking that everything is made up, even the air. History. Politics and Religion, are the main ingredients of society on this world but technology is controlling all the aspects right now. The held view is that life is a simulation and already humans are relying on technology too much. By the end of this century there will be such an expansion of it that where we are now standing could well be made somewhere else in the future." Smiled the doctor dreamily. "You should see the movies they make here Max..."

Max born interrupted him quickly. "Hey! Doctor! Don't forget the mission that I've sent you here for. *There is no predetermined way in which absolute predictions can be made, as in classical physics. These humans on Earth are all part of a plan you know. If your going to spiral off into Quantum Land at least wait until the party."

"Sorry Max, I was just..." The doctor became flustered.

"The Three Breakfasts Corporation was set-up five years ago with the intention of stopping The Comma War before it was started by Mr. Bittrre. You and I have already met Liz and spoken close to God. The fate of the planet is at stake and the only way to stop The Comma War is to locate her. Have you read the details I sent you?"

"They're all in the case sir." Replied Dr. Bostrom.

"Splendid! We have to meet her in a place called Shepherds Bush. I have her address here!"

"What is the plan sir?" Asked the good doctor.

"I am not at liberty to say Doctor." Answered Max drinking the tea. *"Because we travelled in time to get here. We must meet her and fold time, then we see what happened. The real danger is a lady named Britt and she..."*

"...Britt." Asked the good doctor perplexed.

"Yes Britt." Replied the doctor. *"She's one of Bittre's clones. Some of her are working for him freelance, but some of her are working for us."*

"I've met her!" Said the doctor suddenly. *"That character is getting in more places than God."*

"Some of her clones are worse than God. The cloned Britts are gambling with every living thing in the plan... with every living thing in the Universe..." He said as he looked back towards the wardrobe.

Max walked back over to the wooden piece of furniture and reached inside he pulled out a vast stack of compact discs that fell all over the carpet. He then pulled out a large portable stereo compact disc-player and slotted in a disc of the soundtrack to Grease - The Musical. The tones of John Travolta and Olivier Newton-John echoed around the room causing Max Born to smile excitedly. He turned the volume up and shouted across to the doctor.

"MUSIC'S FANTASTIC ISN'T IT THOUGH?!" He yelled as he tried to dance.

Dr. Bostrom placed his tea on a wooden table next to the wardrobe and shouted back. *"MAX! I CANNOT BELIEVE THAT EVEN GOD WOULD PLAY DICE WITH THE UNIVERSE..."**

Max Born suddenly stopped dancing and looked up at him again with an odd expression. *"HEY! WATCH IT PAL!"* He yelled pointing a finger and smiling back to the good doctor. As the two aliens danced in the small tenement building in Hackney the sweet precious cargo of water leaked down from above the clouds and poured over the grey streets of London as yet another alien had been demoted to the position of an X-Chromo Pilot on Earth.

Should anyone have passed the house and looked up at the second floor bedroom window they would have been witness to seeing two of the most powerful aliens in the Universe dancing to the soundtrack of Grease which could be heard echoing down the donkey dark high street below. Yet hopefully they would not have been aware of the thoughts reverberating around the head of the female alien. For as he waved his arms in the air perfectly framed in the dirty window of the house above the shops on the high street, Max Born was pondering on the idea of having another accident. He had already written off two cars since arriving on Earth.

* *"I cannot believe that even God would play dice with the Universe."*

Written to the Physicist Max Born in reply to Quote on page ? by Albert Einstein replying to a letter.

* Max Born was the Grandfather of the singer Olivia Newton-John

TUESDAY 11TH SEPTEMBER 2001
MORNING / BIG NEW YORKER

A CHURCH NOT MADE BY HANDS

*I'll take Manhattan in a garbage bag with Latin written on it
That says it's hard to give a shit these days*
LOU REED

CHAOS. SMOKE. RED Indians. New Jazz. Coffee. Ray Charles. Vietnam. Dancing. Comedy. New York. Grand Canyon. Jack Daniels. Quaint. Sport. Airports. Peanut M&M's. Reebok trainers. Product placement. Woodstock. Big Trains. Pool. CNN. Microsoft. Jack Daniels. Jack Kerouac. Mad Magazine. Dollar Bills. Mickey Mouse. Miami Vice. Kojak. I Love Lucy. Tales Of The City. Tipping. Big. Texas. Kojak. Russia. Bruce Springsteen. Spike Lee Movies. Empire State. Village Voice. Jurassic Park. Madonna. Miles Davis. Capitalism. American Football. Cable TV. The Simpsons. Television. Burger King. Bill Clinton. Clint Eastwood. Shane. The Lone Ranger. Old. Red Indians. Smoke. Chaos. Twinkies. ALL GONE.

Another Britt looked back at the line of people behind her stepping over the rubble and bricks. Standing in her presence amidst the acrid smoke and rising dust, American flag in hand stood a man who had flown directly from London after spending most of a year standing next to a blue blanket stretched on the cold ground trying to sell various bits of rubbish around the market stalls on Brick Lane. A pack of photographers from TIME Magazine rushed around him, cameras snapping and flashing. The scene seemed to have been dropped onto New York straight out of a war movie. A Mexican lady with a fierce expression came and stood next to Britt, she looked over at the paparazzi as various directions and requests were put forward to the figure who Britt immediately recognised as being American George, the lunatic from Hackney who kept handing out five pound notes to people. Without much success.

"Should they be doing that?" Asked the Mexican lady as she looked down to where the feet of George were standing. One of his shoes had been treading on part of a human arm. "That's my arm!" She wailed, looking back at Britt she began to cry. "He's treading on my arm!" She shouted again.

"Well he is the President. Who's going to stop him?" The eighth Britt clone shrugged at her.

"I didn't vote for him!" Moaned the Mexican lady.

"I don't think anyone did darling, did they?" Replied the fifth clone.

"He looks really strange from here, I mean why on Earth would he be having photographs taken in the middle of all this?" Asked the Mexican lady.

"Because he can! Be careful with that anger now." Warned the second Britt. "Let it turn into energy you can use!"

A long line of people continued to walk out forward from the rubble of the building and move towards the various clones of Britt. The firemen and reporters seemed totally oblivious to what they were seeing. The line of people continued to grow as another Britt clone stepped out in front of a CNN reporter who seemed to be crying. The entities all stood around the two clones bewildered by what they were seeing. Britt looked around the group and smiled.

"Okay everyone. Pleased to meet you all. I guess you're wondering what's going on but I can't go into all the details all I can say is first of all, try and not be angry but there's been a bit of an accident involving time and space. We're all going to The Diner Holistic which is in the fifth dimension and once there, everyone can have a latte and another version of myself will answer any questions you might have. Okay?"

A fireman who had just died raised his hand. "Excuse me but are we heading to Brooklyn?"

"Not exactly. The fifth dimension is where time and the Universe began. Once we get there, I'll explain to all of you what has just happened but just keep your attention on me okay? This way please."

The tall figure of Britt with an orange headscarf could be seen leading the entities across the rubble of what had been the ruins of the World Trade Centre two hours previously. Yet as the cameras from television stations transmitted the images all over the world only the form of the tall gently speaking lady could be seen smiling and walking calmly out of the rubble. She seemed to anyone watching television as merely being in shock and mumbling to herself.

Saturday Night Live. Subways. Brooklyn. Yellow Taxis. The dodgers. Snow. Concrete. Irony. Skyscrapers. The Guggenheim. The Projects. The Horseshoe Bar Coney Island. Flags. Dust. Dogs. The Horseshoe Bar. Gold. Central Park in fall. Woody Allen. Brownstone apartments. Sidewalk. Spike Lee. Iggy Pop. Gun control. Declaration of independence. Cats Diner. Tiffany diamonds. The Knitting Factory. Chinatown. Yellow Taxis. The Tribecca Building. The tallest building. Tribecca Hershey Bars. Frank Sinatra. Santa Moncia. Crap. Grand Canyon. Jack Daniels. New York. Comedy. Dancing. New York Public Library. Vietnam. Brooklyn Bridge. Cops. Ray Charles. New Jazz. Red Indians. SMOKE. CHAOS. ALL GONE.

TUESDAY 11TH SEPTEMBER 2001
MORNING / JFK AIRPORT

THE REVOLUTION WILL NOT BE TELEVISED

The earth can be any shape you want it to be
Dark and cold or bright and warm
Long or thin or small but it's whole
THOMAS DOLBY

THE HEAT WAS intense. When the airport doors opened he could almost see the consistency of the air as it clung to his body in much the same way a David Cronenberg movie holds onto the memory. The moisture caused the pours of his skin to start secreting a clear thin liquid which Dr. Bostrom likened to water. He had been warned that America had a different level of temperate zones in contrast to England. Yet he had no idea of the difference until he waltzed out through the smoked-glass doors and into the vast city. His personal stereo had been set for the experience and the alien beamed behind his Ray-Bans as he walked towards the taxi rank outside the Airport.

There had been nothing too strange about the appearance of a well-dressed X-Chromo Pilot walking out of the toilet of an airport. If anyone had noticed the slim built figure in a suit they would have been following him all the way from Hackney in the East End of London where he lived. However the chance of doing so would have only been possible if they had access to one of the only methods of time-travel currently available. The infamous G-WIZ formula. Dr. Bostrom had considered the infinite possibilities of someone doing this but had concluded before he left London that the chances were so rare that he could continue with his persuasive methods of disinformation without worrying too much about other time-folders getting in his way. His long shoulder length hair changed colour depending on his mood swings in much the same way that a human being changes the dilation of the pupils when passing from a darkened room into a lightened room. His hair had faded in its redness after arriving in the big apple.

This particular well-dressed X-Chromo Pilot had travelled the seven-hour flight from Heathrow Airport in London to New York without the tedious business of using any forms of physical transport. Instead the discerning doctor had folded time and simply stepped from his bedroom in England via the wardrobe and arrived in a crumpled heap upside down on the floor of a water closet tucked into the back of JFK airport after swallowing a small orange pill. He had then stepped out of the cubicle in the mens room after getting his foot stuck in the urinal for over two hours. Such were one of the many problems he had been encountering after getting his location co-ordinates slightly out of whack.

The chances of being spotted by anything during such a transformation were infantile. The chances were greater that nobody would be listening to someone who saw such things. Unless they were divine. Usually the alien preferred to keep such thoughts away from his mind. Any time that he thought about the possibilities of being discovered in the urinal he already became highly embarrassed. As luck would have it the enlightened Dr. Bostrom had been developing a serious reputation as one of the luckiest aliens reborn on planet Earth. Let alone in space. Although he seemed to make a point of not telling anyone of his various complications. Such as that of the toilet cubicle incident earlier.

Once the good doctor had persuaded most of the various airline passengers of Flight 815Y that their sudden appearance in Amsterdam had been for the filming of a new movie with free accommodation for a year in one of the best hotels, then the rest had been quite easy. Humans were a pushover for the good doctor. One lady had been easily persuaded by the new life away from her family in China by giving her a picnic hamper and tickets to see Pavarotti in Italy. Although the sight of the rotund opera singer suddenly discovering the good doctor and the young Asian lady in his shower still gave Dr. Bostrom the chills when he thought about it.

What had surprised the doctor had been the way most of the passengers seemed grateful for their magical transportation to another part of the world. He had spent at least one month of Earth time tracking them all down but had been impressed by the various ways that humans adapted to their new surroundings. Some of them explained that their life before the accidental switch in time and space brought in by Three Breakfasts had saved their lifes. These moments he cherished. He also made sure they were on tape for the future meetings with Max Born. A few of these passengers had lived in a place called China and seemed to remind him of the horror that had occurred on Fifty-five Cancri. When he offered to take some of them back to where they had originally been from they had begun to cry and shake their heads. One lady had begged him to let her stay in Amsterdam. Another had threatened to kill herself rather than return to China.

The return journey to New York had been a firm favourite of his since arriving on Earth and as he slipped into the leather and plastic innards of the yellow taxi once again, he watched in wonder at the sight of so many people travelling by air the old fashioned way. Arriving with red bloodshot eyes direct from the various points all over the planet.

He felt assured that G-WIZ would revolutionise the planet Earth and cause it to arrive neatly up to date with most of the Western side of the Universe but at other times he felt a chill when he considered the Copernican revolution required for such a change.

The problem with arriving in Manhattan seemed to be that everyone appeared to be so fashion conscious. If a person had not been wearing a suit that had cost less than two hundred dollars they looked suspicious immediately. The good doctor had heard rumours from other aliens that they had been stopped on the street by the Venetians merely for wearing jeans when in New York. The suit the good doctor had been currently looking snappy and divine in reflected his coolness particularly well. Which had been just as well as it doubled as his skin. Fortunately this fact could only be noticed by another X-Chromo-Pilot. Chance had been his defence. From his outward appearance he simply blended into the city as just another human riding in a taxi or walking down the street.

Occasionally when his hair changed colour people would ask him if he had a band. The good doctor had already been even more confused than usual when people stared at him after he had announced to them that radio-frequencies belonged to no one. Aliens were notoriously literal and language had been the only problem he seemed to encounter in America. Most of the people that the doctor had met in this particular city announced proudly that they spoke English but would then proceed to speak another language entirely.

More often he had been asked if he worked as an art dealer whenever he had folded to New York and he decided to research into why his appearance caused people to ask this. What Dr. Bostrom liked most about this city compared to others had been spotting the locations of many movies that he had seen. Until the doctor had arrived on Earth he had never ever seen a movie before and decided that this could be something that Max would enjoy also. Since his rebirth he had seen over two thousand in one year and had discovered them to be a useful tool for studying human behaviour.

The good doctor had only run into one problem, which had been in a place called Hong Kong. As he had searched for the various passengers that had been aboard Flight 815Y. Arriving in Asia with long bright blue hair had caused most of the city to come to a halt as he had been mobbed by a group of schoolgirls who thought once again that he had been in a band. His usual declaration that bands and frequencies were free sailed swiftly over the heads of most of the people that he had run into at the airport once again.

Any X-Chromo-Pilots banished to Earth should be far too busy working to either compliment each other on their dress sense or to even speak. The general idea being that they were there to simply clear up a blunder which might cause any of the present population of Earth to suspect for a nano-second that there were not only other populated planets in the Universe, but that there were also strange rumours on those very planets that creatures lived on Earth.

Not only that humans lived there but also that some of The Venetians were getting pissed off with aliens treating the place like a hotel. Usually not paying as much tax as they could be and nipping about folding time whenever they pleased. These rumours were usually kept under tight control by his employers at the Three Breakfasts Corporation.

Dr. Bostrom had felt sometimes that through his vague arrival on Earth, the control by the Venetians had been getting a tad too tight considering the extensive freedom available on other planets. Yet this particular alien appeared to be one of the few elements to be benefiting from the hierarchical structure at the moment. After all, The Venetians did literally own most of the place. He had seen the President buy Earth with Max when they had both attended the Planet Xpo on Mars. Max had attempted to convince him to put a down payment on America and now as he thought back to that day he realised that he had to thank him next time they met. He had watched the property prices on Earth soar and had smiled in the back of the cab when he thought of the fact that every living human in the country were actual tenants of his.

He ran a smooth hand of power over his hair as he considered how much he had paid for America and now slightly regretted that he had not also purchased England. Luckily Max had decided to buy Europe which he had since discovered had included England. He had received a text message from Max explaining that The Venetians were annoyed that an X-Chromo pilot had bought the last piece of Earth at the Xpo and so they were planning something big to annoy him. The good doctor had laughed at the message. He knew that whatever The Venetians were planning would be futile simply because he had required a certain little nugget of knowledge about the Earth that they had absolutely no way of comprehending.

As the doctor rode over the New York streets towards Manhattan in the yellow cab he decided that this would be something to mention on arriving at The Diner Holistic. However, he would continue with the current task of disinformation by explaining his notorious blunder to the Earthling Hong Jin Wu who had witnessed the mammoth Tectonic-Freighter above Flight 815Y and hopefully he should find himself back in London in approximately two hours time. Then there would only be Gyro left to deal with. As luck would have it one of the probe-clones who worked for Three Breakfasts had already located him.

Of course without the benefit of G-WIZ none of this would be possible and he would be serving time in a boardroom near Hoth or even worse, on Mars making a documentary explaining to child-aliens everywhere how not to forget to turn the radar cloaking device of their UFO on when landing on Earth. He shuddered at the thought. No. This plan, no matter how pretentious, had been much better. At least he had the opportunity to make some people happy here. Whenever he gave them an orange envelope containing the coloured paper of whatever country their currency came from he seemed to be able to help them. Although why they were still using such a primitive form of bartering on Earth, had been a surprise to the enlightened alien. Especially when two thirds of the planet had been covered with enough of the most precious commodity in the Universe. H_2O.

As the cab rounded a corner heading for the building that his penultimate customer now worked in Dr. Bostrom prepared himself for the inevitable speech which after repeating it to each of the several hundred passengers aboard Flight 815Y he had learnt automatically.

The cab pulled up outside the TIME/LIFE building that Hong Jin Wu had been working in as a journalist since his famous blunder. Doctor Bostrom stepped out onto the sidewalk wondering why a journey which lasted seven hours by plane caused one country to use the word pavement in contrast to sidewalk. He had become convinced that water affected language on Earth. He had heard a large hollow sound that reminded him of the colossal Tectonic-Freighters as they launched themselves off the Earth for the Moon. Perhaps another alien had been reborn. By the distant echo of rumbling emitting from nearby he guessed Max had punished an entire fleet this time judging from the colossal sound.

In the lobby of the magazine publishers the good doctor walked across to the reception desk and smiled enthusiastically at the lady who seemed to be morphing into the technology surrounding her.

"Good day. I'm hear to meet Hong Jin Wu. She's a journalist who works on the seventh floor Editorial Department. Level E. My name is Bostrom. Dr. Bostrom." Announced the rational alien to the receptionist as attempted a wink.

The appearance of an arched eyebrow and a slightly curved lip suggested to the doctor that he could be dealing with one of The Venetians. Not a huge problem however. His codebook, which had been sent on to him via Max Born inside his suitcase, had a listing for some of the main problems to avoid on Earth. One of them had been to always keep a Venetian distracted when talking to them. Max had explained that the Earth had a different gravity from most of the planets since it had been purchased by The Venetians. Most of them seemed to be angrier on Earth as a result.

[Always make some kind of action to suggest that you can run quite fast, if necessary. Max had informed him.] Otherwise The Venetians would reveal their worst side, which included their notorious egos. Hence when they had arrived on Earth most Venetians seemed to find work quite easily in cities such as New York or Paris as receptionists or police. Once again his patter had been rehearsed well.

"Well, I've got a cab running outside, is it possible you could pass this mobile number onto her please and get her to call me in five minutes. I have to get some

flowers around the corner for my wife. Thanks. Ciao." He said as he dashed for the large glass doors of the entrance.

This particular Venetian continued to arch her left eyebrow and looked at the number dropped onto the polished black surface in front of her and sweetly took the piece of paper. Then she notified the seventh floor for Hong Jin Wu. The doctor nipped back out into the New York taxi and sat in the back seat, mobile in hand waiting for the return phone call.

Upstairs the journalist Hong Jin Wu sat at one of the desks in the open planned offices of the weekly magazine Hassle. She pondered and sighed.

She had been attempting to piece together a plausible reason for why she had boarded a flight from Australia to Hong Kong the previous year and had ended up first in Amsterdam and then in New York one hour later. With only a change of clothes. She had then been booked into an unlimited stay at the Chelsea Hotel as if she had been expected all along. Envelopes and instructions had then appeared in the lobby. For precisely one year she had cruised through the seasons of Central Park admiring the style of whomever it had been that had assisted with this new chapter of her life. Her job as a journalist had allowed her to investigate any possible anomalies which had occurred on the night of the mysterious Flight 815Y. So far she had found nothing. Even receipts from the credit card she had used to book the flight had mysteriously disappeared along with her family in China. Which had caused her to wonder on darker evenings if they had been involved somehow with a serious cult group and forgotten to pay the subscriptions. She sighed again.

At her desk in the Editorial Department of Hassle she heard her landline phone ring and reached over to pick it up. The receptionist for the E-wing of the building had a message for her. The receptionist had described the features of one person to Hong Jin Wu perfectly down the telephone line who she had met once before at the airport and who she hoped would reveal some of the unanswered questions which after three hundred and sixty-five of the longest days of her life. She had nearly been driven insane by. She quickly scribbled the numbers of the mobile down and without hesitating pushed the buttons on her phone to return the call.

"Hong Jin Wu?" Asked the voice on the other end. *"Yes?"* Came the reply from the Chinese journalist.

"Greetings. They're coming to get you Neo and I don't know what to do! Just joking! This is Dr. Bostrom speaking. I have a window in my diary free to explain some of the inconveniences which you have been experiencing. I am here for two hours. Do you have time for lunch?" Asked the acute voice.

A huge wave of relief washed over the Chinese reporter. "What? Now?" She asked.

"This very minute..." Said the doctor in his calm but determined way.

"Where do I meet you? Can I bring a friend?" She asked quickly throwing a pen at her colleague Leia on the opposite desk to catch her attention.

"Of course." Replied the voice on the other end. "Although I would suggest to your friend the reason we're meeting is purely for research on a story that you are writing for Hassle. I will meet you in the lobby of Radio City Hall across the street. Please be quick." Informed the alien.

The call she had been expecting for one year had finally arrived and Hong Jin Wu smiled so much that the Irish reporter Leia sitting across from her thought her face would split in half.

"You seem happy." Said Leia opening a window to combat the intense New York heat.

"You wanted to meet an alien right?" Said the Chinese reporter glowing.

"Where're we going?" Asked Leia curiously grabbing a notebook, pen and a small digital camera.

"Across the street to hear the story of the century. How do I look?" Asked Hon Jin Wu.

"Okay let's roll!" She said fanning herself with an old folded copy of Hassle magazine, in the office the heat was intense.

FRIDAY 7TH SEPTEMBER 2001
TIME / THE PHILIPINES

THE TEETH OF GLEN MILLER

*I was once told that you had to have the balls to break down
Now I'm older I'm not too sure*
GOMEZ

AFTER SPEEDING CONTINUOUSLY from the previous night out with his antipodeans chums in Sydney, it seemed obvious that even the pharmaceuticals of the Tropic of Capricorn would in time lessen their impact on his brain. Most living creatures on Earth required sleep at some point in their day and Gyro had been no exception to the rule. Most living creatures on Earth however were not flying at over five hundred miles an hour in the direction of The Philippines and therefore could shrug off any changes to their metabolism as being just another day.

The hangover had been only a fraction of the headache that the artist had begun to experience in major head thumping glory as he first noticed the warm drool that was running out of his mouth. He wiped it away with a numb hand and began opening his eyes which felt as if he had just pulled them from their sockets and dipped them in vinegar over night. His head turned to the right where the Chinese girl had fallen asleep across his chest, dark black hair cascading over his right shoulder. A petrol-blue blanket draped over her warm body.

As Gyro slowly and carefully attempted to move without waking her, she woke up. Then she looked up at him. Embarrassed that she had fallen asleep all over a complete stranger. She quickly sat upright. The plane had landed and the jolt had to be the reason everyone on the plane was now stretching and yawning themselves awake. Gyro thought about the dream he just had and made a mental note to tell Static, his long-time companion next time they met. This one had beaten every other as Gyro remembered how this dream had involved conversations with what had to be called aliens merely because the description of the cute little guys refused to fit into any other categories.

He stretched out his arms and legs and looked around the plane interior as the voice of the Captain announced their arrival into Schiphol Airport Amsterdam with a heavy Dutch accent. Gyro froze in mid-stretch and yawned as he looked at his Chinese companion sitting next to him she seemed to have the same bewildered expression on her face as he had. Slowly he turned his head to the left and peered out the small cabin window expecting to at least see something that looked vaguely Philipines-ish. He gasped out loud and gradually became aware of the growing murmurs of the majority of Asian passengers on the flight, which seemed to be growing louder by the second as they listened to the Captain welcoming their arrival into Holland. Definitely not The Philippines by any stretch of the imagination. Although, some of the customers in the coffee shops would perhaps attempt to suggest otherwise, should they ever be able to speak at all.

However, the view from the cabin window, stayed the same. Gyro and his friend were busy attempting to understand how they had travelled onto Holland from Australia without noticing a change of airline or craft. The artist felt an odd sensation of unfamiliar excitement spreading up from his stomach. He found his sunglasses in his pocket and steadily positioned them over his eyes with slightly shaking hands. Gyro stood up with all the passengers of Flight 815Y who were now drowning out the good wishes of the relaxed Dutch Captain as he wished them a pleasant stay in Amsterdam. Not The Philipines.

Gyro began to smile and laugh nervously as he looked towards his new Chinese friend, who copied him by smiling back, revealing one of the most beautiful faces Gyro had ever seen. The smile seemed so confident and reassuring that whatever they were doing in Holland, the artist knew would be fine just by merely looking at the face before him. Gyro leaned over to her and planted a delicate kiss on her cheek and hugged her with the sheer joy of being alive as five hundred airline passengers attempted to barge past them through the cabin door of the plane.

By the announcement of the new pilot, the passengers had all made the journey in just over one hour. They were supposed to be in The Philippines but Gyro suddenly remembered as he gradually woke up, how a friend had told him of the bizarre laws in that part of the world, in contrast to the country he was now arriving in. There were definitely worse places to be confused than Amsterdam.

As the last passengers crowded off the airplane and down the portable stairway, the Dutch airline crew nodded and waved their cheerful goodbyes. Gyro grabbed his flight bag and held the hand of the Chinese lady. Somehow he had arrived in record time on the other side of the planet. Hong Jin Wu seemed to be the only witness to what had just happened to him but also to her. Without each other neither could prove anything. Whatever had occurred Gyro knew the flight attendants would be unable to explain or even care, the artist knew from friends that worked on planes in the past that the only thing the crew would be giving their attention to over the next few hours would be found in the coffee shops of Amsterdam. After speeding continuously from the previous night out with his antipodeans chums in Sydney, it seemed obvious that even the pharmaceuticals of the Tropic of Capricorn would, eventually, lessen their impact on his brain.

BOOK V
EVENING / CONSTANTS

MAX PLANK / 1858-1947

Max Karl Ernst Ludwig Planck was born on 23rd April 1858 in Kiel, Schleswig-Holstein, Germany. He became a Professor and pioneer of Quantum Mechanics in Berlin for over fifty-five years. By multiplying together Werner Heisenberg's Uncertainty Principle it is possible to actually get Plank's constant.

The outside world is something independent from man something absolute and the quest for the laws, which apply to this absolute, appeared to me as the most sublime scientific pursuit in life

While in Berlin Planck did what is considered by many Physicists to be his best work, he also delivered outstanding lectures. Max remained in Germany during World War II through what must have been the worst of times, his son Erwin Planck was executed for plotting to assassinate the leader of Germany at that time Adolf Hitler. After World War II he again became president of the Kaiser Wilhelm Gesellschaft in 1945-1946 for the second time. During an experiment Max Plank discovered that **the energy of a light wave is always proportional to its frequency.** He died on 4th October 1947 in Göttingen, Germany.

DUTY FREE

ABOVE THE DINER Holistic croaking on a choky, wetback and slicked sideways, perched Clamb-on-bass. Near on seven feet tall, bass-player of Inchworm - hedonist jazz for a bygone era. The band were trucking a grumble grumble problem worry trouble trauma at the reddies and Darwins paid for a fickle recordo-sesh.

Clamb exhaled his cool stick around the room and goggled out the windy at the frantic sounds of The Diner below.

Scenes of the tour made light years across land and sea from Blighty had corroded his mind the gap. His dirkwearswhite took a pale reflection on Yankyland and Landon taan. Electric it had been and easy Sunday but the politics of reddies and Darwins were not music he understood. The root of all shone much grumble, always and ever. Clamb sighed.

Taught on a brush and high and low for the money, all had wanted had been a tour for the Bardos, to drag up the words of an Indian. Viz the land and keep it real. His search engine lead to paths of precious lilies of joy. Clamb-on-bass the genuine draft. An original print from a distance even he knew not. Like his pops before him, the bass-player could only hesitate on the ass wiping bad luck he was about to vedge.

"Er...Clamb?" Enquired a voice a droite, a gauche. Through the haze of jazz smoke and acrid eyes. Through hairy-wairy and satellites of love, echoed the vacuous tones of Duke Garwood. With easy like Sunday morning eyes of stone, Duke fixed his goggle at Clamb-on-bass.

"Er...Clamb, do you remember, where, er...what happened with the Darwins from the recording session?" Duke asked for want of joints.

Clamb-on-bass felt passion flow and home economics of panico magnifico came jisming up his gut. Deja vu all over again and number twos of pullover the car son, we want to have a look inside the trunk thoughts filled the hair of Clamb. Duke requested ready alert. Neine gut.

"Huh?" Served back Clamb-on-bass through eyes of Hendrix.

"The two hundred thousand pound grand piano I handed you at the airport?" Volleyed Duke a tad more rapidly.

"You see the guitar case in the corner?" Nodded Clamb. *"Half of the piano is in there and the other half is in a safe place."* The shiver me timbers cold sweat style left nape of Duke the singer, as he shuffled over to the guitar case and fumbled over the locks. Surrounded by groupies and bodyguard posse.

Clamb-on-bass exhaled his midnight carnival of draw and bouncy-castled the joy back to Paul, the drummer. He goggled at the sight before him of fist on face. As bando-magnifico and roadie and groupie danced with punch and judo at the news of the Monet scruples and casheo retrieval. Buggery. As tooth and piss blue bottled around the hotel room, Clamb found his corner of ringside delectation and perched with cerveza and smoky Joe of glee.

More promising than tactile talk of Darwins, humans cracking the heads of humans. Cheesy wah-wah me jimino indeed. As television box crunch and sideboard back up board, new deco of hotel room became violent style. Clamb-on-bass decided for the first time in his alive alive-oh to alight the train of hotel rumpus, before dust and glass darkly landed at station. He canned on his Camberwell and sally-forthed. Into next reality of beyond the hotel room door, as he caressed handle and whistled his bass over. Projection of light and cinema buzz twinkled on teeth of perfection in jism stained mouth of Valentina, a lovely of frump, passion and Fellini. A couple built for purring. Ramming speed thoughts filled their hair.

Valentina wink of eye and smile of sperm called to Clamb amidst fights of fist, of blood and bone and smells of leather that doffed the interior akimbo. As Clamb tore open the room of room 42 and smiled at the blue Krishnas of limbo captured within the eyes of Valentina. Clamb caught the ear of a packet of California finest law enforcer and lit his hache-eye-jay. He offered a gentleman to her and marched across the threshold.

Windows of souls looked placid as boys of blue sticks of lead galloped into room and assisted in the welfare of all the occupants within. Bagged on the more bleeding.

As ache of humpity-thump and gashy-washy sprayed around the walls of hotel hell, a whisper of shit called OCB coughed under the remaining mattress. Weak, bent in foetal and always blagging, OCB had worked as Inchworm bastard-boy for near on three years. Fourteen of his own had pray and magic spent he, like managers of old and algae.

Sucking and licking used sweets from convents. Panting his masting horses for jisms of hope to wipe his nasa on a bandy wandy of musical delectation. Soul of black windows had noted foxtrot of Clamb-on-bass to the door with planet Valentina. Firing a shot from his sex pistol as he gargoyled her luscious panty tight and leaking. He had a glimmer to hold jerky and thunder after. Yet, wait just a jimminy of wrist and figs. Porqoi und where of hare was Clamb-on-bass kompfing in suchaworry? Outward from reality.

Police and band smash scraps for hard cash and five-finger hand shandy of a moment left OCB under the bed with Q's and P's and a wanton urge of a shotmawod one more time. Erect and oh-eetso big meester. Grunting OCB found a cat-curious of want to trail, want to sniff like the born again. A want to yelp an intrigue. Barking for clues of clues. Eyelids wide and fist of cock he witnessed a groupie handcuffed in wild west style, as blue blazers and steel law instructors forced the face of the madam in line with carpet and frame of porn lined up in mind of a ripe young cop.

OCB gargoyled with grim stink under the mattress hotel bed. The bastard boy jizzled in his tumkin, as the visage of the lady met with his, closer than cigarettes.

"Chrimbo came early!" OCB felched to himself as groupie met vedg with arresting officer of blue. Skirt up and groans of largeness bursting quim squeaked out of groupie as California rammed into Idaho. *"You have the right to remain darling..."* Yelled cop as his pumpy-wumpy began on the maiden faire. Her flushed luck of beginners on all fours caused her to gasp as thrust beget thrust and cuffs dug in on wriths.

"Ohh meeester!" She squealed through ruby red and grins of wire as OCB gawped into doll of face and pig of tails enjoy of enjoy on the law of laws. *"Eeeeet's sooo beeeg!"* Gasped the princess of Idaho. *"You enjoying that darling?"* Grunted newborn as a huff and a puff and the chug-a-luggin of a porn-dog slapped against C and B hind, faster and faster. OCB could contain his shandy no more. As group-oh magnifico drunk out of his pockets and puffs and cuffs of steel, jellybeans from his lips and oohhing and aaarring. As order kenobied on all around hotel riot, only sound came loud as bombs from the porno. *"Bob's yer Uncle!"* Cried out the cop, as bulleteo delishio hot and spicey cream of alive-oh fired up and into the Venus of milo. So bigs and so goods grunted and weaped from under

mattress of lip and tremble, of quick it's my Mother and been to the beach and unprotection and galaxies of Denmark.

OCB begged forgiveness from alien cackles and Daddies of dirge. Stroking and purring confessional fingers of lace and moisten and Brie running from bread and agriculture. Pants up and skirts down and dankas of donkeys. Three arrests and injuries of unknown origin from truncheons of law and keys. One marriage on hotel floor and strange tones astronaut under the foam, lurking like a politician of calm. OCB sucked onhisfingers of love. Sticky and waited, waited for rabble of soreness to quit. As they trickled out of the hotel room. Bastard boy could hear the singer Duke demanding rights and lefts.

The door of 42 snapped back shut and OCB rewound on the moment of eeets so beeeg. Lolli and golly. The squeak of steel and flash of peak and from prom behind. Hot and taught back to nought. On his pool of crust and molten, thoughts filled his hair of replacing the cop with himself. In his wild of dreams and jisms of tease, OCB had many wanky woo-woo dankas, none of bun and cream had he seen like the rush of thrust that had been Idaho. What sound of joy had issued from rubies and gasps of sweet? Was it love?

A memory of steel and panty-hamster jam for one last tug-a-lug make haste for chase. De bastardeo magnifico tugged and squirmed under the sunder and let thoughts of grand pianos fill his hair. Vegas and Idaho, bending over and little Buddhas on the stairs. Reddies and dreamy weamy of swamp planning prior and per say some waiting. Clack on for astral. OCB a slither of shit, Sven teen of age and wasted on he. One quick power nap and then a rubdown with rat chewed rag-water.

In a dreamy weamy flesh of Franco rubbed at Berlin Wall. Face of doll licked on Venus and fire of heat and goo, numbers of two and flame of four. Uniforms of cancer and bearded nymphs. The size of whales screamed from the despair of sea und new and old dancing for a dinosaur of hope. Bending and mending and change and vexxen. Nymphs were sucking on c-hulks. Surf was up and welding of ships carrying rowman to plunder, natives tied natives and hard and long sticks of law pushed between school of shirt and pleated skirt of donkey danka.

Clamb-on-bass and Valentina a droite. Bungie-chord rumble riot of disband and law enforcement a gauche. Parting ways of band and bass.

Corridors of countries and university hotel maze. The new couple of love enriches passed doors like pool hall stitches, with mission to strike eight ball hard into centre cushion of lard.

Breaking through from door came motorbike of night of charlatan of truth namen of Squirrel Drake. Puffed up on liquid cola and half-fat yoghurt. Killer fat of dope on a rope. Crash of helmet on and forever, face had not viewed since fifty-eight. Orange of sick boiler suited and whenever speaking justfullofshit. Squirrel had always as now in eternal, been in the way. *"DON'T RUN IN THE CORRIDORS IF YOU DON'T MIND!"* Howled the gob of day-glow sunshine kiora on legs. Sad visor replaced face and head of black pace. Could suck a pope of reaction from any but the posse of love. Case of bass in crutch brought much folding of Drake and testies at the speed of light aiming for nape of neck to go as whistling passed and onward strove the nuclear family of happiness. Above The Diner Holistic croaking on a choky, wetback and slicked sideways, perched Clamb-on-bass.

FRIDAY 7TH SEPTEMBER 2001
AFTERNOON / HACKNEY

DRUGS WON'T CHANGE YOU RELIGION WON'T CHANGE YOU

Ain't nothing wrong, everything alright...ain't nothing wrong
FLUKE

THE PARTY HAD been a real hum-dinger. As predicted. But in the morning light, the idea of waking-up with a huge hangover and a corpse sitting in a chair had been something most of the rabble of guests had not noticed anywhere on the invitation. Stumbling awake the majority of the guests who had fallen asleep or passed out the night before had been inclined to catch buses home or tubes as fast as they could. Most of them had never seen a dead body before and the sight of O.D. Darren in the chair, farting and dead had been enough to cause even the most hardened of partygoers to throw up. It seemed that there was nothing like death to clear a party.

When the police arrived there were only Barnaby and Claire remaining. The fashion-designer seemed to approach the appearance of corpses with what seemed to Barnaby like sick fascination. He tried talking to her the night before the party but had been too drunk. Now the situation had been reversed and Barnaby had been suddenly too sober and still had no idea how to deal with it all. Claire had an arm around his shoulders and had been comforting Barnaby while holding a whisky filled ceramic cup with her free hand when Officer Stitch walked up the stairs and into the Chill Out Room. She spoke into her radio and Claire could hear bursts of static becoming louder as she knocked politely on the door and entered the room.

Out of sheer nervousness Claire found herself explaining what would have seemed perfectly obvious to anyone entering the room even if they had been as badly impaired as Helen Keller. *"We all woke up and he was just there...er, dead."* Announced Claire in a loud London accent. She sounded almost disappointed in her tone as if she had only stayed awake she would have seen all the action. This had purely been the intonation of her voice which brought a carefree tone to most things she said. The policewoman nodded sympathetically and jotted down the words WOKE UP and the word DEAD. This was the second official day of duty for Officer Stitch and at six o'clock in the morning with the sunshine of grimness shining through the warehouse window onto the corpse of O.D. Darren, the officer underlined the word DEAD for added emphasis. Barnaby sobbed into the shoulder of Claire who continued an amicable ramble of chatter about the body being dead in the morning and the fun of the party the night before.

Officer Stitch surveyed the space around the Edwardian chair in a style she once saw on an English television programme called *'The Bill'* and wrote any notes of interest that Claire managed to hit upon. The policewoman walked across the warehouse floor to a makeshift kitchen sink and looked out across the rooftops of Hackney. Almost exactly like The Bill she thought to herself. The view of East End London on a cold grey morning did very little to inspire most human beings but this particular Police Officer had waited five years just to be in this part of London. She wrote the words WITH BLONDE HAIR down in her notebook. Now for the moves. Dramatically Stitch turned around quickly and focused her attention squarely at Claire.

"Did he...have a gun?" She asked the fashion-designer, squinting her eyes a little as she tried to give the appearance of Clint Eastwood whose films she studied avidly.

"Did who have a gun?" Asked Claire gently rocking Barnaby and stroking his hair. The question threw Officer Stitch off course and the thought that she could be dealing with an arranged alibi crossed her small mind.

"THE ASSAILANT!" Roared back Stitch causing the corpse discovering couple to jump. The cups of whisky dropped to the floor from both of their hands and spilt over the wooden floorboards of the warehouse. Claire stood up furious.

"Now wait a minute! No one killed him, he just overdosed on drugs!" Yelped back Claire. Barnaby returned to his sobbing wreck mode of the previous

hours and the burst of static on the police radio brought a new dimension of sound to the atmosphere of the warehouse apartment. O.D. Darren remained silent for obvious reasons.

"Er...is that Stich?" Crackled the radio on the shoulder of the lady officer. She clicked a button on the side and returned her direction to the window.

"This is Stitch... over." She clicked the side radio button and held it down as she spoke into the mouthpiece.

"Where are you love? I woke up and you were gone." Explained a loud deep voice waking-up. Slightly embarrassed. Stitch attempted to turn the volume of the radio down before the unmistakable voice of her fiancé said anything predictably embarrassing. Instead she accidentally turned the volume up.

"I'm still handcuffed to the bed love!" Sounded out the deep voice. Too late.

Feedback loudly issued from the police-radio as Stitch fumbled with the dial and dropped the radio into the sink with a loud clang. Her back turned to the couple. She tried coughing over the interruption of her boyfriend before continuing with her interrogation slightly red-faced.

"OKAY! So...er, drugs...mmm?" Asked the officer as she wrote the words AND DRUGS in the notebook. *"What exactly makes you think he took drugs?"* Asked Stitch folding her arms officially and looking at the corpse of O.D. Darren. Claire slowly placed her hands on her hips and sighed a little in wonder at how this woman had been allowed to join the Police Force in the first place. She walked over to the cadaver and gestured at the various small wraps and pills contained within the jacket pockets of O.D. Darren. Then pointed at his blue lips and at the pale skin.

"Well, call me naive but when someone has lips that are blue and flesh that is cold, I would assume they have died or were very cold. Considering it is warm and sunny outside it clearly would seem that O.D. Darren took twelve or fourteen pills too many". Answered Claire sarcastically.

Stitch blinked twice at her outburst and wrote the words TOO MANY DRUGS under all the notes she now read back to herself. She seemed slightly worried by the sentence WOKE UP DEAD WITH BLONDE HAIR AND DRUGS. TOO MANY DRUGS. The officer was sure that something sounded strange about the notes she had just taken down.

Maybe a different perspective would be discovered at the police station down on Mare Street.

"The pair of you will have to accompany me down to the station and fill out a statement, if that's alright?" The thought of her boyfriend handcuffed to her four-post bed briefly swam across her mind and a surge of impatience affected her to turn quickly and knock over a capped bottle of Jameson whisky which rolled across the warehouse floor to the exit door of the Chill Out Room. She checked the time on her new police wristwatch and accidentally elbowed the mirror from the window ledge which O.D. Darren had strategically placed only several hours before as part of his plan. All eyes stared hypnotised as the travel mirror bounced off a football some joker had placed in the sink and gracefully vaulted about four feet through the air and then landed with uncanny precision into the front pocket of the chequered shirt of O.D. Darren. Claire let out a gasp and stifled a giggle as Barnaby stopped sobbing instantly after they both witnessed the incident. The rolling bottle immediately knocked against the door that had BINGO written on it with a thud. Silence suddenly filled the room and was then broken by the sound of a long high-pitched fart which came from the body in the Edwardian chair.

Claire experienced a haunting gaze as her eyes met those of Stitch across the warehouse floor. Seemingly an expression of awe and wonder flowed from her out towards the body of O.D. Darren. Claire felt a shiver on the nape of her neck from witnessing such a rare form of physics so directly, which would have to be impossible to repeat. She felt the hair on her neck rise up and shivered accordingly. Officer Stitch had decided to make good use of the miraculous moment to show just how well and truly out of touch with any synchronicity in the world she was by meeting the stunned gaze of the two guests with a slightly embarrassed look due to the fact that she had begun to pick her nose after checking the time and now wondered why she had not done so in the privacy of the bathroom. She turned around and coughed loudly as she marched towards the door.

"Okay then, to the station..." Announced the blonde police officer.

"What about him?" Asked Claire following with Barnaby in tow but gesturing at the farting corpse.

"No, he'll have to stay here for the moment and wait for the ambulance." Said Stitch.

Several cups of tea later an ambulance arrived outside the Sigdon Passage residence as two ambulance men dressed in uniforms and both wearing Ray-Ban sunglasses made enquiries about any women in the area who were about to have a baby. The neighbours seemed to have heard the party or called over with drink the night before but Derek eventually took directions from a bearded man who appeared in the doorway of a nearby house, seemingly dressed as a Musketeer. He seemed to watch Derek with a tentative stare until the ambulance man removed his sunglasses.

"Excuse me sir, sorry to bother you, but we received a call in this area from a pregnant lady who was having a baby. You wouldn't know of anyone would you fitting that description?" Asked Derek as officially as possible.

"Er...pardon?" Replied the neighbour.

Derek had virtually no understanding of French as a language but loved the people. He always made the effort to at least show he could be bilingual even though most of the time his approach had been to merely shrug his shoulders and say *"Oui"* occasionally as if he knew more than he could remember.

"Oh, tu Francais?" Replied Derek stepping back a little from the door.

"Oui. Oui!" Exclaimed the Frenchman. *"Tu parlez Francais?"*

"Un peut! J'ai er...regardez la enfant?" Asked the ambulance man.

The neighbour looked slightly bewildered as a pregnant pause rose between them both.

"Er.. Madame est avec un enfant?" Attempted Derek again.

Suddenly the Frenchman forced his eyebrows up and slammed the door he had been standing behind shut, leaving Derek bewildered standing still outside of the house. Clive began to shout across from the ambulance pointing at the warehouse next door. *"Del! The hospital just radioed in. That's number eleven. We should be at number one!"* He pointed over at the warehouse. *"It's not a birth... it's a death!"*

They both entered the warehouse with apprehension and walked up the inside staircase walking past the large wooden sign with BINGO written on it. Clive pushed open the door of the Chill Out Room with a loud creaking sound and they both peered into the dimly lit interior where the corpse of O.D. Darren sat staring back at them. Derek felt his jaw drop slightly. In all his years of moving people to hospitals this had been the first time he had been called to move a dead body. The shock hit him as he recognised instantly the face of one of his old pupils from the Isle of Wight.

"Great galloping Gods..." He said in shock moving over to the figure in the Edwardian chair. *"It's Darren!"*

The party had been a real hum-dinger. As predicted.

SATURDAY 8TH SEPTEMBER 2001
AFTERNOON / THE RITZ

THIS IS A PERSON TO PERSON MESSAGE

It's a one-time thing it just happens a lot,
walk with me and we will see what we have got
My footsteps are ticking like water dripping from a tree,
walking a hairline and stepping very carefully
And something is cracking I don't know where,
ice on the sidewalk brittle branches in the air

SUZANNE VEGA

AS LIZ CLOSED the door of room 236 softly behind her Darren sat down on the end of the double bed. She looked at him carefully with as much attention as she could muster and attempted to stop her brain leaping out the top of her skull. He really did look dead. She rested herself against the door and slowly let the entire weight of her petite body slide down the wooden surface until she was crouching and resting on her haunches. Then she placed her palms on her face, calmly closed her eyes, took a deep breath and exhaled slowly outward. Then tried to stop herself crying. With little success. "Oh Darren...what happened?" She asked as tears streamed down her face.

"As Spandau Ballet would say. To cut a long story short I lost my mind!" He smiled back at her.

"That's poignant but it does little for an explanation." Said Liz looking up at the dishevelled figure.

"You know the campaign your working on for the new drug?" Asked the ghost of O.D. Darren. Liz nodded through mascara and tears. "Well, it has something to do with that. In fact, it has a great deal to do with that!" He stared out the window.

"You took it? That was pure base chemical!" She barked at him with her famous laugh partly in disbelief.

O.D. Darren nodded bashfully and fiddled with the buttons on his jacket looking like a lost child. She then stood up and moved over to the window and looked out over the rooftops of the West End.

"There's more to it than that but for now that's all I can say. The drug's incredible but I wouldn't recommend mixing it with narcotics, for that matter. It seems to have a fatal reaction with humans. There internal structure just melts and although it feels great...so much damage is done, that the body just shuts down." He said as he tried to recall dying at the party that morning. "I just fell asleep and melted, on the inside."

"Fantastic..." Liz raised her eyes upward and wiped her hands across her eyes, mascara smudged across her face. "I finally fall in love and it lasts three days but I don't get dumped this time...,oh no, instead my boyfriend dies of a drugs overdose and I now have to promote the drug that killed him. Wonderful! I think I need a drink..." She stood up and moved over to the mini-bar and began to drink three small bottles of whisky from it in succession, one after the other. Small cans of soft drinks fell out of the fridge and all over the carpet, causing Liz to momentarily feel taller than she was as she looked down at them.

"Imagine how Jackie Kennedy felt!" Said O.D. Darren wondering why he had suddenly remembered such a thing.

"Oh purr-lease!" Guffawed Liz.

"No really. She was sitting next to her husband when his brains ended up all over her face with most of the world watching and still the killers haven't been found. Imagine how that felt!"

Liz found herself laughing and threw to Darren a miniature bottle of Jameson Whisky. He caught it with surprisingly sharp reflexes. Then she watched as the bottle also fell to the floor after bouncing off the window and through his torso. Liz gawped in amazement at what at had just happened.

"Every atom or molecule, every single pro-ton or neutron has a single related spirit. A copy." He undid the cap and drained the miniature bottle in one. "Splendid whisky, I must say." He said.

"What happened then? After I left the party? Did you just die?" Liz was still in shock at how this particular Saturday was turning out.

"Not exactly, the argument after your leaving didn't have that much of an effect. I think it was around four, when my heart gave out but the rest of me kept melting until six o'clock this morning. My body's still in the warehouse I think, although it might be in the morgue by now." He seemed to be in remarkable form. "For the first time, I actually am in two places at once! The strangest things happen when you're dead you know. Weirder than when you're alive."

"Who found out you were dead?" Liz was finding the conversation surreal but fascinating. She made a mental note to recommend Jamesons for the 'dead market'.

"Some couple. I didn't catch the names. A blonde girl with glasses called the police and helped clear the mess up. I think her name's Claire. Which reminds me, I've got a request." The hippy said conspicuously.

Liz looked slightly apprehensive. "I'm not sure how to take that..."

"No, nothing kinky, I'll explain on the way but it's going to need some planning and some serious acting. I need you to get to the body, which should be in the morgue by now. There's a mirror in the pocket of this shirt, the real shirt, here..." O.D. Darren pointed at the pocket and pulled out a rectangular compact mirror. "It looks like this and it has your name written on the back. I need that mirror."

"I'll explain on the way. Without the mirror though, I'm fucked." Liz held her head. "Ohhh come on Darren don't do this! First I find out you're dead and now there's problems?"

"I promise it's not that bad. If we get the mirror, things will be much better..." He sat on the bed.

"Which morgue would the body go to?" She asked.

"Hopefully it should be in High Holborn. Near Lincoln Fields." He said more than amazed. "I was in the ambulance with it and you'd never guess who was driving the ambulance? My old art teacher!"

"Wow! Okay, we'll get a cab!" Liz found herself going into professional mode again.

O.D. Darren walked back around the bed, out of habit and over to her and looked poignantly into her eyes. *"Have you dyed your hair by the way by the way?"*

The hippy reached out to brush his hand down over her orange hair and Liz could see some of the hairs move by the touch. The aura which pulsed around her, made her feel as if each individual hair on her body were standing up and seeking attention. Darren bent his head down closer until his face was close enough to Liz to enable a more intimate conversation as he kissed her on the mouth. She could feel the momentum suddenly of their union in the toilet of her local pub and began to wonder why they had met at all, if only to be separated immediately. Liz looked up at his pale drawn out face and she realised that timing was pretty much everything in a relationship.

"Darren, what is the story with the mirror?" She asked.

"Well..." O.D. Darren stroked the side of her face.*" It's how I've managed to appear here for the moment. It's not really a mirror. It's a reflector for temporary storing of all of my physical molecules until they can be regenerated. Max Born dropped it in the stairwell at the party."* He said trying to understand the explanation. *"Once a person takes the G-WIZ, it acts like iron-filings over a magnet. It's difficult to explain but it allows a person to fold space."*

"Why on Earth did you take it?" She asked.

"Baby steps Liz. Baby steps!" The hippy said winking at her. *"There is a time frame to the drug. Once five days pass I can't come back to Earth. So we have to move fast."*

"I have one quick question..." She said raising a finger slowly as if she was at school.

"What?" Said O.D. Darren standing up.

"Where did you learn all this stuff? I thought you were a hippy? "

"A little penguin told me." He said smiling.

"A penguin..." She felt herself becoming curious again. *"Tell me more..."*

As Liz closed the door of room 236 softly behind her Darren sat down on the end of the double bed.

SATURDAY 8TH SEPTEMBER
2001 NIGHT / GERMANY

AT HOME WITH RAY CONNIF

There's something strange going on tonight
There's something going on that's not quite right
REM

RAY CONNIF SAT down on an exuberant lounge chair in the hotel room and sighed. He had over twenty-three scripts to read over within the next four days and it was not an immediate prospect he had been looking forward to. He stared down at the mountain of paper at his feet and momentarily thought about having a designer convert the stack into a chair or coffee table. Then he began to consider the amount of paper itself that had once been a tree. From the beginning of this task for the weekend it would be something he would find himself returning to again.

Being back in the cold still quiet of Germany and away from the hassle of frantic London, the country had given him an immediate new perspective before heading onto New York in three days. Ray loved his homeland. On the outer rim near The Black Forest, dates, times and fashion consciousness of the city fell away here. Time seemed to have frozen solid along with much of the landscapes covered in snow. Everything about Meissen Ray loved. The quiet and the porcelain. This part of Germany seemed to be still held in 1944. The year he had been born.

Ray had been feeling a little despondent since handing over the reigns of Big New Yorker to Liz. He was trying to be more optimistic. The tall German reached out for the script at the top and perused the title on the top sheet. O.D. It read in classic uppercase type in the centre of the white page. There had been no name of a writer and no other details an unusual prospect and one of the main reasons he had chosen it. In the fifteen years he had worked as an Advertising Producer, this had to be the first time Ray had ever witnessed a writer not claiming credit for a story.

Picking up the script he walked into the kitchen and began idly leafing through the opening of the film script to see if the paper it had been printed on had been worth the suffering the tree had gone through. German people were notorious for their methods of recycling and Ray Connif could not stand the idea of a tree being wasted needlessly. He opened the fridge, the prospect of a snack seemed to present itself as having more potential for a great idea. He retrieved a packet of Waitrose plastic-wrapped prawn sandwiches which Liz had given to him in Heathrow from the shelf and turned to find the light from the refrigerator had illuminated the top part of a paragraph which Ray had understood to be representing the opening of the film. He froze where he stood in the kitchen as he read the opening.

SO NOW FADE FROM BLACK

The audience sees a man dressed in a dark grey suit, in his apartment, walk from the lounge into the kitchen. The illumination of the refrigerator shows that he is reading a film script. He calmly strokes his tie covered with yellow stars. Close-up of the man reveals to the audience that he is in his late forties and German with black hair and a weathered complexion, possibly working in advertising. There is a knock at the front door of apartment. Although he cannot see beyond the door, when he touches the handle it is hot and the audience sees that on the outside of the house an incredible spaceship has descended from the night sky and has landed at the forest edge.

Ray Connif felt a chill of apprehension on the back of his forty-eight year-old neck. Something he had not experienced since he had begun this line of work in the seventies. The knock on the door of his apartment at that exact moment nearly caused his heart to leap out of his throat. Working in an industry where dreams were made on a daily basis, meant that this sort of thing happened to the middle-aged German all the time. There was still nothing like reality to make a person jump out of their skin. Nervously Ray walked down the long hallway with the script in his hand until he reached out to unfasten the locks of the front door. He thought about turning the music coming from the lounge down momentarily maybe it was just the neighbours complaining.

The fact that he had no neighbours and was staying at the furthest reaches of the German countryside near The Black Forest, was a thought that had been pulling on his coat in a nagging fashion for some time. He decided once again to ignore it. Whoever was at the door, knocking in a fairly urgent fashion might be the bringer of bad news. In the deep countryside of Meissen in Germany at ten o'clock at night with absolutely nobody knowing where Ray was except Liz. He realised he could in fact continue reading and fire his secretary on Monday, who had obviously been bribed to give out his address. Be a man about it Ray, he told himself under his breath, open the door.

As he unlocked the bolt of the apartment door words of black ink on white paper seemed to be leaping off the page and boaring into his brain. He threw the script quickly into the bedroom but not before his attention was momentarily distracted by another line which read; *the audience can see the haunting figure standing outside the apartment but the sound of light music lulls us into believing that nothing too horrendous will happen. The close-up of the gun the figure is holding however, reveals to the audience that something terrible is about to happen.* For some reason the apartment of Ray had not been built with paranoia in mind. This was South Germany not New York. The worst that had happened in this part of the world had happened over fifty years ago. There was a letterbox although looking through the thing whenever guests arrived was not something a forty-eight year-old Advertising Executive was inclined to be doing at this time of night. Deep down Ray was still a gentleman and decided that safe was better than sorry. He lifted the flap gently and took a peak through the rectangular hole while he nervously stroked his tie.

Even though it was night, the amount of bright light steaming through the letterbox did not seem natural but briefly reminded Ray of the movie Close Encounters of The Third Kind. As he slid the last bolt back, still holding onto the prawn sandwich which had been squashed between his fingers, the build up of weight from behind the door had become too much. Ray had seen a lot of movies. None of them seemed to suggest the shear terror that was emanating from the other side of this piece of wood. He made a mental note to bring the scene into the script of O.D. somehow.

Suddenly he could smell a scent of cooked onions and noticed that white light was pouring in through the cracks between the hinges of the oak door. Ray Connif grasped the handle of the door firmly, almost oblivious to the heat coming from the metal handle and pulled the front door open. The light jazz playing in the background cast a soundtrack quality to the scene while his impulses were telling him to run in any direction that was not where he was standing. Instead he shielded his eyes from the screaming white light and instinctly shoved the prawn sandwich into his mouth to enable him to focus on the source which seemed to be filling the entire area from the front of his house to the edges of the Black Forest about one hundred metres away. In the still night of Germany.

"Ray Connif?" Asked a commanding voice from somewhere within the light.

Ray nodded whilst squinting into the light his right hand guarding his view, blinded by the light. For the moment he forgot about the prawn sandwich which was half sticking out of his mouth. *"Whm fghe rrth wmhnn?"* Then instinctively placed his arms in the air.

"We mean no harm, we love your music!" Said a familiar voice from the light.

Ray squinted again in quizzed wonder and proceeded to take the only option open for a forty-eight year-old film producer during moments like these. He fainted.

After regaining consciousness Ray found himself standing inside a translucent Zoa-Pod from a Tectonic-Freighter. Apart from a cartoon like sign which was being held up by one of the two bored-looking aliens standing in front of him which read YOU ARE STANDING INSIDE A TRANSLUSCENT ZOA-POD FROM A TECTONIC-FREIGHTER, there was little else to describe. The tall German Advertising Executive surveyed the immediate area and then looked back at the chair he had just been sitting in. Ray had no idea what the sign held by the aliens meant. He watched as one alien shuffled the various boards revealing more sentences in English. WELCOME TO SPACE...LOTS OF IT. WE'RE PROCTA & GAMBUL...FREELANCE ALIENS. WE WOULD LIKE TO EXPLAIN SOME THINGS TO YOU. One of the aliens coughed loudly, spread his arms out and began to sing.

Ray Connif sat down on an exuberant lounge chair in the room and sighed.

SUNDAY 9TH SEPTEMBER 2001 EVENING /
THE FIFTH DIMENSION

THE PATH OF LEAST RESISTANCE

If you ever get close to a human and human behaviour
Be ready to get confused
BJORK GUDMUNDSDOTTIR

TWO POWERFUL LESSONS had been taught to O.D. Darren over the years as one of the larger drug dealers in the Western World. The first had been based on the primary rule of drug dealing. Never shit on your own doorstep. The second had come through on the path of knowledge, a little bit slower. In fact O.D. Darren had been inspired to travel a great distance just to understand the basis of the only water-tight plan a major drug-dealer could really come up with should he want to increase his chances of survival past the age of twenty-six. Death.

He had told associates in London that the two years he had spent away from Hackney were down to a prison sentence spent at Brixton Remand Centre. The truth was a tad less sinister. The hippy had travelled to Tibet in order to educate himself in the teachings of the Dalai Lama. Luckily when he arrived back in Hackney he returned to a place that had one major benefit going for it. No one really cared.

Understanding reality had been something a large portion of the East End of London were constantly attempting on a daily basis. In South London there had always been the architecture and the clothes shops, the decent coffee and the traditional figureheads of finance and power for a person to lose themselves in. Finding a decent cup of coffee in Hackney seemed to be almost a mystical journey in itself, that seemed to somehow contradict the date of the millennium. In this part of the world however the calendar was still visibly stuck on 1947.

When in Hackney you usually had to forget about anything modern. Unless it was Vietnamese DVD shops a person required or anything from Turkey. In the opinion of O.D. Darren there had never been a great deal of understanding as to why anyone would live in Hackney out of choice. Now that the hippy was dead, the only exception he could notice was the fact that the rent was cheap. It also held audiences captive to one of the more popular modern conveniences of East End London. Drugs. Shit loads of them.

Furthermore O.D. Darren could not understand why an area the size of New York could hold so many drug-dealers and so little in the way of convenience food and cafes. Even Brixton allowed you to have a latte option with your smack. There had been only one cafe that served food which only gave you food poisoning for three hours instead of the unusual seven and that was Mandys' Kitchen. Unless you wanted Turkish food every waking hour you were alive. Yet somehow no one in Hackney really knew how, the liquid that Mandy had been passing off to builders and workmen, as *'coffee'* seemed to defy all possible theories of chemistry. It was definitely instant.

There was little denying the speed which you received your *'cup of mud'* at Mandys'. Yet how someone could make such a disgusting drink out of instant coffee after simply adding hot-water had been a mystery that even the Dalai Lama could not rectify when O.D. Darren had attempted to ask him. Tenzin Gyatso had merely smiled at O.D. Darren and replied *"I don't know."** Maybe someone had mentioned this to Mandy but it had been difficult to tell. How could they explain though. What could you use as a comparison for her to understand that what she had been calling coffee for years had not been quite what over 800 million people around Earth would be in agreement with.

In shape, form or even taste.

In true Hackney fashion however the ghost of O.D. Darren was now standing opposite the notorious Mandys' Kitchen in true wonder at the subject of timing, rare moments of joy were indeed rare to discover in this part of the world and sights like the one he the hippy now a witness to were even more typical once you were dead. Mandys' Kitchen. Knocked down. Maybe the Health Department of the local council had visited and tasted the *'coffee'*. Whatever the outcome had been, O.D. Darren would never have the misfortune to taste the poison again.

As he stood in the rain at the end of Ellingfort Road he began to experience a strange elation similar to food poisoning. There was a plus side to being dead after all. Maybe he could haunt Mandy as punishment for serving the worst coffee that side of creation. Instead he decided to do what he had discussed with a monk in Tibet and always thought he would do once he died. He was going to frequent all the places in London he could never afford to get into when he was alive or those that he thought were ridiculously overpriced and scare the owners. Beginning with the Odeon Cinema in Leicester Square via a Hackney carriage. Then Garfunkels Restaurant. He had a list in his pocket and the name of Winmau Diamond was at the top.

Then he remembered what the monk had told him about compassion and decided to head for the cinema. He had no money but he had become convinced that he could materialize himself into the building from where he was now standing at the bus stop. O.D. Darren looked up at a Jamaican woman carrying her shopping and could see her own personal ghost shifted to her right and nagging her along with dead Cousins and Uncles as she walked down Mare Street. Then he realised why it was that some people looked so haunted in London This was no good. He opted for the Odeon. His favourite film-director Horst Klimt was appearing with Dead Daddy Badger and Dexter Wexford at a film screening and after waking-up and feeling like death, there seemed to be only the seclusion of the cinema in London to find some sanctuary. The hippy assumed the lotus position and levitated upwards over the rooftops of Hackney and towards the West End.

As he floated over the warehouse that his physical body had been left in O.D. Darren thought about the plan that he instigated on his two year sabbatical in Tibet. He had been fascinated by the plight of Tibet as a child at school on the Isle of Wight. A teacher called Mr. Orange. Derek Orange had taught him about the country and Darren had become fascinated almost immediately. In Geography he had managed to locate the location of Tibet and had been amazed to discover the country had been next to Nepal on the plastic globe that he studied in a geography class at High School.

Politics had been the key. The discovery had been in a class that had introduced the subject of consumer durables. The basis for a huge amount of frustration for O.D. Darren. The problem had not been in understanding the subject but in wondering why anyone would have thought of such reasoning as producing products that would consistently break. O.D. Darren had been amazed to discover that televisions, hairdryers, toasters, airplanes, technology and especially light bulbs had all been specifically designed in order to break in the Western world. The economy had been divided into two areas. Things that broke. Things that killed.

Karl Marx had discovered that War had always been an essential part of the economy. Without it the West would crumble. Yet with it, the West would be obliterated by its own eventual destruction. Empires were built up only to collapse. Much like any teenager with an understanding of the basics of the subject, O.D. Darren had understood what nearly everyone in his class understood. The system was bollocks.

On a school trip to East Germany he had discovered a light bulb at house of a student that lasted three years and continued to work. He had also discovered a new passion. Travelling. At the age of fourteen he had decided that somehow he would one day travel to this place of mystery called Tibet. As O.D. Darren levitated above the lines of traffic that refused to flow through the arteries of London he pondered on the consumer durables all designed to not work made by factories that used to make weapons of destruction. From this height it was easy to understand and see the bigger picture. London; the heart of England was destined for a huge bypass operation. The Dalai Lamma might suggest the best solution to the problem would be to stop the problem at the root. Exercise more. Walk the dog. Live your own life well.

On travelling through China there had been nothing but learning for O.D. Darren. The terms of the World Trade agreement had been explained to him and he had been amazed. Every country included had been able to produce a product of some kind. Some countries had industries using materials at such a rate that a future collapse was inevitable. Yet that could be then turned into another product. Television. Movies. The pharmaceutical industry. Things that broke. Things that killed. A person could breakdown just thinking about Capitalism. Or Communism.

Yet with all this going on, life on planet Earth continued. The big discovery had been Tibet amidst all this. Tibet seemed to be the only place on the entire planet that generated one commodity. More precious than all the other countries combined and without it even the last moments on Earth for a dying human could be mysteriously transformed from a living hell into heaven. Compassion and Love. Not easy things to see at times on a planet that had more credence for money or hair-gel. Yet without them there was indeed a fair chance that the Earth would kick off the mortal coil before 2011.

Most of the West was still patting itself on the back for inventing mobile phones, digital watches and cancer. While Tibet had spent most of its time receiving a severe kicking for loving everything on it. O.D. Darren had been amazed to discover that the Tibetan monks had translated a guidebook for the dead. Even the mere idea had made things easier to cope with and after he had travelled there, he had made his mind up pure and simply. Earth could not be saved. Not by him.

The only solution as far as the hippy had been concerned was to leave and the only way to leave was to die. Once you had the guidebook, visiting a country was much easier and sometimes once you studied the book there really was little else to be gained from visiting the place. Sometimes a person had no reason to go to a place once they read the book or saw the film. Yet the fact that the Tibetans were doing little in the way of joining the industrial revolution seemed to suggest that they would be doing little to join the World Trade Agreement. The Tibetans were there for the harder things in life. Death.

Compared to how well your trousers fitted or what kind of missile your army would be using this year. In the book of O.D. Darren, the Tibetans were the only sane people on the planet, in his opinion. They loved everything and everyone and insisted on doing little else. The monks of Tibet would prepare painstakingly intricate sculptures out of different coloured sand taking months and sometimes years, only to sweep them away and return the sand to the sea.

However, knowledge had led the hippy back onto the path a little bit too quickly. O.D. Darren had made some poor choices in life. Drug dealing had to be the worst one of them. He had no idea the number of people he had accidentally killed or caused to have relationships that had failed. In a book on Tibet, he had discovered one simple idea that had stopped everything around him. The Tibetans believed that when a person died they had to experience all the suffering that they had caused to any living thing on the planet. Multiplied.

This one idea had been enough for O.D. Darren. He had reached thirty and understood at last that his own mortality had to reach a turning point. He had sat up at night worrying how much suffering he had caused incidentally just by selling drugs. Without doubt the figures were reeling around his head and had somewhere reached into the region of millions. Not good. If he was not careful the numbers would cause him great suffering. Yet he had one choice. He had decided to return to Earth and try and get it right next time. His actions had spoken louder than his words had ever needed to as he gracefully sailed down over Oxford Street towards Soho for the date he had arranged with Liz the previous night, he thought about all the planets he could now visit. He was unsure as to how Liz would take the news but he was resilient. He knew she was pregnant. He could feel it. She was also financially secure. In nine months time he would be back although unable to explain the entire plan he had put together in Tibet until twenty-six years had past which is why he had to act fast. If the monks were right O.D. Darren only had a short time to be a ghost and then it was onto the hard stuff.

One of the bigger shocks for O.D. had been the discovery that all this would be happening in his own head. Close to the world of dreams. He had dreams where it was possible to meet old colleagues who had died and the business had already spawned an incredible number of these over the five years had become involved with it.

His spirit began the descent down towards Charing Cross Road and he landed smoothly. The hardest part of the journey would probably be telling Liz the bad news. Two powerful lessons had been taught to O.D. Darren over the years as one of the larger drug dealers in the Western World. He only hoped he was a good enough student and that he had revised enough to take the examination.

---

*When filmmaker Gideon London visited A Dalai-Lama Public Lecture in India as part of a Channel Four documentary. The Dalai Lama said "I don't know" to three questions from the audience. Gideon later said; 'Surely this is the one person on the planet that you never want to hear say those words! Yet everyone laughed.'

MONDAY 10TH SEPTEMBER 2001
EVENING / NEWTOWN

THE DISTANCES OF THE STARS

There are some days that catch the light...days like diamonds
LOOPER

CLAIRE HAD NEVER been to a crematorium before and had been curious as to what would happen next. Barnaby was still crying occasionally and she continued to comfort him as best she could by pointing out some of the famous people gathered in the church. Everyone listened patiently to the Vicar who seemed to be unable to contain his enthusiasm that so many people were present. The day he had prayed for had finally arrived and he glowed with pride. Then realised that had been marked as a sin and quickly returned his expression to concern. He climbed slowly up to the pulpit and began to read aloud from a folded sheet of paper he was holding in his hand.

"A telegram from a friend of Darren here on the Isle of Wight, which reads; 'Good luck Darren mate. I know this is a difficult time for you and your friends and I wish you all the best.' Love Tony Webb." Read Vicar Fricker aloud in his best English public schoolboy voice from the pulpit.

Although most of the creative clique recognised the huge American seated at the front from the mass nobody knew that Winmau had merely turned up in order to be certain O.D. Darren was dead. Winmau Diamond had been given a plane ticket by The Madam heading to New York tomorrow and was wrapping up any last minute deals before catching his plane. He hated funerals although he had been impressed by the fact that O.D. Darren had managed to pay him the hundred and twenty-five thousand required. He had thought it best not to mention to anyone that he had lied about the fatal situation he had put O.D. Darren in. There were no deposits on the cases. Winmau had simply decided to take his hate out on O.D. Darren for Challenge getting killed. He had never thought O.D.

Darren would die as a result. He still had no idea as to how he managed to hate someone so much when all he had ever done had been to help. Or why he felt the same hate when he thought about the journey he was about to make up to Heathrow Airport to catch the plane.

Winmau looked around nervously in the church at the guests arriving. The Madam had told him to attend the service and sell as much G-WIZ as possible before getting the plane to New York. He hated the idea of travelling to New York but with the money he now had with him he could easily invest into heroin or maybe armaments when he got back to the States. He had about an hour left before he could leave this whole horrible mess before the police would turn up at the house and then start asking questions. Yet when he had last seen O.D. Darren at the warehouse party he seemed to be relieved. People continued to arrive at the church and sit down with bewildered expressions and quiet words to Claire and Barnaby some of them mistook the obsequies of the scene for a wedding.

"Another tele-gram from the staff of Big New Yorker who have gracefully sponsored the proceedings this evening which reads; 'Darren, you were a true inspiration to many people and you will be no doubt missed by a lot of people. We hope you find peace and happiness within the journey you are currently undertaking."

The Vicar adjusted his glasses as he fiddled with the opening of a bright-orange envelope. A pocket-sized card fell wistfully through the air and onto the altar causing one of the guests at the front to jump up from the his seat and hand the card back to Vicar Fricker who thanked him. His voice echoed loudly over the feedback of the microphone.

"This message comes from..." He squinted at the card held at a distance from his glasses. *" Er...oh it doesn't say..."*

With absolute perfect timing, the doors of the church flew open and silhouetted the forms of both Chris T and Ben standing in the cool September evening. The sun setting picturesque behind them. They walked down the centre of the aisle and sat behind Claire who felt herself slightly attracted by the new bright blonde hair of Ben. Both the artist were dressed in immaculate black suits and ties. The Vicar coughed politely and continued to read the announcement looking over his glasses in a way a teacher would at two pupils arriving late in a class.

"...who have the following message for all friends of O.D. Darren..." He paused, reading the message quietly to himself for a moment, his lips studied carefully by the congregation. The expression of the Vicar seemed to suggest that this was going to be quite tricky. He sighed and then read aloud into the microphone;

" Nothing which we are to perceive in this world equals,
The power of your intense fragility
Whose texture compels me
With the colour of its' countries
Rendering death and forever with each breathing
I do not know what it is about you that closes and opens
Only something in me understands
The voice of your eyes is deeper than all roses
Nobody, not even the rain, has such small hands..."

When he returned his attention to the assembly Vicar Fricker noticed a change in the atmosphere of the candle lit church. Just the reading of the words had caused a shift somehow in the proceedings within the church and the vicar found himself pleasantly surprised by the stirring of emotions within himself. For a split second a voice in his head told him that the multitude in front of him had given him their undivided attention. He decided to use a line from the sonnet to make a link with his hastily written speech. He repeated the line.

"Rendering death and forever with each breathing..." He paused and thought of something the vicar who had inspired him when he was a child said. *'In life, you should always try to be good, it makes more sense at the end of the day.'* He had entered the church with this mission in mind and now at the age of fifty-four had gradually begun to understand what his original inspiration had meant.

"There are few moments in life that help us to form an understanding of what happens. As humans we experience so many emotions and thoughts on a daily basis that it is easy to be distracted from the miracle of what we are capable of. Regardless of what has happened to us. Life is simple. We are born from woman and man and spend our individual journeys on this planet searching for answers to questions when it would seem, at times, that there simply are no answers to." The Vicar paused with great authority and suddenly decided

to improvise by thinking of a film he had seen recently. "*That happiness is rarely on the cards. Or even in the equation.*" He paused and rested a hand on the edge of the wooden pulpit steadying himself and thoughtfully addressed the packed church.

"I have often thought about death and I have wondered why it is that humans and animals die. Yet, if you attempt to question everything about the world, there is a danger that you will unravel too much too soon. You cannot understand the end of the film halfway through. Life is for learning and growing, regardless of any other plans that you have while you are here. Darren's life seems to have been one amongst all of you who decided that, for him, life on Earth had little more to offer. I dearly hope now, that which ever place he has moved onto, he has found some happiness and that whatever level of the search you are currently on yourself, you enjoy it as much as he did."

The Vicar stepped down from the stand onto the altar and everyone stood up. Most of the actors and actresses gathered were on the brink of tears as the coffin, supposedly holding the body of O.D. Darren, began its slow and steady glide under the curtain of the crematorium. A slight distortion once again, came over the speakers as the music requested by Ben and Chris T began to echo throughout the church and lifted upwards to the high ceiling. The lyrics of a favourite song of O.D. Darren began to play and most of the artists laughed. One person had at least surprised them since his arrival in Hackney five years previously.

"I come awake with a gift for womankind, you're still asleep, but the gift don't seem to mind..." The distinct voice of Ian Dury and The Blockheads drifted out of the speakers as the lyrics to Wake Up And Make Love To Me, sounded out for all to hear. O.D. Darren had finally left the building.

As far as funerals went the inhumation of O.D. Darren had been similar to the man himself. Disorientated, highly entertaining once the drugs turned up and full of surprises. The wake at the house after however was much better.

The Vicar was halfway through a list of yet more telegrams from some well-wishers. All of who had been notified immediately of the situation. Although most of them expressed sorrow and deep regret from the news, none of them could really believe O.D. Darren had really died. Yet no one seemed surprised that an overdose had been the cause.

Claire had called some numbers in a black book that O.D. Darren had left in his jacket pocket with the poem on a piece of orange paper with some strange results. One voice had laughed solidly for two minutes when she spoke the news. Another had informed her politely that she required no insurance of any sort and missed the announcement entirely. Yet nothing had prepared her for the number of guests that arrived once they had been driven to Southampton Airport in limousines, where each group had then been flown across the Solent by private helicopter to the island where they had landed in a place called Newtown. As the vicar read aloud the remaining notices Claire had been more than surprised by the meticulous details undertaken at first and had then become gradually dumbfounded at some of the people who were arriving and slowly piecing together a life of a person who seemed to reveal himself when dead as a bigger mystery than when he had been alive. Most of the Hackney artists had made the journey down from London to the Isle of Wight after meeting back at the warehouse the previous day and had been stunned to discover that the preparations for the funeral included a list of details with the names of so many guests, along with herself and Barnaby, that surely spanned into the reaches of the impossible.

Most of those at the party had reported receiving text messages explaining that once they reached the warehouse they should only bring the outfit that they were wearing and one single piece of luggage containing a tape of music they love, along with a change of clothes.

Due to the time that O.D. Darren had died and the circumstances, each of the artists were harbouring all manor of guilt for not helping Claire and Barnaby clean up the mess and wait for the police. There was a lot of unnecessary shame gathering in the hallway of the manor house, which had been previously rented, although any enquiries about who had arranged everything seemed to be kept under the tightest scrutiny.

The atmosphere created by the guests had changed drastically from that of the drum and bass party although she had been surprised to discover the microphone, speakers and the wardrobe, which had been brought along for the performance of Gyro and had been as everyone else returned the lounge of the house to a replica of the warehouse in Hackney. Almost as if everyone had been magically transported to a new location.

As people gathered into the enormous front room they acknowledged each other excitedly and stood almost subconsciously in the same places that they had stood in the night of the party. Yet there was still a murmur of excitement gathering within them all as people exchanged stories discovering that each had thought the other responsible for the text message invitations as well as the various famous stars who were arriving.

They had also been informed by the appearance of small orange envelopes at each one of their homes containing a list of typed instructions. Which included details of accommodation, schedules and a gift of one thousand pounds each for the inconvenience of leaving London for two days. The ceremony of the funeral would proceed to a strict schedule of six o'clock the following morning.

Due to the nature of the various artists that had been invited, dress codes differed wildly along with hairstyles. Claire sat in an Edwardian chair, which nobody else felt that comfortable to sit in. Static, Gyro, Derek and Clive and Glenn Campbell, a friend of Liz joined her. Claire held onto one of the flyers in her gloved hands and felt strangely excited.

They had all arrived at the location within three hours of being told about the funeral by Gyro who had announced the instructions into the same microphone he had used at the party during his stand-up routine. Bewildered and curious, hardly anyone disputed the request for such a send off for O.D. Darren. Claire thought it strange that the only people who were not around to appreciate wakes were the ones who had died.

"*Wow! Its like Tombraider this place!*" Said Static giggling as he moved over to sit down next to Claire. There must have been around two to three hundred people arriving at the house. The rest of the crew were arriving from two other houses nearby and were chatting excitedly about their accommodation and the journey down to the island. Each wondering what had been about to happen at twelve o'clock. Italian Waiters were already offering drinks on trays and the highlight of the event for Ben had been the metal urns stood on tall stands around the room filled with marijuana and blocks of the finest hash he had ever had the pleasure of smoking. Along with enough cigarettes to avoid any scrounging.

"*Chris T! Look at this stuff!*" He exclaimed over to his creative colleague lifting up the lid of one of the tarnished metal containers. King-size rolling papers were also neatly left next to the urns with the title of The Diner Holistic printed on them in gold next to books of matches that bore the same logo.

"*Ben man. Pinch me, pinch me! I cannot believe any of this.*" Shouted Chris T finding it difficult not to laugh as the artist held a glass of red wine in one hand he had been explaining the journey by limousine from Hackney with much amusement to Michelle the French neighbour of the warehouse who had been still dressed as a Musketeer from the previous party. Chris T had travelled to Newtown with two students from Oxford University. "*There were two wolves in the limo man. Two wolves! There were these three girls sitting in the front with them! Unbelievable. I think the wolves are around here somewhere...*"

Michelle stood near a medium-sized wooden table and had been gently explaining to the Astronomist Sir Patrick Moore and Professor Magnus Pyke that crop-circles were man-made.

As Ben sat down in an Edwardian chair and began to make a joint he read discreetly over the instructions in his orange envelope. Smiling knowingly at the writing. He checked nobody had been watching and muttered to himself nodding with approval.

"*Way to go doctor. Welcome to Earth.*" He said quietly to himself.

In the kitchen, a group of caterers were rushing around preparing food. The elegant form of Britt sat next to one of the cooks talking and drinking red wine. The largest of the cooks seemed somewhat concerned.

"*Who was the boy who died?*" Asked the cook in a low whisper as she poured some fondue dip into a bronze bowl.

"*O.D. Darren. You never met him? Oh, I think you might. He was hardly a boy though. I think he was about twenty-six. You have to see the cabaret act that he's prepared for everyone- it's going to be amazing! Have some wine.*" Offered Britt, holding up the bottle.

"*I thought it was a funeral!*" She said slightly worried. Preparing some humus and pita bread. "*It's such a shame when young people die like this, it always makes me wonder.*"

"*Its a FUNeral. O.D. Darren wanted specific emphasis on the FUN...*" Said Britt.

"*But there are drugs being smoked in there!*" She whispered this last part of the conversation so seriously that Britt found it difficult to keep a straight face.

"My God no! Have you never been to Amsterdam? There's drugs smoked everywhere there too and no one seems to mind." Said Britt sarcastically standing up and leaving the kitchen with the bottle. She quickly stood up and left the kitchen holding onto the bottle.

As Chris T walked up to the third floor to find the bathroom he became momentarily dazzled by the various actresses and actors amongst the crowds of well-wishers from film and television and smiled at them each in turn. Today was indeed a special day and Chris T thanked his Father and Mother under his breath for creating him. A man of simple pleasures - he had found a bottle of wine in the limousine marked for the attention of CHRIS T. All it said under the name had been DRINK ME. LOVE O.D. For a quick moment Chris T had wept for the sheer style of one of his best friends. He had the bottle in his hand and had been swigging from it and laughing as he thought about O.D. Darren. When he arrived momentarily behind a line of three women waiting to use the toilet. They all turned to shake his hand in turn. The author Naomi Klein was wearing a bright red dress with a white covering T-shirt that read WHOEVER DIES WITH THE MOST TOYS WINS and seemed to Chris T to be seriously stoned. Slightly drunk he quickly cornered her on her book.

"Pleased to meet you Naomi. I'm afraid I didn't get a chance to read your book but my friend who's a graphic designer hated it. He said he thought it was immoral that you could write about Reclaim The Streets and not give them any money for printing photographs of one of their protest marches!"

Naomi seemed too stoned to care and burped. *"Jesus, it's supposed to be a bleedin' party Chris T! Cheer up."* She said ignoring the comment as she wobbled into the toilet. Cigarette in hand. His curiosity was heightened enough now and Chris T had been shocked to spot the brief appearance of a pair of new Nike Trainers peeping out from under the hem of her red dress. He winced to himself when he realised the second woman standing waiting to use the lavatory was Kate Bush and felt an overwhelming urge to ask her what her relationship to O.D. Darren had been. She was holding onto a can of Guinness Draught and laughing at the snubbing he had just received from Naomi Klein.

"Never mind love do you know any jokes?" Said Kate in her cute London accent.

Suddenly Chris T felt his mind go blank as he stood on the landing between Kate and a very pleasant looking French woman who he was certain had appeared in a recent film he had seen somewhere in Camden. He found himself abruptly put on the spot. He then recalled the joke O.D. Darren had told him at the party.

"There's a Cowboy and an Indian riding across the desert and they both see smoke signals rising from the distant landscape. The cowboy asks the Indian; "Can you understand and translate the smoke signals for me?" and the Red Indian says; "Sure." He looks again at the signals and turns back to the Cowboy and he says; "The smoke signals say WE......ARE......... ALL OUT......OF...... FURN...IT...URE!" Chris T smiled and drank some more wine.

Kate and the French actress giggled politely and Chris T found himself looking at Juliet and into the darkest and most incredible windows of soul he had ever seen. Kate had politely excused herself from the obvious moment of attraction between the couple, mentioning something about gooseberries as she left and stumbled into the lavatory still giggling.

The third lady held such a mystical beauty for him that he was certain she could only be the actress Juliet Binoche. He could feel himself shaking slightly as he offered her the bottle. She blushed and took a swig from it.

"You are Juliet Binoche aren't you?" Chris T asked suddenly forgetting about the reason he had run upstairs.

"Oui. Tu as l'artist de Hackney? Are you Chris T the artist?" She asked as the line to the toilet went down leaving only the two of them together on the landing of the second floor.

"Er...yes. Er, oui." He squeaked. Unable to stop himself staring in wonder at how a human being could possibly start life as an embryo that looked like a tadpole and yet over time could develop into such a creature as this. As the two of them chatted on the landing in front of the paintings hanging on the wall of the stately manor house, Chris T wondered to himself whether he might actually be in heaven.

Juliet sipped once again at the bottle of wine labelled and bottled by the late O.D. Darren and smiled her unique smile at Chris T who noticed that she appeared to be smaller in real life than when he had last seen her projected fifty feet across a cinema screen in Camden. As the artist retrieved the bottle from the actress, he looked down to her feet and felt a strange twinge of perspective distortion similar to when a person looks down onto a miniature bottle of Baileys Irish Cream after drinking a full seventy-five Cl bottle. He blinked again and stared in astonishment as Juliet Binoche began to shrink right in front of him. Chris T looked around bewildered and quickly placed the suspicious formula of red wine down on a small table at the top of the stairs of the manor house, which Juliet was already able to stand under. Fortunately there were no guests witnessing the sight of one of the greatest actresses of Europe shrinking in perfect perspective. The artist resorted to the only action available and quickly bent down to pick up Juliet Binoche.

He was already able to place one open palm around her waist and managed to pull her up from the surface of the carpet. *"Oh Chris T, I feel so small."* Said Juliet.

The artist had never felt so embarrassed in his life. He headed for the back room at the top of the stairs with Juliet in his front suit pocket. Fortunately again when he looked inside there was a selection of cakes with Eat Me written on small tags attached to them. Chris T grabbed one and quickly handed it to the French actress, who had already become the size of his hand. She took a bite and managed to halt the process of reverse growth. Chris T sighed with relief as within minutes Juliet Binoche returned to her usual sized glory.

"Mais non! Sacre bleu Chris T! What is that drink?" Asked the actress adjusting her dress.

"I'm so sorry, I had no idea that would happen, Juliet. It was a gift from O.D. Darren." Said Chris T embarrassed but pleased that nobody had been hurt from the experience. He could only guess that because he was not a huge star yet the contents had little effect on his size. Although, he had a strange feeling suddenly that his head had become slightly larger since meeting Juliet Binoche.

They both walked back out on to the landing in search of the bottle of shrinkable aperitif. The artist found it exactly where he had left it on the small table. As he bent down to pick it up and read the label on the back, he noticed the small print for the first time. 'G-WIZ PRODUCTIONS PRESENT A FORMIDABLE DRINKING EXPERIENCE IN THE FORM OF NEW MINIATURES - GET REALLY SMALL WITH G-WIZ.'

The sound of the guests gathering downstairs had begun to increase to an amicable excited mass. Laughter echoed like sunshine around the huge lounge. Claire had been reminded for a brief moment by the party at the warehouse in Hackney. She had only spoken to O.D. Darren for about fifteen minutes but already decided then that she had felt a strong maternal urge to watch over him, in much the same way a Mother on a crowded London bus watches over everybody. Claire had rarely seen anyone so lost in London as the hippy. She had found herself frowning as she recalled the expression on his face once she heard the argument that he and Liz had been having on the stairwell outside the dance room. As she sat in the Edwardian chair drinking with Glenn Campbell on her lap smiling she wondered where Liz had disappeared to since the warehouse party. Barnaby had stopped crying for a brief moment as he sat next to an actress called Bonnie Langford who had offered him some crisps from a large glass bowl.

The audience made of artists, musicians, actors and actresses began to relax after the funeral. For a brief second she was certain that she could see O.D. Darren laughing and enjoying the scene from the corner of her eye. Glen Campbell fell over the arm of the chair and collapsed into her lap like a large baby.

"Claire baby! What is happening?" Asked Glenn holding a glass of tequila.

"I think there's some kind of show again." The invite was held in her hand and she read from it aloud.

"Cabaret begins at 12 p.m..." She said to the clique of artists gathered near the fireplace.

"Have you seen Chris T anywhere? I've got a wicked idea!" Said Glenn Campbell to Claire with a sparkle in his eyes.

"The last I saw, he was laying into Naomi Klein about her No Logos book on the second floor landing, although that was about half an hour ago." Replied Claire.

"Oh I was going to phone his mobile." He said drinking the tequila in one swoop. *"Oh what the heck! I'm drunk enough I'll do it anyway."* Glenn Campbell scrolled down the numbers appearing on the mobile screen until he reached the number of Chris T and pushed the call button. As he held the mobile to his ear Britt walked across the busy room mingling with the

masses still holding onto a bottle of red wine from the kitchen. Her orange scarf had slipped from her head and fallen around her shoulders, giving her a slightly Mexican appearance. She walked over to the fireplace where Claire and Glenn were sitting and planted herself down onto the arm of the Edwardian chair. Glenn glanced up at her as he spoke into the phone.

"Hey Britt. Do you want to speak to Chris T? He's upstairs!" He said through his perfect white teeth.

"No thanks I don't need head cancer!" Replied Britt tersely. *"Does anyone have a bottle-opener?"*

Glenn returned his attention to Chris T who had answered his mobile. *"How are you doing with Juliet? Well Claire says you're definitely in there mate! What? Where are we? We're in this huge house on the Isle of Wight in a place called Newtown...downstairs. I'm sitting with Britt, Claire and Barnaby after O.D. Darren's funeral. Of course he's dead."* He turned back to face Claire. *"He's asking what he's wearing..."* He said slightly confused.

"A black suit of course it's a funeral Glenn!" Replied Claire reaching for a handful of peanuts from a nearby bowl.

"You're wearing a black suit Claire says. There's loads of people here man. Oh...bugger!" Exclaimed Glenn. *"It's like O.D. Darren! the things gone dead! My batteries have run out. Isn't it amazing that you call someone a hundred feet away and there's nothing but a bad line and yet if you call Australia, the telephone lines work almost perfectly."*

"Has anyone seen Liz yet?" Asked Claire looking around at the hundreds of guests in the house.

The multitude of people gathering and standing in the lounge were now being served drinks from a host of Italian waiters who held black trays that also advertised the words The Diner Holistic. Everyone speaking brought an air of sophistication to the wake and Claire was reminded suddenly of the movie Titanic as she stood up and gestured to one of the waiters for a glass of champagne. As the handsome Italian swayed over to her with the tray she asked him whether he had seen a petite Jewish looking woman with long bright orange curly hair.

The waiter nodded and pointed silently and slowly towards the wardrobe and microphone, which had been set-up in the centre of the room. Claire became suddenly aware of a wave of silence that seemed to be descending onto the crowd. Almost exactly the same formation as the warehouse party was developing around her. The rows of guests at the front of the audience began to sit down and a circular arch was being formed around the microphone stand and wooden wardrobe. As she drank from the crystal glass held in her delicate hand she could see Ben and Barnaby steering a huge metal spotlight from the staircase. The interior of the old manor house was becoming darker. Gradually without any direction, the hush of expectation before a show had descended onto the crowd and she peered for a view between the shoulders of Glenn and Michelle. For some reason she felt a chill of anxiety as the entire room was enveloped into darkness.

The white spotlight patiently circled the area around the microphone, giving the impression of a searchlight looking for an escaped prisoner. The sound of strange and beautiful but haunting music drifted over the crowd and suddenly the circular shape stopped on the wardrobe, which began to shake slightly and then rock left and right as if it were attempting to walk. The wardrobe became suddenly still and then the door creaked open slowly. The petite figure of a lady with long orange curly hair stepped out, closed the door behind her and moved gracefully towards the microphone peering into the audience with a hand guarded over her eyes deflecting the brightness of the spotlight. She held the microphone in her right hand and spoke calmly.

"Ladies and gentleman. Damon und Herron. Madames et Monsieurs. Boys and girls. Artists and actors. Bodies and corpses. Religion and politics. Fruitarians and vegans. Chalk and cheese. Cheese and pineapple. Pelicans and penguins. Electrons and protons. Coffee and tea. Senor a senorita. Actresses and bishops. Nebulas and aliens. Life and death. Yes and no. Positive and negative. Past, present and future. Here today and gone tomorrow...I would like to introduce to you one fifteen minute miracle...which now that I have spoken will last..." Liz checked her watch. "...Perhaps four minutes. A big hand for...O.D. Darren!"

Nearly everyone in the room felt an uncomfortable silence build up as the ex-girlfriend of the dead hippy outstretched a hand in presentation and bowed in the direction of the wardrobe. As the door creaked open once again. O.D. Darren stepped out into the spotlight and smiled at the audience who were all suddenly frozen still with shock.

He walked up to Liz and took the microphone from her and spoke into it. "Hello everyone from the fifth dimension. Thank you for coming to my funeral. I know you're probably asking yourself why I'm not dead. The fact is I am. Sort of. This message is being relayed from The Diner Holistic. Yet hopefully Liz will explain how it's all happening during the party, which is about to happen. I'd like to thank Vicar Fricker for a great service and all of you for coming to the wake. I hope you have a great time. God willing lots more guests will be arriving and I think you'll be pleasantly surprised by the end of the evening." He flicked the chord of the microphone in a similar way that Las Vegas comediennes do and waved to the crowd. "Oh one last thing...I'll see you all in The Diner Holistic...lattes are on me! Ciao!"

The microphone dropped to the floor and O.D. Darren faded from view. Suddenly the house lights came back on and the atmosphere of the house returned to its previous relaxed setting. The audience paused for a second squinting at one another and then began to applaud. Gyro walked into the arena of the wardrobe and picked up the microphone. "Thank you O.D. Darren and the gorgeous...Liz. I've seen a lot of acts die on stages around the world but nothing like that! We hope you enjoy the party now and remember to enjoy life. Dance, sing and if I may, I'd like to read to you now some quotes to give you advice on the one subject that everything living must face at some point. There's no going back unless you continue on! The first is from the brilliant poet John Lennon...

And we all shine on like the Moon and the stars and the Sun

The next is by another poet, writer and comedian called Stephen Hawking whose theories crack me up most of the time. Yet I must say, he has his moments...

There was a young lad of Wight who travelled much faster than light

He departed one day in a relative way and arrived on the previous night*

I'm sure you'll agree that he perhaps shouldn't give up the day job! Just kidding Stephen. So, enjoy yourself and remember the words from O.D. Darren there from the Isle of Wight. We are all janitors really, passing through this world and hopefully looking after the place for the next relay team to visit. I'm available for children's parties and barmitzvas and you can catch me in Taho the week of the seventeenth. Ciao!"

Gyro fitted the microphone back into the holder on the metal stand and walked over to a large tape recorder and pressed down on the play button. The soft and truly valid sounds of Eine kleine Nachtmusik by Mozart began to slowly fill the interior of the old manor house as the various guests began to eat and drink from the various trays carried by waiters.

Claire stood still almost unable to speak. She had just witnessed O.D. Darren stand nearly twenty-three feet from her and talk into a microphone. Yet she had seen and checked his body in the warehouse and he had been dead. She had seen the corpse. The fashion-designer had heard and seen a great deal in London but she had never come across anything so unusual as this. She had to find Liz and ask her what on Earth had just happened. She looked down at her left hand only to see that it had started to shake and the champagne in the crystal glass spilled out onto the carpet. Maybe she thought, funerals were always full of such surprises, she had no way of knowing simply because Claire had never been to a crematorium before and had been curious as to what would happen.

* ' Somewhere I have never travelled' - E.E.Cummings

* Told by Stephen Hawking in a public lecture on time-travel

TUESDAY 11TH SEPTEMBER 2001
AFTERNOON / MANHATTAN

BELIEVING THE STRANGEST THINGS LOVING THE ALIEN

They say that planets will collide whenever I am by your side
Notes from a distant sun shower over everyone
TIM FINN

THE YEAR SHE had spent working in Manhattan researching had been filled with much personal adulation. The kind usually set aside for journalists such as Sydney Sheinberg who wrote about the atrocities that had occurred in Cambodia during the time of The Killing Fields or Noam Chomsky who had alerted the students of Australia to the possible outbreak of civil war in Indonesia at the end of the nineties.

Hong Jin Wu knew she had been onto something due to the size of the desk she had been allocated and the numerous calls she had received regarding offers of work, she had never been so busy in her life and had little time to understand what had become of her past life. The opportunities posed however had given her little chance to investigate her own story. That of Flight 815Y and she had since learnt that it was important to tell your own story More recently the Chinese reporter had lost a huge amount of weight during her time in America, which was unheard of for people arriving in the country. Hong Jin Wu suspected that even due to the fact that even the tap water might have had sugar in it. Finding something to eat without sugar in it had been about as easy as finding a twenty-dollar bill that had no traces of cocaine on it in New York.

She and Leia rode the lift down to the entrance of the TIME/LIFE building. She had attempted to explain some parts of the events she had been experiencing since arriving in America. She had to tell someone.

Even if at times she could hardly believe what had occurred at the airport. Fortunately Leia had been a good listener of tall tales.

As the lift descended the reporter adjusted her hair as if she had been about to meet the date of her life. *"Right. The guy we're going to meet is someone I followed after I arrived off the plane in Holland. He walked into this tiny closet at the back of the airport and just disappeared through a solid wall."* She said excitedly.

"Like David Copperfield?" Asked Leia doubtfully.

"What?" Said the Chinese journalist.

"He's this incredible magician whose engaged to Claudia Schiffer, although I heard that they split-up..." Said Leia.

"I guess the magic has gone from the relationship. He once walked through The Chinese Wall though. He also made the Statue of Liberty disappear in New York once."

"You've seen him to?" Said Hong Jin Wu dumbfounded by the possibility.

"No, it was on television! On a magic show." Said Leia.

As the lift descended through the innumerable floors of the building. Hong Jin Wu raised her eyes to heaven.

"What is it with this country?" She exclaimed. *"People don't see anything unless it's on television!"*

Exasperated, she dashed out of the elevator doors with Leia following and walked quickly through the sliding doors of the entrance and out onto the intense streets of New York. The humidity reminded her of Hong Kong.

Outside most of the population of Earth seemed to be breaking for lunch at the same time and Hong Jin Wu still felt excited by the feeling of walking down the bustling streets of one of the most incredible cities in the world. The cool September breezes were soaring down between the tall buildings of Manhattan creating a wind tunnel. The air blew around them from sky of blue causing mini whirlwinds to appear all over the streets. Leaves and plastic bags swirled and jigged near their feet they seemed to head off down the long streets as if rushing to somewhere important.

As they all crossed over the street to the Radio City Music Hall, Hong Jin Wu was abruptly reminded of the first time she went to see a movie in New York she had come out of the cinema with the strangest sensation that she had just walked out of the cinema and back into the film. Under the light bulbs of the canopy stood the penetrating figure of Dr. Bostrom. Smiling in dark suit and sunglasses, practising his best impersonation of a confident alien who owned everything around him. Waiting patiently. His long peacock-blue hair blowing in the breeze. The good doctor shook both their hands warmly and smiled, introducing himself to Leia. He then escorted them across the street in the direction of a diner, which he had recommended to Hong Jin Wu, made the best latte this side of the Universe. Something about his penetrating voice persuaded her to believe him.

As the three of them walked towards the hoards of oncoming people in the midday heat the good doctor would occasionally wave at people as if recognising them. Or would point his finger and wink. Hong Jin Wu would hear the welcoming shouts and cries of far too many people for one person to know in one city constantly as they followed along with him. A voice inside her head had been telling her that she was merely being paranoid and she had quietly convinced herself of the fact. There were countless doctors in New York she told herself. She must have seen at least three walking this way on a regular basis. Maybe he was just trying to impress her.

They rounded a corner and Dr. Bostrom opened the glass and metal-framed door for both Hong Jin and Leia to walk through. Then chaperoned them both over to a table at the back. The Diner had been decorated in fifties style Americana. Dr. Bostrom had been fascinated by the service in America. Finding it hard to believe that his purchase from the Planet Xpo had been so fruitful. He chuckled as he recalled the memory of an alien who had purchased something called Antartica.

However the towns of Hackney and Manhattan were as diverse as men and women. Inside The Diner, the good doctor gestured for both his guests to sit down and took off his long black overcoat before he joined them.

They ordered coffee and food as the distinguished doctor exuded an air of grace and charm towards everyone in The Diner giving them the distinct impression that whatever his purpose on Earth had been, they had better understand first that they were blissfully ignorant and after that he would start things rolling for them. When he lowered his Ray-Bans the windows of his soul caused Hong Gin Wu and Leia to almost fall off their seat opposite him from the impact. His eyes seemed to suggest the last thing on his mind had been lying. He spoke in his best reassuring voice.

"First - your spotting of the UFO over Flight 815Y. I was piloting the UFO. My employer is Max Born of the Three Breakfasts Corporation. Currently in the process of saving your planet. I've been sent to Earth in order to apologise for the inconvenience caused. The knowledge of water being taken from the oceans of Earth is far more important than anything else." He reached into the side pocket of his suit and withdrew an orange envelope, placing it on the table. *"My employer's purpose is to clear up any discrepancies that occur during this operation. I can only say that an irrigation project is in operation and its purpose is to stop an immense disaster occurring in the date 2011. Do not be alarmed by what you saw. There are Tectonic-Freighters arriving and departing to and from this planet every week. Your arrival in Holland was deliberate and carefully executed. Along with your arrival at the hotel in New York."* He said carefully checking that Leia was able to keep up. The alien lifted his coffee to inhale the warm sweet aroma, accidentally catching some of the foam on the end of his nose.

"Without causing a disturbance to personal missions. We are now able to return you to your original time where you were about to settle with an Earthling called Gyro. That is if you so wish. Oh and your family are fine. Because you have been held travelling in time they will always be experiencing your departure in a loop. Until we have your permission to notify them of your new existence." He smiled reassuringly at her. Hong Jin smiled back and affectionately wiped the foam of the coffee off his nose with a napkin.

"In this envelope are the details of our mission. You are allowed two choices. One is to follow everything inside the envelope and become an employee of the Three Breakfasts Corporation. Inside are details of a bank account which is yours if you accept. You continue your job at Hassle and report as instructed or..." Dr. Bostrom paused for the required effect. *"Or, you come with me now and return to the exact point where the UFO appeared over Flight 815Y and ignore what occurs when the ship appeared and arrived in Hong Kong to meet your parents. Each passenger on the plane has been offered the same exact solution to the problem."* He began to drink his latte.

"What have they decided?" Asked Hong Jin calmly.

"That is not a liberty I am able to divulge until you decide." Dr. Bostrom observed the time on his watch with careful consideration. *"I will give you ten minutes to reach a decision."*

Suddenly all sound in The Diner stopped. Leia and Hong Jin looked around the Diner interior with a shocked expression. From their position at the back of The Diner they watched as everyone around them froze in position. Then Hong Jin Wu noticed even the coffee being poured from the glass containers by waitresses into the cups, slowed down and stopped. The silence was golden. Leia felt as if they were in a painting.

Hong Jin Wu nodded calmly and continued to sip from her coffee as if nothing too unusual had occurred. Then she turned to face Leia.

"What do I do?" She whispered to Leia, sensing a slight bitter taste from her coffee.

"Woah! What was back in that time exactly? You've got free accommodation and a job in New York! That's success in Andy Warhol's book." She whispered back uncertain if she had just lost her mind.

"There was a guy on the plane. He helped me. at the airport." Hinted the reporter.

"You speak of the Earthling Gyro...he is due for the same interview in..." He looked down officially at his watch. *"...four hours Earth time."* He calmly sipped at his coffee.

"What will happen to all the money I've been receiving?" Asked Hong Jin, ever the cautious journalist.

"Payments will continue. Arrangements have been made. This is your home life now, if you want it. Until your meeting later at The Diner Holistic. I will notify and approach you about your mission details when they occur." Suddenly an expression of heartbreaking sincerity came across his face. Hong Jin found herself suddenly thinking about lost puppies. *"Flying those ships is not so easy. Lots of aliens make mistakes. You'll have plenty of work coming in..."* He offered.

"Give me five, I'll be back in a minute." Said Hong Jin Wu calmly. After one year in New York she had heard every conceivable chat-up line possible. She had no idea how many had been from aliens.

"You have ten minutes..." Announced the good doctor as he accidentally knocked a spoon from the table and onto the floor of The Diner with an eerie silence.

Hong Jin stood up and walked past all the mannequins of people in The Diner and opened the door. Outside on the streets of the big apple cars had stopped moving. People halted in mid-step. The Chinese reporter looked up into the sky where she saw birds and planes held in mid-flight. All frozen in time. As she walked up to a middle aged man in a suit who had been smoking a cigarette she covered her mouth and giggled to herself with excitement. She stamped her feet with joy at the sight of the wisps of smoke rising up into the sky motionless. The expression she observed on his face seemed the saddest she had ever witnessed. The entire city had stopped, still as night.

Whatever the outcome of this experience would be, she felt that a relationship with an Englishman she had briefly met on a plane hardly compared to an alien who could freeze time. She headed back into The Diner and walked over to where she could hear the remnants of a conversation Leia had been having with Dr. Bostrom. She returned to the leather seat. Her eyes fixed on the orange packet on the table.

"*...Okay, if she doesn't object...*" Said Leia.

"*Object to what?*" Asked Hong Jin concerned.

"*Your friend here has just been making enquiries as to how she could work with you for the Three Breakfasts Corporation and I was suggesting that she could work as your partner. We need as much help as we can get. Did you make your decision by the way?*" Enquired Dr. Bostrom blowing across the top of his latte.

"*Yes. Is there a contract to sign?*" She asked politely.

"*Sort of. You just have to press your thumb print onto this.*" Replied the alien.

Doctor Bostrom casually produced a slim black box from his hand, which was about the thickness of a pack of playing cards. The object reminded Hong Jin of a light box the art department used near her office for looking at photographic transparencies. Both of the women pressed their turned down thumbs onto the surface as a small beam of light worked its way across, scanning their imprints. Suddenly the sound of the planet roared back into their ears and Hong Jin was reminded of emerging from under water. New York and the world began again.

Dr. Bostrom stood up from the Diner and left an unnecessarily large group of American dollar bills on the table. As they all walked back out of The Diner and returned to the bustling streets of New York. Life continued as if nothing had happened. The doctor continued to speak as he strolled along next to them repeating the process again of greeting people as he walked along the avenue. All three of them arrived back outside the front of the TIME / LIFE building. The good doctor shook hands with his two new employees.

"You'll be notified of your next mission by text from Max Born my employer. See you soon and welcome to Earth." Announced the good doctor with a firm smile. *"By the way I have read your work Hong Jin Wu and I can only see a good future for you with a career that will flourish. Your observations on the UFO phenomenon has contributed greatly to the Three Breakfast Corporation already. I thank you."* He smiled again.

Two steps had been taken by the two women when immediately Hong Jin Wu and Leia recalled the earlier conversation at the table. They both then turned in unison and shouted after the doctor who had returned to his previous position camouflaged amidst the crowds of New York inhabitants.

"What did the other passengers say by the way?" Yelled Hong Jin Wu. But the well-dressed form of the X-Chromo-pilot had already become difficult to spot in the camouflaged surroundings of what seemed like half the population of the world. The growing mass of people appearing around them seemed already to have concealed the acute Dr. Bostrom as he blended into the hustling crowds of Manhattan.

"Wow!" Said Leia as she stood next to her smiling. *"He really likes you..."*

Hong Jin Wu stood and stared into the crowds of people rushing around in the heat of Manhattan. She felt a familiar sense of wonder about her life returning once again. The Chinese reporter looked around the city as her confidence began to return. Time-travel takes a lot out of a person but she suddenly felt a great love towards the people that she had worked with at the magazine and towards everyone she could see walking around New York. Perhaps it had been because the year she had spent working in Manhattan researching had been filled with much personal adulation.

* **News Chronicle, 14 Mar 1949**

FRIDAY 7TH SEPTEMBER 2001 TIME / HOLLAND
ANOTHER LOST WEEKEND

I got my head checked by a Jumbo Jet
It wasn't easy but nothing is
DAMON ALBAR / BLUR

IN SCHIPHOL AIRPORT everything was Dutch, of course. The bewildered passengers of flight 815Y were not difficult to find. They all remained as one group wandering aimlessly around the floor of the large fabricated building, staring blankly at the monitors and attempting to decipher any information at all as to where The Philippines had been moved to. Gyro and his Chinese compadre headed over to the KLM check-in desk where an attractive Dutch lady, appeared to be wearing a uniform of orange and blue, with a white felt biscuit-tin on her head. For a brief moment he thought the KLM representative might just smile back at anything he asked her. Yet what he was about to say, he was well aware would sound more than a little bit strange. There was no harm in trying.

"Er... Halloo..." Gyro began anxiously.

"Halloo sir." Beamed the lady behind the desk.

"Er... myself and my friend here have just arrived from Australia and we're wondering where to go to retrieve our bags. We fell asleep on the flight and just woke up. I think we missed any announcements..." He said coyly.

"What was the number of your flight sir?" Asked the lady politely.

"815Y..." Said Gyro trying to sound as if he had not time-travelled over ten thousand miles in fifteen minutes.

The KLM attendant pushed a number of keys on her keyboard. *"Mmm... from Australia, are you sure you don't mean Austria?"* She enquired rather tartly.

"Er... no, I think I remember... it was definitely Australia!" Said the Englishman.

"Australia...not Austria." The KLM assistant smiled again.

"Definitely!" Gyro replied in an attempt to keep calm.

"Mmm..." She typed in a few more keys and tutted to herself. *"Flight 815Y you say?"*

"Yes." Gyro replied starting to feel rather tired and leaned heavily on the check-in desk counter.

"Well, there are only flights arriving from Austria today. Your quite sure it was Australia?" She asked again as she was joined by another employee of KLM wearing a large moustache. A man.

"YES! Look, you see all those passengers over there...they were on the same flight.." He nodded.

"Which people sir?" Asked the lady looking up from her desk at Gyro.

"Over th..." Gyro stopped in mid sentence, as he looked around the airport. The crowd of jostling passengers were nowhere to be seen. Suddenly he felt rather embarrassed. *"They must've left the airport."* He smiled uncertainly at her.

"Yes sir?" Came the patronising reply.

"Well...where would my, er, our bags be then?" Asked Gyro.

The lady adjusted her hat slightly as she read from the monitor. Her work colleague interrupted and whispered something into the ear of the KLM assistant. They both looked at him again and laughed.

"Ahh...there you are. Flight 815Y. Just arrived. You should head over to carousel E. The bags are just unloading from the plane." He said in a deep American voice.

"Oh...thank you very much." Replied Gyro. Turning around to his new friend, he became startled suddenly to discover that he was holding the hand of a large Texan man, wearing a white cowboy hat and smiling at him. Startled beyond belief, Gyro dropped the large hand of the stranger and moved slowly backwards away from the desk. Looking startled and quickly span around, he could see a long line of passengers impatiently waiting to check-in.

"Wh...?!?" Asked Gyro searching the immediate vicinity of the airport and wondering if he had just gone insane.

The man smiled with a strange distant expression and lifted his hat. *"See you on television..."* The man said in a heavy Texan accent.

"Er..." Gyro attempted to speak out loud but felt suddenly speechless. The Chinese girl he had arrived on the plane with was nowhere to be seen and his eyes quickly darted around the airport searching. She must have headed to the carousel he reasoned.

"Okay...er...thank you very much. Sorry to be a nuisance. Thank...you for your help..." He stammered and turned sharply then headed in the opposite direction, stumbling into a tall slim lady dressed in a multitude of different layers of bright clothing with an orange shawl and scarf covering her hair. Knocking her to the floor. He apologised and helped her up dazed.

"Jesus, sorry... are you okay?" Asked Gyro helping her to stand up.

The woman was fine and started to laugh. *"Yar! No problem. Are you okay?"* She smiled back.

"Yes...er..sorry. Look I'm in a real hurry...okay? Sorry er, again!" He called out to her as he turned and ran towards the baggage reclaim area.

Gyro felt his own heart pounding now and as he read the signs hanging from the airport ceiling which showed the direction to Baggage Reclaim, he hurried frantically through the airport until he saw the sign marked for Carousel E. A white sheet of photocopied A4 paper had been attached below it with the flight number 815Y printed on it, hanging above the black rotating conveyor belt. His eyes followed the black arrow down to where a lone crumpled rucksack sat moving along the rubber belt. Gyro walked over to retrieve it and pulled it off the carousel and onto the polished floor of black linoleum. Tired and bewildered yet relieved that at least one thing had remained constant throughout his journey, his bag. As Gyro grabbed one of the supports and lifted the bag up he looked back up to the E printed on the plastic square above. The sheet of paper with the name of flight 815Y printed on it had vanished.

Standing on the linoleum floor of Schiphol Airport, Gyro stood alone. As he walked passed the other baggage claims and steadily headed in the direction of the Customs area he realised he could not spot one passenger that had been on the same flight.

Walking in complete silence under the Nothing To Declare section of customs, Gyro passed the lady that he had previously knocked over in the airport, who had her back turned to him as the customs officials asked her a barrage of questions which she was calmly answering. He rounded the screens that separated the arrivals section from the rest of the airport, and was met by a crowd of faces peering out at him. They awaited the arrivals of various loved ones from all over the world with such expectation that Gyro felt as if he was on a stage about to perform. He had been to Amsterdam many times in his thirty years on Earth but this had been the first time in his life that he was arriving in such a bewildered and lost state.

He headed towards the sliding doors of the arrivals entrance and as the glass doors opened, in the centre of Amsterdam felt the distinct chill of Dutch air on his face. He pulled his suit jacket together with one free hand in order to warm himself as he walked towards one of the taxis parked at the rank outside. He muttered some instructions to the driver to head for Amsterdam Centraal Station still amazed to be ten thousand miles off course from his destination. Somewhere near the station there had been a coffee shop ten years previously called The Greenhouse Effect and he was now more than curious to see if it still existed.

As the huge moustached Dutch taxi-driver took his bags and placed them on the backseat, Gyro opened the front side-door and sunk into the leather upholstery, exhausted. The driver got into the vehicle next to him and pushed a cassette into the car-stereo. The sounds of wonderful jazz filled up the car and the driver turned his large friendly face to look at his new fare.

"Good flight?" Asked the driver as they pulled away from the kerb smoothly and drove onto the motorway.

"Mmm...definitely original I guess, you could say..." He replied politely running his hand through his bleached hair and feeling more than a little bit flustered from time-travelling.

The next taxi in the line outside Schiphol Airport slowly cruised up to the front of the line. A tall and elegant woman dressed as if she had arrived directly from South America opened the front door of the second taxi and seated herself inside. She calmly rested a black leather briefcase on her lap and spoke pleasantly to the driver.

"Did you see a blonde haired gentleman who just drove off in the cab in front of you...?" She enquired in a soft calm German voice. Idly fiddling with the luggage tag that read Flight 815Y tied to the handle.

"Yar." Replied the driver.

"Could you follow that cab bittre?" She asked as the Dutch cab driver nodded in approval. Then smiled to herself. *"Sier shun - I've always wanted to say that!"* She said checking her reflection in the mirror.

The Dutch taxi-driver spoke something but it had been difficult for Britt to understand exactly what he had said, in Schiphol Airport everything was Dutch, of course.

BOOK IV

NIGHT / SIMULATIONS

NICK BOSTROM
1973

A PHD Graduate and doctor of Scientific Philosophy of Yale University where he continues to teach science. Nick Bostrom was born in America. He published a paper in 2001 entitled *THE SIMULATION ARGUMENT: Are You Living In a Computer Simulation?*

*If advances in computer technology were to
continue at close to present rates
there would be a strong probability that
we are each living in a computer simulation*

Some of the points raised are:

1] the human species is very likely to become extinct before reaching a post human stage

2] any post human civilization is extremely unlikely to run a significant number of simulations of their evolutionary history *(or variations thereof)*

3] we are almost certainly living in a computer simulation. It follows then that the belief that there is a significant chance that we will one day become post humans who run ancestor-simulations is false, unless we are currently living in a simulation.

Nick Bostrom, PhD is a Lecturer at the Department of Philosophy at Yale University. He is the author of many academic papers and of ANTHROPIC BIAS:Observation Selection Effects in Science and Philosophy. He will be a research fellow at Oxford University from December 2002.

CUSTOMS

IVAN VAN THE Man fought logarithm of tooth and rumble on greenie bent for Jamaica and Mittvoch City. Stacks packed of green piece fitted snug around mid-riff, bomb happy. Cruised and bruised seeking of heat was he. For Ivan had one wishing on a star. Bullet holeo magnifico connected four stylie across his Bruce the boss. Nine to five of hard slog at HASSLE as body of dog and pen trainee pusher journo had grown a slow wedge of discord betwixed the Editor und he. Bunsen burner heat of magnesium experiments through window of soul had pried slowly on Editor Joe and all his dirge of dirt of lackaday for much of skiving, running to bog und bomb on bomb dealings.

Ivan sulked mitt cappacheenie on dark and dank within HASSLE head and hindquarters. Anteater of puppy clue for much rumble. Trunckie wanting big bun fantastico, hunting big snark with mucho Roberto. One fine discovery of scandal could be jumpstart of fresh career paths ahoy. Editor Joe long of tooth played swing ball with bastard-boy had tittered manacle at attempts to lure and trap door swingy. Written out in lines of chunky Helvetica clues for Ivan. Another year for hunting high and lola quipped Joe. Purple kopf après another twelve wine of bottles. Joe edited in his pants of wool behind desk of scroat, back of school but never left. House points for whores yapped Joe for his fat neck and toes. Marking down through Jimi haze to diary for HASSLE.

Lunch for HASSLE was drunk out of pockets, sick and hand-shandy-city. Cokey-wokey and hoodwinked at forty. Touch downed in Chico. A beached whale of an office for every diatribe of shoot and pen dandy, would only reach critical on its last days of hell-sodden dishcloths.

Computer turtle tutor pinged around the offices as nine to five of hard slog rang out from the gurlz of Friday pump and Bolivian crematorium all for the delectable hot panty lust of HASSLE. Maggot rag chewed up best wood of bark and figs oak along the Valley of California red white and green and groan.

HASSLE mucus of bumble covers spread across interior office walls along with awardy bastards of fake gold and bronze praising its last days of great cheese. What a tight fishnet. Nineteen thoughts filled fat little head of Editor Joe as liquor and lecker fudge smoke loomed from cigars and all but a waistband of fifties fat throbbed the corpuscles around his box girder kompf. *"Shit sucking!"* Belched Joe. *"I want, I need, I crave, me me me!"* Flem of lust and spit of rat brewed for a cricket of ideas of disease on who to bring down with what and when, filled his love nuts. What had the young chicken squawked he had mounted at lunchtime? A grunt and a crutch-rub brought it all back. Some sack of a Senate hearing?

"Bastard-boy!" Squawked Joe. *"This is your missionary. Expenses and excrement Vegas-stylie. Play ball!"*

Brain and caffeine met for Ivan with coat and hat of journo-loopy, per chance of vexxen sure to be a land of Vegas and slots-o-fun...gurlz and wimen lose! *"Making it so chief!"* Chirped Ivan the bastard-boy.

Coffee Moca trip kick and lucky medallion of goat Charlie and Turkey board-game of shesh und besh in baggy waggy for Elvis was a calling, was a ripping, was a tearing a new reality eight ball. Gliding on concreto fantastico, toward the junction of fourteen and Oak, chugged Ivan avec cake and games of board. Sucking sess of future vision and greenback city, caffeine pumpy and gurlz of wet legs thoughts filled his hat of beige and lackaday for south for north, betwixt and between, up and away, or train of line and track.

Vegas und expenses should tell of how not why, where, but how much of Roberto could tight fit in snug as bug and suit of case, with cokey wokey and ice as cool as smokey chokie. Air of port and dinky drinks all around would seem to be puncture repair for Senate hearings of old and new lolly bashing. Ivan trucked to Taxi wank, ignoring filter of thoughts filed in hat of Editor Joe and previous trap door springy.

Crackling back of purple veined, in swivel chair grinned Editor Joe. Alchy woo-woo pulsed in vein of sick and tongue of reptile clacked and clucked. Tosser thoughts for swing ball on Ivan Van The Man made for toast and pate, as had a bologna headlines filled his hair in Europa bold style of happiness.

BASTARD BOY IN METAL BLOOD SMASH. JOURNO GETS GOATED. DAISY TO FOLLOW!

Humans were such fodder thoughts filled scales and hair of Editor Joe as porking humping young puppies of taught ness pulled the beam wide of smiley and teeth, oh teeth pulled back. To make a whale proud were picked and manicured. Joe loved the souls of fresh and the naive to plunge in lust of five tunes or more. Closing wounded windows of soul. His palms of Pilate behind kompf Joe felt a bonnie boner rise up thoughts of cards and penguins filled his hair. As fear filled HASSLE offices, keeping M and F straight on computer tutors.

Tucking on a sarnie and namma for journeyo fled Ivan to a of air and p of port. Taxi discussions had flown up driver black and news of senate metal airbus emerging and how. Criminal Sunshine as your Father and Holy Ghost no doubt bit on lip of Ivan. Vexxen of plan or cool in stride. Transport that could beat on the wings of desire.

Looking through boiled sand door of taxi, numbers ascended towards the beat of primary. Fourteen and Ant forged memory backlog back-up and drunken ramblings from an army general of meat about a Diner on the crossroads nearby one party with too many heaps of alchy-woo-woo. He had mentioned a form of travel and relativity or herbal. *"HALT!"* Yelled Ivan. Chucking twenties of Abraham at the driver, all the Kings' horses screeched to a corner, that merged with night air and a hotel above stacked up with floors of eight.

Clunking of cab door, tyres pip squeaking away as Ivan mit reflector in glasseo of neon buzz and gee whiz stood in appreciation of large tickle at the sight before him, on the corner of fourteen and Bardo. Attention goofball on hat-head and smile of bloody mucus for Mr. Bittre in windy. The Diner Holistic read sign of times.

A naive melody sprang out from Diner and night of electric pancake Summer rolled a royal carpet to Ivan cat-curious. Mr. Bittre owed him reddies and there were Ques and Peas within.

FRIDAY 7th SEPTEMBER 2001 MORNING / SOHO

I WAS LOOKING HANDSOME SHE WAS LOOKING LIKE AN EROTIC VULTURE

I see the people working and see it working for them
And so I want to join in but then I find it hurts me
KATE BUSH

AT THE HEADQUARTERS of Big New Yorker Liz dashed through reception ignoring Deb the Australian receptionist who made attempts to catch her attention. The petite figure moved quickly into the office. Chaos had already begun breaking out in usual fashion at Big New Yorker. A quick check of the coats hanging in the cloakroom revealed that Ray Connif her boss, had not yet arrived much to the relief of Liz. She ran over to her desk and hid the black suitcase underneath it. All the phones in the office seemed to be ringing and she hastily worked through the calls on hold, calls coming through and voicemail messages, some from people she had never heard of and then the ones directed specifically for Ray Connif.

Four minutes passed and swearing at the receptionist announced the arrival of Ray Connif. Dressed immaculately in a black pinstriped suit and petrol-blue framed glasses. Ray was wearing one of his many designer ties. This one bright red emblazoned with little yellow stars all over it. He waltzed into the office dancing with an invisible dance partner.

"Ahh Liz my little cabugion, you are here! I thought you'd be trashed in the East End and unable to come in." His German accent seemed to allow no intonation of humour to come through correctly. Liz winced inwardly at any of his usual attempts to be friendly in this way. Instead she forced out her infamous barking laugh as a retort.

"Did you see my black suitcase anywhere the one with scripts inside?" He asked looking past her.

His tall frame moved with such speed towards his own section of the open-plan office that she could only follow with a notebook prepared for the orders of the day. She hoped that she could sneak the case under his desk later, when he had gone to lunch. Nothing prepared her for what happened next. Jez his current flirtation announced loudly across from near the other end of the room. *"Here it is Ray!"* She cooed. *"You left it in the taxi last night when I dropped you off outside my flat!"*

Liz stood in a stupor as she felt her mouth drop open slightly and watched as Jez handed over the case and Ray opened it in front of her pulling out twenty-three separate film-scripts.

"I've got a real good feeling about this one called 'O.D.' It's written by this English guy and two studios are already interested in producing it. We're going to set up a meeting for Monday. Liz get on the line and tell Deb to hold all your calls. I want you to look after this project. 'O.D.' is your baby okay? I've got to go to Germany tonight. So can you be an angel and book me a flight for six or around then?"

Liz slunk back over to her desk perplexed, aware that she had a suitcase under her desk and she had no idea who it belonged to. Then another wave of paranoia and questions swept over her. Who did the case belong to? What was in it? It could even be a bomb. *"Does anyone want a coffee? I'm buying?"* She announced, scratching her chin. Amidst the chirps of happiness, she sneaked out of the office mildly panicking. Mobile phone in hand Liz awaited the realisation that she had just helped change the events of life somewhere in London a little bit more than at any other point in her entire existence. The case must belong to O.D. Darren thought Liz. That had to be it. She must have picked up his case by mistake.

As she waited outside for the coffees on the corner of Denmark and Old Compton Street, none of the suggestions her memory attempted to make, made any sense. Obviously she had picked up the case from the pub, the barman had given it to her when she came out of the toilet with O.D. Darren. Something had not added up here and Liz had been having enough problems in September, usually her busiest month, without having to solve this problem as well, especially with the hangover she was currently harbouring. If Liz wanted to keep her job, whatever had been happening, would have to wait until lunch. Still three hours away.

On her return to the office, another infamous meeting of Big New Yorker had already begun. Everyone from the company had been in the boardroom. Liz brought in the coffees and took a seat at the back, listening curiously. The atmosphere of the office seemed to be charged with excitement although Liz had had enough of that for one day already. Running on four hours sleep had caused her to be more than a little wired already.

"Ah Liz. Glad you're back. I didn't want you to miss this." Ray announced as she attempted to enter the room without being noticed. *"I've got some news for everyone here about some of the changes that we're going to be making in the oncoming months at Big New Yorker. First of all, I'm heading over to Germany and my hometown of Meissen tonight, to read over the scripts for our move into film production. After five years as head of this company, I'm handing over the reigns to someone else and so as from Monday, Liz Goldberg the wunderkind will be the head of Big New Yorker. So, you'll all have to be late everyday!"*

Liz dropped her jaw again and went slightly red-faced as everyone in the boardroom looked at her.

"Er... thanks!" She barked out an unusually loud laugh.

"I'm concentrating completely on my movie project and so have decided to head over to our New York offices, at The World Trade Centre. Once I'm there, Britt Johannes, the angel that came over in May to this office will be promoted. I will be based there from the remainder of the year. You can still talk to me through Liz and if there are any queries about projects you can take them up with her. Any questions?" Liz beamed back at everyone and nodded, especially Jez, who had a question. *"Do you believe in God?"* Asked Jez.

Although a quick incredulous silence descended onto the room. The question seemed relevant when Liz considered the morning that she just had. Ray Connif had always been direct.

"Yes. I do." He smiled. *"Any other questions? Yes Liz?"*

"I was just wondering if anyone lost a black suitcase from the office? Er... a client was asking." The words were out of her mouth before she knew it. Yet the response was negative. Liz scratched her chin nervously.

"Okay anything else to go over before I leave you wonderful people and move on to the next place? Fine. Liz if you would join me for a few minutes? The rest of you can get back to your various roles."

The solid oak door closed shut with a solid clunk behind Jez, who seemed more down in the mouth than usual. Liz felt sorry for her and made a promise to herself to go easy on her from next week. Already she felt slightly nauseas at the prospect of running a production company at the age of twenty-five. The truth being that she had been well capable of running it in her sleep for a number of years. Ray pulled out a small vial and placed it on the black table between the two of them. The white powder looked peculiar in the light from the fluorescent bulbs shining down from the ceiling. *"Any idea what this is?"* Asked Ray Connif as he gestured to the powder.

A horrible sinking feeling ran around her stomach and she kicked herself metaphorically for believing any of the tricks that Ray Connif had just made her fall for. She felt as if she had returned to school and decided to feign ignorance. *"Washing powder?"* She asked cautiously.

"Interesting answer. But no, my angel... try again." Said Ray.

"Sugar?"

"Closer. Try once more." Hinted Ray, stroking his designer-tie.

"A white powder that looks like washing powder and tastes of sugar?" Asked Liz refusing to comply.

"I can tell you're a copywriter! But this is the new campaign you're going to be working on Liz."

"Sorry?" She asked incredulous.

With eyes sparkling, Ray stood up and walked over to the only window in the boardroom. *"It's a sample from the manufacturers in Germany. A pharmaceutical company have named it Phenylalainemontovia Dymulsive Cronoconiff. For the moment, we're calling it FX. They want an advertising and marketing campaign set-up over the next month concentrating on the soft drinks market."*

"A pharmaceutical drug?" Quizzed Liz awaiting a film crew to spring through the door

"They want it marketed as a recreational drug. Similar to Red Bull and the energy series of soft drinks."

"Is this a wind-up?" She asked, looking first at Ray and then back at the powder on the table.

Ray laughed out loud as he attempted to contain his secret. "I know exactly what you mean Liz! I couldn't contain myself when the manufacturers told me. They are paying fifteen million pounds to Big New Yorker for the marketing contract. And get this. They're not sure of its release yet!"

"So we're going to do a campaign for a drug that might not come out?" Asked Liz divided.

"Yep!" Beamed Ray returning to the seat opposite her.

"Do we get paid?" Asked Liz with her best professional face.

"Yep! Ve get lots of money." Smiled Ray.

"Even if the drug doesn't come out we'll get paid?" She asked.

"Bingo!" Exclaimed Ray Connif smiling.

Liz found herself strangely excited by the prospect of marketing a pharmaceutical drug. She had no idea what she had been asked to deal with. Ray seemed to be getting more excited by the second and had the pitch ready. Liz swung her legs in the chair, too petite to touch the floor with her feet and felt slightly excited.

"This is what they told me. They are opting us with the contract because of our success with the Telecom, Apple campaigns and the Mini marketing work you did. When I told them that you were the lady behind the Bacardi marketing... that clinched the deal! Every one of their noted clients, were your clients Liz. Then they asked for you to take it onboard personally, so I thought it over and thought I'd better ask you first. The brief outlines what they're after. Logo, Corporate Colours etc. Even the name is up to you. What it looks like. Everything."

"Hang about Ray! You're asking me to come up with a campaign for marketing drugs to children? This sounds like those strawberry cigarettes that were released in Japan years ago." Disputed Liz and barked a laugh.

Ray ignored her flatly and moved onto the details of the contract. "They're offering two point five million pounds to you personally, paid directly into your bank account as an employer arrangement and they'll pay all your taxes for five years. They are also offering you a car. You have two weeks of the month for three months research covered by expenses of five thousand pounds, each day, that you do research through recreational drug usage. They're also offering free medical insurance for any problems which might arise from your research and free accommodation in Switzerland should you need to have your money placed in a bank account there."

"What was the drug research bit?" Asked Liz, the rest had turned into babble for her.

"They're offering you five thousand pounds a day to take recreational drugs in research as a comparison to Phenylalainemontovia Dymulsive Cronoconiff." Ray Connif repeated, laughing. "You know, marijuana, cocaine, ecstasy, heroin, oh yes and LSD."

"Have they drawn up a contract?" She asked trying to contain her excitement.

"I have it right here. Once you sign, the work must be done over thirty days. This is big Liz. I've worked in the business for over twenty years, I've never seen a contract like this. They offered one million into your account, which will be there by twelve o'clock today... if you want to sign!"

"Burning flies man! Who the fuck are these people?" Liz gasped aloud.

"That's the catch. They'll pay for you to have a lawyer look over the contract but they won't say who they are."

For the first time in her young life Liz discovered that there really nothing to say. Yet she knew that the questions would come thick and fast later.

"Oh, I couldn't say anything in front of the rest of the office, but the black suitcase you were asking about? That's the sample case and without that. There's no deal. That's the catch. As your employer, Big New Yorker gets twenty percent of the campaign budget, which...is," Ray quickly pushed buttons on a calculator sat on the table and slid the calculator over to her side of the table. "...about one hundred and twenty-five thousand pounds."

Liz gulped. Her annual salary was already twenty-five thousand pounds per annum after tax, as an assistant.

"There is the question of two other campaigns I'm giving you and I'm also promoting you. So you'll get your raise today of one hundred thousand pounds *which will be in your account from twelve o'clock. I still need a plane ticket though for tonight, so you'd better get onto that first. After you've sorted that out. I'll give you an hour to think it all over okay?"*

"Er.., right. Thanks." Said Liz, attempting to stop her voice from shaking. Adrenaline and caffeine were causing her stomach to tell her brain that it could be her Birthday.

Liz wobbled out of the boardroom with a slightly pale look on her face and planted herself at her desk. Then proceeded to dial up phone numbers desperately trying to remain composed, amidst sudden bursts of laughter. She looked down at the black case and idly ran her fingers over the top, next to the handle and felt the initials of P and G embossed into the leather surface. She finalised the flights from London to Berlin for Ray, then onto New York for September 11th 2002. The date seemed familiar until she realised, it was the signing of the World Trade Agreement O.D. Darren had been speaking about in the pub, last night. She walked back over to the desk of Ray Connif and told him the flight details.

"I don't think I need an hour to think about it. Where do I sign?" She asked her yapping laugh reaching ear-splitting level and forcing the rest of the office to groan inwardly. Ray smiled up at her and pulled out the contract, placed it on the desk and stroked his tie.

"Right there..." He said pointing at the bottom of the paper and handing her a petrol-blue fountain pen with the initials of P and G faintly printed at the top.

Liz signed the contract as her eyes quickly surveyed the last page of the document. As she quickly scanned down the page she noticed a few words that stuck out one sentence had the words Fifty-Five Cancri written in upper case and she could see 'planets' and 'Universe' printed in small type at the bottom in the last paragraph. However, with the millions of pounds she would have access to by midday she had become sure she could locate a lawyer somewhere in the world who would translate it all for her.

Ray Connif smiled back at her and handed her one of the thin undersigned light orange sheets that had been impregnated with blue carbon paper.

"Welcome to the business." He said as he put the contract back into his suitcase and locked the lid.

"I think I'm just going to get a coffee to celebrate if you don't mind?" Said Liz preparing herself to run out into the street and jump in the air as she had seen done by an actress in one of the adverts made by Big New Yorker.

"Whatever makes you happy Liz. I'm sure you can afford to buy the entire cafe after twelve o'clock!" He smiled again.

At the headquarters of Big New Yorker Liz dashed through reception ignoring Deb the Australian receptionist who made attempts to catch her attention as she moved quickly out the front door of the office.

FRIDAY 7TH SEPTEMBER 2001
AFTERNOON / BRISTOL

THE ECSTASY OF DANCING FLEAS

Don't work hard. Don't play hard. Don't plan for the graveyard
Remember - everything, everything gives you cancer
JOE JACKSON

THE ARTIST CHRIS T had moved to Hackney four long years ago after the split from his hometown of Portishead. His parents had opted for divorce as the last stage of a disastrous marriage and Chris T had been fifteen when he had heard the news unexpectedly found himself homeless. His father had been forced to move into smaller accommodation with his new girlfriend in order to pay the bills of a solicitor firm called P & G. The mother moved West across the great pond of the North Atlantic Ocean into an apartment in New York with her new boyfriend Ray Connif, who had originally been born in the quiet village of Meissen in Germany. A town famous for the invention of porcelain which curiously enough the Chinese invented one thousand years previously. Chris T had met Ray only once. It had been on the last day the family who he had spent seventeen good years with in Portishead, were finally disbanding and moving in separate diretions.

The artist and the Advertising Executive had met in the lounge while the last weekend they were a family had been separated into two equal halves. One had involved saying goodbye to his mother on Saturday. While Sunday would be farewell to his father who had already transported most of the furniture to his new house in Bristol. Chris T had been a skinhead in appearance from the age of twelve and took an immediate disliking to Ray. In such situations humans have a defensive streak a mile wide and what Chris T had been disturbed by had been the simple way that when Ray walked into the room, he kept stroking his tie when he had spoke. That moment had been three years ago. Now Chris T had grown to the age of eighteen and had been living in Hackney in various squats ever since.

Art had been the saving grace of Chris T. He discovered a huge love for it as an expressive medium for his anger from the break-up of his family and had devoured nearly every book and gallery he could find on the subject. He had discovered an interview with Picasso in a library when in London and had been impressed with the manner the way the artist had handled an persistent questions of an interviewer after asking him to draw a 'quick doodle' on a napkin. Picasso had obliged and after one minute the interviewer had held the napkin up to the camera and the audience as he had pointed out that the great artist should be disgusted by the simple fact the drawing he signed had become valuable to the cost of a million dollars at least and the interviewer forced the point that Picasso had only spent one minute making it. As Chris T viewed the library monitor showing the videotape of the interview, his life had abruptly taken a new turn simply by the reply to the question from Picasso.

"A minute? It took me fifty years to learn how to do that!" Exclaimed the artist.

Chris T had decided to treasure the moment and displayed the tale to the smartly dressed gentleman that stood next to a large canvas in the main gallery where he now stood. The dark suit had blue hair, Ray-Ban sunglasses and was holding a glass of red wine in one hand and a joint casually smoking in the other. Ben had been impressed by the wicked sense of humour of Chris T. They both stood talking in the art gallery situated near Clifton in Bristol. The X-Chromo-pilot had developed a tremendous love for art since his rebirth on Earth and the theme of *'Rich Art'* he had found difficult to resist. Ben had travelled from London in his new Mini and had met Chris T by chance at the opening of the new exhibition.

The two of them struck up an immediate friendship with each other once the initial misunderstanding that Chris T had not been not a musician from a band called Portishead was cleared up. He set Ben straight on this immediately by explaining that the name came from a small town near Bristol. Chris T had been intrigued by the talk of squatting, which Ben told him he had been involved with since leaving school. However the truth about the original birthplace of Ben would probably have ruined the moment of social normality. Over drinks at the bar of the gallery the two of them exchanged numbers and arranged to meet in Hackney the next day.

"There is more to life than London you know Ben..." Said Chris T, never a person to hold back on his personal opinions. *"How long have you been living in the big smoke?"* He asked the blue haired alien.

Ben toked on his spliff and thought hard for a moment. *"Probably about five years..."* He said cautiously.

"What made you move there? What about Manchester or Liverpool?" Asked Chris T.

Ben laughed and most of the smoke spluttered out of his mouth at the suggestion. *"Nah, too far North for me. I'm from a small village near Portsmouth. My Mother still lives there, I have to travel home sometimes and anywhere further than London would do my head in."* He mimicked the accent of the East End perfectly.

"London always reminds me of The Bill whenever I see it on television." Continued Ben. *"It always amazes me how many times it's on national television. If anyone was arriving in the country for the first time, they'd probably think London was England. That's the power of television though, you can't beat it. Brookside has always had a profound effect on my visits to Liverpool however."*

"You've been to Liverpool then?" Enquired Chris T as they strolled around the exhibition.

"Nope. Never. From television I always think I have enough of an understanding of what a place is going to be like. Usually, it's inaccurate, but America is a place I would never want to visit, after having watched it on TV. So I think most people end up in situations simply because they like the programme. Which inspires them." Said the alien.

"You don't have to visit America these days. It's already here. England is the fifty-first state." Said Chris T proudly.

"Mmm, but what's so bad about that? Imagine what England was like before America's support in World War II. Massive unemployment and scurvy and rickets for everyone!"

"Rickets?" Enquired Chris T laughing.

"Rickets..." Repeated Dapper Ben profoundly stoned. *"...quite a strange word really isn't it?"*

The joint seemed to be having its desired effect and the newly formed alliance paraded slowly around the exhibition. Within the space were four separate galleries that displayed a variety of wealthy artists from across England. The main theme of the exhibition had been to show art from the frame of reference of artists that had a minimum of one hundred thousand pounds in their personal accounts. Like all exhibitions some of the art had been stirring, some bland and some extraordinarily powerful.

Most of it had not impressed Chris T, whose only admiration had been directed towards his new associate. His dress sense of blue jeans and white T-shirt had caused him to ask Ben where he had purchased the dapper suit he had currently wearing. *"Oxfam of Hackney."* Ben had replied smiling. They were both gradually being unimpressed by the *'art'* on display to such a degree that Ben was forced into observing that a mattress with some vegetables on it was about as artistic as a fart and merely seemed to reveal less talent in the exhibition, yet it did stick in the mind in much the same way the word haemorrhoids or rhino plasti does.

They arrived in a small room built onto the side of the main gallery, which held a dark atmosphere that Ben found extremely appealing. Inside were a number of fluorescent bulbs dimly flickering on and off. *"America holds a great deal of appeal to me."* Chris T continued as the two artists stepped into the darkened installation. *"I love the culture and the music. The movies are incredible."* He said.

"Would you go there though?" Asked Ben suddenly curious. The joint hanging from his mouth.

"Well, I used to live there. It's nothing like television. The appeal of England to America was something I became fascinated by since my Father married an American...eventually."

Ben laughed, as he sat down cross-legged in the middle of the room. Mesmerized by the flickering bulbs.

"Man, I think I have little time for America. The movies are like sugar. They seem to be designed for an audience of people who like sugar a lot. After seeing how overweight some people are there. I sometimes think I can understand enough about the country without having to visit the place. Plus,

some Americans are so loud. I do however, love The Pixies from Boston. If it weren't for that band I would really detest the place. They're the saving grace of the place."

"That's just the image of America you see on television though." Replied Chris T as he joined his new associate seated on the floor. *"When you're in the country it's incredible!"*

"Which part did you go to?" Asked Ben offering him the joint.

"Well, I went to visit my mother in New York and then travelled to Austin Texas. It's an oasis of liberal in a sea of fascism. Texas has to be one of the strangest places on Earth. You can fit Europe into that one State over three times. I had trouble the minute I arrived though, being English."

"What happened?" Asked Ben as he sat in a meditation pose on the floor opposite to the electrical light bulbs.

"I was filling-up my pick-up truck with gas. I owned a pick-up truck then. I'd just driven through the border of Texas and this guy pulled up at the garage next to me. Huge guy. He just walked up to me and asked where I was from and I said, 'England'. He then asks me in this broad Texas accent. 'So how does it feel to be in the most powerful country in the world?'" Chris T took a pause to inhale sharply on the joint.

"What did you say?" Asked Ben.

The face of Chris T broke into a broad grin. *"I said, 'I don't know, I've never been to Japan!'"*

Ben burst into a huge smile and laughed a deep rumble of a laugh.

"In Texas? That must have gone down really well."

"Like a fart in a spacesuit." Answered Chris T quickly.

"Where did you get that? That is not one of yours!" Retorted Ben referring to the sharp reply.

"I know! It was something my old teacher Derek from school used to say!"

"You called your teacher Derek? I know a Derek in... Hackney." Said Ben profoundly.

"He was a great teacher! The first person who got me interested in art." Replied Chris T.

The joint forced both of them to laugh harder. The small room they were now sitting in had a mysterious atmosphere generated by a low sustain coming from the amplifier which had been plugged into a tape-player and then connected to a sampled recording of two foxes mating. The details of the installation were all printed on the wall under the name of the artist. This had caused even more laughter for the pair. Ben read aloud the details of the entire project to Chris T. Who exalted at the name of the artist alone.

"Dead Daddy Badger?" Asked Chris T about to burst with laughter.

They were dragged into a stoned laughing frenzy, which was broken by the sound of polite coughing from the connecting door of the smoke filled room.

"Is this art?" Enquired a gentle German voice softly.

"Good question!" Guffawed the two in unison through tears as they rolled on the floor.

Chris T and the alien both looked up to see a tall, elegantly dressed woman peering her head around the opening of the darkened room. The light from the gallery behind her with the flickering of fluorescent bulbs, seemed to bring an ethereal quality to the whole scene and something similar to recognition passed over her pale expression as the sweetest smile either of them had ever seen spread across her face. Ben found himself instantly mesmerized and stood up slipping into his best suave impersonation that he could find.

Chris T stood up and turned quickly to face the heavenly vision. *"Is it art? Did you say?"* He repeated, quickly passing the joint to Ben, who purported it to be something unknown.

"Yes, I had been wondering if either of you were the artists?" Asked Britt, looking at the two of them.

Chris T looked back at Ben wide-eyed. Although judging by appearances he had to admit that the suit forced an image of dealing and buying onto Ben. He turned back to Britt and offered an outstretched hand to shake.

"Yes, that's right...we're the artists!" He said smiling with red bloodshot eyes.

"Please to meet you, I'm Britt. I really like your exhibition." She said calmly.

"Er...thank you very much." Said Chris T as he escorted Britt out of the small extension and back towards the main gallery. As he held her hand he experienced a sudden flash of an image appearing somewhere in the back of his mind. He dropped the hand politely and passed his attention to the paintings in the gallery.

"What do you think of the penguin?" He asked politely.

Britt cupped a hand over her mouth and giggled lightly. "I'm sorry, did you say penguin?"

"Chris T's a little bit stoned..." Said Ben in a slight patronising voice. "He means exhibition."

The young skinhead fired a look of hard appreciation in the direction of Ben and felt as if he had returned back to the house of his parents the last time he saw them together.

"Yes sorry I meant to say what do you think of the exhibition?" He asked again.

"Oh I love it!" Said Britt in her cute German accent. "I really like Bristol, especially Clifton. I live in Hackney and it's nothing like this. It's my first time here."

"Hackney?" Said Ben stunned he had never seen such beauty there before. "Me too!"

The concurrence of three people standing in an art gallery all from the same part of London hit each of them immediately and Ben found himself staring blankly at a lady who he would have proposed marriage to on the spot if he could only persuade his brain to function properly. As the German accent drifted eerily throughout the gallery. A strange sensation crawled up the back of each spine of the group as they smiled at each other politely nodding.

The artist felt as if it had been only four minutes since he left home but in reality Chris T had moved to Hackney four long years ago after the split from his hometown of Portishead.

FRIDAY 7TH SEPTEMBER 2001 NIGHT / THE FIFTH DIMENSION

DEAD DADDY BADGER

*There must be a way I can dress to please him
It's hard to walk in a dress it's not easy*
P J HARVEY

AT THE ODEON in Leicester Square, the most expensive cinema in London had begun showing a new piece of American propaganda by an up and coming flavour of the week, named Horst Klimt. Born in the United States and raised by wolves until the age of ten years Horst had become one of the sensational new Feral Directors launched onto the public after an article in a weekly magazine named him as the hottest of the new emerging wild young Feral Film Directors. The others were Dexter Wexford and Dead Daddy Badger, the youngest of the sect. Dexter had been raised by bears in the heart of Washington State and Dead Daddy Badger were a gaggle of three sisters who had been brought up by Swans in Omaha. The critics were torn between all three, loving each of them equally as they showed the press and public how the Swans had taught them to eat little chunks of bread gracefully and paddle ferociously, whilst always remaining deeply poignant. Just like their films. They always dressed in white.

The first major release of a movie by Horst had arrived at the cinemas and O.D. Darren had become a major fan after reading an interview with the new wunderkind. He had shouted *"Cheesebeads!"* over and over at the journalist interviewing him to every question thrown in his direction, almost immediately. The opportunity of watching the new work had caused the press to praise the film as *'harder to understand than David Lynch and weirder.'* What more needed to be said for bums on seats. O.D. Darren had become fascinated after reading the reviews and witnessing the poster outside the Odeon as the PH of five of rain fell from the sky. People were arriving in limousines and the Square had already become packed with half of England screaming their knackers off for a look at the new media darling of the United, Horst Klimt. O.D. Darren stood next to a journalist who seemed to be braving the elements of rain and wind, in order to shout into a digital camera how excited she was to be standing in Leicester Square in the pouring rain. Lucky me thought O.D. Darren. He had never been this close to glamour before and was amazed to have access to such a vivid sight, as that of the journalist reading from a clipboard. She seemed to be introducing the various celebrities, as they waved behind her to the camera, filling in anyone watching with every scrap of knowledge that was possible to muster up about the Feral Directors. Now that he was dead O.D. Darren seemed to discover that what appeared on television as glamour was merely a woman standing in the rain.

"Now also, you can just see Dexter there, waving at the crowd gathered at the front of the Odeon. Now, arriving there is one of the actresses from Horst's first short movie 'Rain' which a lot of critics loved and expressed strong beliefs that it held a good chance of taking an Oscar should it ever be released in America."

Rain had been shot entirely in Scotland for a budget of thirty-five pence and entered the grandiose prestigious halls of fame via The Guinness Book of Records as the cheapest film ever made. Not bad news for Horst who heard the news on his ten-year-old Birthday last week. What had made the film so special, had been the fact that it had bee all shot on tissue paper. O.D. Darren decided to exploit his full ghostly talent by walking into one of the limousines parked outside the cinema and witnessing what was behind the smoke-screened windows. He had always been curious.

Inside the white stretched limo, he witnessed a real professional at work. Horst was operating two mobiles at the same time and seemed to be negotiating a film deal in Hollywood on each line. His manager sat in the front of the vehicle ordering various types of steak from a restaurant nearby while next to Horst on the back seat sat two of the wolves that had raised him as one of their own cubs. O.D. Darren felt honoured to be amidst a real talent, instead of the usual bunch of London smack heads he hung out with when he had last been alive.

The two wolves began to growl and O.D. Darren noticed a change in the negotiating procedures being held on the phone. One of the phones slammed down and then a high-pitched voice squeaked out. *"What do you mean? They're all here? But I only invited the eldest sister!"*

O.D. Darren hopped out of the limousine and walked past the reporter who was wearing a petrol-blue dress and still shouting at the digital camera in the rain. She seemed to be sticking her finger in her ear and jumping up and down with excitement. The throng of people outside the cinema became intense with squeals of pleasure, as she screamed into the camera. *"OHMYGOD! I don't believe it. I've just been told that Dead Daddy Badger have all arrived for the screening. Oh yes! There they are!"*

The crowd roared and cheered with excitement, cameras flashed, as one hundred and twenty-five thousand people tried to stand next to three tiny girls all at the same time. Ages ranged from nine, ten through to eleven.

"I don't believe it!" Continued the journalist. *"They're here tonight from Omaha, live in London and look...ahhhh, how sweet! The crowd are throwing little chunks of bread at them and the girls are picking them up and eating them, just as their foster swan parents taught them. Aren't they adorable?"* She cooed.

Cameras flashed and the press crushed in closer to the three sisters straining in an attempt to get pictures of their segnant shenanigans. As O.D. Darren headed into the cinema all the security in the area had become oblivious to the fact that one of the largest ex-drug dealers in the Western World had just walked into a cinema in the West End of London without paying live on television. The hippy stood in front of the crowd and gave a huge victory sign with both arms raised outstretched up in the air. The French film actress Juliet Binoche walked directly into him and continued onward into the cinema. For the briefest of moments O.D. Darren wished he had stayed alive. He watched as Juliet Binoche turned and smiled at the crowds of people gathered outside in Leicester Square and wondered to himself how the molecular structure of such a creature could be so divine.

The hippy knew that most of the flashes came from the various cameras around but as he stood on the steps next to the star from France O.D. remembered a time in Germany when he had travelled with a school trip to discover the concentration camps of Krakow. He had looked up at the stars of the night sky over the walls of the camp and cried. The lights appeared to be so peaceful and he had considered the possibility briefly that if each star had been a sun shining down onto a separate planet then each planet could easily have a population of people and life covering it. He just could not see it from such a distance. They would be aliens from where he stood. From the perspective of these planets he would be an alien to them. Surely that would be easier to believe than what had occurred in Krakow or Aushwitz. As this thought began O.D. imagined himself at the age of fifteen as a prisoner of war in the camp looking up at the night sky and seeing it for the last time. He sighed and wondered if maybe people on the other planets had gotten anything right. Or if mistakes were made there too.

The bright flashes reflecting from the smiling face of Juliet Binoche bounced back towards him and he could feel water coming from his eyes as the actress smiled and looked directly into his eyes. She waved in slow-motion to him to follow her into the cinema and O.D. Darren wondered briefly for a moment if he was in heaven.

"Come on O.D., the film's nearly starting..." She said.

At the Odeon in Leicester Square, the most expensive cinema in London had begun showing a new piece of American propaganda by an up and coming flavour of the week, named Horst Klimt.

SATURDAY 8TH 2001 SEPTEMBER
MORNING / THE MORGUE

I CAN FEEL ONE OF MY TURNS COMING ON

Even though you've made it pretty obscure
Baby it's clear you're losing your atmosphere from here
You're losing it
AIMEE MAN

IT WOULD PROBABLY have been faster to walk or crawl. The situation that morning however required some discrete preparation. Liz had always been conscious of her appearance to nearly everyone she met in London. Advertising has that effect on people. She had thought of the idea to pretend she was actually an actress rehearsing for a movie. In order to show anyone who might pass her on the street that she had not gone mad. If they wondering why she had been running towards a taxi shouting at the ghost of her ex-boyfriend. She became aware as she headed through Soho that it looked to a lot of people as if she had been talking to herself.

She had seen enough movies where this sort of thing happened and after the looks she had been receiving outside Cafe Nero it had taken her a few minutes to understand the situation. Her reflection had caught her slightly off guard. O.D. Darren had been missing from the picture. In order to prove to the cab driver that she had been an actress rehearsing for a film and not talking to herself in the back of the black taxi. She had also quickly grabbed the G-WIZ brief from the offices of Big New Yorker after checking with a few tourists in the street whether they could see O.D. Darren. None of them had. So she really was dealing with a ghost.

She need not have bothered really. The days when a London cab driver had taken any notice of what a customer in his cab had been doing were long gone. All that this particular cab-driver seemed interested in had been how to travel the longest distance between two points. Fortunately the scenic route gave O.D. Darren an opportunity to explain what had previously seemed to be just the drug-fuelled paranoia of Liz.

"This is going back over the last few years." He explained to his ex-girlfriend. *"I met a really sweet old lady in Hackney one day who was having trouble getting a huge suitcase from her car into a house. So I helped her. There was this big American bloke at the door with her. He was huge. He still is huge actually. The two of them invited me into the house and explained how they had to get the case to the lady's house in Hammersmith. They asked if I could help. So I played the good Samaritan and helped. We kept in touch and two weeks later she calls again and explains that there's this other case that she left in Hackney."* Darren took a mouthful of beer from a pint he pulled from under his jacket drank it and lowered his voice as he continued. *"She told me that they both contained CD's. Imports. Which she was bringing over from Holland for her son whose a DJ. Anyway. About two more weeks go by and a routine starts up where I would visit Winmau and pick-up a case and deliver it to this lady's house..."*

"Didn't you look in the cases?" Asked Liz amazed as she held up the makeshift script for the cab driver to ignore.

"Never. It just never occurred to me to do that. It's someone else's property. Also, the cases were locked, with a combination. The fifth case I moved wasn't locked properly and after carrying the fifth case onto the tube, curiosity got the better of me.." Said Darren, seemingly distraught when he recalled the story.

"What was in there?" Asked Liz as her voice lowered.

"I couldn't believe it. It was packed to the top with sealed packets of white powder. All wrapped in petrol-blue cellophane. So I carefully pulled a flap down and took out a smidge of the powder and wrapped it in a rolling paper."

"What was it? Heroin?" Whispered Liz. She looked at the blank script again. *"No, no, that doesn't sound right."* She muttered to herself shaking her head and performing for the cab driver.

"I had no idea. After I dropped the case off, The Madam, which is what I called her, still carried on as if it was CD's, so I assumed she thought it was. After I left her house, I phone a friend who is working as a chemist in London and arrange to take the powder over to her. She takes it into work and analyses it and... guess what?" He paused.

"What?" Liz asked hanging onto her script. "Er, I mean, what kind of a time do you call this?" She pretended to try the line a number of different ways.

"It's unidentifiable. It doesn't appear anywhere on the periodic table." Continued the ghost of O.D. Darren. "All she can say is what it isn't. It isn't heroin, cocaine or any derivatives of any drug ever recognised...on Earth. It is a base chemical though."

Liz felt a strong sensation of deja vu come over her and suddenly knew what O.D. Darren was about to say next. She finished off his sentence for him. "*Phenylalainemontovia Dymulsive Cronoconiff!*" She yelled waving her arms dramatically.

"Bingo! *This excited her so much, I thought she was was winding me up.*" Said Darren as he continued to drink his beer casually. "*She was raving about the Nobel Peace prize and how something like this was the greatest discovery you could ever come across. Big shock! I think I could have handled it if it was cocaine or heroin, or speed, you know? Something normal. Suddenly, I was looking at these two in a whole new way. Obviously I couldn't tell anyone what I knew. I just hoped something would work itself out.*"

"But why is this drug such a problem?" Asked Liz keeping an eye on the cab driver who seemed to have taken the words 'take your time' and given them new meaning.

"Can you imagine what some mortician's going to think when they take a look at me and discover that half my body chemistry is extra-terrestrial? Stop the cab, the morgue's near here." O.D. Darren literally leapt out of the taxi.

Liz asked the driver to stop and felt momentarily like a small girl as he pressed a button in the front of the vehicle, which allowed the back door to be unlocked with a loud click. She stepped out onto the pavement and handed over a Darwin to the driver with an embarrassed smile. She gestured with the pile of blank paper in her hand.

"Well I hope I get the part. I'm going to an audition!" She said hoping the cab driver had not thought her insane.

"I'd get rid of the ghost if I were you love!" Said the gruff East End voice of the driver. "He's liable to put you off!"

The expression on her face froze divided between shock and bewilderment. He disentangled some lose change from a leather moneybag and stretched across the driver seat to count the change back to her.

"You can see him?!" She said stunned.

"I can see them all love. I have to chase most of them out of me cab miss!" He coughed and winked at her. *"They're always in the back trying to get a free lift. My old gal sometimes rides up in the front. She died in the eighties."* Liz wondered if momentarily if today had been declared national insane day and she had simply forgotten.

"But I just checked with some tourists and they couldn't see him." She said diplomatically.

" Well, death's a funny one. I could never see the ghosts in London until my wife died. Then she introduced them to me gradually. Sometimes they make the day easier. Sometimes they make it hard. But it depends on the weather I find. The trouble is they don't know they're dead at times and getting them to shut up at night can be a problem. Boyfriend was it?" He asked smiling at a black and white photograph attached near the meter.

"Sort of..." Liz answered discerningly.

"Thought so, there actually more trouble. I get a lot of them coming here, to the Morgue. It's all part of life though innit? Like the banks and the taxes, there's no avoiding it." He laughed. *"I had Einstein in the back last week. Nice bloke. Couldn't understand a word he was saying though. German. Said he wanted to see Buckingham Palace. He's never been busier apparently. Said something about a big plan that's going on."*

"Thanks I think I needed to hear that. Keep the change." Said Liz wondering if she should laugh or cry.

"Oh thanks love. Well, mind how you go. We'll probably meet again...on the road." He winked at her as the taxi pulled away from the kerb. Then called out again.

"REMEMBER LOVE YOU'RE LIVING IN A DREAM THAT SOMEONE ELSE IS HAVING!"

Liz watched the sensible black vehicle turn around and drive back towards the direction of the West End. Then she turned to face the building the cab had pulled up in front of. They had parked directly opposite the John

Soanes Museum. As both herself and the ghost of O.D. Darren walked along the road next to Lincoln Fields, Liz glanced around at some of the tourists enjoying the Saturday afternoon sunshine. Smiling and kissing. A cautious thought occurred to her suddenly which she remembered thinking once before at the bahmitzva of her cousin when she had been twelve years old. Yet she had never spoken to anyone about it.

The thought had been more of a theory. She had been curious enough to ponder on it the moment a friend had told her the expression. *"It's all in the mind."* She said it aloud. *"It's all in the mind."*

She turned to face the ghost of O.D. Darren and carefully held up the script, continuing with the actress charade.

"Darren, what do you think that means? It's all in the mind? I mean where is the mind?" She asked tactfully.

"Ahh, now that's a great question. The ghost in the machine!" Replied O.D. Darren. *"I've always thought everything you see, touch, eat, watch, smell, taste or even everyone you meet or see or talk to. Everything that can and will exist. It's all in the mind. We all live in the mind. Travel the world and you travel in your mind."*

"So right now, you're in my mind and your dead?" She asked with the honesty of a child.

"Restaurants sell dead food then yeah?" Rather touchily.

"I have no idea what they sell..." She said with a wary smile.

"You might as well ask where's the future? Where's the past or where's the present?" He placed a hand above her skull. *"A lot of what you see and hear in life is right here and nowhere else!"* He said patting her on the head affectionately.

"Where's the Morgue Darren?" She asked as they hurried along the pavement. *"I'm getting hungry."*

"You see that building there? It's underneath. Down the steps. Have you been to a Morgue before?" Asked O.D. Darren with apprehension.

"Oh, all the time. I live in Hackney. There's probably more death in that part of London than there is in here..."

Without any further hesitation she ducked down the cobbled stone steps and into the front entrance of The Morgue.

London fuelled Liz up at times but then again the coffee at Cafe Nero could probably propel a rocket ship off the planet because it had been so strong. She had felt edgy getting to The Morgue until the cab driver had delivered such a sermon of knowledge to calm her down, but she held onto the belief still that it would probably have been faster to walk or crawl.

SUNDAY 9TH SEPTEMBER 2001 TIME / SPACE

DON'T YOU POINT THAT RAY-GUN AT ME

Does love ever end when two hearts are torn away?
Or does it go on and beat strong anyway?
KIM DEAL / THE BREEDERS

"I TOLD YOU it was the wrong one! You never listen!" Announced a rather camp voice close to Ray as he slowly stood up and peered into the dark red light of the tall cave he had been transported to. *"Hello?"* Called Ray in the direction of the two figures standing in front of him. *"Er... where am I?"* He asked.

"How do you like surprises?" Chuckled a second deeper voice back.

"What?" Replied Ray cautiously peering up from the spongy floor he was slowly sinking into.

"He said do you like surprises?" Giggled the voice of Procta.

"I guess it depends what the surprise is really." Answered the German as vaguely as he could.

" Well, I don't want to be pertantic but it wouldn't be a surprise then really would it?" Replied the first alien tartly.

"True. Er...where am I?" Asked the German again.

"Your in Liz." Replied the voices in near perfect harmony. *"Your assistant. Sorry, I mean, your partner...she was promoted don't forget!"* Corrected Procta.

"Wh...What?" Asked Ray as he moved towards the spongy wall, through the warm soft floor. *"Look is there someone in charge here?"*

"Oooh hark at him! Someone in charge? Where you are, we're as 'in charge' as your going to get pal!" Returned Gambul, one of the two aliens who

now leapt forward ballerina-style through the air in slow-motion until he landed in front of Ray bent on one knee as if in a musical presentation arms outstretched. The alien opened its mouth wide and wailed aloud. *"Ta-dahhh You're in Liz!"* "Sang the alien as if performing in front of a huge audience. *"L.I.Z. Liizzzz!"*.

Ray smiled back and attempted to not sink into the squidgy pink surface he was now standing on without much success. Which had already engulfed his black hush puppies and was now engulfing his ankles fast. He smiled, not understanding a word of what the alien was singing. The second alien hovered cartoon-like above the pink soft floor, held in the air by a propeller sticking out of its head, which rotated at such a speed, that a high-pitched whine could be heard coming from it across the cavern. The alien smiled and focused all attention in the direction of Ray who was becoming aware that whatever he was now dealing with had been attempting wildly to make him laugh. Due to Ray being German however the attempts were proving to be a little trickier than the aliens had first anticipated.

Suddenly a pink spotlight picked out the hovering alien as it descended downward towards Ray who was now up to his knees in the soft cavern floor and sinking further down by the second.

"Quick quick! Pull him out otherwise we're in serious trouble." Yelled Procta.

"Okay. Ray sorry about all this. You'll have to give us a chance - it's only our second go..." Chimed in Gambul.

Both aliens now stood either side of him, grabbing him under the arms and pulling him out of the pink and red surface until his hush puppies resurfaced with a loud wop sound. They continued to hover around the cave interior until they both reached higher ground and dropped the Advertising Executive down onto a more solid base.

"She is definitely ovulating huh?" Yelled the first alien, slapping Ray on the back with a wink.

"Man, you still have to rectify the situation. He isn't supposed to be here - he's the wrong one!" Continued the second alien through gritted teeth until there was another sound. That of an audible cough, loud enough to shake the walls of the cavern. *"GENTLEMEN! What is happening here?"*

Yelled the voice suddenly. Both of the characters froze and hunched their shoulders as if expecting to be yelled at again.

Ray turned his attention to the sound of the coughing and was surprised to see a brown-suited figure looking slightly dapper cross-legged in a lotus position, levitating above the pink surface of the warm and moist cavern, dressed in a fifties style suit, white spotless Italian shirt and dark fedora hat. Mr. Bittre held a black cane in one red-gloved hand and used it to gesture at the three of them as the spotlight lit him perfectly, showing his pale face, with blood and mucus dripping continuously from his mouth. The spotlight turned to a crimson shade of red, just before it picked out the distinct shape of a fifties-style cartoon ACME Ray-gun held in the gloved hand of Mr. Bittre.

"Please feel free to be extremely worried if you are not already doing so Ray." He grinned at the German through broken teeth and dripping blood.

"Are you in charge?" Ray asked in his German accent.

"Yar! You could say that Ray! For the moment, we'll assume that you are still unaware where you are and that I have the Ray... gun so to speak. Ho Ho. Ho. Which you invented! The name's Bittre. Unfortunately, you are in the totally wrong place at an exceptionally wrong time. Then again, having employed the aliens from planet stupid, what would you expect?" He spat at the aliens.

Mr. Bittre laughed and stepped down onto the pink surface from nothing. He continued to point the gun at Ray, chuckling at the reversed joke.

"So Mr.Connif - firstly may I apologise for your abduction from Meissen at such short notice. There was a slight misunderstanding as to which Ray Connif you really were. Yet I'm sure you'll agree, the situation is not too far removed from what you would like to be doing with Liz, you just happen to be a little bit teeny-weeny to be of use to her at the moment and yet...of course, now I see! You dirty old man!" Mr. Bittre walked directly up to face Ray as he continued to point the space gun at him, he took out a handkerchief from his suit pocket and offered it to Ray for no apparent reason.

"You're the one!" He announced triumphantly. *"All that buoyancy with O.D. Darren and it was you all the time! Well we will have to rectify all that. Aliens! Get him back to the ship before he works it out and get that hippy bastard. QUICK!"* Spat Mr. Bittre again.

Ray winced as he felt blood and mucus splash across his face and glasses he took a step backwards to avoid the rancid breath of Mr. Bittre who was already walking off hurriedly down a tunnel off to the side of the cavern.

"We will meet again Mr. Ray Connif. Everybody meets me at some point, but it won't be today. If you get to meet Liz again - apologise from me personally about O.D. Darren, it gets lonely at the top you know? Tell her that O.D. Darren is on his return. Ciao!" Called Mr. Bittre over his shoulder.

Ray Connif suddenly found himself back in the white floating interior of the previous room alone and floating in zero gravity. With the mobile phone and a dark briefcase, which span past narrowly missing his head along with a copy of a book entitled G-WIZ - THE ADVERTISING CAMPAIGNS OF LIZ GOLDBERG. The cover pictured a silver can with worms pouring out of it. He reached out as the large book bobbed past his head just out of reach. As he floated in perfect isolation he noticed the control panels of the rebirth transporters below him and decided that tumbling in weightlessness of space meant the only way to take control of the situation was to swim.

After a few manoeuvres of the breaststroke he managed to gracefully travel towards the panel of flashing lights and dials and grabbed hold of the front panel. Then he pulled himself underneath and sat cross-legged with his head pushing against the surface. Just as the case and mobile phone crashed to the floor. Ray could feel his body return to a normal weight as the gravity returned and the cylindrical door opened. Looking upward from the floor he could see the legs and boots of a tall lady. Who seemed to be standing and waiting for him to come out from under the control point. Her left foot was tapping impatiently.

As Ray stood up slowly he found himself acknowledging the presence of his employee Britt from Big New Yorker. The shock nearly caused him to fall over.

"Britt! My God how did you get here?" Asked Ray.

"On this vessel. How do you think I got here?" She replied appearing slightly more aggressive than usual. The short black leather pants mixed with a white polo-neck and heavy eye-liner seemed to suggest this particular Britt clone had arrived at a more teenage phase of her life and decided it was time the world suffered for her torment.

"Oh yar, right!" Replied Ray slapping his forehead. He looked around the room and then back at her with a perplexed expression. *"Where is... here?"*

Britt sighed and stamped one of her boots on the ground. *"Oh not this again!"* She exclaimed and proceeded to pace up and down in front of him whilst pulling out a long cigarette filter and twisting a perfectly rolled cigarette into the end. *"Okay..."* She said reluctantly raising her eyes upwards as if she was about to explain how to boil an egg to a very stupid person indeed.

"Would you like a light?" Ray asked thankful to see someone he recognised at last.

"I'm fine thank you. I have some matches somewhere..." She patted her pockets on her jacket and finally found a book of matches that Ray noticed had the words The Diner Holistic printed on the cover in gold. Britt lit the cigarette.

"Okay Ray. You're probably asking yourself lots of boring questions like 'Whose in charge here' and 'Where am I' right? Well to cut to the chase, you're in a Zoa-pod." Said Britt tersely.

"A Vhat?" Asked Ray his accent slipping.

"Neine. Please shut it just for a moment Ray...I'm explaining." Britt adopted an expression of such cool boredom that a person could well have been tempted to hand over power for the entire planet to her just to attempt to cheer her up.

Mr. Bittre had just landed us on Earth where there is an excellent party that I am about to attend. I am still working at all your offices of Big New Yorker around the world due to the simple fact that I've been cloned. Even I don't know where the real me is, so don't get into that okay?"

She dragged hard on the cigarette and blew smoke into his face with a blank expression. She seemed lost suddenly. *"Right where was I? Damn this time travelling. My memory is completely fucked!"* She exclaimed stubbing the cigarette out on the floor of the Zoa-Pod and letting it hiss.

"The party?" Asked Ray expectantly.

"Right! Yarhvol! The party! Mr. Bittre my employee has just abducted someone from the party and he is impersonating you. With the intention of locating some

of the other Probe-clones like myself in an attempt to take over the world. You will now be working for Mr. Bittre in space for the meantime." She finally smiled.

"For any particular reason? I'm an Advertising Executive not an astronaught!" Exclaimed Ray.

"Which is why you are here my little bean-bag!" Cooed Britt patting him on the head. *"We need your genius brain for helping us with our plan for Armageddon. Your in charge of the marketing department!"* Britt walked over and turned to the elliptical door and patted one of her thighs with a loud slap as if she was calling a dog. She clenched the cigarette holder between her perfect white teeth.

"Come on boy! I'll show you the new offices. We're going to need some sunglasses for the troops and you've already invented them...they're called Ray-Bans!"

Procta and Gambul cowered in the corner and then breathed a sigh of relief as they watched the two Germans leave.

"I told you it was the wrong one! You never listen!" Announced a voice close to Ray as he slowly followed Britt out of the dark red light of the tall cave he had been transported to.

MONDAY 10TH SEPTEMBER 2001
NIGHT // NEWTOWN

ANOTHER GREEN WORLD

Hear my whisper when I tell you I'm your sister
Fly me first class over to your pad Hear me now I'm an alien lover
LUSCIOUS JACKSON

THE DEEP BACK garden of the large manor house seemed to stretch far off into the infinite away from the Victorian building into the still deep endless dark of the night. Static, Gyro and Laurie Anderson had stepped outside for some air following the intense discussion in the dining room from the Physicists. As all three walked out of the back entrance and onto the garden path they noticed the number of cars that seemed to be arriving at the front of the house.

"Do you live here?" Asked Laurie Anderson walking arm in arm between Static and Gyro.

"No." Replied Static. "I live about half an hour away by car in a place called Carisbrooke, in the town of Newport..." Static said in his broad country accent as all three of them strolled along the path of the garden.

"... the capital!" Finished Gyro laughing.

"That's right. The Las Vegas of the island!" Returned his friend smiling. "It's hardly the likes of New York but I like it. I was born here but I've never travelled the lengths of the planet as much as Gyro. He's been to New York loads..."

"Strange that we never met before, you all being artists..." Said Laurie.

"Well that's where you might be surprised." Continued Gyro. "I saw you once in Manhattan when I was waiting outside a cinema to see Terminator II and you walked passed, but I couldn't think of anything to say I was so surprised at seeing you...in real life."

"No way!" Replied the performance artist.

"Yes way!" Answered Gyro.

"Is Manhattan that big? I mean the Isle of Wight is about thirty miles by sixty and I read that Manhattan was only a small island in comparison." Enquired Static as they walked past groups of smartly dressed people sitting at tables on the lawn, drinking and laughing in the cool night air.

"Well it's compact. There's a lot of tall skyscrapers. Things are more up than spread out." The American turned to Gyro as they continued to stroll. *"Were you living there...in New York?"* Asked Laurie.

"Oh yes." Sighed Gyro with a misty look in his eyes. *"I fell madly in love with a young lady from Gettisburg called Sara. We lived in Brooklyn for a short time."* He said.

"It didn't work out?" Asked the American.

"Does it ever?" He sighed again, then suddenly stopped on the path and nodded over to where a group of people were sitting and chatting under a fruit tree. *"Laurie there's someone I would love you to meet..."* Said Gyro.

"Yeah... you must meet this guy. He's a legend on the island." Agreed Static.

The small group walked off the path and headed towards a large twisted tree at the centre of the garden where the figure of a strongly built man could be seen sitting calmly cross-legged in discussion with several monks dressed in bright orange robes. Static recognised the warm face of the Dalai Lamma and the long bearded features of Charles Darwin, sitting cross-legged with him and laughing. As they all walked over towards the group, the clear night sky shined down countless stars displayed over Newtown. The light from the Moon was enough for the small congregation to show were listening intently to what the man had been saying. Laurie was reminded of the Red Indians of North America by the appearance of Tony Webb, the host of the party sitting under the tree. They stood politely as he immediately stood up from the discussion slowly and acknowledged their presence-shaking Gyro warmly by the hand.

"Ahh. Monsieur Scope! Pleasure as always and Mr. Static and...I don't believe I've had the pleasure but I am well aware of your work Ms. Anderson. Are you having a good time?" Asked the legendary host.

"It's been incredible...sorry I don't know your name?" Said Laurie shaking his hand. Gyro introduced her.

"Laurie Anderson...meet Tony. This is his house. He's a good friend of O.D. Darren." Announced Static.

"Oh...right. What can I say? It's a fantastic party!" Replied Laurie.

"Many thanks m'aam." Said Tony suddenly. "Where are my manners? This is Charles Darwin and er... Mr. Gyatso."

The group sat down cross-legged forming a circle on the grass and greeted each other. The sounds of the music from the party were drifting over to the gathering under the tree.

"So how are you enjoying England?" Asked the Dalai Lamma adjusting his robes.

"It's wild. I've become fascinated by the music." Answered Laurie.

"Yes indeed. Music is the food of love." Replied the smiling monk.

"I'm a big fan of rock and roll myself." Said Charles Darwin. "It's evolved from the blues in the South of America I believe. Have you heard that kind of music? It's great for dancing to!"

The American sat down on the grass next to them. "Well I make music but it's not like rock and roll. I love that music but I mix classical styles with observations about life. I tell stories." Said Laurie.

"Oh I have a friend who does that called Lewis. I think he's in the kitchen. You must meet him. He has some fabulous stories. One about a girl called Alice." Beamed Charles happily.

"Not that again please!" Said Tony laughing. "It's great but it goes on a bit. He wrote it after he arrived on the island and went out harvesting mushrooms with Tennyson and Byron. Man what a night that was or still is!" He said winking and laughing to everyone.

Britt appeared again and walked towards the group holding a mobile phone in one hand and a bottle of unopened Oxford Landing in the other. She zigzagged past all the bodies scattered across the lawn and made a beeline for Static slightly drunk as she walked over to the tree. Britt sat down and held a blue mobile out towards him.

"Guess what? Someone wants to talk to you about your movie script. They say they're at the party but I'd be buggered if I could find them amongst all these people. They keep saying they've text you already...one hundred times."

Static felt slightly foolish and quickly took the phone from Britt.

"...You left it in the first floor bathroom." Said Britt.

"What? Gosh, thanks!" Replied Static looking at the mobile. A text message said simply GREETINGS. WE ARE COMING. DO NOT BE ALARMED. He looked back up at Britt bewildered. Then the phone vibrated in his hand. At first he dropped it with surprise onto the grass and then quickly picked it up again walking away from the tree and the small group who were gathered beneath it.

"Hello?" He asked walking off down the garden and attempting to find a place where someone was not standing or talking in order to hear the mystery voice clearer on the other end.

"Hello? Yes? I'm Static. Yes I read the text message... I just got it from Britt." He replied into the phone.

As Static entered further into the foliage at the end of the vast garden towards the hedges and trees that ran around the edge of the vast garden as the phone signal became stronger until he could hear the distinct sound of two voices on the other end singing.

"No, it's my turn to use it...Static? At last we meet." Sang the first alien.

"Hello yes? Who am I speaking to?" Asked Static politely.

"I can't read that! What does it say? 'Look up towards the Moon...ya buugger!' I don't get it." Said one of the voices arguing.

"What?" He asked. Static was certain now that the voice was singing.

"Look up towards the Moon...in the skyyy. Wee'reee herrreeee! Coooeeee!" Yelled the voice.

Static turned his head in the direction of the Moon and squinted up into the darkness. In the sky all the bright shining stars were displaying their usual alignments and giving the appearance of pinholes in a huge dark sheet of black foolscap. Static almost dropped the mobile in shock as he blinked hard and watched one of the stars suddenly move and separate themselves from what he had thought before was only the three-jewelled belt of Orion. The star was moving at incredible speed and zigzagging across to the Moon where it began to grow in size heading towards him. Within a split second it was growing to match the size of the Moon. The definite shape of a circular vessel was now heading directly for him. Static backed away stumbling towards the bushes, snapping the small branches of the foliage. Then he fell to the ground and sat still in shock and as mere seconds passed Static stared dumbly at a huge white Zoa-pod hovering and glowing above the field next to the garden. The colour of the vehicle began to change and camouflage itself with the surrounding area to a shade of green Pantone 361 CVC. The glow emitting from the craft filled the entire surroundings of the field and Static looked up and found himself staring at a tall German man in a suit who was stroking his tie and standing next to him at the edge of the field.

As Static looked up at the windows of the craft he could see the shape of two aliens smiling and waving back at him through the tiny round windows.

"Gutten Tag Herron Static! You are Static aren't you? At last we meet." Said the tall German helping him to his feet.

"Yeah..." Said Static dumbfounded by the sudden arrival.

"Sere shun! I'm sorry to interrupt the party but I wanted you to meet some aliens. They want to talk to you about the script you sent me. I'm Ray Connif of Big New Yorker." Said Mr. Bittre offering a gloved hand to shake.

He extended a large warm hand and shook the hand of Static. Slowly and eerily, the bottom of the craft began to open as the outside tones of the hull were already changing in appearance as he walked with Ray to the entrance of a warm shade of Pantone 032 CVC red that enveloped the outer shell. Static felt himself being steered towards the thin elliptical opening. Soft music emitted from the warm interior.

"By the way, the mobiles don't work very well where you're meeting will be held." Warned the suited figure walking back away from him as the craft began to rise. *"Don't worry we'll get you back to Earth in time. I've got to go and meet some people at the party and talk about something that's happening in America tomorrow. Don't worry if they seem a bit strange. They're big fans. They have a deal lined up about your next film as well. Something about disciples! I'll tell Gyro you'll see him later."* Called Mr. Bittre after the vessel.

As the hatch began to close with Static inside, he looked back out at Ray Connif standing in the field in his suit and turned to see the aliens, one of whom was still holding a mobile in his hand sitting around a ball of electric coloured petrol-blue in the centre of the interior. The alien came flapping over to him enthusiastically. Looking up at the stunned face of Static who could see the first alien operating some controls at the front. Suddenly the transient tones of beautiful music echoed out from all over the vessel.

"We looooove your scriiipt daaaarling, eeets faaaabuuuulus!" Said the other alien as he shook his hand.

"Do you like music? We're big fans of it. Especially The Pixies." Said the first alien as Static peered through one of the cabin windows and saw the garden fading smaller into the vast reaches of space as the Hammond organ of Klaus Wunderlick blasted out from the interior.

The deep back garden of the large manor house seemed to stretch far off into the infinite away from the Victorian building into the still deep endless dark of the night

TUESDAY 11TH SEPTEMBER
2001 NIGHT / BRIXTON

TROMPE LE MONDE

Bands, those funny little plans that never work quite right
MERCURY REV

CLAMB-ON-BASS was back-stage in the dressing-room of The Brixton Academy searching for his lucky plectrum amongst the collection of coats, magazines, cases, bottles and flowers that were piled onto the table in front of a large mirror, decorated by red light-bulbs mounted around the frame of the mirror, in the dressing room. Something was about to fall apart and Clamb-on-bass had a terrible feeling that if it was Luke or Paul, they were doing an admirable job of keeping it quiet. Tensions were frayed tonight and as the various members of the band were crammed into the small back-room, the usually placid bass-player tore the room apart trying to find the plectrum. He could hear the rain pouring down outside.

The Manageress of the band knocked on the door urgently. The lights over the stage had lost electrical power for the last hour and she had just fired two American roadies, who for some reason had chosen tonight of all nights to call in sick. Tonight had been the last night of a gruelling American and European tour, which had lasted three months. In the United States, the Hackney based trio were riding a successful wave of controversy over their latest album Jonathan Tower Block which had stunned everyone in the band by turning triple platinum. They still had no understanding as to why this had happened.

The mix of jazz and ear-splitting beats had been arranged by the lead-singer Luke, a forceful cool figure permanently dressed in 1969 into a hugely commercial single called *'Love In My Kitchen'* which had been recorded as a one-off joke. Somehow, Luke was still asking anyone he met now, the song had been used in an advertisement for the new English Mini and had grown into cult status, a mere four weeks after the release onto the airwaves. The joke had backfired massively as the results developed into a recording and publishing contract that each member of the band had signed instantly without reading any of the small print.

Paul the drummer had cursed that day for three solid months of touring. He hated the music business with a passion that had been only matched by his hatred for the hit single, which he could now hear on the television permanently switched on in the dressing room. In unison the group all turned their attention to their manager as she stormed into the claustrophobic room.

"Hi guys...I hope your ready for some bad news...water has leaked in through the roof of The Academy and flooded the stage. There isn't time to mop all of it up, so try not to let any of the leads to the amps drag on the floor. Okay Clamb?" She forced the point by placing her hands on her hips.

The bass-player absent-mindedly nodded as he continued his plectrum search.

"Luke, you have to start with Love In My Kitchen tonight okay? Not like Amsterdam again. The representatives of A & R are out there tonight and they've mentioned that any Tomfoolery will result in a serious revival of the contract. Oh and the plane that flew into the World Trade Centre has forced a major setback as half the country has decided to hold all flights throughout the rest of Europe. So we've had to cancel the last week of the tour. Bad luck guys."

Luke stared daggers of hate back at the manager. He hated being told what to do by anyone. Especially this strange woman who had appeared in America and refused to leave him to his artistic endeavours. The pressure to follow-up the success of Love In My Kitchen had resulted in a serious addiction of hash, which had been his only salvation throughout the remains of the tour.

Paul the drummer was still pining for his family after hearing the news that they had all moved to the States after he had returned to London, with no numbers or addresses. Their support was usually all he needed to get through the day and now he was joining Luke in a slow demise of health through drugs. The music was suffering as a result. The last five concerts had forced their old manager to quit after Luke had walked on stage in New York and announced that he was sick of American food and burnt an American flag live on stage in front of a shocked audience. The concert was being aired on prime time television and Clamb-on-bass and Paul had reprimanded him afterwards backstage simply for the fact that their parents were watching the show.

They had all flown back to London with serious debts, somewhere in excess of two hundred thousand pounds. An unstoppable urge to murder their record company A & R men had developed in Paul due to the unseen details which explained they must record an album to pay off the debts, once the last concert had been played. Luke checked the papers at the airport and discovered that now they were being slagged-off so badly for selling out, the last concert had sold only a quarter of the previous ticket sales. He was beginning to see the flag-burning incident as a ludicrous career move. Unsure of what to do next, Inchworm had court orders up to their neck regarding an incident on the returning plane which had been down to a journalist claiming that Clamb-on-bass had attacked her unprovoked during the flight. Of course, the Media had sided with her due to the size of the personal fortune of Clamb and possibly his name but mostly due to the amount of albums the band had shifted.

Luke shivered to himself as he recalled the name of Criminal Sunshine and how this particular lady had pressed charges on all three members of the band. He had never even seen the woman. So, their incentives to play a set, which the audience would find offensive, had become their only hope to be fired from their label. Luke and Paul had argued consistently through the tour from America and the bass-player had now lost his lucky plectrum. They had five minutes to find it. Patience was wearing mighty thin.

"Clamb-baby, use one of mine in the case...we don't have time for this!" Exclaimed the singer strapping on his guitar.

"I can't, Valentina gave me this one...it's lucky!" He replied.

"LUCKY?" Luke had lost it now. *"How is it lucky? You've had it all through the tour and up until the manager telling us the fuckin' stage is flooded, I would have blamed everything going wrong on that bloody plectrum. Stop, look and listen Clamb. Since you have lost the plectrum, nothing bad has happened!"* Exclaimed Luke grabbing his guitar.

"It's important Luke. If it was you who'd lost it, we'd have to call the cops!" Answered back the bass player.

"Yeah right! Like you did in Ohio and Kentucky you mean?" Luke had lost his trousers and refused to go on stage until they were handed over. Missing

one of the better concerts of Inchworm as Paul and Clamb had played an acoustic set without him.

Fortunately, Clamb found the plectrum with three minutes before the curtains went up. It had been tucked into his right ear, although why or how, was beyond understanding with anyone in the band.

"Thank Christ!" Yelled Paul, as they filed out of the dressing room and headed to the stage of The Brixton Academy, all set to play the worst concert of their young lives.

The second that Paul stepped out onto the stage towards the drum-kit, Clamb-on-Bass dropped the lucky plectrum and watched in horror as it fell down between the floorboards of the stage. He held onto his bass guitar, bent down to try and pick it out of the crack in the board, caught it between his fingers and miraculously pulled it out. As he stood up, the neck of the bass went directly in between the legs of the drummer, banging him painfully in a very private place and lifting him up. Paul lost his balance due to the unexpectedness of the blow and turned crashing into the drum-kit. The lead of the guitar trailing to the amplifier wrapped around one of the ankles of the singer and as Paul tumble back over the drums and cymbals crashing all around him, he landed face first in the water which leaked down from the huge dark domed ceiling. The electric current passed directly onto Clamb, who flipped like a ballerina and was thrown back across the stage in shock, still holding his bass. The force of the jolt threw him at least twenty feet in the air and the audience gasped as they watched him land directly on his head with the solid wood backing of the guitar. The sound of Luke breaking his neck sounded out across the front rows of The Academy as Luke and the already dead body of Clamb fell down into the orchestra-pit, Luke was holding as they both landed in the dark ten feet below the stage, dying instantly.

The whole incident took no more than three minutes and a ghastly hush fell over the audience as security men ran quickly onto the stage and the fire curtain dropped with a thud. The A & R men from the record label all raised their eyes to the heavens and shook their heads in unison then left the building.

Inchworm had performed their final gig and as the music industry shifted gears into quickly re-packaging there farewell tour CD's and videos, a young German lady sitting at the front of the audience, decided that

The Diner Holistic would benefit greatly from one the most unique live performances she had ever seen on the planet.

Britt loved jazz. She had followed the band from America but had more recently enjoyed herself immensely following them from the dressing-room where she had been hiding the small triangular piece of clear plastic when Clamb-on-bass was back-stage in the dressing-room searching for his lucky plectrum amongst the collection of coats, magazines, cases, bottles and flowers that were piled onto the table in front of a large mirror, decorated by red light-bulbs mounted around the frame of the mirror, of the dressing room.

FRIDAY 7TH SEPTEMBER 2002
EVENING / AMSTERDAM

OUT OF MY MIND ON DOPE AND SPEED

You can buy a dream or two
To last you all of the day
RICKY NELSON

SITTING INDOORS ON a red metal chair with his legs crossed, reflected in the window of The Greenhouse Effect sat Gyro Scope. One of only 752 passengers from the cosmically tainted Flight 851Y. As he sat blended into the light orange coffee shop interior, feeling worse than a hangover brought on by drinking with Jeffrey Bernard, Oliver Reed and Jack Kerouac for fifteen consecutive years without a break, he looked out at the grey morning of Amsterdam and sighed. He had just purchased some of the strangest hashish he had ever seen. Black and squishy.

Even the name had already escaped his memory along with two of the longest years of thirty-four spent on planet Earth. He had arrived at Schiphol Airport a mere one hour before and although nobody in the cafe noticed anything particularly odd about his appearance at the window, they might have been surprised by the discovery that they were sitting nearby to one of the only humans on the planet Earth who had experienced time-travel and had been still alive to talk about it. Except talking in a coffee shop in Amsterdam was indeed a rare experience. People did not say a lot here. They tended to stare into the distant reaches of time and space which Gyro had just been dragged through and almost never spoke. This was useful because the experience of time-travel had left him with one thought on his mind. To head for a coffee shop and get ripped off his gizzard as quickly as possible.

Gyro took one of the King-Size skins from the tray in the centre of the table and broke a Marlboro Light cigarette into the lining. Looking at the black squidgy lump in the cellophane sealed packet, he pondered on how he was to roll this into the doobie and smoke it. Hopefully halting all signs of jet lag buzz in the process.

"*Roll it on the table...like plasticine!*" A soft German sounding voice announced. Gyro looked up through dark sunglasses and eyes of stone to see a surprisingly tall, slim woman sitting on a stool next to the table. She seemed to be wrapped in a variety of different layers and brightly dyed garments. Although he had never been to any Latin American countries on his travels, well, not that he could remember, he had however seen pictures and the way this lady was dressed immediately reminded him of words such as Cuba and Peru. The orange woollen scarf wrapped tightly around her head suggested that whatever this heavenly creature did for a living, a large part of her day was spent getting ready for it. He suddenly became conscious of seeing her somewhere before.

"*I beg your pardon?*" He asked as politely as possible.

"*Like plasticine or clay you know? May I show you?*" Continued the German.

He watched fascinated as Britt pulled up a chair, sat down and then proceeded to take the lump and roll it on the table surface with an open palm until she had changed the shape of the hash to a long thin strip, which now reminded Gyro of a fuse. She then placed part of this into the joint and completed what he had half begun. Licking the glued edge she passed Gyro the most perfectly executed spliff he had ever seen. He lit it and exhaled the smoke off to one side.

"*Pleased to make your acquaintance. The name's Britt.*" Said Britt in an accent that seemed to be a mix of maple syrup and figs heated gently in a golden saucepan on a steady flame.

"*Gyro Scope. Have we met before?*" He asked.

"*I get asked that a lot. Are you English? You're accent sounds slightly Australian..*" Asked Britt flatly.

Gyro found himself having to concentrate in order to reply. "*Er..yes...I mean, I'm from the Isle of Wight. It's a small island off the...*" He began.

"*Southern part of England, near Southampton. Across from the Solent. Yes?*" She continued.

"Wow! You know your geography. I know people in Southampton who have no idea where it is." He offered her the joint and idly noticed how none of the usual fireworks of exploding hash jumped out of the end. *"Mind you, I also know some people on the Isle of Wight who don't know where the Isle of Wight is."*

"Danka." Said Britt.

"Bitter schune." Replied Gyro.

"Oh, you speak German?" Asked Britt curiously, joining him at the table.

"Not really. I lived in Berlin for a year, but I can never get an angle on the language. I think it's beautiful though. Berlin is the coolest city on Earth." He answered politely.

"Have you ever been to London? I think it has its moments."

"Oh yes, most of my life has been attempts to escape the place. I'm not a big fan, really." He said, feeling his feet growing too large for his shoes.

"No, you're a human being!" She turned smiling and elegantly pointed at one of the fans dropping down from the ceiling. *"That's a fan!"*

Gyro found laughter suddenly bursting from his mouth, as he received the joint back from what he could only describe as the most curious woman he had ever met. Not a hint of sexuality came from any part of her and yet she looked as if she had stepped off the cover of VOGUE magazine after having first art directed every page within.

"Have you been to Australia?" She asked calmly.

Gyro felt a strong urge to smoke come over him whenever people asked him that particular question.

"I've been living out there for about two years." He replied casually.

"How did you manage that? I thought European citizens could only stay there for six months?"

"Marriage." He answered with the knowledge of someone who knew too well what was coming next.

Almost immediately, the dark eyebrows rose up to the hem of her makeshift turban and her face seemed to glow slightly. *"Mmm, marriage... is your marriage here? I mean is your wife here?"* Asked Britt as she chuckled softly.

"I fucking hope not." Gyro grimaced.

"Oh dear. Did it not work out?" Asked the German.

"Oh no, it was great if you enjoy being married to a deeply disturbed and unfaithful smack head."

Whether it was the tone of his voice that suggested the conversation could do with a change of direction or Britt was a natural psychic Gyro could not easily tell. Suddenly the woman placed a pack of cards on the table.

"Have you ever had your fortune told?" Her stunning face took on the appearance of wild excitement.

"Many times. It's never been accurate though, unless you count the time when a fortune teller told me I would be hungry one day." He sounded more than a little cynical on the subject. *"You're more than welcome to convince me otherwise..."*

"Well, you pick out five cards and if I'm wrong about your future, you can tell me the next time we meet." Said Britt.

"Okay. Where do you come from?" Asked Gyro politely, extinguishing the joint and becoming more hypnotised by the nano second.

"The Diner Holistic, of course." Replied Britt calmly dealing out the cards. *"You seem to be pondering on how you came to be in such a place as Amsterdam. But really, you have to be honest to yourself and ask where it was you wanted to be in the first instance. Choose five cards."*

As the cards were chosen, Britt shuffled the pack and slipped it back inside her shawl. She then placed a hand gently onto his as it rested on the surface of the table. The sound of jazz drifted from the jukebox of the cafe and Gyro nodded at the familiarity of the tune. He found himself wondering about the journey on the plane.

"Have you ever met a complete stranger and felt as if you have met them before and then wondered what it was you supposed to say or even do?" She asked.

"Yes. That's how I met my wife, I mean my ex-wife." He replied. *"She asked me to marry her."*

"There are many circles in life you know. People often think that as they walk down streets and through fields that everything they see and everyone they meet are on the outside but really, where is that? If you ever have a dream where you are floating over seas and running down cliff faces and mountains, where are you? I mean, you could be dreaming and then wake up and then fall asleep but never leave one room in your house. Yet you would experience just as much as when you work and earn money and then go to the airport with a ticket you purchased yourself.

Tickets and money are only made of paper and aeroplanes are only made from metal and glass...isn't it strange how you can be born on a planet you have never been to before and yet so much of it is familiar? Remembering where everything is kept all the time is so difficult. Where are my keys? Where are my children? Where are the buildings? Is that mountain supposed to be there?

Take a journey that a person makes through their life as an example. You leave your house and you have so much to worry about. Yet what are you looking for to leave the house in the first place. A job? Food? A wife? A husband? Surely if you were to find those things you would continue looking for something else? Maybe you are inspired and need to travel. Maybe you have to look for answers physically but have you noticed how all that you see in the day disappears at night and then when you are dreaming...well, it's so difficult to remember anything about your life isn't it? Even, where you are. Journeys through time. We return to the past physically and move onto the future physically. Yet we can do all this without moving...even without breathing. Even without living. Yet if we get lost or scared or find danger we simply come back and have to do it all again. School is fascinating. You move up a level once you get all the answers right but you move to a lower level if you find it all too difficult.."

"Or there's a teacher who makes a mistake."

"There might be a huge mistake on it's way already. Are you happier knowing about it before it comes or after you see it happen?" She finished the joint and stared out at the grey overcast weather.

"You might as well ask is the movie any good before you see it." Said Gyro amazed to meet someone in Amsterdam who spoke English so well. He was reminded of Berlin.

"I do that all the time." Said Britt in her best bored voice.

"Why?" He asked.

"Safety. My time is precious and I don't want to waste it. I don't like people wasting my time." Replied Britt tersely.

"What else are you going to do with it?" Gyro asked sitting indoors on a red metal chair with his legs crossed, reflected in the window of The Greenhouse Effect.

BOOK VI
TWILGHT / PROBABILITY

MAX BORN 1882 / 1970
RECEIVED THE NOBEL PEACE PRIZE AGED 72

Max Born was born in Breslau on the 11th December, 1882, to Professor Gustav Born, anatomist and embryologist, and his wife Margarete, née Kauffmann, who was a member of a Silesian family of industrialists. Max was awarded the Prize of the Philosophical Faculty of the University of Göttingen for his work on the stability of elastic wires and tapes in 1906, and graduated at this university a year later on the basis of this work.

An appointment as professor to assist Max Planck at Berlin University came to Born in 1915 but he had to join the German Armed Forces.

> *If God has made the world a perfect mechanism*
> *He has at least conceded so much to our*
> *imperfect intellect that in order to predict*
> *little parts of it, we need not solve innumerable*
> *differential equations but can use*
> *dice with fair success*

QUOTED IN H. R. PAGELS, THE COSMIC CODE

During the years 1925 and 1926 he published, with Heisenberg and Jordan, investigations on the principles of quantum mechanics (matrix mechanics). The year 1913 saw his marriage to Hedwig, née Ehrenberg, and there are three children from this marriage. From Nobel Lectures, Physics 1942-1962. Max Born died in 1970.

He won the Nobel Prize in Physics in 1954 and was the Grandfather of the New Zealand singer Olivia Newton-John who starred with John Travolta in the movie Grease.

ARRIVALS

Stetson BP was an ugly wall of bourbon fat and anger that loved oil. On business class flights, he drank heavily from the backs of air stewardesses and pondered on slamming his gargantuan dick. A dinosaur reborn over and over until he evolved, his wings became thick arms of flesh and his tail of spikes hooked up between his fat scaly thighs. In the toilet of the private leer-jet, he mounted a young Philipino maiden from behind and as he slowly slid his spiky tail into her, he lazily chewed on the girl's long-flowing hair.

Outside the toilet door of muffled shrieks of reptile lust lurked Criminal Sunshine of journalistic quadrant rage HASSLE. Reporting chips of salacious vomit and mucus for all its weekly readers. Criminal tuned her radar in towards the direction of beyond the bathroom cubicle door, sounds of lizard porno pumping and salivated. She thought of her readers dribbling over the shocking news, as they discovered oil tycoon BP bumpy-wumpy whacked-out on all manner of pharmaceuticals en route to a senate hearing.

Yet more juice would spill once she revealed the proud husband and Father of two, was now handing over half internal affairs of his oil corporation to his new business partner and publicity associate Ms Sunshine. The young nubile unqualified sky-waitress's Mother to be.

Smiling sweetly to herself like a fox eating shit out of brace and metal, she noted number of lizard grunts and teenage gasps, along with sounds of plimsolls kicking that were now beating against the door in a steady rhythm, before quickly returning her tray to it's upright position and dribbling all over seat.

"More dinky drinks!" Screamed two detectives at the back of winged sailor, mission for drunken fumbling of the lost wings of Icarus were calling the two Joes. D1 had flown once for a bet in a helicopter of black machine-gun for bubblegum. This being second shot at above the skylark and he hated every turbulent second, vomit chuck a sicky on suited lap bag. He awaited inevitable return of lunch. D2 was an ex-army barmy nut beer-barrel whose hatred of people outweighed his admiration feline-style of winged steel and bolt.

Hats of feder stapled to heads of pinhead Zippy, couple held mirth as dinky drinks arrived from tall dark sky-waitresses amidst squeals issuing from the in-flight dunnie. A case of chase and missing pianos sniffed their wigs of Lego hair and ties of black shoelace.

Pouring down through cables electric, crooned baritone mid-fifties and into headsets of in-flight terminal cack. Older women mid-way of girth gave freely on laps of reporters and politicians. A steel air capsule of free and four love roaring through upper Ritz of California head spaceo magnifico. Pumping for the Senate.

Cheering on a chokie as BP grunted thrusting into maiden nubile held down tight and taught in toilet private with much squealing as gush of oil from Jurassic loin struck pay dirt quim within Philipino ghetto. Jiz of spurt on pantie-fantie up back and down in front as chromo of dino hit bingo. *"Sorry about the turbulence,"* cried out Captain, *"but we're all smacked-up back here!"*

Zipped-up and pants up, bronto-burger weight of bulk that was BP, continued munching on teenage scalp back kicked toilet door open, leaving his prey, dazed and confused in sink. Reversing out from cabin WC, Stetson BP lolloped back to class of numero uno upgrades and chewed on rocket surveying next potential surrogate tycoon junior carrier.

FRIDAY 7TH SEPTEMBER 2001
NIGHT / THE EAST END

THINKING ABOUT SEX AGAIN

I don't care about the way you look
You should know I'm not impressed
There's just one thing I'm looking for and he don't wear a dress
ANNIE LENNOX / DAVID STEWART

AFTER ARRIVING AT Bethnal Green O.D. Darren caught a taxi with some of the money in the case Liz had given him. He had no idea how much had been in the case but he estimated that it was somewhere near three or four hundred thousand pounds. He had to go to a bank and check the joint account set up and had been stunned by the zeros on his electronic balance. There were at least seven. Documents in the container explained that there were over twelve separate accounts each in a different country. The figures in his head were somewhere in the region of a few billion. When he arrived at the pub in Hackney O.D. Darren had never been in such a need of a drink in his life. He felt as if he had experienced a ten-year life span compressed into a twenty-four hour period. He sat at the bar and ordered a pint of London Pride, watching as the barman pulled the handle of the pump back and the dark ale flowed steadily into the glass.

"Busy day today then sir?" Asked the barman. "You were in here last night weren't you?"

O.D. Darren nodded and patted the bag of ecstasy tablets in his combat trouser pocket for reassurance. He looked up at the clock behind the bar and checked the time with the barman, who turned and looked at his watch. He nodded.

"Yep. It's a bit fast, but only by a few minutes. It's ten to nine. Liz usually gets here at about nine. Are you expecting her?" The hippy nodded in the affirmative.

"Well, I'm sure she'll be here soon enough. That'll be three pounds for the ale." O.D. Darren winced at the price. For the life of him, he could never understand why prices of anything increased the closer you got to London. Coffee, tobacco, even drugs and rent all seemed to increase dramatically once you entered London. As if some magic border of expense went up around the city. Yet the quality never improved anywhere else in England. If anything, it was always worse. He had enough of the place really. The thinking behind pricing a sandwich at two pounds alone, when bread cost around eighty pence a loaf, was revealing to him now just how stupid the idea of coming to London in the first place had been. Even New York must be cheaper than this he thought.

The pint of beer was placed on the bar in front of him and for the first time in his life, O.D. Darren realised what a million advertisements revealed about a product. O.D. Darren stared in disbelief. It seemed almost alive. The way the froth showed off the colour of the beer, but also the way the entire pub surroundings seemed to be held in the reflection of the dark ale. He closed his eyes briefly and opened them again, muttered a short prayer and then began to taste the ale. He turned to see Liz sit next to him at the bar and outside realised as the policeman had said on the Bakerloo Line, he was indeed a lucky man. He turned to face her and suddenly realised that he had been thinking about her all day.

"You're never going to believe what happened to me today!" They looked at each other and laughed after having said the same sentence to each other. Then laughed as the action was repeated. *"What?"*

The barman automatically pulled another pint for Liz and smiled. O.D. Darren stood up from the bar and offered Liz his hand D Van D style. *"Would you care to adjourn to the garden?"* He asked.

In the beer garden, the sun was setting over the rooftops of Hackney. The air was surprisingly warm for May in London and Liz was reminded of the beauty that was hidden all over this city, you had to search. Most cities she had visited across Europe seemed to make a habit of displaying the beauty to the tourists, but what Liz loved about London and especially Hackney, was the little pockets of natural plant life that she would discover throughout this part of the capital. Hidden treasures.

The garden of this East End pub was unlike any she had come across anywhere in the country. When O.D. Darren walked out of the pub holding his pint glass, he nearly dropped it. He had the feeling that he had just walked into the countryside and rediscovered what he liked most about going out with women, they always seemed to surprise him. They sat down at a table next to a concrete fountain of a man in a uniform, which O.D. Darren felt held a slightly uncanny similarity to Adolf Hitler. The statue forced him to make the observation a little louder to Liz.

"I'm not sure, if it's me Liz, but does that statue look like Hitler?" He asked, placing her beer on the table for her.

"Well, luckily I've never met him, so I don't know, but if you read the plaque at his feet, you might find a fine clue!"

The answer surprised O.D. Darren and he put his beer down on a beer mat on the table and stepped over to the plaque, which had been cast in bronze. Set into the surface were the words.

THE BIGGER THE LIE
THE MORE PEOPLE WILL BELIEVE IT

He came back to the table smiling. Liz had obviously visited this part of the pub before and seemed to get a great deal of fun from taking people into the garden and showing them this little piece of history.

"Why did you say 'luckily'?" Asked O.D. Darren. *"When you mentioned it before?"*

"Well, I should tell you that I'm Jewish and obviously, the subject of the old Charlie Chaplin look-alike there, is a strong link with my own investigative ness in life."

"Oh right, Goldberg is a Jewish name!" Replied the hippy a little slow on the uptake.

"Bingo!" Yelled out Liz.

"Has it always been here?" He asked.

"I guess so. It looks pretty old. I thought it must have been there since World War II." Replied Liz as she sipped on her beer. *"When I first came here, about five years ago, I was going out with a Jewish bloke and he arranged to meet here. I thought he had decided to do my head in a bit, you know, like*

going to see *The Sorrow And The Pity* on a date. He swore that he was just as surprised as I was."

"I can imagine..." Said O.D. Darren.

"I met a historian through an advert I was working on and I asked him to come and have a look at it one evening and he stated that it had to be over fifty years old at least. He knew quite a bit about them."

"Them?" Asked O.D. Darren with surprise, drinking from his pint.

"This historian reckoned that there were over one thousand of them made in Germany and shipped over to England, and placed throughout Europe in the late nineteen thirties. In Hackney, there's about ten of them scattered throughout the borough, in different places. I've only seen three."

"Are you serious?" O.D. Darren could hardly believe that he had missed statues of the biggest sworn enemy of England scattered over Hackney after living here for five years. He now understood how much of this wonderland he had actually seen.

"Where have you been O.D. Darren? It sounds like you walk around with your eyes shut. Don't you like to investigate your environment at all?" Asked Liz, crossing her legs.

"Well, I've been investigating, I've just been doing it in other countries..." Replied the hippy.

"Such as?" She prodded.

"Tibet..." Answered the hippy.

Suddenly Liz sat up straight. "Tibet? Wow... I've just been reading about that place, it's fascinating. How long were you there?"

O.D. Darren was stunned, he had never gotten to the point of explaining any of his journey to anyone. Liz had been the first person in Hackney that had listened to anything he had said and after the day he had just experienced, he was unsure if this was a good or a bad situation. He became agitated thinking of the older Madam in Shepherds Bush.

"I stayed there for about two years. I had been always fascinated by the Governmental powers of the world really after reading about Bill Lazar. He was a lecturer from California, who had been presenting lectures on the subject of World War III and the countdown to 2011. A deeply fascinating lecture he gave seemed to paint a picture of mass destruction coming and nothing really was going to survive past 2011. So the only option left open to survive seemed be death."

"You're kidding?" Now it was the turn of Liz to feign disbelief.

"Well, if I'd had a girlfriend five years ago, I might have been saved. Instead I was reading and researching anything I could get my hands on, an old habit from school. I began to get all sorts of information about all manner of things, but one of the key points that kept coming up was this thing called The World Trade Agreement. This is where every country in The World is recognised in producing what it does best. Tibet seemed to be a country that was being wiped out simply for the reason that it contradicted nearly every part of the agreement. Tibet didn't produce anything! All that this one country did, was love. It also seemed to know more about death than anyone else. So, understanding that every living creature on the planet dies, I thought that Tibet would be the only country that would be able to teach me what I needed to know."

"Wow. I thought The World Trade Agreement had already been decided." Said Liz.

"Well, the final agreement is about to be signed at a Senate hearing in New York. Once it is signed, the United Nations which is really America, has the power and ability to do whatever it sees fit to the entire world."

"When does the signing occur?" Asked Liz, feeling important.

"September 11th. In three days."

"On a happier note. We have a date at one of the best parties of the century. The Miniscule of Sound are doing the music and two DJ friends of mine called Gyro and Static are coming up from the Isle of Wight to perform some tunes. Here's the flyer!"

Liz produced a colour printed invitation from her ever-present bag, which had the words TOOT and CLICK written on it in huge black letters. O.D. Darren held the invite and read it aloud.

GREETINGS AND SALUTATIONS EARTHLINGS. TOOT AND CLICK.

YOU ARE CORDIALLY INVITED TO THE COSTUME PARTY OF THE CENTURY AT THE WAREHOUSE IN SIGDON PASSAGE. MUSIC & PERFORMANCE BY DJs GYROSCOPE, UNIVERSAL BEING, THE

MINISCULE OF SOUND. DRUMANDBASS. IN PROTEST OF THE WORLD TRADE AGREEMENT. ART INSTALLATIONS BY DAPPER BEN AND CHRIS T. THE MORE THE MERRIER. THE GREY AREA WILL LIVE AGAIN.

"How do you know Gyro Scope?" Asked O.D. Darren curiously.

"Oh, through an ex-mutual friend. He was one of the first people to show me around Hackney when I first came here. He's a legend on the squatting scene in these parts. Strange bloke. You'd like him, he seems to talk in this really strange way, but he has the most amazing music I've ever heard. He performs surreal comedy, when he's not making people dance their nut off."

Darren finished off his pint of ale and offered Liz a top up. "By the way," Said O.D. Darren, "I've procured of some unbelievable ecstasy if you'd care for some?"

"Gimme gimme gimme..." Replied Liz.

With a quick fumble in his pocket, he produced two tablets and popped one into the open mouth of the young Advertising Executive. Checking his watch, he noticed that it read nine-thirty and the party invite announced eleven as the time for kick-off.

"Well, we've got just over an hour until the pub shuts and then we can walk up there, Sigdon Passage is just round the corner really..."

"Splendid! That's just enough time for another pint and a shag in the toilets if you don't mind." Said Liz, leaning forward and kissing him on the lips.

"I do mind actually! I need chocolates and flowers. I need to be wooed you know!" Laughed O.D. Darren

"Get the beer!" Growled Liz. "I'll tell you some good news..."

As O.D. Darren walked past the statue of Hitler he had the strangest sensation that the face of Adolf winked at him. Not that strange he considered as the pill he had just taken had been the forth one since leaving Shepherds Bush and he could barely walk straight. Only nine to go. "Suicide is painless..." He whispered to himself as he entered the toilets of the pub.

In the beer garden Liz closed her eyes as she sat on the bench and thought about a dream she had the night before where the hippy and herself had been sitting in an open field talking about world domination. She recalled an old lady who had arrived in the scene somewhere. Then she had begun to have a huge argument with Darren and found herself eating a pizza. When she looked down at the pizza, it appeared to look like the Moon. She had sprinkled white powder over it and continued eating it. She recalled how bitter the taste had been as she drank from her pint of ale looking down at the small case that O.D. Darren had left on the seat next to her.

The initials P and G were embossed at the top and after she realised the lid was open she decided to have a look inside before O.D. Darren came back from the toilet where the hippy was standing in the urinal attempting to stand straight and at the same time stop is stomach from exploding out through his mouth. Mr. Bittre knew the mix of beer and ecstasy had already created a toxic combination in the bloodstream and once O.D. Darren had finished pissing, he had to remember to tell Liz to keep away from the G-WIZ. He tried to work out if he had some money in his pockets to buy more beer, then realised that after arriving at Bethnal Green O.D. Darren caught a taxi with some of the money in the case Liz had given him.

FRIDAY 7TH SEPTEMBER 2001
TIME-TRAVEL / HACKNEY

ARTISTS ONLY

I'm counting numbers all those numbers to give me guidance
So much guidance oh Lord I need that now
GENESIS

LEARNING ANYTHING ON Earth could be a painful experience compared to most other planets. Yet after the initial shock of rebirth had worn off and from discovering something, which had been referred to as his Mother, Dr. Bostrom had survived the process of rebirth remarkably well. Along with the various pains of growing a new body and developing such skills as speech and walking. To the credit of the good doctor a great amount of knowledge had now been crammed into a brain that had some strange technicalities, which he had since discovered, he had to learn all over again. Such as memory.

His least favourite part of the process had been the humiliation from Max Born over what the doctor had considered to be a simple mistake that could have been rectified in a much easier way than the traditional methods of rebirth. He sighed with his new lungs. A year had passed since the famous cloaking device mess-up. Now he had the genetic spacesuit of a human man, genetically halted at the age of twenty Earth years and had been stunned as to how easy the development of his physicality had been.

Most of the people that he had been contacted by over the year on Earth had been reborn pilots and fortunately his Mother had been living in the East of a place called London, which he had to admit was a city. Nothing near the incredible sights he had witnessed on other planets. Yet there had been something unique about the place he liked. The oddest part so far had been something called *speaking*, which it seemed everyone on earth thought of as highly intelligent, when, for most of his life as a doctor he had been trained into believing that not speaking had in fact been a sign of intelligence.

Most of the operation to reach the witnesses of flight 815Y had been a success and his receiving of a black case of supplies, tools and time capsules from an X-Chromo-pilot named Ben on Earth had been highly useful. The capsule had allowed him to travel quickly around the planet, rearranging the entire tragic events of his demise. The oddest part had been seeing the Freighter from the Boeing aircraft over The Banda Sea. Once that had occurred, the good doctor knew that the punishment had probably fitted the incident.

Most of the time after the alien had been shocked of how gigantic the Freighter appeared from Earth. He had spent most of the year in London kicking himself. All he had to complete as part of the journey now was understand how to get hold of something called a Job. Ben had explained the process to him on their occasional meetings but he still could find little comfort in knowing that most of the planet had been subject to such a ludicrous idea.

Another blow had been the discovery that most Earthlings seemed to be oblivious to what was happening to the planet. Any times the alien had tried talking to them or making contact, regarding the plans for Earth, they would back away from him or simply stop talking. This had been noted in his data record and returned to the base on the Moon as a consistent diary which he had been reviewing in his Mother house, on Ellingfort Road. Ben was also introducing him to some of the customs on Earth from a perspective he could understand. Such as *'smoking'* and another one called *'drink'*. The effects of which he had been suffering from in the form of what was known as a *'hang-over'*.

The alien walked over to his sleeping quarters and unlocked his black suitcase of orange envelopes, which had been sent after him from Max Born. Each contained five thousand pounds in Earth currency, for each recognised country on the planet and enough packets of time-capsule formula to last until his eventual demise, which would return him to The Diner Holistic and enable him to return to the normality of anywhere off the planet.

Ben had given him a brief description of the humans Gyro and Hong Jin Wu, along with details of Captain Li located in a place called Sydney. The names of locations made him chuckle. He had been given written instructions to explain which things were positive and which were negative to mention and was now quickly revising them in order to time-travel, meet Gyro and explain in detail what had occurred and how he could assist in the Irrigation Project. Hong Jin Wu had been easy to speak to and had thanked the doctor with something called kissing, which had some peculiar effects on his human form. He marked it in the diary as positive. Along with the subjects of music, kissing, mountains, dogs, Barcelona, trees, coffee and something he had recently discovered called art. Next to this he had written a question mark and had been amazed to discover that its appearance in Hackney seemed to be a constant. So far the only subject he could mention under his negative title had been the words *'television'*. Ben had been attempting to convince him otherwise by explaining that, with the help of art, viewing television could be seen as highly positive.

Dr. Bostrom dressed himself in a black suit and tie and his traditional dark glasses, which helped him to see in the light of Earth and then undressed as he had forgotten the material layer of clothing, which was called a shirt. Then the alien repeated the process again. As he was placing the shoes on his feet, his Mother knocked on the door of his room.

"Er...your friend's here dear...Ben?" She asked cautiously.

Ben entered the room with an expression on his face that suggested something was up, as they said in London.

"Fancy going to a party?" He asked popping hi head around the bedroom door.

After closing the door, Ben explained laboriously how the evening was going to work and how a year of searching for the last member of the witnessing aboard flight 815Y would be arriving from a place called Holland. All that was required now was that the good doctor had to be prepared for something possibly more shocking than his original rebirth procedure. A drum and bass warehouse party in Hackney. He handed Dr. Bostrom a flier.

"See the list of names printed? One of them is Gyro. They were printed by a friend of his called Static and the location is on the opposite side of London Fields. No problem with getting into the party and thanks for the orange envelope by the way...I thought that American George had left it on route to the States. Did you hear about the World Trade Centre?" He asked sitting down on the bed.

"Mr. Bittre." Said the doctor with a heavy sigh. "He was behind it. There was a document in the briefcase explaining the details of everything but I have no idea where it's gone. Max Born had the whole thing written down to the last detail but for some reason the Three Breakfasts Corporation won't allow any of it to surface. He's tried several times to be reborn here and knowing him, he's attempting another right now."

"Bittre?" Ben suddenly allowed his hair to turn from black to pale white, matching his complexion. "I thought Benedicto had taken care of him."

"Alas not every penguin is so gifted as Benedicto. I believe from what Max Born has sent to me that The Academy have enough to work on without checking on The Diner Holistic and chances are, he will escape in time. Once you consider what happened in New York. There's no telling what will happen if he arrives on Earth. I don't believe all the ex-pilots down here can achieve a balance after that." Dr. Bostrom shook his head wearily.

"Perhaps there is a solution at the party?" Offered Ben. "It's a costume party. I'm staying in character as an artist..."

"Maybe I'll go as an alien." Replied the good doctor.

Learning anything on Earth could be a painful experience compared to most other planets. Yet, after the initial shock had worn off for what he had discovered was referred to as his mother, Dr. Bostrom had survived the process of rebirth remarkably well.

FRIDAY 7TH SEPTEMBER 2001
NIGHT / AMSTERDAM

HOW CAN THE ANGELS GET TO SLEEP WHEN THE DEVIL LEAVES THE PORCH LIGHT ON?

It's time to move on, time to get going,
what lies ahead I have no way of knowing
But under my feet baby the grass is growing
It's time to move on, time to get going
TOM PETTY AND THE HEARTBREAKERS

The journey from the coffee shop in Amsterdam had been the smoothest Gyro had experienced. After the initial shock of walking out onto the streets of Amsterdam had worn off, he wondered to himself how this one city in Europe could be run so differently from everywhere else on the planet it seemed. He embraced Amsterdam with a warm heart. Just walking through the streets of the red-light district with its crowds of football supporters seemingly terrified by the women displaying their wares in the windows. Britt had disappeared as suddenly as she had arrived in his life and after the enormous craft he had seen after leaving Australia, the sight of windows displaying hardcore pornography next to cafes that sold drugs seemed to lose the impact he could see it still having on most of the tourists around him as he meandered in the direction of Dam Square.

Amsterdam as a loud neighbour without morals who had moved in next to the home of the Pope. The place seemed to practically throw morals out the window while other countries embraced them. Holland even made Euthanasia legal. The choice to commit suicide had become freely available. In Holland it had not been illegal to kill yourself. However, in Korea a person could be remembered as a hero if they died at work. Gyro had thought about this paradox many times and had friends in the past who had succeeded but now understood that they had not had to see the devastation that the act left behind. It seemed that they had all never realised during those last moments that life was a gift, that the world existed inside, not outside once you died, the world died with you. Perhaps once you died, the world died with you.

The truth had been long in discovering and had been keen to discover now what lay ahead and became excited by the prospect that one day he would die and as he had read somewhere you really could not expect to understand the movie until you reached the end. Unless David Lynch had been directing. Yet what had happened on Flight 815Y had brought a bigger mystery into his life that reminded him of one thing. Either a person knew what had been going to happen or they did not. After he had met aboriginals in Australia he had begun to wonder just how much he had to learn. Meeting them had been similar to going back to school. Gyro had journeyed to the ends of the Earth searching for answers and smiled as he recalled the words Gregg, Allanah and Chris had held up for him to read as he left the country. A NEW BEGINNING.

The night had already been swallowed by the past and he thought about the meeting with the mysterious German lady who seemed to have secrets within her that were greater in size than the mammoth vessel he had seen hanging in the air over the Jumbo Jet. He walked over the bridge and looked across at the narrow houses of Amsterdam in this strange Disneyland for adults.

He had opened the orange envelope only to be dismayed by the discovery that instead of any details explaining the location of Britt or even a phone number, the contents had consisted solely of a large stack of hundred Euro notes. He had taken them to the bank immediately, expecting the news that they were counterfeit. Disappointment had not arrived however and the teller on the other side of the counter had merely counted them, placed them in a file and handed another stack of paper back to him. The printed image of Charles Darwin had been on some of them and the rest were now replaced with one hundred English pound notes instead.

Gyro had then walked out of the bank and headed for the nearest clothes shop in Amsterdam, whereby he purchased a spanking new dark navy blue pinstriped suit. A white shirt exported from Bologna in Northern Italy and a petrol-blue coloured silk tie with a small hardly noticeable embroidered penguin on the front. All extremely esteemed and eldritch thanks to the instructions left in the envelope.

After much deliberation he decided that whoever had been generous enough to leave such a gift at the bar with such meticulous details to follow, had been obviously far more concerned about his appearance than he had. The instructions also included a detailed budget, which Gyro had been considering, held a fine clue to the whereabouts of the gorgeous Britt. Purely because from the experience of being married once before he now foolishly thought he understood a great deal about women. From his adventure in the bedroom at Hotel The Crown, he had been fifty percent certain that this particular soft-spoken woman from Germany, had indeed been a woman. Even if she seemed obsessed with the idea that she had been a clone. The sheet of orange paper had also told him to visit a manicurist and get a haircut and brush his teeth. Then there were the details about using the tickets for another airbourne flight, which had caused him to momentarily flounder, and head for one last visit to The Greenhouse Effect coffee shop.

The current problem being that the mandate in the orange envelope had dictated that he also visit The Greenhouse Effect. Then the day-glow sheet of enlightenment began to explain of a slight anomaly with the twelve points to follow. He had been sitting at the coffee shop when he learnt that he had been expected to take a small pill, which had also been inside the envelope contained in a neat slim black box. [*EAT THIS WITH COFFEE*] the instructions read [*and it will half the desired toxicity. Take your belongings and walk into the toilet of the cafe. Wait exactly one minute and open the door*]

Gyro stared at the note, as he sat in same spot he had sat in when he met Britt the day before. He had already considered that if Britt had not been the one who had left the envelope in the bar then someone had been watching him the entire time. Whatever the orange pill that looked like a tic-tac sweet appeared to be he decided that the choice had been given to him.

Gyro had opted for following the advice of his Antipodean friends and had decided that these instructions were part of THE NEW BEGINNING. After he had finished his latte, grabbed the rucksack, opened the wooden door and stepped into the toilet of the coffee shop, Gyro discovered that he had now arrived at a different level in the game of life. There had been an immense noise and neatly refreshed he had found himself in a crumpled heap peering out between the gap of a wooden door from inside a wardrobe in a warehouse with approximately five hundred people gathered in front of the wardrobe in a circle around him.

Slightly removed from the new situation Gyro closed the door of the wooden wardrobe and stepped back inside. Quietly hyperventilating to himself in the dark and attempting to stop his head from exploding with laughter, he looked down at his rucksack, which seemed to be as normal as ever and patted the envelope in his new suit inside pocket for reassurance. The journey instructions had been marked on a light-blue sheet of paper and had mentioned that he could only go forwards in time still until he found a person at the costume party known only on the instructions as Dr. B. The sound of the crowd outside had changed from a noisy bustle to a slightly lower levelled bustle. Gyro sat pondering what would happen if he opened the wardrobe door again. The pill or the coffee had made him feel slightly elated and so he decided to go for it. If only to get out of the confinement of the wardrobe.

As he pushed the door open a jar with a low creak, he heard the sound of a settling crowd, sitting down and standing in an arc in front of the cabinet. Some were still chatting amongst themselves, others were drinking from glasses and talking. There had been a distinct cabaret atmosphere in the large warehouse room. There was also a hushed tone of expectation falling across what he could see now was indeed an audience. There had also been a microphone stand. A bright yellow spotlight flooded the interior of his new hiding place and he heard someone speaking across the room through the microphone.

"Now ladies and gentlemen! A large welcome for one of the highlights of the party tonight in Hackney. He will also be mixing the decks later with Static. From the Isle of Wight, a warm round of applause after his successful tour of New Zealand and Australia, for....GYRO!" Announced the voice.

A warm round of applause drifted across the room and Gyro decided that whatever would occur next had already been just a matter planned by a higher force. He followed the typed instructions and placed the dark glasses on his face and stepped out of the wardrobe. Into the spotlight and grabbed hold of the microphone.

"Good evening er...humans! You are humans aren't you?" A few of the crowd shouted *'yes'*.

"Splendid. Wonderful to be here in... Amsterdam..." Gyro paused suddenly amidst huge jeers from the crowd and referred to the blue sheet of paper in his suit pocket causing everyone to laugh. *"Sorry...Hockney. Wonderful to be in Hockney tonight. Er...a camp painter!"*

As he turned around, Gyro realised he was surrounded by an audience of people forming a circle and the wardrobe he had just stepped out of. The crowd seemed to be a mix of different faces but from the heckles he heard occasionally he could hear accents from England. His home country.

"I've had the most surreal week of my life and most of it happened inside that wardrobe, I think. Good to be back in the poorest borough in Europe though." A huge cheer went up as Gyro spotted his long-term friend Static in the audience smiling back at him with quiet confidence. *"I have just arrived back from Australia on the plane flight from The Twilight Zone. Never fly with Korean Airlines unless you want your reality severely altered. I tell you. Is there a doctor in the warehouse? If there is, I will tell you what you need to know. Meanwhile, I will begin the amazing intelligence trick and then I will introduce the finest DJ in the world apart from my good self."* He moved the microphone from its stand and approached the most beautiful lady in the audience he could find. *"Now madam, I want you to think of a number between one and ten, are you thinking of one?"* He asked a beautiful lady in the front of the audience who had an orange scarf wrapped tightly around her head. *"Okay, now I will prove I am more intelligent than anyone else in the room..."* He passed the microphone quickly under the mouth of the young lady to allow her to speak into it. *"Okay what's the number?"* Asked Gyro.

"Eight." Answered the lady in a soft German accent. *"WRONG!"* Came the reply. The crowd roared with laughter and Gyro could hear the bark of his friend Liz from somewhere in the audience. *"Now for the music!"*

On cue the audience began to blast out of two of the largest speakers Gyro had ever seen and everyone started to dance to the irresistible sounds of Muddy Waters mixed with The Two Ronnies theme music. Two people, one dressed as a musketeer and the other dressed as a dinosaur, moved the props from the floor allowing more people to get up and dance

As he turned to face a tap on the shoulder, he looked into the face of the well-dressed soft-spoken Doctor Bostrom.

"Nice entrance Gyro. I see you found the envelope." Winked the good doctor wearing the same Ray-Bans.

"Dr. Bostrom I presume?" He enquired bowing slightly.

"The very same. I think we need to talk. It can wait. I have all night and I do believe you have experienced a great amount of inconvenience already. I do humbly apologise. The fault was all mine." He said gracefully.

"It's quite alright doctor. I believe you' ve given me a new perspective in life I had no idea about before." Said Gyro.

"Obviously, that was what I came here tonight to explain. First you must speak with your colleagues, they wish to celebrate your return...for the moment. Meet me by the wardrobe and we'll talk okay?" Announced the good doctor as he adjusted his shades.

"Very well." Replied Gyro as he began to dance.

"Meanwhile, enjoy the party. By the way, Hackney isn't the poorest borough in Europe anymore!" He smiled through rectangular glasses.

As Gyro reached out for a glass of champagne he looked around at the dancing and cavorting guests on the dance floor. Static waved over to him as he stood at his twin decks playing music and quickly smiled. In the corner of the room he thought he could see his old school friend Liz and O.D. Darren arguing. They seemed to be the only people in the room who were not having a good time amongst the sea of smiling and laughing faces around him.

Gyro walked over to Static as the sounds of Mannish Boy blasted out of the large speakers at the back of the room. Gyro thought for a brief moment how the music seemed to fit his mood perfectly. He felt as if the sudden arrival in a wardrobe in Hackney made little sense but since leaving Australia only twenty-four hours ago, Gyro had given up on anything in his life making any sense. Static seemed pleased to see him regardless and as he hugged his old friend he shouted in his ear over the music.

"Hey! Smooth entrance man! I like it! Where's your lion and your witch?" Asked Static.

"I think the witch is here somewhere..." Said Gyro still bewildered and scanning the mass of faces for one particular stunning German lady he had previously spotted. "I've no idea what happened with the lion, but I think I'm about to find out..."

"Well, come over in the break. I'm on until we change over at eleven okay?" Asked Static beaming.

Gyro nodded and strode across to a small alcove near the dance floor where Dr. Bostrom waited as promised. Something about his manner seemed to remind Gyro of the air of confidence that physics teachers exuded towards students when they asked in a University for directions towards the toilet. Teachers of any other subjects seemed to always pause before handing out such information. Dr. Bostrom spoke in a way that made Gyro feel as if he had begun to talk with someone who could actually handle the obvious questions he had.

"Dr. Bostrom? A pleasure as always." He said officially shaking his hand again.

"Gyro. I have just spoken with Hong Jin Wu about two hours ago and I'm afraid I could not get her to join us!"

The shock of hearing the name caused him to momentarily separate himself from the crowds of people around him.

"IS SHE ALRIGHT?" Yelled Gyro. "I WONDERED WHAT...." Suddenly he felt himself shocked by the sound of only his voice echoing around the walls of the warehouse as every single sound and action, every molecule in the world froze solid. Gyro turned his head in absolute wonder at the sight of people stood still and holding impossible positions without movement. Wisps of smoke held in the air like fractured ice draped across cobwebs.

"Did you never study physics at school?" Asked Dr. Bostrom smiling through his glasses.

"No. I studied art. The nuclear bomb kind of put me off physics." Answered Gyro. "I don't think Science could help explain to me how I got here and landed in a wardrobe so expectantly. But art might."

"G-WIZ." Announced the good doctor.

"I'm sorry?" Desperately trying to remember any paintings called such a name.

"The pill you took in Amsterdam contains a chemical that allowed you to fold time. It's like this..." The good doctor produced a pen and began drawing a standard diagram on the wall they were both standing next to. "Let's say this is your head and through your eyes you're able to perceive reality which your brain interprets. Yes?" Gyro nodded at the diagram, which the good doctor had drawn revealing his head as a projector. "Your brain is vast in scale. Large enough to hold the Universe and surrounding Galaxies but only if your memory is emptied to allow for the space. Much like a hard disc in a computer. Or an attic in someone's house. Once you make the space you can perceive more dimensions and therefore travel. The possibilities are indeed endless." Explained the doctor.

"Yep! And the atomic bomb was progress?" Asked Gyro.

"Perhaps. What was done with it however... that's another story. There is the Rub Down Transfer Principle though which comes with the new territory of time-travel. This means that copies of people can be seen walking around unattached. To some cultures they would be known as ghosts." Said the good doctor.

"Why do I get the feeling that you've met me before?" Asked Gyro.

"You saw the Tectonic-Freighter I was flying over The Banda Sea which is why we've met. Myself and Max Born my employee are currently enlisting individuals to help Earth with a little thing called the Irrigation Project. Hong Jin Wu has already signed up. You have some time to think it over and if you want to get in touch, just whistle." Winked the good doctor.

The sound of the entire planet slipping back into operation blew Gyro clean into the alcove wall and he lay collapsed in a pile on the floor as Dr. Bostrom bent down to help him back to his feet.

"Oh sorry about that." He said. "I forgot humans are affected by the sound waves."

He politely dusted the bewildered Gyro down and introduced his friend Max who had dressed for the party as Sandy from the movie Grease. With studded jacket and tight black leather pants, along with bright blonde wig.

"Excuse me for asking, but which way is the toilet." Asked Gyro as he felt himself suddenly alone at the party. Disorientated. Suffering from time-travel fatigue and now without memory he realised that by comparison the journey from the coffee shop in Amsterdam had been the smoothest Gyro had experienced.

SATURDAY 8TH SEPTEMBER 2001
AFTERNOON / HOLBORN

FEELING YOURSELF DISENTIGRATE

*Sunshine came softly through my window today,
could have tripped out easy but I'm changing my ways
Cause I've made my mind up you're going to be mine
I'll pick up your hand slowly and blow your little mind*

DONOVAN

INSIDE THE MORGUE an unusual atmosphere of excitement had been generated by the presence of the Federal Bureau of Investigations from America who were dazzling the rest of the staff with their accents and teeth. Morticians and doctors in white coats were frantically rushing about the place. The corpse had already arrived and looking at the amount of bright yellow police security tape stretched across one of the doors seeking entrance to the cadaver would be trickier than Liz had anticipated. O.D. Darren walked quickly through each door and wall until could hear cries of discovery from the ghost of O.D. Darren.

"*LIZ! They're all in here. They've cut my head off!*" He shouted back to her through the walls.

Liz walked up to the reception and bawled her eyes out as best she could and attempted to look like a distraught girlfriend as much as possible. The woman at the counter seemed to behave even more distraught than she did.

"Excuse me. I'm the fiancé of Darren...er.. I understand, he was brought in here this morning." She sniffed.

"Ahh, yes... oh you poor thing...are you family?" Asked the receptionist.

"No. I'm his fiancé..." Sobbed Liz.

"I'm sorry, but only immediate family are allowed to view the body." Came the expected reply.

"What? What do you mean? I was talking to him yesterday!" Asked the disappointed Liz.

"I'm sorry, but those are the rules."

Liz took a deep breath and spoke as slowly and politely as possible through gritted teeth. The ghost of O.D. Darren stood next to her nearly hysterical. "I cannot believe what they're doing to me in there!" He whined.

Liz barked out a laugh trying to keep the situation together. "Okay, look. I know you're just doing your job, but I am afraid he was my boyfriend and he had a mirror which belonged to me in his pocket, a gift, we were engaged and I promised that I would... er, always treasure it. Is there any chance I could just see if he has it on him?" She asked as two of the uniformed members of the FBI ran passed her.

"All the personal artefacts are kept in the room over there. If you fill out this form, then you can take any of his belongings. But you must remember, its just material. He's not here anymore!" She said weeping slightly.

Liz thanked the receptionist, sniffling and took the sheet of green paper into the room opposite, closing the door behind her. Which the ghost of O.D. Darren walked through, furious.

"The dirty buggers. Can you believe it?" He asked pacing around the room. "You pay your taxes and this is how they thank you at the end of the day!"

Liz looked up at his ghost with her best schoolteacher expression.

"Did you pay your taxes?" She asked.

"Well...no, not exactly. But that's not the point really is it? I mean, what right do they have to cut my head off?"

"Darren, this is not the time really. I have to fill this form out and I have no idea about any of your personal details. When was your Birthday, you never told me!"

"September 10th 1978..." He said meekly. "They've found the traces of the drug in my blood by the way..."

"You aren't serious...already?"

Suddenly his attitude took a new turn. *"Bloody hell! Look! It's the mirror!"*

Sitting on top of the rest of his clothes, was the pocket travel mirror. Liz picked it up and turned it over, seeing the handwriting of O.D. Darren where he had written her name on the back. Suddenly she experienced an unexpected emotional surge of overwhelming sadness come over her. She placed the mirror quickly into her pocket. Liz felt herself start to collapse inward slightly. For the first time that day, she slowly realised that O.D. Darren was really dead. Her own mortality began to flake slightly as she stared down at the stack of clothes on the table. She wiped a hand across her face, crying.

"I think I'm going mad. What's happening?" She asked sadly trembling as she looked up at O.D. Darren who seemed to be fainter in appearance. He seemed to be shouting yet his voice sounded as if it was outside the building.

"You're dead. What the fuck am I doing?" Liz shook her head slowly, backing away from the memorabilia and with eyes full of tears and her long orange hair falling down over her face. She quickly opened the door, she was finding it difficult to breath, ignoring the queries of the receptionist.

"Miss. Can I have the form back please?" She asked.

"Fuck off!" Liz shouted back, running for the door and fresh air. *"He's dead!"*

The tears in her eyes blurred her vision so much that, as she headed out of the stone steps of the morgue entrance, she seemed oblivious to the fact that she had walked straight past an old lady walking in through the wooden doorframe. Strong emotions had just saved her from meeting the most dangerous woman in Europe, The Madam.

Liz just kept running while inside the morgue an unusual atmosphere of excitement continued brought on by the presence of the Federal Bureau of Investigations who had been dazzling the rest of the staff with their accents and teeth.

SUNDAY 9TH SEPTEMBER 2001
AFTERNOON / ANTARTICA

THE OTHER SIDE OF MIDNIGHT

I don't go for fancy cars for diamond rings or movie stars I go for penguins
O Lord I go for penguins
LYLE LOVETT

THE FISH LAY on the ice lifeless. Benedicto Perky Eco picked at the fins with his long black beak, stripping away the hard scales and fins until he could separate the flap of the head away from the aquatic remains. He looked down at the ripped bloody carcass of the expressionless creature as the one glass glazed eye stared back at him, then he looked up, craning his head towards the starry night sky. An incredible night sky. He watched as another UFO whizzed past overhead and chuckled to himself. The constellations were looking more beautiful tonight than ever before.

The fish had taken patience and delicate skill to catch. Benedicto had bewildered a number of his colleagues as he had heaved his monomorphic body out of the cold water and onto the ice. He had stayed under the water for longer than usual and had swum far deeper than any of the other penguins in order to find the largest fish of the school. The hunt had paid off however and now as he looked down at the catch beside the smaller fish, he smiled to himself. The Emperor would be pleased. He quickly picked up the small fish flipped it onto the cold hard ice and caught it gracefully in his mouth and then gulped it down in one go. He clapped his fins together and laughed. The fish tasted better when fresh from this planet called Earth than at The Diner Holistic and he pinched the large tale of the bigger catch by the tail and dragged it towards the largest of the rookeries on the iceberg. The office of the Emperor.

King Benedicto stood at the entrance of the chilly interior and waited for the stars above to show their alignment. Once the UFO moved towards the Moon from Orion he could enter the rookerie and present his catch to the Emperor. Then he would hear the great leader of the Empire tell him of the location co-ordinates for Big New Yorker and he could fold time to where his confused friend Mr. Bittre would no doubt be working away. King Benedicto sighed in the freezing night air of Antartica and looked out over his colony. He would miss all of his troops during his next mission but he knew that Max Born from The Three Breakfasts Corporation would need all the help he could find on this planet called Earth. The very battle for space itself had become included in the stakes. Something that no creature on Earth could ignore. The King turned as a guard shuffled out of the rookerie and acknowledged his presence.

"*My Lord.*" Said the guard. "*The Emperor will see you now.*" King Eco looked up and saw the UFO dart from the usual location near Orion.

Inside the icy cavern a large image of The Emperor had been displayed on a large colour digital screen sunk into the far wall of snow and ice. The interior of the cave was quiet from the howling winds outside and King Benedicto dragged the large dead fish inside. Setting the carcass down before the image of the screen where he settled it onto the raised platform. The fish immediately dematerialised and appeared on the screen next to The Emperor. He inspected the offering and smiled back from the screen.

"*Well done Lord Benedicto. You have served The Empire once again and displayed your vigilance towards us with this great offering.*" Said The Emperor filling the screen with his full height and weight of fifteen kilograms.

"*Thank you my Liege. I am indeed your humble servant.*" The penguin stroked the front of his orange plumage.

"*I suppose you are awaiting the co-ordinates for your quest to find Mr. Bittre...*" Smiled The Emperor knowingly.

"*Yes my Liege.*" Replied the King.

"*He is growing stronger on this planet by the second. I have felt a great disturbance in the force of his actions directed against the Empire.*" Announced the penguin touching a curved flipper to his bill and stroking it.

"*He is confused my Liege yet I feel he can be converted and returned to The Diner Holistic.*"

"*He will do so... or die!*" Commanded The Emperor.

King Benedicto Perky Eco bowed his head humbly and shuffled back to the entrance of the icy white cave turning momentarily as a short burst of static from the monitor caught his attention. The King looked back up at the screen as the image of the monarch filled the screen once again.

"Oh one more thing King Eco" Said The Emperor smirking. *"...You look as if you are wearing a tuxedo..."*

"Perhaps..." Replied King Benedicto turning around with a wink. "...I am."

Outside the warmth of the shelter, the majestic stars gleamed down onto the iceberg in Antartica. This had been a good home to King Benedicto during his year of growing. Now he had to fold time and search for his friend Mr. Bittre. Benedicto craned his neck around and acknowledged the stern presence of the guard as he returned to his watch over the rookerie. The guard passed one last fish to him with his large feet and smiled. A gift before he prepared for his leave across time and space. Benedicto bowed down to receive it as the guard brushed past him into the cavern. The fish lay on the ice lifeless.

MONDAY 10TH SEPTEMBER 2001
NIGHT / NEWTOWN

SCISSORS CUT PAPER BUT PAPER WRAPS ROCK

Big science hallelujah
Big science yodellayheehoo
LAURIE ANDERSON

ALL THE GLASSES were filled at the table as David Icke poured the red wine from the bottle he had been offered by one of the Italian waiters in the large private house in Newtown. Several groups of the guests were dancing on the stairs to the music of Tom Waits across the landing of the second floor. Hardly anyone had noticed the arrival of three old German gentlemen at the house, who had sat down at a table in the backroom near the kitchen. In the Dining Room several guests were following the evening after the wake of O.D. Darren into the night and seemed determined to watch the sun rise on the following majestical morning, unless the alcohol ran out. The music of Brian Eno drifted from a compact disc player near the sink and filled the interior snugly with a polite atmosphere, which had become ripe with discussion, led by the Physicists.

"You seem to forget Mr. Icke that we have all come from a background based in physics, most of the ideas that you have proposed in your books have all the style but none of the facts are provable!" Said Erwin Schrodinger.

"There was a series of facts that Albert there came up with years ago and you were all convinced that he was wrong when he suggested his findings on relativity." Said Mr. Icke in his soft Coventry accent gesturing at Einstein across the wooden oak table. Niels Bohr quickly bit into a prawn sandwich and looked at Albert. "Sorry Albert. I never meant to say that you were wrong, just that..."

"David you can suggest whatever you like, it's a party. We're listening!" Said Erwin Schrodinger sitting near the compact disc player and offering an empty box of After Eight mints to the assorted guests at the table.

"I am merely saying that my predictions for society in the future include a computer-chipped society controlled by one government and the dissolving of money as a usable currency. This already seems to be developing at an incredible rate. We now already have a society which is revealing itself in the lead up to 2012 as being more easily manipulated than that of previous societies." Continued the controversial speaker.

"If most of the people allow such an occurrence then we can hardly say it is not required..." Replied Erwin.

"This control of society sounds familiar.." Said Albert Einstein drinking from his glass.

"How do you mean?" Asked David.

"Life is full of circles you know Mr Icke. When you consider that your entire life, much like O.D. Darren's today, may well be remembered as a good thing because he threw a great party for all the people he had ever met." Said Albert.

Everyone at the table nodded and smiled agreeing that it had been an incredible party.

Gyro flicked ash into an ashtray and lifted a glass of red wine to his lips as most of the guests looked up from the table as an elegant American lady named Laurie Anderson entered the room with a four-pack of Boddingtons lager under her arm. She offered a can to Gyro who turned in his seat to face her standing-up and wobbling. As Gyro and introduced her to a chair. He asked her a question that had always been on his mind.

"Do you think we're born onto this planet Laurie to find an ultimate answer." He asked drunkenly.

* "I'm glad you asked about that - it's really been on my mind lately," said the artist. "There are so many ridiculous things that get in the way of finding that answer and so many events swirling around people that prevent them from actually thinking about it." She continued to talk to Gyro as she sat at the table next to Juliet Binoche.

Niels Bohr leaned forward and whispered drunkenly to Juliet. *"What's she going on about?"* Referring to the comment made by Laurie who overheard the question and became slightly intimidated by the German Physist. The French actress quietly finished what she was saying to Gyro as she sat down next to him.

"... it's a long way of saying, performance art is about joy, really, about making something that's so full of kind of a wild joy that you really can't put into words." Whispered Laurie, looking around at the guests of the table with the air of a student who has interrupted a lecture.

David Icke drank from his glass and considered the funeral that day. *"Yet most people believe that they are in control of their own lifes..."* He said distantly.

"We always have choice and free will in our lifes should we require a moment just to think of how uncontrollable most of it is." Announced Werner Heisenberg.

"Oh come on Werner! Free will? Choices? What choice do all the people in Africa have dying of aids? What about the jews in World War II? Do you think they had a choice? What about the simple fact that you have to get a bank account in order to eat? You can no longer simply live from the land because everyone's built on it..." Said David.

"In Germany things were harder than they have ever been in this country...or America." Said Stephen Hawking sullenly.

"Well I'm sure we're about to discover how much weirder life will get." Interrupted Icke. *"There is no one leading the good fight anymore."*

"What about the atomic bomb? I thought things had developed into a stalemate due to that at least." Asked Werner. *"You could argue that..."* He was suddenly interrupted by David, who was homing in on everyone at the table.

"Nasa was supposed to be a corporation developed for the people right? The great discovery of space cannot be bought and yet a terrestrial planet finder space telescope is to be launched in 2012, not by or for the people of Earth. Where is the money coming from? If that plan is already being prepared then who is planning this and not planning an Aids vaccine? The incentive is suspicious..." Said Mr. Icke as he refilled his glass.

"You don't believe NASA's intentions are wholesome?" Asked Juliet Binoche.

" I believe a lot of the intentions of corporations are similar to the media's purpose on this planet, which is to withold information not to reveal it to the public, which is subjective and immoral." Answered David.

*I think computer viruses should count as life. Maybe it says something about human nature, that the only form of life we have created so far is purely destructive. Said Hawking.

"Speak for yourself..." Said Quentin Crisp.

Albert sat up and joined the opinion. "Are you a pacifist?" He asked the question directly to David Icke.

"Of course, how could anyone argue any other point?" Questioned the x-goalkeeper.

"Around the time of the war, I really had no idea that an atomic bomb could be built from the knowledge that was acquired and I don't think any physicist from our era did. *If only I had known, I should have become a shoemaker."

"Werner did..." Answered Stephen Hawking. All eyes suddenly fell on the slightly embarrassed face at the end of the table. Werner drank and feigned sudden interest in a painting on the opposite wall. "Er...what an interesting painting...I wonder who did that?" He asked attempting to change the subject.

"Well, the war was wonderful, of course. I wrote about that." Said the writer Quentin Crisp, unperturbed by talk of the War. "You see, you were in danger, which is lovely, because you look your last on all things lovely every hour. And that's nice." Said Quentin offering some eggnog to Stephen Hawking.

Britt entered the room swinging a bottle of red wine in one hand. "What's up Gyro? Is everyone hiding back here now?" She asked sitting between Laurie Anderson and Gyro.

"Would anybody like another glass of wine?" Asked Icke. "It's Oxford Landing..."

Everyone murmured in the affirmative.

Gyro asked if it was possible to have a latte and one of the Italian waiters took his order and walked off to the kitchen. Laurie Anderson asked if she could have one as well.

"You know I've been trying to cut down on drinking coffee." She said fiddling with a teaspoon on the table.

" Why? I love the stuff I can't think of what I would do if I didn't drink it..." Replied Gyro sitting next to her.

* "Well I got this idea from some friends who work in an office and they said that they were getting really nervous from their coffee breaks. Every time they had coffee, it made them feel more and more driven. It wasn't relaxing at all. So they started to have 'wig breaks' instead. Around 11 o'clock every morning they all went into a small room and tried on wigs for 15 minutes. After a while they weren't really certain about who they were anymore and they found this pretty relaxing." Said the performance artist.

Gyro stared into her eyes as the wine he was drinking brought a warm feeling to the back of his head and he wondered why he was not married do this woman.

"...So that's Wig Therapy..." Said Laurie, aiming for the After Eights. Gyro considered for a moment that the dimples in her cheeks had to be the most beautiful feature of the day.

Stephen Hawking was speaking to Quentin Crisp as he asked for Gyro to order a pot of Earl Grey tea from one of the Italian waiters when they return. "I don't know a lot about art but I know what I like and I like your hat. It's very flamboyant." Said The Professor. Quentin politely thanked him.

*"You see, it may be true that artists adopt a flamboyant appearance, but it's also true that people who look funny get stuck with the arts." Said Quentin with a debonair stroking of his grey hair.

"I've been offered a job in America and I heard it's a bit dangerous. But I think I would miss England..."

" Oh, I never miss England. No, someone said to me, 'Don't you miss anything about England?' And I thought, "My gas fire..." Quentin continued. "Yes, it's written into the Constitution that you're allowed to pursue happiness. In

England it would be considered a frivolous objective." Stephen laughed and had to explain to Albert Einstein what had been so funny.

Laurie looked across the table at Erwin Schrodinger and smiled. *"What do you do?"* She asked.

"I'm a physist...sort of...I don't do as much as your good self..." He stuttered bashfully cleaning his glasses.

* *"Mmm that's strange...a lot of people don't do things because they say, well, I'm just not the kind of person who would do that, just I wouldn't do that. I think, but why wouldn't you? It's because you've made this sort of picture of who you were and what you would do under various circumstances."* Said Laurie.

The Physist nodded in agreement. Suddenly Erwin Schrodinger realised that no one he had ever met had spoken in such a way to him before. The German felt himself becoming gradually fascinated by this charming American lady.

"A lot of people just follow that sketch and they don't go and say, 'I'm going to get out of my thing here for a minute, I'm going to do something really different.'" She continued. *"Whether you're a writer or a critic or whatever, the world sort of pushes you in that direction because stylistically you're supposed to be a little bit consistent. "But it's too bad. I think it locks people in - it limits their lives."* Said Laurie. Erwin nodded enthusiastically.

Britt decided to sit next to Albert Einstein and asked him what he thought was going to happen tomorrow after everyone had left the party and headed back to where they came from.

* *"I never think of the future. It comes soon enough."* Said Albert winking.

As David Icke walked over to the cabinet and pulled out another bottle of wine he saw an orange envelope marked with the words PLEASE READ THIS MR. ICKE. He opened the envelope and sat back at the table with a short note in his hand.

"What's in the envelope?" Asked Erwin Schrodinger. *"Don't tell me, don't tell me, I'll guess."*

"Its a set of detailed instructions explaining the location of The Holy Grail and an open cheque made out for ten thousand pounds..." Announced Icke.

"That's right gentlemen! Either of you can have that cheque if you can answer one simple question." Replied the voice of Ben as he and Chris T entered the room with Juliet Binoche. Everyone at the table stood up and smiled as a chair was arranged for Juliet who sat down. A glass of wine was offered to her immediately by Chris T.

"Albert, could you put some music on?" She asked the actress coyly. Albert blushed and stood up, nodding enthusiastically.

"But of course Fraulien..." Replied the Physicist and walked over to the CD player accidentally knocking a number of discs to the floor. Picking up one by Tom Waits he slotted it inside the machine and pressed play.

"The question is quite simple and you have one hour to decide amongst all of you the answer." Announced Ben the alien as Chris T made a drum roll on the table edge with his fingers. The room fell quiet as everyone listened.

"The question has been left by O.D. Darren and is, he believed the hardest question of his life..." Ben paused enjoying the attention of the greatest minds of the last century gathered around the table. He felt at home. He smiled at everyone in turn.

"What is love?" He waited for the discussion to begin.

* *"When you are courting a nice girl an hour seems like a second. When you sit on a red-hot cinder a second seems like an hour. That's relativity."* Answered Albert smiling at Juliet.

"More wine anyone? " Asked Britt entering the room with another bottle smiling and winking at Gyro who had found himself not only in heaven but discussing writing and art with the American artist Laurie Anderson.

"...So I think writers sometimes want to summarize, 'What does this mean? What did we learn from this? What is this really about?" Said the American artist as she drank from her coffee. *"But that's a very 19th-century way of thinking about art, because it assumes that it should make our lives better or teach us something. I think maybe school has that application, but artists don't, 'cause if you did, you'd just be handing out propaganda to make people's lives better. You'd be giving them coherent tips about how to do it instead of vague ones."*

"Er...yeah. That's an interesting theory. However, trying to find a theory that..." Began Gyro although.

Stephen Hawking interrupted. * "...when a complete theory could be found understandable to everyone. If we find the answer to that, it would be the ultimate triumph of human reason - for then we would know the mind of God." The eggnog had obviously begun to have an affect on the Professor.

Britt turned to him and asked what he thought of time-travel after having just folded time from the future.

* " The only way to get from one side of the galaxy to the other, in a reasonable time, would seem to be if we could warp space-time so much, that we created a little tube or wormhole. This could connect the two sides of the galaxy, and act as a short cut, to get from one to the other while your friends were still alive." Answered the professor.

Gyro interrupted in return after drinking some more of the Oxford Landing and asked Quentin Crisp what advice he gave people in life after he had arrived in America. For some reason the room had become quieter and Gyro noticed as he looked around the room, that everyone had begun listening intently to the words of the two Englishmen. Quentin ended the momentum of the conversation.

" Well, I tell them not to do any of the things their mothers tell them and not to clean the place where you live, and not to wash the dishes, and all that. It's all a waste of time. I never spend my time doing anything." He seemed deeply reflective suddenly as all eyes around the table fell on them both and smiled a charismatic debonair smile revealing a human being who had seen a great deal in life and learnt much about Earth.

He sighed. *"I'll have to do again tomorrow."*

All the glasses were filled at the table as David Icke poured the red wine from the bottle he had been offered by one of the Italian waiters in the large private house in Newtown.

---

* Laurie Anderson interview by Greg Cahill From the August 20-26, 1998 issue of the Sonoma County Independent. Copyright © Metro Publishing Inc. Maintained by Boulevards New Media.

* Quentin Crisp: © Copyright 2002 Onion, Inc., All rights reserved. Media Kit Privacy Policy

* Stephen Hawking public lecture courtesy of the University of Oxford

* Courtesy of News Chronicle, 14 Mar 1949

* Reflecting on his role in the development of the atom bomb Courtesy of New Statesman, 16 Apr 1965, 1965

* Courtesy of. Interview, 1930, 1930

FRIDAY 7TH SEPTEMBER 2001
TIME / AMSTERDAM

YOU KEEP COMING BACK UNTIL YOU GET IT RIGHT

Je ne 'taime plus mon amour je ne t'aime plus tous les jour
Mother was Queen of the Congo Papa was King of the bongo
MANU CHAO

THE BEEPING OF the travel alarm clock woke Gyro from a theatrical dream of two highly animated characters that seemed to be singing. He turned over in the bed and reached out for the form of Britt next to him, she had already left. Looking around the hotel room, he realised the black suitcase she had been carrying was also missing. An orange piece of paper sat folded on the wooden dresser next to the square double bed inviting him to sit up and read it. The note had been written in capital letters, in black marker pen. As his eyes followed the short sentences, Gyro began to experience the feeling that he had seen the style of writing before. The note was brief and simply read;

NOTHING WHICH WE ARE TO PERCIEVE IN THIS WORLD
EQUALS
THE POWER OF YOUR INTENSE FRAGILITY
WHOSE TEXTURE COMPELS ME
WITH THE COLOUR OF ITS COUNTRIES

RENDERING DEATH AND FOREVER WITH EACH BREATHING
I DO NOT KNOW WHAT IT IS ABOUT YOU THAT CLOSES AND
OPENS
ONLY SOMETHING IN ME UNDERSTANDS
THE VOICE OF YOUR EYES IS DEEPER THAN ALL ROSES
NOBODY, NOT EVEN THE RAIN, HAS SUCH SMALL HANDS*

Although no other words explained what had happened to the mysterious German lady, a sinking sensation in his stomach was informing him that Britt had headed off to Berlin, to say farewells to her family before heading on to her job in New York as she had mentioned she would the day before. Gyro sighed. There had been few women in his life that had touched his heart and brain in such a way as this woman had within the first few minutes of their meeting and now even that event had become a memory. Even standing by the window and looking out at the various oddballs on the street below, would become memory once time had gotten hold of the image.

He lifted himself off the bed and mooched over to the window of his room, still holding the note. He looked out at the bridge over the canal that he had walked across in the rain with her the previous day and attempted to understand what had occurred on the plane as Britt had explained it to him. He had never studied physics in his thirty years on earth but suddenly felt a symmetry with the subject. As he listened to the sounds of Amsterdam waking-up, he wondered how on earth he would explain this problem of time travel another way.

An entire year had gone by in the blink of an eye. If Britt had been telling the truth then nothing could be predicted as certain throughout the rest of his life. He was beginning to doubt whether he had even met her already and the discovery that he had spent his entire life not living one life, but living in a duality was something he had never even considered before.

Now it seemed obvious. He had time-travelled and although the chances were slim. He knew that Hong Jin Wu and the stewardess, along with the Asian passengers were scattered somewhere around the planet attempting to understand exactly the same dilemma. Had he understood the affects of the UFO then surely he could travel back. The idea seemed to strike a resounding gong in his head and he watched as a squadron of pigeons were startled and scattered skyward by the sound of church bells striking. Their echo sounding out over the rooftops of the houses on Voorburgwal Straat.

The bell had struck once and he looked over at the travel alarm clock, which also read one o'clock. The only person he could tell anything to without being judged was his friend Static and Gyro decided to try calling him as quickly as possible. The chances were he would still be living on the Isle of Wight, but of all the phone numbers of people he knew, only Static had them at his house in Shorwell, stored for his return from travelling to Australia. Gyro had decided that travelling such a distance required him to break all contact with this side of the world. A bill for drunken long-distance phone calls and the torture of travelling so far would have not helped when journeying around Australia. Obviously, he had not considered that time-travel would cause him to over-ride such details.

While all this had not explained the casual appearance of his rucksack, with his belongings intact. He had travelled to France once, when he was at college years ago and the ferry company had managed to lose all of his bags. Typical that now he had travelled one year in time and lost nothing except parts of his sanity.

Dressing and briefly checking over his pieces of luggage, he headed down the narrow insanely steep steps and into the bar of Hotel The Crown. Leaving the small hotel room as he had found it.

In the bar the sound of extremely cool jazz echoed around the wooden interior. Gyro decided to collect his thoughts at the table he had sat at the day before over coffee and the last of the hash in his pocket. Enquiries at the bar revealed Britt had paid for the room for one night. He smoked another badly rolled joint waiting for his coffee. Gyro realised there were more clues on the back of the orange note. He read the words; GOD SPEED. SEE YOU IN THE DREAMING GYRO. BRITT. Under the words was what looked like a phone number for a mobile and Gyro felt the feeling of optimism surge in his heart again, in a similar way as when he had the idea of returning to his own time.

He moved quickly towards the public phone at the bar and began to dial the mobile number, shoving the strange new Euro fifty-cent coins left in the orange envelope into the slot. He decided to play it cool, once Britt had picked up the other end he would speak as calmly as she had yesterday, first he would thank her for paying for the room and then he would casually round onto the subject of how he was madly in love with her and would enquire as to the possibility that they could be married as quickly as possible. As the distant echoing tones of telephone connection across the land and sea from Holland made their way through the atmosphere of Earth and the vacuum of space, relaying from satellites and returning back to Earth. Gyro felt the waves of worry and trauma from the time-travelling experience wash away and turned to face the tall Dutch moustached barman. Who seemed to be clicking his figures and signalling to him with his coffee.

"The German lady told me to tell you that the number of the mobile's not her number..." Spoke the relaxed Dutch accent of the barman.

Gyro heard the ringing of the mobile and then the click of an answer machine come on the line and cursed quietly to himself. What was the point of having a telephone you could be reached on at any time and yet refused to have turned on so that you could speak to someone, he thought to himself. If the number did not belong to Britt then whose was it? The requests of the voice on the other end caused Gyro to be none the wiser. All he heard was the sound of music coming down the earpiece. Loud music. Then a distant voice shouting *'Friday 8th September 2002. One Sigdon Passage. Warehouse. Hackney. London. Tonight. Nine. Party of the century. Be there!'*

The line went dead as the answer-machine clicked off and Gyro felt himself returning to the slightly bewildered state he had been in when he first woke up. He hung the phone back on the cradle. At least he had some information. Perhaps this cryptic message had been left by Britt. The voice had sounded anything but German and he had no idea who it belonged to. Perhaps the barman had some clues. He placed the receiver back on the handle.

"Did she say anything else?" Gyro asked the barman, pretending his guts were not spilling out of his mouth, heartbroken.

"She said she was travelling...onto Berlin and then New York on...Monday. Very pretty girl." Replied the barman.

"No phone numbers or anything?" Asked Gyro.

"No. She said something though to tell you when you came down from the room..."

"Really?" He hoped he was not sounding too much like a young schoolgirl.

"Yar. It's a bit odd!" The barman laughed aloud as took the money for the coffee. *"She gave me this to give to you."* He slid a thick orange envelope across the wooden bar surface. *"Said it was important that you followed the instructions inside carefully"*. He winked.

Gyro looked down at the envelope, on the back was the same handwriting in black pen again, it read simply;

GO TO THE PARTY. TALK TO DR. BOSTROM. SEE YOU IN THE DREAMING.

Taking the orange envelope, he walked back over to the table and sat down. As he looked out at the canal he thought about the beeping of the travel alarm clock that had woken Gyro from a theatrical dream of two highly animated characters that seemed to be singing.

---

* *'Somewhere I have never travelled'* - E.E.Cummings

MONDAY 10TH SEPTEMBER 2001
PROBABILITY / THE GARDEN

TOMORROW WILL BE LIKE TODAY

*With your mind you have ability to form
and transmit thought and energy far beyond the norm*
KAREN CAPERNTER

THROUGH THE TREES at the end of the garden strode the intimidating figure of Ray Connif. The guests sitting at various points on lawn-chairs across the green Pantone 361 CVC grass were still talking amicably under the warm September night sky. From where Ray Connif was standing the arrangement gave the impression of the Nebulas near Capricorn, which he had been looking at previously for around two hours. The flight in the stolen Zoa-pod had left Ray Connif slightly disorientated and had also caused his ears to pop every few seconds. He stood near the trees attempting to force the pressure back into his head as he held his his nose and forced the mucus out of the sinus canals of his head. After doing this Ray realised the sensations of time-travel sickness and the journey down to Earth brought forward a sudden urge to vomit. Ray doubled over and threw up into the bushes. Suddenly he felt all better. He pulled out a cigarette and screwed it into his holder and let it stick triumphantly out of the corner of his mouth clenched between his yellow and broken teeth.

What had been originally of complete importance to him, somewhere around the Nebula of Capricorn stressed the urgency with which Ray was now scanning the garden, in search of the Physist clones. Of course Ray would blend right in. He had a suit on modelled from Ray Connif himself, who was still onboard the Chromo-vessel nicely tucked in with Static and the real Ray Connif. Unless Mr. Bittre smiled his disgusting smile of pure despair, there had to be a good chance that he could not only get the Physicists to listen to one of his twisted plans but he could also check-up on how they were functioning. Only one person in this entire Galaxy would be mad enough to clone Albert Einstein, Erwin Schrodinger and the rest. If anything, Mr. Bittre scored high on that test. Nothing of course compared to what his next plan would be.

As the shell of Ray Connif walked down the garden path towards the chatter of guests controlled by Mr. Bittre, he looked over to his right and at the small group talking under the fruit tree with the host Tony Webb. No time like the present, he thought under his hat. Mr. Bittre walked towards the voices, grabbing a glass of wine from one of the waiters. He could hear the voice of an American amongst them.

* *"Well, it's not a pretty picture. But maybe I've gotten jaded. Maybe I've been attending too many tech conferences. Because everybody at those things has like these glowing visions of how cool everything's going to be, but it comes off to me like just a way to get people to get more stuff."* Said Laurie Anderson. *"Which disturbs me, because I look forward and I see technology splitting us pretty cleanly into people who have the stuff and people who don't. And for the people who can't keep up, life is going to get really, really hard."*

Ray Connif took a seat on the lawn amongst the guests. The suit had already been recognised by Gyro who was listening intently to the words of Laurie Anderson, along with the others.

"What do think of music such as Techno?" Asked Tony Webb reaching into his pocket and pulling out a small packet of tobacco and some cigarette papers, as the host listened he began to make a small roll-up.

It's cool in the background. Techno is music without a foreground. But that's all right. I've got plenty of things to do in the foreground.

"What about Hip-hop?" Asked Charles Darwin smiling warmly and pouring wine into his glass. *"I love the old school of Eric B and Rakim. 'I know you got soul..' is truly legendary as a line of poetry in my opinion."* He offered some wine to the Dalai Lamma who politely declined. Showing he was content with his carton of Tropicana orange juice.

**"Definitely cool."* Continued Laurie.*"Especially, if the words are good. Of course they're usually not that good, but in a lot of cases it doesn't matter 'cause the hip-hop attitude comes through strong. It's like "Look at me! I am so cool."*

Everybody should think they're ultra-cool. The world would be a much better place." Replied Laurie.

Gyro looked over and waved at Ray acknowledging his presence by lifting his glass to him. He nodded and raised his in return, chewing on the plastic filter in his mouth. A pause in the conversation allowed Mr. Bittre to speak in the deep German accent of Ray Connif. He drank a little of the wine before speaking.

"I always thought that Americans hated having fun at parties or situations they weren't in control of." He said provocatively, winking at each of the group in turn who seemed surprised by the comment.

Laurie sensed the animosity coming from the new arrival immediately. *"I think that in spite of our puritan roots Americans are pretty fun-loving. We genuinely like fun. We value it. Go to some place like Germany, where it's really all about work, and you'll see that loving fun is an amazing achievement for a people to make. Another big achievement America has made over its puritan history is that we're friendly."* She volleyed back to Mr. Bittre, smiling calmly.

Gyro sensed the tenseness coming from the suited stranger and decided to move over closer to Ray in order to discover what was bothering him.

"Hey Ray man I thought you'd be chatting with Liz and the Big New Yorker staff. Have you lost her?" Asked Gyro politely. He could hear Tony attempting to change the subject of conversation slightly as he smoked his roll-up.

"No. I'm just looking for the professors. I've got some ideas I need to discuss." Said Mr. Bittre.

"Well the last time I saw them they were in the dining-room next to the kitchen. I'll take you to meet them if you want but you only have to head into the back of the house. Follow the path. You can hear them talking." Replied Gyro.

Mr. Bittre stood up quickly and marched towards the house, glass in hand as Gyro returned his attention to the group under the tree.

"My apologies Laurie, he works in advertising and he gets a bit stressed sometimes." He said to the American lady.

* *"There's a startling difference in that respect between Americans and some Europeans. I think a lot of Americans experience that when they travel

Friendliness just comes more naturally to Americans. Strangely enough, to Tibetans as well." She nodded at the robed figure sitting next to her. *"That's one of the reasons I think Americans and Tibetans have this strange sense of kinship. Anyway, seeing that friendliness rise out of this democracy is a thrill."*

Tony laughed suddenly. *"I guess it's not a time to mention that my bladder is bursting."* He stood up and stretched in his T-shirt and shorts. *"Please excuse me while I go and have a slash."* He said walking towards the house.

As Gyro looked around the group and occasionally stole a glance at the hundreds of guests talking and laughing around the garden, all he could see was happiness, people enjoying themselves. His Mother and Father always told him that was what life was all about. That laughing was the most important thing. Gyro wondered about O.D. Darren. He had always thought that O.D. Darren had become lost as a person at the odd times when he bumped into him in Hackney. When had he decided that life had nothing more to offer him. There had been comments from people at the funeral about suicide but whenever Gyro had spoken to him he had thought that suicide had occurred to most people at some point in their lives. People were always living or dying depending on how they looked at life. It had a lot to do with perspective. Whether a person treated the planet like a hotel or a house to pass on to the next generation. Gyro suddenly felt anxious for the future of the planet. He thought it was because of the conversation. He continued to listen to the group under the tree.

"Restlessness. I have this sense that people are very restless these days, and that's always a good sign. Because it means they're questioning and some of the answers are making them uncomfortable, and that's the only way things ever get better on a large scale." Said Laurie as Charles Darwin and the Dalai Lama continued to listen, nodding occasionally. *"I see this growing lack of fear at making contact with other people. It took a while to build, but I think it's become more and more pronounced."* Laurie smiled. *" So there — that's one solid, good thing about the future."*

Something about the way this woman spoke seemed to eliminate any worries Gyro had been having and he could begin to understand why some artists on the planet could lead the good fight while others merely followed. Gyro offered some wine to Charles Darwin whose eyes seemed to be sparkling with enthusiasm for all things living. The conversation was returning to the funeral earlier in the day.

"Yes please." He beamed at Laurie Anderson. *"I haven't listened to a lot of music but I know what I like and I loved your album with 'O Superman' on it. There's poetry comparable to Tennyson and E.E. Cummings on that. Let X=X has to be the best song to play at a funeral I've ever heard. A true classic. Well done!"*

"Vinyl is always superior sound..." Said Gyro slightly drunk. *"Always more of an event."*

"If there's a choice between digital and analogue, I guess I'm more of an analogue kind of guy." Replied Charles Darwin tipping what looked like small mushrooms into his glass of wine.

"You'll have to excuse me but I also have to use the toilet." Said Gyro standing up.

The Dalai Lama stood up, politely adjusted his robes and leaned forward slightly and smiled softly.

* *"I see a good journey ahead and I see a safe return."* He said.

As he wobbled towards the direction of the garden path, Gyro could hear the conversation continue behind him.

"Have you ever heard of Klaus Wunderlick?" Charles asked Laurie Anderson.

Through the trees at the end of the garden strode the intimidating figure of Ray Connif.

* **Quote from the movie KUNDJUN directed by Martin Scorscese**

* **©1996 Tweak Magazine Laurie Anderson Interview**

TUESDAY 11TH SEPTEMBER 2001 NIGHT / SOHO

LISTEN TO THE VOICE OF BUDDHA

*No it ain't Judgement Day no it ain't Armageddon
Just the apple stretching and yawning New York putting its feet on the floor*
GRACE JONES

THE FERRAL FILM directors had set Dexter Wexford up for at least two more years. Some of the meetings that Dexter had recently been attending with the dashing Ray Connif in Soho were taking the future of advertising to such dizzy heights that he had been almost tempted to call on a priest for the moral dilemma he had found himself currently in. A company from Albuquerque in New Mexico had recently called his office and given him the entire pension scheme, company yacht and even a possible Nobel Prize for the oncoming century. As he sat in his office he had been considering the possibility of marketing on Mars and then moving onto Venus. Nano-Advertising. He swilled the Buckyball Brandy around in his decanter and chuckled to himself. Even his archrival Ray Connif would have to admit that Big New Yorker had been slow on the uptake with that one.

The Institute of Practitioners in Advertising had better get the red carpet ready for the announcement he would make tonight live from the Bafta building. The company in Albuquerque had finally discovered how to fix an advertising trailer for a movie onto a group of atoms and were able to inject the combination into a goldfish. Somehow causing it to appear in the very cinema that had been about to show the film on the Moon. The chances of the fish using free choice in such an experiment were statistically mediocre to say the least and the floodgates were now open. Advertising was indeed the most influential aspect of mass popular culture. Now advertising could be passed onto the clients with a handshake, literally in a femtosecond. Hair lice and germs could be selling products.

In fact the original proposal of the idea had been a happy accident. A blessing in disguise. Dexter Wexford had discovered that magazines and newspapers could be injected and not only could The Media be transferred genetically from generation to generation but the possibilities were endless. Movies were already great advertisements for guns, weapons of mass destruction and food. But product placements inside the consumers on this level meant that a person could eat or swallow a product without realising that they had eaten enough advertising campaigns to last a lifetime. Once they were dead the product could steer them to keep buying and consuming right through to the next level. Even when they were aboard a Bridgett.

Dexter looked down from his smoke-glassed windows over Soho and laughed. The consumers were now moving into a new era and they had no idea how busy they were. They would be born with a desire to buy the right brands by the age of three months after being bombarded with product trailers while they were still in the womb. Of course by then the new viruses would be hatched and the ability to consume would grow and grow.

The Mini campaign had originated the whole thing for Dexter. He had called the offices of King Penguin Media in Albuquerque with the plan to build the first Mini on Earth, which could finally live up to its name. The Mini could be squeezed into the bloodstream instead of the client squeezing into the vehicle. Parking had been a slight problem in London for years. Now the problem had been instantly eliminated. The experience of having a car driving around your body as you walked had been a classic and thanks to the beautiful Britt clones working on the campaign. There was only the developing of Fluidic Text Biscuits, Foglet Catalogue Snacks, Nuclear Powered Ray-Bans and Fractal Robot Trailers. A full range of Fullerene Internet-Meals, The Louvre Trips were his favourite. An entire art gallery experience with sleeping French wardens included and confused tourists, the surroundings up to the Eiffel Tower and all in a delicious hazelnut coating. He rubbed the small spare tire of fat around his midriff as he leaned back in his chair and chuckled. Dexter had eaten the simulations of The Guggenheim all the way to the Tribecca many times.

Dexter loved advertising and he loved beating the competition even more. The Feral Directors had been a good start but the beauty of Nano-Advertising was that it all worked on such a level that Deja-vu had been doing nicely in sales of perfume and the compact discs of bands that littered his office were doing unbelievable business. The copyright laws could be curved. How could you sue a company if you could not even find it? If it had been sitting literally right under your nose the entire time? Tower blocks were indeed big bogies on the landscape.

The problem for Dexter had been that he was the only person enjoying the non-reality and most people hardly believed him when he told them about it all. He could hardly show anyone the Mini except when they fell asleep and it kept appearing in their dreams. The part the young genius liked about the Nano-Mini was that now a person drive in while asleep and the streets of London were always free of traffic at last. Although there seemed to be a lot of people in the roads being run down by consumers of Citrone drinks as a result. The free car in every can - literally! campaign Had been a bit of a turkey though. A mere hic-cup. His new campaign for The Pipe-Cleaner would put him back on top. If he got bored he could always rewind and watch the speech he was about to give at the Bafta building.

As Dexter looked over at his new mobile phone that had already been tested in space and emitted a low gravitational force field causing ripples from the fifth dimension to echo towards him. He realised that he had to fold time in order to speak to the lady who had made a lot of these technological break throughs possible. Liz Goldberg. A lot of people would be gradually understanding that none of what they had previously thought of as life was really life at all.

She had already been calling his office all day on track eleven, for fifteen seconds and Dexter pulled out a small digital orange disc and pushed it into the mobile as it hung in the air. The best part about life when you understood most of it had been a simulation was that you could just play recordings back to people and they had to take that reality and like it.

London had been a classic disc to watch. Dexter had always been a hopeless romantic and had decided to view one of his favourite years again. Just for the eighth time. Viewing the year of 2001-2002 on Earth was a classic track. From September 7th the orange disc he was watching at the moment in 2050 had become stuck after he left the disc on his coffee table and accidentally spilt some G-WIZ on it. When he scanned the disc through the Bridgett-Detector he had seen a short scratch and unfortunately his favourite part of the year just played over on a loop. That was technology for you though. Hardly perfect.

Dexter wondered for a brief moment where his rival Ray Connif had been for the last few days. When he called by the office on Denmark Street there had only been Liz running the show. Now she was calling from the future and after watching the scene eight times he knew too well what this part would be about. He had actually gotten her to make the disc she was calling in to interrupt him on after she had landed on the Moon. He had been surprised however to discover that she had started The Three Breakfasts Corporation without listening to O.D. Darren though. That part had really interested him. The sex scene in the toilet had been nearly worn out and the moment where O.D. Darren died still managed to get Dexter weeping.

He looked around the unreal interior of his office that he had King Penguin Multi-Media fold from another part of space. They were doing a sideline in Space Instillations and they entire fluctuation was coming live from some place called Fifty-Five Cancri. Chris T the artist assured him this was at least forty-one light years away from Earth. Dexter had been watching the battle scenes of bloodshed circling around him with fascination. He forgot how much it had all cost to fold it direct but as he spat the Buckyball Brandy out onto his office desk with disgust Dexter decided that it had to go, he had already become bored by it.

He looked down at his miniature silicon model of Manhattan positioned on his desk and realised the sell by date had expired again. Every time on the simulation this happened and already had caused the island of Manhattan to go off and decay. Dexter had also accidentally dropped his model Jumbo Jet into the skyline of the New York structure and had probably demolished the Twin Towers again. Bugger.

Outside on the rainy streets of Soho the simulated old bricked corner of Old Compton street and Frith street looked relatively normal from the outside. Inside however, the ten-year old tyrant of the future of advertising stood on the big chair and stared out at the people who looked like ants below him. Bored and terribly alone.

Soon he could retire and head back to school, folding time was fun but in the year 2050 Dexter still had exams to take after the holidays were over. The ten-year-old decided to fold over to the Leicester Square simulation and watch his first movie. Then he would fold back to his home of 2050 before his Mother found out that he was playing in the simulator again without asking permission things were not so bad after all and if anything, the Feral Film Directors had set Dexter Wexford up for at least two more years.

TUESDAY 11TH SEPTEMBER 2001
EVENING / NOTTING HILL

SEND IN THE CLONES

*Took all the trees and put them in a tree museum
And they charged the people a dollar and a half just to see 'em*
JONI MITCHELL

BRITT SHOT DOWN the stairs of the Big New Yorker offices from the toilet and ran towards The Clean Room holding her blue and orange mobile phone. Albert Einstein had suggested an idea to her during a brief interval from the party on the Isle of Wight in England and Britt was now calling her directly from the bathroom of the huge manor house where the Physicists were discovering the joys of a game called Beer Hunter in the kitchen. The eggnog had been already finished and they were now moving onto Tequila slammers. Britt had made a subtle request to Albert and had managed to piece together the last of the information required to bring a reign of terror and destruction throughout the world, once the threat of imminent destruction had been placed into the hands of Mr. Bittre who seemed convinced that the oncoming apocalypse would be brought about by graphic design.

Britt pushed the wooden buttons into a central locking keypad which opened the oak wooden door to The Clean Room and entered the laboratory, carefully constructed to take on the appearance of a deep forest during the Autumn. As she located the first tree on her right Britt listened carefully to the instructions she was receiving via satellite from one of her many probe-clones stationed around the planet. Number forty-one was in Newtown. The entire room had been so carefully designed by her employer Mr. Bittre that anyone passing the open door would have fainted from the sheer overwhelming madness of a complete replica of The New Forest built into part of the building. From the outside of the grey stone construction on Portobello Road, the appearance of a normal semi-detached Victorian house converted into a split-level office with a Prêt A Manger sandwich shop beneath it, would have done little to catch the eye of any of the hundreds of tourists. They were too busy marching from the tube station in search of the book shop that Hugh Grant and Julia Roberts had spent a gruelling week at, pretending to fall in love during the filming of the movie Notting Hill.

From the inside of Big New Yorker, if anyone had managed to locate one of the clones using the phones at the reception area, or even walking down the winding staircase to get a sandwich, they would have assumed probably that Britt had a sister or twin-sisters. The secret that the soft-spoken German had researched before being cloned had been to make sure that all the clones were always dressed in different uniforms. Or to be certain that she would never be in the same room for long enough to be asked questions about any doubles who were in the room with her.

Parties had already been a breeze simply because no one really bothered asking anything of much importance. People were usually too busy talking about themselves or somebody famous. Most people had thought cloning to be mere science-fiction. The odd times that Britt had been caught out by the appearance of one of her copies, she had been able to convince the witness quite easily that they had only seen someone who resembled her. Most people on Earth were only after a quiet life anyway. They had no desire to get involved. Britt had slipped out and tested the theory by getting drunk in pubs and explaining that she had arrived on Earth as part of a huge plan to wipe out the human race with MGD - Molecular Graphic Design. A lot of the customers in the pub had found this hilarious.

However, the Millennium was making it easier for clones to get work. Apart from the occasional photographic shoot for a film poster or appearance in a music video, Britt had been forced to rely mostly on any powerful and highly insane projects to take over the planet Earth. Whereby she worked freelance. Fortunately world domination had begun making a huge comeback and she had now found herself backing a huge winner. This plan had the stamp of genius all over it and she had been slightly impressed by the select and delicate way that it had been sealed together.

Mr. Bittre had finally called her on the mobile phone and asked her to wait before beginning the procedure of splitting the atom and holding it within the logo of G-WIZ in preparation for The Comma War. The intrinsic methods of doing the almost impossible required just one more piece of the formula and that had turned up in the form of the drug itself. Which came from the fruit of the Singularity Tree that Britt was now standing under. The surrounding view had been folded through space directly from the New Forest via a handy little idea called the fifth dimension by King Penguin Multi-Media. The original birthplace of the big bang.

The part Britt liked most about the idea of the apocalypse of Mr. Bittre had been the setting. She had listened intently as they had both journeyed in the Zoa-pod to Earth where she had been pleasantly surprised by the simplicity of the scheme. Simply fold time back to the original creation of the Earth and the Universe and then look out for the very thing that started it all rolling. The bonus from the first visit by Mr. Bittre had been the drug taken from the Garden of Eden called *Phenylalainemontovia Dymulsive Cronoconiff*. Or G-WIZ.

Once the drug had been manufactured, then all the time in the world would allow Mr. Bittre to build one of the largest corporations in the known Universe. Folding time and collecting the various parts whenever he wanted. One of the more useful parts of the plan had been that Mr. Bittre need not worry about the moral perspective of the great plan because a certain physicist had proven that God would not interrupt due to being proven unnecessary. So the plan had all been coming together rather splendidly. It had been around this point when Britt had read an advertisement placed in an English magazine named Creative Review requesting several clones to assist in his plan to take over the world. The advert read like this;

The one part of the advert that had caught the attention of Britt had been world domination. She had already made enough money with most of her clones by getting them to appear as extras in various movies all over the world. Some of them were already working freelance for the Irrigation

Project but the important thing for Britt had been that most of them were following the rich path of decisions rather than the poor. Soon they would all be part of history.

She stood under one of the silver birch trees and watched as the forest completed a circuit of the computer program currently running. First the random wind element blew the leaves from the tree, which fell to the ground. The acorns and the apples were already rotting on the grass and a grey squirrel ran out from the hedgerow collected some of the acorns as two crows flew overhead. Over the tops of the trees. Britt followed.

She arrived at the edge of a small pond in the clearing and looked up at the nest the two crows had landed in. As the birds bounced on the branch, a small piece of bark floated down to the grass and landed next to a tiny metal wire framed cube poking out of the ground. The entire forest was a simulation currently set on track five playing through to track eight and could never be interrupted once a person set the program running.

Britt crouched down and pulled the long elongated silver Hurrier out of the soft wet Earth. The device had been used to measure time and could trap particles and molecules from entire eras of history. Britt took a reading off the side. Inside, electronic diodes read out the vast number of centuries and millenniums on the display. They were already a number of such devices buried throughout the forest. Each revealing the only true history of the Earth. Each from the future. Down the side, the logo of The Diner Holistic had been embossed into the surface, along with the elegant signature of Mr. Bittre. The words Limited Edition were printed on the top.

Orders had come direct from the entity himself on her mobile that Bittre was on his way back and wanted the plan for world domination to begin once the forest had completed track eight of the program. Britt was no scientist. She still held onto a marginal cluster of brain cells that functioned relatively well. She was constantly surprised by the unfolding of the plan but recognised the reading of the Hurrier. Mr. Bittre had been right all along. The years from both 2050 onwards had completely disappeared and the period known as The Dark Ages from 1000-1500 A.D. had vanished from sight but only from the country of Ireland.

Britt quickly checked the bark around the base of the conifer for interference and gasped. Words of English had been carved into the bark of the tree.

She scrambled around the bottom of the tree trunk to read the sentence. Bewildered.

THE COMMA WAR HAS BEGUN, LONG LIVE THE COMMA

Britt knew she had the only access code to The Clean Room apart from Mr. Bittre and also knew that The Comma War had been such a vast war, that it had altered time and space already. This one War had caused such disillusionment that The Great Blur had been forced into preceding it. She had already studied the reports from the future files of the Hurriers during her coffee breaks and her head reeled thinking about what would happen next.

The simplest thing in the world had started the onset of the most devastating war of all time and as Britt stood up with the Hurrier in her hand she almost dropped the device with shock. She closed her eyes and tried to breathe calmly.

The images from The Comma War had already been seen by two of her clones. The concentration of information came pouring into her mind and she dropped the Hurrier onto the ground and fell to her knees. Automatically she pushed the balls of both hands up into her eyes to divert the flood of devastation, which continued unabated to flash across her memory cells. All the dead bodies. Mountains made of people, of corpses. Years of fighting which would continue. Ripples of destruction reaching out across the entire planet. Families divided. Friends torturing friends through methods learned and passed from generation to generation. Continuously. Forever. Attempts by the resistance to quench the fire. Hair pulled from scalps and sold. People turned into furniture.

All because of a comma in a sentence which would finally return the silence after years of destruction. Bringing the era of The Great Blur with it. Whereby nothing would appear as it seemed. Nothing would be true. Truth would always be opinion. Opinion would be objectionable and only in time could answers be found. Chaos from order and devastating, gut-churning, wrenching, negative, over-loading panic. Pain. World pain. Holocausts. Fire. Showers.

Her whole body shook as her adreno-glands began to work overtime to enable a giant concrete wall to be built over the images. She squeezed her eyelids and her whole face tightly as brief images flashed past in the dark. Connecting all the horror to positive thoughts. Medicine. Headaches. Tense nervous headaches. Have you sent your children to have their medical experiments done yet. Asked a voice.

The insanity and terror of such destruction over something so simple as to where to place a comma in a sentence forced itself like a hot bullet of light shot into the centre of her mind. Then calm and peace flooded through her whole body. She could hear the wings of butterflies beating. The sound in the air. Held in the oxygen. The atoms. The molecules. Electrons. Carbon. Airwaves. Rays of light. Break it down. Impossible. Each cell rejuvenated. Each eyeball had already seen. Nothing can be kept so secret. Nothing can end. Off with the wind, blending. To the sea. Merging. Day into night. Music made from hydrogen bombs. The atoms of carbon blended into ink, put words on paper and printed. Let the whole world know. Let them read it. Let them not forget it ever. Vexxen. Change.

Calmness. The waves on the beach came crashing to the shore and passed the beach once more.

Britt knew already what would come and knew suddenly that she had repeated this action at least eight times. Her hand felt weary as it lifted the mobile phone from the ground and her thumb weighed heavier than the entire forest cubed and crushed. Yet a fallen star, a black hole could not forbid her pushing skin cell to rubber emergency button as the click of radio signal sent itself out across the forest to every member at Big New Yorker throughout the world. The crows cawed from their nest. Escaping the tidal wave of blame yet again. The birds looked down at the perspective of a tall German lady marching quickly towards the exit door near a cluster of golden daffodils and shouting into a mobile.

"SEND IN THE CLONES!" Yelled Britt into the mobile giving the code signal that one of the clones patched through to all the offices around the world as she ran under the branches of the silver birch trees. She thought briefly for a moment and then added. *"And make sure they look cool and there hair is nice and neat."*

Then she realised that this entire situation involved world domination, The Comma War and The Great Blur rolled together and would require some serious demands. As she left the Clean Room and headed for the office staircase, she spooke politely into the phone. *"Oh and one of the clones bring me a latte and some Quark bittre..."*

Britt shot down the stairs of the Big New Yorker offices from the toilet and ran towards The Clean Room holding her blue and orange mobile.

WEDNESDAY 12TH SEPTEMBER
2001 PROBABILITY / IRELAND

A BIG HAND FOR THE TIME DISCIPLES

This wrinkle in time can't give it no credit
I thought about my space and I really got me down
I got me so down I got me a headache
FRANK BLACK

THE CLOCK ON the wall of the pub read half past three. Yet the large Moon held in the night sky outside seemed to contradict this by its simple appearance as it reflected the seven-minute-old rays of light down from an incandesant ball of gas called the Sun down onto the rooftops of Galway. The light of the afternoon had blended quietly with the warm milk of the evening and the deep notes of the wooden clock ticking seemed to reflect the weighted tones of conversation around a large round wooden table near the fireplace of the Kings Head.

The goblets of Guinness were lined up on the stand of the bar and were settling down nicely should anyone have been timing the good work of the barman they may have noticed that he had been pouring them for approximately five hundred and twenty-seven years. Apart from the occasional difference of opinions he had heard over the centuries none counted as interesting as those he had heard at these meetings. Unfortunately and fortunately he could never decide how long they would go on and the fact that most of the customers would order one pint of Guinness during the course of the meeting explained that the following nights after the barman would have to put the price of the bar drinks up in order to make the difference. He was a practical man. Even though he had not been outside the pub since King Arthur had been in and ordered a shandy some centuries ago. He looked across to the meeting, which had already begun at the back of the room. The Time Disciples were holding one of their rare meetings in the abandoned pub on King Street in Galway on the coldest and rainiest night in Ireland. It was Summer.

"So gentlemen...I guess I need not mention some of the recent occurrences of anti-matter which have turned up..." Said a bearded figure. A general murmur moved around the darkly lit atmosphere of the interior and settled back on the shoulders of Dermot who sat closest to the fire. *"We have discovered anomalies in time which seem to be increasing in size and frequency around the planet Earth. Brian has spotted two already in New York while he was working undercover at 'Michael's Pub'. He also said he saw Woody Allen playing clarinet there and if you ask him later, he'll tell you all about it."*

All smiles and eyes in the room shifted over and up to the grand sight of a man in a white shirt and black trousers who was grinning with a huge satisfied expression on his face.

"We have, for the first time in over two thousand years been called out of retirement by the great artist himself to sort the mess out. It would seem our old friend Mr. Bittre has made an appearance on this planet and is causing disturbances in TIME and LIFE and SPACE...again." Continued the deep Irish accent of Dermot as he supped slowly on his goblet of beer. *"I, for one, have a serious bone with the chaos that he has brought to the place out of order although I wish him no harm. The poor lad is simply lost. We must therefore find the location of his next appearance and encourage him back to The Diner Holistic."* Murmurs of agreement rang out across the pub.

"How is he getting into the Earth plain? I thought yer man had sorted that out." Asked a voice from the back of the room as murmurs of agreement spread around the circle.

Dermot stood up and placed his pint of stout on the wooden table and cleared his throat as he produced a sheet of paper from his inside coat pocket. *"Bittre is stronger these days. He's even learning at such a rate that he has written these words and left them in this very place."*

There was a burst of disapproval as most of the mass inside the room began to raise their voices.

"Gentlemen please..." The noise of voices dropped quiet again as Dermot held up the note. *"I will read out what was written, but the handwriting speaks for itself..."* A hush enveloped the crowd as everyone waited to hear the words of their nemesis and as Dermot coughed again the only sound

in the pub came from the crackling of the fire and the clock on the wall ticking.

"It would seem of late that I know nothing. The slate has been wiped clean and we are all on the run. I lost my GUT and thank the maker someone stills this night for the planet. When Moon keeps barking and no love will comfort too soon...where is love? This willow-wick candle gives little light to fuel my tale. Where are the knights so virtuous and true. Are there no knights? None to be here on this tale of death." Another murmur of disapproval rang around the crowd. Dermot let the unmistakable words of Bittre echo into the souls of each member present and then continued. *" Fandoople your fries butcher. I am mere flotsam to your jetsam and cat curiosity barks. Gosh and gibbly. You have no virtuous knights and I know this. The ripping is a tearing. This world has fallen once before into darkness and yet without our horses of sweat on steed there will be no demons snuffed out by the brethren on the crystal night air. Does the Moon make you bark? For the sun is also needed on this quest. You are not scared though. Can you taste it?*

Men machines show love. Fall to the willow-wick. Fall to the planet again. For there are images coming through and they speak louder amidst this jumble of mixed emotions than any noble curse of armoury. Yet where is love?

Still we trip in darkness and leeches of faith are needed to suck on your true love. What will it be mankind? A pitiful cough. A gasp at what is lost and a last look at life through ale? Oh snoozy-woozy mankind. The noble thoughts of women and what they must burden in your life is not enough? Come on fucker! Where is love?

A ripping is a tearing and a cracking is a thundering and the sound of hoofs on stone and across wood far off in the distance is no sound to fear. Bring it closer now and let your knights enter. For they will fight the good fight with honour and you cannot lose." Dermot looked up at the faces around him. No one had made a sound through the entire reading. *"For they fight for true love and there is no more noble a cause on any world - you cannot lose. Believe me, you cannot lose."*

A deathly hush fell over those gathered in the room. Dermot sat back down and let the paper lower to the table with the solemn expression of a weary traveller who had just missed the last ferry to Ireland and had been forced to spend the night in Holyhead in a tent. One of the lecturers from Galway University stood up.

"Sounds like the positive electrons have shifted position into a negative state..." Said a voice at the back.

"Every action has a reaction...I can understand that two of the time holes have appeared but where do we begin the search for the others?" Asked another.

"London, England. Superior, Wisconsin. The United States. The Philippines. Australia and Hong Kong. Oh and Newtown on the Isle of Wight...and..." Spoke a calm German female voice from somewhere at the back of the crowd. Everyone shuffled and moved trying to find the location of the voice. *"...a place somewhere in Europe called Paris. Of course those are only the time-holes that have been presented by the good doctor and Max Born..."*

"Who are you and where is that person speaking from?" Commanded the voice of Dermot as the crowd of bearded disciples stood up around the table.

A tall and slim elegantly dressed lady entered into the circle wearing a long dark coat. All the men stood around the circular table and as all the eyes in the room fell on her she placed a bottle of the red wine she had borrowed from the big manor house of Tony Webb in Newtown.

"Hello. I'm Britt and I'm here to help. Does anyone have a cork-screw?" Asked Britt.

"She was on television during the World Trade disaster!" Spoke another of the time disciples.

"How do you know of the time-holes?" Asked Dermot.

"I've been observing the artists at work but you only have to watch Top of The Pops these days to notice the loops and the time-traps occurring." Said Britt flippantly. *"I've just used one to get here but to be honest that is the least of your problems. There is something far greater to be worrying about right at this moment."* She said.

"Far greater than that which we've just heard...far greater than the arrival of Mr. Bittre...?" Asked another disciple.

"Where do you want me to start...? *Human demand for resources of this planet in the year 1961 stood at 70 per cent of the Earth's sustainable capacity. By the year 1970 it had risen to match the global supply of the entire planet and in 1999 it had exceeded it by 20 per cent. Now that's just for beginners..." Britt said and looked at all the people around the bar. Everyone looked

embarrassed. "On Earth the enervation of agriculture is equivalent to the destruction of a football pitch every twenty minutes. It cannot sustain life forever you know unless people start looking after the place." Britt inhaled deeply on her roll-up and blew smoke into the air forming a perfect diagram of the Earth and the surrounding planets, which began to orbit the flame of the match she was still holding. Everyone in the bar gasped in bewilderment and watched as the elegant German lady demonstrated how the turning of the Earth revealed the various mapped out countries frozen and perfectly carved from grey smoke. A spotlight picked out the country known as Greenland.

"The way things are heading here, there's going to be a situation on this planet that even the greatest minds of the century might be able to help with if they stop walking the same path as previous worn out roads and focus their energies in a more positive area." She said looking at each of the faces around the room.

The smoke drifted away showing the surface of what was unmistakably the outline of a gigantic Tectonic-Freighter, under the ice of the surface of Greenland shaped like a mammoth Mantor-Ray. Once the ice had broken away the diagram revealed how the vessel was moving together and joining with other sections to form a vast ship even bigger in scale than the original ship. Everyone became hypnotised. Britt continued to smoke and blew out perfect balls of smoke that turned into globes representing yet more orbiting planetary spheres.

"Everyone on this planet who is human is walking the same path. All die eventually and there is nothing that can be done to stop that." Britt breathed in yet more of the smoke and exhaled. "Everyone on this planet must learn to calm down. Mr. Bittre is trying to teach this, yet as the planets turn he is getting more powerful and only one thing can stop him. Otherwise..."

Gradually the diagram that could be seen forming was being pieced together. Each country was shaking off a camouflage of rock and river as it rose up and linked together like a three-dimensional global jigsaw puzzle made of smoke. In turn forming another planet. All that was left spinning above the table was a ball of water.

"This is a diagram formed to explain the future plan of Mr. Bittre. He is already getting stronger each day that passes. But he can be stopped. No one must kill him for without him we would not learn about ourselves and what *we are all truly capable of. There are doctors who are here to help also. There are X-Chromo-pilots from Fifty-Five-Cancri and they are well aware of the plan. You shall meet them all. Any questions?"* She asked.

"You said one thing could stop him..." Asked Dermot. *"What is it?"*

Britt turned her calm expression to face Dermot.

"How did you stop him, two thousand Earth years ago?"

"We didn't...someone else did." Said Dermot bashfully.

"Yet that being did show you a way of stopping him... from ever emerging again." Hinted Britt.

Everyone looked around at each other nervously attempting to explain how Mr. Bittre had been forced away from Earth. Britt continued to build the floating holistic puzzle above the round wooden table. Smoking and exhaling yet more planets. Forming Galaxies and Universes. The names of each star and Universe began to gradually build a picture of an immense Multi-Universe each with a planet similar in appearance to Earth and orbiting a separate Sun.

"What do you think keeps all this working and stops people crashing planes into tall buildings every day of the week?" Asked Britt.

She looked around at all the disciples who had sat down and begun to listen attentively as if they were in a classroom knew the answer but were too worried at being looked at to actually answer the question. Britt looked around the table and waited in the silence, even the smoke could be heard in the silence as it span in the air.

"There is only one force that can be used against the most powerful demons. Only one force powerful enough to stop them all and the likes of Mr. Bittre from their gradual emergence..."

Suddenly the mouth of Britt blew at the diagram sending one of the planets hurtling towards another, which in turn caused the Earth to wobble from its axis and hurtle into the Sun. The next effect was a powerful explosion, which dissolved all the planets in the diagram and in turn continued to expand outward until all that was left above the table was a cloud of smoke, which drifted and dispersed upward to the lights of the candles around the pub. The apocalypse had been seen.

"...*Love.*" Said Britt calmly as she looked around those gathered at the table.

Almost immediately as she spoke the word the dispersed vapours of smoke drifted backwards to their original settings and reformed the diagram as if nothing had happened.

Britt spoke calmly reaching into her shawl and pulling out a book. "*Excuse the pun but you are running out of time. You also have to sort some style out. You can't go out and save the planet dressed in big sweaters and beards. No one will take you seriously. You all need a severe makeover. I've read some ideas in this...*" She threw a large thick sketchbook onto the table, which landed in the centre with a loud thud destroying the diagram yet again. All the disciples stared at the dusty cover dumbfounded. It read;

SAVE CHANGES AGAIN
THE TIME DISCIPLES SEARCH FOR GYRO & THE HOLY GRAIL

"*What is that?*" Asked Dermot suspiciously looking down at the cover.

"*Well that's the next adventure that you're going to be having... I've also just signed a great deal with Paramount, which includes merchandise such as T-shirts, Mr. Bittre car-stickers, bath mats and watches.*" She turned to a disciple nearby and smiled at him." *The T-shirts are so cool. They say, 'I'M NOT BITTER. I'M Mr. BITTRE!'* " Laughed Britt. The disciple smiled back although slightly bewildered. "*The profits from all that and the movie rights should fund each of your journeys to the various locations all over the planet in order to fix the holes and meet back in time to stop Mr. Bittre but most of the details are already in the book.*"

"*What is a Gyro?*" Asked a disciple cautiously. "*Is it like the quarks we've been hearing about.*"

"*It's not a what, It's a who but it's about as difficult to get hold of as a Holy Grail these days.*" Said Britt with a chuckle as she rolled a cigarette between her fingers. "*Gyro is the man that you have to go and locate. There's a picture of him in the book. He's just folded to a place where your quest should begin called Tibet. The problem is, if you read the book then you'll just copy exactly what's already happened and it's important that you don't copy but lead they way.*" She nodded matter-of-factly at her new pupils.

"Where is the Grail?" Asked Dermot.

"At the moment, it's in a pub in Hackney in England, London. The alien who has it thinks it's fake but it shouldn't be long before he works out that it's the actual Grail. The really big problem is that he's getting very close to Mr. Bittre."

Outside the old cottage she sighed pub the rain was beginning again and now that Britt held the attention of every person inside she decided that most of the plan of Max Born was coming together and stood up from the table.

"Now to the business at hand... gentlemen. Does anyone have a cork-screw?" Asked Britt as she looked around the pub. The clock on the wall of the pub read half past three. Yet the large Moon held in the night sky outside seemed to contradict this by its simple appearance.

---

*Tuesday 25 June 2002 Proceedings of the National Academy of Sciences

FRIDAY 7TH SEPTEMBER 2001
AFTERNOON / AMSTERDAM

SIX GNOSSIENNES:
No.2 AVEC ETONNEMENT

It took a lost weekend in a hotel in Amsterdam
and double pneumonia in a single room
And the sickest joke was the price of the medicine
Are you laughing at me now may I please laugh along with you
LLOYD COLE

BRITT AND GYRO glided around the corner to Voorburgwal Straat in the heavily built Dutch rain. Following the cobbled street until they reached the bridge that crossed over one of the hundreds of canals that ran though Amsterdam crowded with elegantly painted barges and stoned motorboat enthusiasts. Across from where they were standing a vertical sign smiled Hotel the Crown back at them sleepily, hanging from the front of the hotel. Two large soaked flags hung under the sign. One American and one English.

Through stoned, jet-lagged and time-travelled eyes, Gyro squinted around at the various assorted dealers gathering on the bridge and was momentarily reminded of being in a zombie movie. As they both wobbled across the bridge Britt gestured at a fast food outlet, which was set on the corner. Huge red Pantone 032 letters shouted out the word FEBO loudly from the shade of yellow that Gyro usually associated with the jerseys of German cyclists he had seen in the Tour De France. He had read in a magazine on the plane that people often wore yellow more than any other colour when they committed suicide and had pondered for a brief moment on why articles about suicide were leaking out from his memory whenever he got on an aeroplane.

"Have you ever wondered what they put in the food in those places?" Asked Britt.

Gyro was still giggling from the joint they had both smoked in the coffee shop. *"Isn't it obvious?"* He replied. *"They put FEBO in the food! It's all made from the finest quality FEBO that money can buy!"*

"But what is FEBO?" She asked staring back at him suddenly sounding like a girl at school he had once known.

"I thought, someone who worked in a diner would know the answer to such trivial questions. I mean, Dutch as a language sounds as if it would be closer to German than any other... to someone English that is." He replied as politely as possible. Then he attempted to read the words underneath the large red letters and immediately fell over.

"I thought FEBO was an English word, maybe it's an initial. Maybe it stands for something?" He pulled himself up from the surface of the bridge and leaned against the icy metal railings of the canal. He thought he could see his hands turning light blue from the cold.

"Maybe..." The way his brain was feeling the interest stopped right where the question began. *"Where are we heading in this wonderful Dutch weather Britt?"* He asked.

"Hotel the Crown." Replied Britt as she walked over to help him walk forward. *"This way."*

The coldness of the rain on his face and hair felt like a baptism. Gyro made a mental note to himself never to complain about the weather in England again if he ever got back there. The distance to the hotel seemed as if it would take light years to travel. As they attempted to get to the hotel every creature they passed was either growling or trying to sell them something. From machine-guns to heroin or even people. Such was the price it seemed for changing the laws on drugs and prostitution. Gyro thought he was in a documentary about World War II. He suddenly remembered the images he had once seen in a library textbook about the holocaust and how bodies of Dutch people had been hung from telegraph poles around the edge of the towns.

He reached the steps of the hotel and looked up at the typically tall building, which looked like a difficult enough task to conquer without being stoned. Either it was the architecture or the hash they had just been smoking, but something seemed oddly familiar about the place to him. Britt helped him up the incredibly steep steps of the hotel which lead into a large wooden bar at the front. Pictures of European beers were posted all over the walls and a man with the largest moustache he had ever seen was polishing glasses, calmly passing the time.

As they entered the most relaxed hotel in the world, Gyro dropped his wet rucksack down on the floor and noticed his reflection in the large mirror behind the various bottles of alcohol on display. He looked like a drowned rat. Britt was laughing gently stood behind him at the image in the mirror, with the affection a Mother looking at her son after playing football. She pulled the scarf from her head revealing short-cropped orange hair interspersed with crops of varying lengths. The style suited her. She held the material out for him to dry himself off. That was when he noticed something peculiar. Under half the North Sea that had been falling down onto Amsterdam and the two travellers not one molecule seemed to have landed on Britt anywhere. He realised even when they had been standing outside that when she had pointed at the FEBO sign on the bridge, the rain seemed to just fall around her somehow, not on her. A cold shiver shot up his neck as he wiped even more of the cold water away.

"Shall I book you a room?" She asked in a soft German accent, which would cause even a hungry great white shark to flop over on its back and expect its tummy to be rubbed. Gyro found himself nodding, struck dumb again by her beauty as she leant against the bar and spoke in perfect Dutch to the man behind it. Forgetting completely for the moment that he held within his pockets of clothing not a single cent of the new Euro. He had forgotten to get any currency after the shock of waking up on a plane approximately ten thousand miles off course from the initial journey. *"Would you like a coffee? Have a seat and I'll bring it over to you..."* She said calmly.

Something about the way this lady spoke or even moved or even dressed was so graceful. As Gyro collapsed at the table by the window, he looked out back at the canal they had just walked across. His gaze drifted over the table to an Italian newspaper which a guest had left perhaps in the vague hope that someone here would like to learn Italian and for a moment thought his brain would leap out of his head and slap him rudely. The date at the top read exactly the same as when he had left Australia but there was something almost illegal about the year. In a moment of pure terror usually reserved for when he left his cashpoint card in the bank machine, Gyro noticed the year had changed. The type at the top of the newspaper calmly showed him the numbers 2002. Instead of the 2001 he had on his plane ticket. As he looked up at Britt and tried to persuade his brain to stay in his head he located the ticket and focused on the date. It did read 2001. He sighed with relief and then looked back at Britt.

Gyro found himself constantly looking over at her fascinated and bewildered. He retrieved a tobacco tin from his soaked jacket and proceeded to make another joint. Attempting to roll this one as perfectly as Britt had shown him before in the cafe. Outside the rain seemed to have a real mission set aside to drown everyone in Amsterdam. Gyro was reminded of the line from a movie called Taxi-Driver.

"Someday a real rain will come and wash all the scum off the streets..." Spoke Robert De Niro. Looking out at the canal the effect it was having on the living dead outside was miniscule. *"Someday a real rain will come and cause people to go indoors, until it passes..."* somehow, had less of an effect.

"Are you going to try that again?" Asked Britt as she slid a small cup of coffee across to him with her left hand. Matching the one she was stirring with her right. She sat down opposite him and winked.

"When in Rome..." Gyro replied.

"What would you say, if I told you that in two days time, the world was going to be very different?" Asked Britt with another mischievous wink.

"Is it something that you are likely to say?" He replied as he rolled the hash with his open palm.

"Perhaps." Spoke the German gracefully.

"Britt, I've just met you, but I have to tell you, I think you could say anything to me and it would sound fine." He said dreamily then suddenly remembered to ask her what day it was.

"You have to roll the joint like a cone, not a roll-up and it is Thursday. " She said smiling. *"September 7th..."* She continued to stir her coffee. *"...two thousand and two."* He dropped the hash on the floor and reached under the table to pick it up, immediately banging his head on the underneath of the wooden surface. Britt offered assistance.

"Thankyou, I think I can manage." He said as he began to build one of the worst constructed joints ever made. He felt his memory cells straining to remain in his skull. *"Sorry?! Did you say two thousand and two?"* He asked in a stunned voice as he looked back at the young lady who was calmly

nodding and smiling knowingly. Britt pulled a variety of newspapers off the bar and dropped them down onto the table with a thud. They all read 2002.

He handed her back the scarf about to apologise for making it so wet. Then he noticed how the piece of coloured textile was as dry as it had been when she originally handed it to him. Jet lag mixed with the smoking was causing him to hallucinate. That must be it. The sky outside appeared to be getting darker as if the clouds were a married couple setting up for a huge storm just as the only television in the house broke. The lobby of the Hotel the Crown took on a Gothic appearance.

Britt looked slightly glazed. *"The Earth is coming into an interesting time. A journey is being made along a train-track each day from today. Crowds of people will die or they will be saved. If they know which way to turn. What happened when you visited Newtown?"* She asked.

Gyro looked at her surprised spluttering smoke out the window and had a coughing fit. *"How did you know about Newtown?"* He asked. He had not told anyone about his dreams before, especially one where a figure had told him to visit a place called Newtown. The wooden lobby was getting darker by the second, he looked over to where the receptionist was lighting candles around the bar and felt as if he was in a church. When he looked back at her face, he noticed her eyes were closed. On the table she placed the five cards that Gyro had selected from the pack in The Greenhouse Effect coffee shop face down.

"There are many circles in life Gyro. All the best stories finish exactly as they began. Some continue. The ones who need to leave, who can see the change are not needed here. They have finished their part of the story. Like the Russian dolls. We live inside each other. What is coming will be hard for some, easy for others. Search and you will trap a fine clue. Mr. Bittre..." She winked again at him.

"Who told you about Newtown?" Asked Gyro again ignoring most of what Britt had said in a stoned fashion. *"There was a dream I had in Australia where someone told me to go to Newtown but I told no one about that. How did you know? And what year did you say it was?"* He read the top of the Italian newspaper which confirmed that it was indeed 2002. His heart began to beat quicker.

Britt seemed nonchalant but within the scene commanded calm attention. *"Let's have a look at your future, shall we?"* She turned over the first card. The ace of spades. Quickly followed by another. The ace of clubs. *"In pontoon the ace can be used as eleven. The middle card represents a clue of great significance."* As she turned over the third card Gyro spotted the words The Diner Holistic written on the underside of each card in gold letters.

"The ace of diamonds. Then the eight of diamonds and finally...a five of hearts...mmm. Can I have go on that joint now?" She asked chuckling. *"Do you have the time by the way?"*

Gyro looked down at his watch, which read 1:15PM exactly. The same time as when the plane had left Australia. The second hand was frozen as if the watch had all the mechanisms removed. He paused looking up at Britt.

"Er, it would seem not...no..."

Britt leaned closer to Gyro enjoying the intimacy of the situation. Suddenly a powerful sensation began to enter his forehead and he could feel an overwhelming surge of happiness and peace flood through his body. He naturally closed his eyes and had a vision of an Americana styled Diner at night. White spotlights lit the edge of the silver art deco roof and the building seemed to be floating on a black background.

Through the windows he could see the interior packed full of activity and muffled yells and cries to waitresses were made by a collection of different characters all bustling and moving. As his view floated and bobbed through the front silver entrance and over the jukebox. He heard the most exquisite jazz music and slowly manoeuvred and weaved over the seats to a table towards one end.

His vision recognised friends and actors and actresses from old Hollywood movies. There seemed to be an atmosphere of great celebration within the ornate building and the walls almost wobbled with the vibrations created from the sounds around him. Gyro could see O.D. Darren a friend from the Isle of Wight and a large dark skinned man sitting smiling. Inchworm a band he loved from Hackney were setting up their instruments and arguing. Journalists and reporters were running around shouting and taking notes. A baseball player ran passed. Then his attention was drawn to a table were he was certain of the sight of a penguin sitting opposite a man dressed in a fifties-style suit. Smiling the most horrible smile Gyro had ever seen. Red blood flowed from his broken teeth and onto the surface of the table. The cute and fluffy penguin looked up at him and smiled.

"That's the ticket! Don't miss the party now or you'll meet him too soon! " Chirped the penguin and winked.

The face of Mr.Bittre smiled harder and harder cracking the sides of his mouth. A fierce presence seemed to be coming from him directly towards Gyro and he felt a strong urge to leave. As he moved backwards the voice of Mr. Bittre echoed after him. *"See you on television"*. Called the voice.

Gyro opened his eyes startled as his body jerked back against the seat of the hotel bar. He looked up at Britt in the fading light of the hotel interior. She smiled and took on the appearance of a china doll. Every part of her face and body seemed perfectly designed. The smoke from the joint drifted up past her visage and out the window.

"Shall we go to bed now?" Asked Britt coyly.

Gyro thought about the possibilities of time travel and the UFO he had seen over the vast distances from Australia. Along with the proof of the newspaper date and could only nod dumbly. Time travel really took a lot out of a person.

"Hold on a second! We just met, I need to be wooed you know before I leap into bed with mysterious beautiful German women." Said Gyro tugging on the raincoat of reality for some answers. *"I think there's more in that vision you just gave me...what on Earth was all that about?"* He asked shaking his head and sitting up straight.

"Okay. I was on the flight with you from Australia. You've seen a UFO - actually it's a Tech-Freighter. The largest vessel for space travel between here and the Moon. It's owned by the Three Breakfasts Corporation. You and the others saw it and they've employed me freelance to watch out for you for one night. I'm a probe. I'm also a clone. You're currently being held in a Bridgett which is a cheaper model of a holographic simulator. You're actually aboard a transport vehicle called a Zoa which enables aliens to fold time and space where you have been temporarily held until Dr. Bostrom the pilot of the UFO gets in touch and clears up the anomaly. He sends his apologies by the way. He is also currently relocating the various passengers aboard the flight in order to...."

Gyro interrupted the flow of her speech missing most of it.

"You're a clone and you just invited me to go to bed with you?" Asked Gyro bewildered.

"What? You think clones don't have sex?" Asked the Britt clone.

"It's not something I've thought about much." Said Gyro, glad to have a new idea to ponder about.

"Sex is all in the mind anyway." She said placing the key of a hotel room on the table. *"Have you never done it with a clone before?"*

"How would I know?" He asked curiously.

"Ahhh...." She winked at him again. *"Trust me. You wouldn't!"*

Britt stood up suddenly and began to wrap the woollen scarf back around her head. *"First thing is that you have to see this incredible cinema. It's called The Zuchinski and it's the very cinema that inspired the scene in Pulp Fiction where they speak about buying a glass of beer. Not a paper cup, but a glass of beer. I'll buy you one. Come on!"*

Outside the rain continued to pour down over the streets of Amsterdam and flow into the canals. Gyro was reminded of the theory that Static had come up with once that the rain was really leaking out of giant containers from mammoth space vehicles outside the atmosphere of Earth as part of a huge irrigation project. He wondered where Static was and why the theory seemed possible when he was in Amsterdam. He loved Amsterdam simply for the fact that you could head in one direction and get totally lost just like life. They ran down the hotel steps laughing. Britt and Gyro glided around the corner to Voorburgwal Straat in the heavily built Dutch rain.

BOOK VII

BEGINNINGS / DAWN

ERWIN SCHRODINGER / 1887-1961

Brilliant physicist with extraordinary and versatile intellect who wrote a useful wave equation and profound book on quantum physics and genetic structure

I know not whence I came
nor whither I go
nor who I am

His famous 'thought experiment' proposed that a cat be placed in a sealed box containing a small flask of cyanide gas which might (or might not) be shattered by a hammer that might (or might not) be activated by an emission from a lump of potentially radioactive material & the experiment be run long enough to give the cat a 50/50 chance of survival - observation kills the cat

[ON QUANTUM MECHANICS]

I don't like it
and I'm sorry
I ever had anything to do with it

CHECK-IN

THE TICKLE OF leaf dancing on leave wisped out on a treacle of wind. And belief, oh belief was an itching was a scratching and a creaking. All of a car door on the car park linoleum floor of a crusty Americana Diner in Paradise.

Rancid and puking his gut into the hedgerow announced the arrival of O.D. Darren. Reborn again and a million light years from home. Chuffed he had a huge want fulfilled a growing kidney of a need had left and returneo to where his howling fitted snug and cosy around his shoulders and under his arms like a new born babe. O. D. Darren evolved upward from the bush of leaves and sick and burped out his arrival of truth on a carcass and focused his little jiggy eyeballs at the neon across the way. The Diner Holistic read the sign of majestico magnifico, buzzing and clicking its vibe across the way to his car park distant relationship.

Lecker, lecker thoughts sprang eternal. Woozy woo-woo were dribbling down his hips and once again the burps came flying out of his mouth, inspiring him on. There will be flies of hope and lemons of love within thought O. D. Darren. His sewn-up fifties suit was bearable and black pinstriped and tight fitting perspective on the humpety-hump night. It was time to sally forth. To make it so. He barked off to one side a last slice of vomit and with cane in fist focused on the reality of the neon 'D'. This time we egg ourselves on tongue and bread ourselves in mouth he giggled to himself inward under his hat. Feet on forward and march it into reality. O. D. Darren serpentined towards the front entrance of The Diner Holistic and all it stood for.

Stripping fast around The Diner O.D. Darren and Winmau with egg on face and broad of smile due to Challenge of long gone. and out of bullet target sieved he. Holier now and reunionised. O.D. Darren grinned until flip-top headed. Flashing the broken teeth of one achieveo magnifico direct from Tibeteo. He jigged across to the penguin of cool who pointeo directed a flipper of noir and chirping with delight a la the view.

"O. Deeee baby you were and can bee-buzz again and again if you wish?" Suggestedeo Benedicto Perky Eco.

"Thanks but I can wait a while Bene it be crowded down those stairs." Replied the hippy.

"Would you latte with me? Sadly Mr. Bittre left us for Britt..." The Penguin winked.

"As eggs is eggs. Don't worry." Replied the hippy. *"We bring him back running."*

With that Benedicto chirped and clapped his flippers together and banged a rhythm on the surface of tabletop as the cups of coffee arrived.

FRIDAY 7TH SEPTEMBER 2001
PROBABILITY / NEWPORT

GODS PROVIDENCE

You've got to tell your story boy before its time to go
NEIL YOUNG

OUTSIDE GODS PROVIDENCE in Newport, the rain was pouring from the sky and Static was convinced that most of it had at one time been on the Moon. Of course he had become certain from this by various studies he carried out as a hobby but thought it best to keep such thoughts to himself. At the age of twelve many years ago, Static had spoken to a farmer called John Angel in Shorwell who had given himself and Gyro a lift back to Newport on his tractor. Static remembered the journey well. It had been in Spring and Gyro had been bombarding the farmer with questions about subjects of life and philosophy. The farmer had dropped them off in the park of Church Litten nearby and advised them to head to Gods Providence if they needed answers to such questions. They had both walked off in the direction of the football ground instead and had missed the point of subtlety entirely. Now so many years had passed from that day and here were both Static and Gyro walking in through the front door of the cafe for the first of three breakfasts. Arranged by the still grieving Liz who had approached not only Gyro but also Dr. Bostrom and Max Born into meeting here in the cafe interior during the funeral of O.D. She had only said so far that there was a plan being executed which required his help.

The interior of the cafe was empty of the usual clients and members of the public drinking tea and chatting thanks to a hefty pay-off from Liz to the owner for the current meeting. Static walked in through the side entrance. He could smell the history of the building and wondered of many decisions, which had been made in over the years.

Dr. Bostrom found himself having to stoop most of the time and had already banged his head twice on the old wooden cross beams as they all entered into the main dining area as Liz was preparing the first continental style breakfast and was boiling the water for the tea. There was only one round wooden table in the Dining Room, which had five chairs strategically placed around it and names on folded pieces of orange paper placed on the tablemats.

As they all sat down in the ornately carved wooden chairs Liz decided to break the ice with a joke. She coughed politely and welcomed the group.

"First of all, thank you all for coming today." Said Liz. She looked around the table through her azure blue eyes and acknowledged the four guests sitting around her and continued with her joke. *"There is a penguin walking across the ice in Antarctica, with another penguin. As they walk at night across a particularly big iceberg with the light of the day just emerging over the horizon. The first penguin, who is called Benedicto Perky Eco turns to his friend the second penguin and says; 'You know, all this time that we have been together walking across Antarctica I always wanted to tell you something.' And the second penguin, who was not baptised, so he had no name, turned and said; 'What do you want to tell me?' And Benedicto says; 'You look as if you're wearing a tuxedo' and his friend says with a knowing wink. 'Well, maybe I am...'"*

Something familiar about the joke made everyone at the table laugh. As the first breakfast arrived Dr. Bostrom spent a detailed few minutes explaining with a diagram drawn hastily on a napkin for the benefit of Max Born, who finally got the joke during his first encounter with a croissant.

"First on the agenda gentlemen...and lady, is the product G-WIZ. How do we get it to stop?" Asked Liz, lightly buttering a croissant and reaching for the marmalade. She sighed looking suddenly at her plate and then at Static. *"Is it me or does toast and croissants come with marmalade everywhere in the world except England?"*

Static smiled in return, he was having strong deja vu all over again.

"I have one suggestion allowing twelve of my finest X-Chromo-pilots to take the containments of G-WIZ to a planet called Neburi which contains a lake of solid steel, which freezes and expands once every hundred years. The powder can be tipped into the lake just before it freezes. The main problem seems to be that in a century, the lake defrosts!"

"When does the lake freeze next?" Asked Liz hopefully.

"Precisely at 19:27 Earth time. Friday 11th September 2011." Replied Max smugly.

Everyone at the table stared silently at Max as if he had just farted.

"I have the only containment of a time-travelling powder under the table and we need a water-tight plan to dissolve it..." Liz asked again. "Come on people. How do we eliminate the problem?"

"We could set-up a fund or a dynasty which enables the drug to be kept in one location and then check on its progress over a period of time..." Suggested Max. "Something that has been tried many times in the past..."

He suddenly felt a sharp kick to his left shin under the table and winced.

"What about using the G-WIZ. We all use it and fold time and see if any ideas come up as we travel?"

Everyone stared at Gyro as if a large blue whale had appeared on his head.

"Give it to a dog...or a cat!" Said Static. Everyone at the table stared at him.

"Sorry...?" Said Liz bewildered. "Give it to a dog...or a cat?"

"I'm suggesting that after considering the vast distances and time and not forgetting trust required in the Neburi plan I have a dog called Copper that's at a neighbour's house and he will eat absolutely anything. Give him the G-WIZ and maybe it'll dissolve with him." Replied Static sensibly.

"I thought we just understood that this stuff is toxic and helped kill O.D. Darren?" Said Liz attempting to keep calm.

"Oh yeah...right..." Said Static glowing red with massive embarrassment.

"How about mixing it with sea water? The salt in the water could have give assistance in breaking down the chemical base... I've already been trying some experiments in my house in London. The drug would be diluted enough to not cause a toxic effect but would then be able to be taken from the planet with the Tectonic-Freighters that are currently in operation..." Said the doctor.

"But you'd surely kill anything living in the sea..." Said Liz reaching for the tea.

"Not exactly...we could only do it once however, with the one case. Should any more G-WIZ appear after that, we'll need a bigger planet. But the Moon could be irrigated with the sea water and it wouldn't really harm that operation."

Everyone at the table looked at Dr. Bostrom silently as the second breakfasts arrived at the table.

"Have you seen what the Venetians are doing to the place already? With nuclear waste? You think we should be like them?" Asked Max Born smiling at his old friend.

"Where do we dispose of it?" Asked Liz.

"Here? There was a place of the island's coastline... I think the Earthlings call it Compton Beach." Replied Max.

"Okay. Dr. Bostrom and Max Born will oversee the disposing of the G-WIZ. We'll drive out there straight after the third breakfast." Said Liz.

"The FBI and New Scotland Yard are making enquiries for an extra-terrestrial cadaver and its all over the papers, I don't need to say anymore do I? Suggestions please...pass me the sugar." Said Liz.

"Dump it in the sea?" Static felt four pairs of eyes on him again. "Sorry..."

"O.D. Darren did ask to be taken to Tibet when he was dead..." Gyro had spoken.

"Okay, how do we get him there?" Asked Liz pausing.

"I've thought of a plan." Said Gyro leaning into the table and reaching for another croissant. "I fly with O.D. Darren's body to Tibet, via a time fold, I'll bring him myself. Its what he would have wanted. According to Dr. Bostrom, I should then be able to return to The Imperial bar in Erskinville, Sydney and not head for the Airport, therefore not seeing the Tectonic-Freighter. I stay in my own time."

Static beamed. "Wow man, you really have been thinking that one out... why not fold straight to Hong Kong?"

Dr. Bostrom coughed politely warming to his subject. "To return to his own time of September 7th 2001. Gyro has to be in the place he was intending to get to, in order to get to where it was he was originally going. Which was Hong Kong from Australia. Once he gets to the airport, he must fold time and he'll reach the co-ordinates I've given him."

"Thanks Gyro.." Said Liz politely.

"No problemo." Replied Gyro tucking into a plate of Quark and brown cobbler bread. The third breakfast of Metropolitan Ice Cream arrived with optional blueberry bagels.

"I'm pregnant!" Said Liz laughing. *"The child belongs to O.D. Darren."* She cupped a hand over her mouth as she tried to contain her excitement. *"It does strange things to a girls appetite."* She said explaining why she was eating ice cream for breakfast.

"Well I'm not...so you'll have to forgive me if I don't join you..." Replied Max smiling.

"We also have a problem with time holes appearing. The drug G-WIZ enables humans to travel through the hole like a cat through a cat-flap, but unfortunately...er, the cat-flap is still swinging... so to speak."

He coughed slightly embarrassed and sipped at the Earl Grey tea. *"Which is, I guess something that myself and Max will attempt to resolve."* Everyone at the table sighed with relief.

As silence fell over the group at the table as each person enjoyed their various meals. Static had opted for a muffin made from blueberries and highly buttered it as he noticed that the sound of people eating in relative silence seemed to describe an atmosphere better than words ever could.

He wondered for a brief moment whether language was indeed a virus. Whether the weather was imported. Then he wondered whether weather had a nationality. How could Spain own hot weather while Germany owned cold weather. He sipped at his latte as he briefly considered how anyone could actually recognise a nuclear weapon without seeing it explode, preferably from a distance or was their a remote possibility that a war could begin between two countries over something as simple as a comma. Then Static returned to the weather.

Outside Gods Providence tea rooms in Newport, the rain was pouring from the sky and Static was convinced that most of it had at one time been on the Moon, of course he was certain from various studies he carried out as a hobby but thought it best to keep such thoughts to himself.

FRIDAY 7TH SEPTEMBER 2001
PROBABILITY / TIBET

MOVING THE RIVER

I'm starting to see a bigger picture I'm beginning to colour it in
MIKE SCOTT / THE WATERBOYS

THE CADAVA OF O.D. Darren lay still and covered in the black body bag. In the cargo-bay aboard yet another Jumbo Jet airliner. This time bound for Hong Kong. Gyro sat alone and pondered for a brief moment the possibilities of seeing yet another Tectonic-Freighter descend from the heavens. He pulled the grey plastic cabin cover down over the window of the plane knowing that right next to the plane yet another X-Chromo-pilot was descending towards The Banda Sea on its mission to remove water and return to the Moon for part of the Irrigation Project.

However his first official job for The Three Breakfasts Corporation had given him strict instructions to ignore the sightings of any more UFOs for the moment until he began the return from Tibet and as he looked around the sparsely filled seats of the airliner, Gyro realised he was the only Western male aboard the craft. The passenger Jet had already flown over European airspace and Asia. Gyro checked on the body several times just to be sure that O.D. Darren was still down in the holding bay.

Although the conditions for the flight were fine, past experiences for Gyro had taught him to always be careful on noticing a coincidence appearing in life and be cautious should a pattern emerge from any actions. The flight from Australia had begun safely enough and yet here he was still in the wrong time. Missing a year from his life. The only occurrences, which had remained the same for the time-traveller, were his brown suit and his hair. Which had not grown since he had arrived in Holland only days before.

As Gyro sat in the plane and looked out over the dark cold landscapes of China below through the white wisps of clouds, he thought about change. The experience of the UFO had taught him to be prepared for its next appearance.

Somewhere far down below him were the parents of the Chinese girl he had lost at the airport in Holland and he wondered if he was doing the right thing moving O.D. Darren to such a vast distance from his original birthplace. Yet the alternatives of letting the FBI or any other Government organisation get their hands on it would mean God knows what for the people of the planet. O.D. Darren was a friend and friends were supposed to help one another. Especially when they died.

As Gyro patted his inside pocket for the reassurance of the orange envelope in his jacket that contained the co-ordinates passed onto him by Dr. Bostrom, he thought about what O.D. Darren had told him at the party in Hackney. O.D. Darren could have told anybody anything in his life but somehow Gyro had felt instinctively that what O.D. Darren had been saying during the moment they spent talking together was the truth. The hippy had known or had planned his entire demise all along. That he had wanted this one thing in his life to be a certainty. Looking back at the promise Gyro had made to him at the party, he decided it had been interesting that the only time a person seemed to get what they wanted in life was when they were dead.

Gyro still had in his suit what he hoped to be the very last packet of G-WIZ on the planet. He had reserved the vial of orange powder for the unveiling of the body, once he had arrived in Hong Kong. In the country which O.D. Darren had asked to be taken to.

From the height of thirty thousand feet in the air, China looked as mysterious as the people. Off into the distance he thought he could see Mount Everest and from the comfort of the craft he pondered briefly on the journeys made by mountaineers to the summit. As a child Gyro had dreamt about one day seeing it, but only because it was on television. He was sure if someone had asked him at that age what he had wanted to do in life it would have involved sitting in a field and staring at the cows in the day and the stars at night.

The flight began its descent down into Hong Kong Airport where O.D. Darren would fold time and reappear one last time. If all the co-ordinates held in the calculations of Dr. Bostrom were correct, they should both appear exactly where O.D. Darren had been standing over three years previously. Then Gyro could return to his own time. The chances were high that O.D. Darren had planned the entire journey from the moment he had arrived in Tibet.

The plane landed without any hitches and Gyro waited outside by the large wheels for his old inanimate colleague to be lowered down onto a containment trolley. He calmly wheeled the trolley with O.D. Darren inside through the customs of Hong Kong Airport and showed the police all the necessary documentation papers and his passport. He then wheeled the body out of the airport and into the warm humid night air towards the bus stop where he had been instructed by Dr. Bostrom to wait until precisely eight minutes past five.

The following instructions had been to place the G-WIZ in the mouth of O.D. Darren, wait one minute and then do the same for himself. Compared to Hong Kong the cities of London or New York were nowhere near as packed with people and Gyro smiled as he realised that the instructions of the good doctor seemed be made purely this part of the city. Near the bus stop seemed to be the only immediate area that a person could actually stand.

Gyro left the trolley next to an advertisement for the new British Mini, which seemed to make as much sense in Cantonese as it had in English when he had last seen it in Heathrow before boarding the plane. He checked the time on his watch, which read 8PM Hong Kong Standard time. Then proceeded with the plan. He took the bag of G-WIZ from his pocket and swallowed half the contents.

Then he unzipped the body bag just enough to see the face of O.D. Darren. Opened his mouth then placed the small orange cellophane bag over his mouth and poured the rest in.

Gyro quickly held onto the handle of the trolley with both hands and waited for the minute to pass on his watch and then closed his eyes tightly. Pressing the handle down and releasing the brake. He could hear the sounds of time folding around his ears. He then quickly pushed the trolley, O.D. Darren and himself towards the Mini advert. Disappearing into the poster.

An incredible sound swam all around him as if he had been underwater. He opened his eyes, both of them were standing in the bright sunlight of a mysterious landscape scattered with incredible stone carvings and temples. The sky of deep azure blue stretched overhead. Desert faded into horizon, in either direction. If this was not Tibet then the pictures Gyro had seen over the years had all been lying. Gyro took a white hanker-chief and covered his nose then he unzipped the leather bag and stepped back from the trolley seating himself on a large stone. Then waited.

The sight of O.D. Darren stepping out of the bag and onto the ground was a sight to behold. Gyro smiled to himself as he held up a small cardboard travel camera and clicked a button as Darren stood up straight and stretched, then yawned and turned to face him. Gyro quickly did as instructed by Dr. Bostrom and placed his Ray-Bans on before he faced Darren to speak to him, but kept his eyes cast down to the ground. Remembering the words of Erwin Schrodinger at the party in Newtown. Observation kills the cat. Gyro looked down at the tall unmistakable.

Shadow of Darren cast onto the orange sand of Tibet. The colours of this country were incredible. O.D. Darren could be seen walking around and he turned suddenly to face Gyro who kept his eyes cast down at his shoes as the good doctor had instructed. *"Always look away from death, but don't ignore it."* The good doctor had told Gyro. *"Darren is death now. Don't ignore him."*

"Gyro man, where are we?" Asked O.D. Darrren.

"O.D. Darren. We are in Tibet...as promised! You are free to run around if you like. I don't think the monks are up yet though. It's still pretty early." Replied Gyro with his eyes looking only at the shadow of the hippy cast over the sand.

"G-WIZ!" Yelled O.D. Darren waking up to the situation. "So it worked. I'm in Tibet again! Excellent!"

"Exactly! I have to get back to Australia now." Said Gyro fighting temptation to look at his friend.

"Don't you wanna' meet Tenzin Gyatso?" Asked Darren.

"I'll see him next time around." Smiled Gyro stepping back and fading from view slightly.

"Do you have to go so quickly?" Called O.D. Darren after him.

"You've got a new journey to be making Darren." Said Gyro. "I'm still here... on Earth at least for a while, I hope."

"I thought you always wanted to see Tibet man." Said O.D. Darren.

"Nope. That was you..." Exclaimed O.D. Darren as he jumped up and down.

"You told me at the party that you wanted to come here and now we're here. Don't tell me the great O.D. Darren has changed his mind again." Gyro smiled.

"No Way. I'm pleased with the way things are now..." O.D. Darren said happily.

"You don't want to come back?" Asked Gyro.

"No way!" Said Darren.

"I just thought we could talk for a bit. There are some things that I need to make sure are working out..."

" Such as? " Asked Gyro closing his blue eyes behind the dark Ray-Bans.

"Well what about Liz? Is she okay?"

"Well she is pregnant!" Replied Gyro.

"Do you think she believes I'm coming back through her?" Asked Darren scratching his head and looking around the landscape.

"Perhaps...she's not a Buddhist really Darren, she's Jewish." Gyro didn't feel like lying to a ghost. The Sun began rising up over the temples as the start to a new day in Tibet began.

"Do you have any cigarettes on you?" Asked O.D. Darren suddenly.

"Nope. I think it's time to stop smoking." Said Gyro.

"Sure. Good idea. It's Tibet isn't it! What about the funeral...? Was it good?" He sounded happier.

"It was excellent! Best one I've seen. Actually, it was the only one I've seen. Strange act." Laughed Gyro as he picked up a stone from the ground.

"Yours or mine?" He said laughing.

"Yours...of course." Replied Gyro standing up. He only had a few minutes remaining to fold time.

"Okay I'm ready to go onto the Temple. I guess I'll see you in nine months then." Said Darren.

"Of course...I might seem taller, but I will look out for you both." Said Gyro as he began to fade.

"Excellent!" Beamed O.D. Darren. "I forgot to ask...where do I go?"

"You see that smaller Temple over to the left?" Gyro shouted as he became like a ghost.

"Yeah...?" Asked Darren unsure.

"Don't go into that one..." Said Gyro. "Just joking!"

"See you in nine months...promise?" Said Darren as he walked back towards the temple.

"Promise..." Yelled Gyro as the sound of time folded all around him.

Gyro faded from view as O.D. Darren ran up the steep orange stone steps of the temple. At the top of the steps he could see a figure dressed in dark red robes. Tenzin Gyatso The 14th Dalai Lama of Tibet smiled warmly back at him. Shaking his hand warmly.

"Darren at last! We've been expecting you. Come in." He said. "Welcome back!"

"Hello..." Said Darren laughing. "Any room for one more?" The cadaver of O.D Darren lay still and covered in the black temporary body bag.

FRIDAY 7TH SEPTEMBER 2001
EVENING / TIME POCKET

THE ROUGH DANCER & THE CYCLICAL NIGHT TANGO APASIONADO

Change is inevitable for each one of us
We should direct it rather than let change direct us
GILL SCOTT-HERON

THE CONVERSION RATE of the Euro is currently 1.53727901614. Read the headline of The Financial Times. The newly elected President of the New World Order had been named as President Trust Noone. Who had launched a unique subliminal strategic campaign for years designed by Big New Yorker. *'Trust no one'* had been the first of many launches onto the public consciousness. The time that Gyro had folded from Tibet had definitely brought him somewhere but the year did not seem to appear on the passenger vessel he was now sitting in. As he read the words appearing on the monitor in front of his tired and time-travelled features, he sighed. At least he was finally in agreement with The News which was currently being displayed on the digital screen for his pleasure in glorious Bostrom Vision. They both seemed to have no idea what was happening on Earth.

Thankfully he still had his Ray-Bans on and he also had the knowledge that O.D. Darren had reached Tibet. As Gyro peered out the small round window next to his seat he had been astonished to see the Earth beneath him. The whole Earth and nothing but the Earth merrily rotating in space blue and white and orange. The future was indeed orange. Advertisements rarely lie after all Gyro thought to himself. The in-flight movie had just finished. Damn.

To his left holding a glass of red wine sat the relaxed form of Britt. He smiled and felt the sensation of life joyfully sneaking up behind him and tapping him on the shoulder again. She was also wearing dark glasses and still had the orange scarf tightly fixed around her head. She smiled back at him and raised her glass.

"Gyro! You made it just in time." She gestured towards the monitor. *"Have you seen the news?"* She asked. He turned his attention back to the small screen built into the back of the white passenger seat in front of him and read the headlines of digital words that were fading in and out slowly.

HITLER HAS BEEN CLONED SUCCESSFULLY
DEATH IS ILLEAGAL
UNEMPLOYMENT IS ABOLISHED
GREAT BLUR IMMINENT
PRESIDENT TRUST NOONE LAUNCHES G-WIZ INTO SPACE
DR. BOSTROM SAVES THE PLANET
GLOBAL POLLUTION REDUCED TO AN EASY PILL TO SWALLOW

Gyro had found himself hypnotised by the blank screen and looked back at the soft-spoken German lady. He smiled. Somehow he had been relieved that the only part of the future that had remained a constant had been the use of the words to describe the events of time unfolding as new.

"Where are we now?" He laughed at Britt.

"The future." She announced smiling back at him. *"It's all new here."*

"What's the year?" He asked.

"Oh that's been abolished. The calendar has been replaced with file numbers. It's much easier. All the resources on Earth ran out around the time of The Great Blur."

"The Great Blur?" He asked bewildered.

Britt adjusted her seat and relaxed back into it. *"Yep. The folding of time caused an international catastrophe. Due to the inevitable realisation that time was indeed a mere tyranny. The Government had announced to much confusion that there was no option for the future other than to introduce a loop into the continuum..."* She sighed. *"It was officially announced on television in 2009. The P & G Building society was held irresponsible for the catastrophe. But actually its because a waitress named Holly Grail at The Diner Holistic forgot to change the Earth simulation disc. Which had caused the disc to jump back to somewhere during World War II and play through to 2011 again. The next year had never been seen by anyone and had become a legend merely by not being seen."*

"So Dr. Bostrom was right?" Asked Gyro.

"It would appear that he was merely a back-up file in the program designed by Procter & Gamble. Two freelance aliens. Once the disc was analysed by a company called King Penguin Media they discovered that all the wars on Earth had been viruses and the disc simply needed cleaning."

"But Max Born and Liz..." Asked Gyro as he sat on the vessel trying to comprehend the idea that the only way to stop a war had been to merely run a disc under a tap and clean it.

"She's on the Moon running Big New Yorker. She's behind the whole operation. It turned out that everyone on Earth had died in 1945 during World War II and the few hundred thousand humans that remained had been taken to the Moon by the Building Society P & G. Liz developed the simulation programme which is why she ended up with all the money. She's actually President Trust Noone. Her office is next to mine." Britt said smugly.

"Is that where we're heading now?" Asked Gyro.

"I am. You're going back to the simulation. The waitress at The Diner Holistic has finally changed the disc this time around, but because she was too busy, the entire simulation has to play through one more time. After that you can meet me on the Moon when we'll go through this part again..."

Gyro felt very tired. Exhausted by the time travelling.

"That's why everyone on Earth is going a bit mad. They've been through the programme from 1945 to 2011 about eight times. The waitress Holly Grail sends her apologies for the inconvenience.

"What about the time-folding...is that simulated?" Asked Gyro.

"No that's real. You're in a time-pocket. Whenever you fold time you take yourself off the programme. Like now. The Moon is on another disc. Right now we're the fluff on the needle, so to speak. Because its all a simulation, the disc became damaged after someone mistook it for a coaster and left their coffee on it. Well, that's what the President announced. Hence time has been jumping and skipping and months on Earth had just been lost. Then the next play through would be fine. But hey that's technology for you!" She said as the

sipped from her glass of wine and leaned further back into the passenger seat.

The Zoa-pod was landing on the Moon in three hours and from the what Britt told him, nothing sounded more horrendous than getting stuck there. With only two ways of accessing food - McDonalds or Kubrick and only one Chip point Machine which was the new and improved version of currency.

"What about the G-WIZ? I thought I had the last packet." Said Gyro forgetting if he had already told her this.

"Calm down Gyro man. I have some on me here." She said reaching into her shawl. *"These are the new prototypes from Big New Yorker."* She placed a carefully compact and handy container of what looked like prescription pills into his hand with G-WIZ NEW FLAVOUR printed on the side in orange. As he studied the container he could see a small penguin on the side. *"Hey, that's my idea!"* Said Gyro. Around the bottom of the label read words in blue type.

BE THANKFUL YOU HAVE PEOPLE AROUND YOU WHO STEAL YOUR IDEAS FOR WHEN YOU DIE YOUR IDEAS WILL LIVE ON AND SO WILL YOU

"What's the idea with this?" He asked glancing back up at Britt surprised.

"The new prototype...the G-WIZ is now available in Subliminal-Oracle Packaging. The product analyses your brain waves and then gives you advice to dispute any emotions your experiencing when you hold it. To calm you down. Cool huh?" Said Britt smiling back at him. Outside the Zoa-pod in the black surrounding space Gyro could see metal piped structures floating in a grid above the atmosphere.

"What the hell are those?" Said Gyro as he looked out at the huge structures floating silently above Earth.

"They're the Bridgetts." Said Britt. *"Temporary holding pods for Earthlings. You're in one of those at the moment suspended in time in a place called Amsterdam 7th September 2001 with one of my naughtier clones. Awaiting the meeting in another pod of Dr. Bostrom."*

"But I'm here with you now." Said Gyro turning to face Britt.

"Exactly! Because you're travelling in time not space. The Bridgetts are part of the simulation. They work in a similar way to a desktop on a computer holding files, which are not in the main running of the programme. They were built by the humans for any mistakes made by the Chromo-pilots. Humans are transported there should they have a glimpse of the bigger plan that's currently in operation to help the planet. When you saw the UFO leaving Australia they transported you there. It's designed to distract the person until they can be returned to Earth."

She opened the container of G-WIZ and pulled out one of the orange tablets. Gyro stared down at the tablet as she held it in her delicate palm. *"Be careful when you arrive on Earth Gyro, you'll be in World War II yeah? You'll see some seriously weird shit going on that will make everything so far seem like a picnic. The pills will only take you forward though and the only numbered co-ordinates I have for your arrival are in my home town of Berlin. You can visit me when I'm my Great-Grandmother."*

"You mean I've got to go through all that again?" Gyro felt exhausted just thinking about the mission ahead.

"Well you did sign up with Three Breakfasts Corporation. You can fold time to the Moon for a holiday in about 1969. I wouldn't mention it before then however you'll probably be called a witch. When you get to Germany one of my clones will attempt to locate you." Said Britt.

"Can't Holly Grail just fast forward through to this moment again?" Asked Gyro.

"Why do you think you got here? She already did." Said Britt.

"THAT was fast forward?!? I had to live through all that and you call that fast-forward? What about catching the ferry from the Isle of Wight...there is no way I'll believe that was fast forward...what about The Miner's Strike and the Poll Tax Riots?" Laughed Gyro. *"That was all simulation?"* He felt himself becoming nearly hysterical.

"Gyro calm down it's an old simulator okay? The Diner Holistic is the first attempt to have them introduced. You have to think about the impact such knowledge could have on people if they were told they were merely being run on an advanced piece of technology. Especially when you mention that the reason,

say, their friend had been killed by a tree falling on them in a storm is purely part of a developing software problem." Said Britt.

"Okay then where's the keyboard pusher who wrote the program?" Asked Gyro.

"As we're speaking, he's folded to a place called Soho. On the corner of Old Compton Street and Denmark Street. His name's Dexter Wexford although he prefers to be called Command or ZED and he's the closest thing to a God that you're going to meet on this Earth. He's ten years-old and he lives in the year 2050 on Mars, his birthplace."

"God's ten?" Asked Gyro slightly bewildered. He had always pictured God as a wise old man.

"Not the God. A God. They used to rule Earth before the Technetium Comet hit. It's all in the great book."

"What The Bible?" Asked Gyro.

"No the dictionary!" Answered Britt with a loyal smile.

"Technology developed so quickly that Dexter started developing a cloning programme which ran simulation software by the age of seven. His father Darren marketed me actually as the first toy clone. Until the abolition of clone-slavery act around 2030." She sipped at her wine.

The sight of the continuous smile of Britt throughout the joke calmed Gyro as he placed the orange G-WIZ tablet on the tongue of his mouth and felt it dissolve leaving a pleasant mandarin flavour in his mouth. He looked down at the container of G-WIZ for some last advice and was surprised to see that it read;

UNTIL YOU DON'T KNOW YOU DON'T NEED IT

"Have you ever heard the story of the Three Spacemen and the Constant Variable. I'll tell it to you before you head back to World War II. My doctor used to tell it to me when I was still in the laboratory." Britt finished her wine and focused all her attention on Gyro.

"Once upon a time there were three spacemen. They travelled to the Moon. They were called Steve, Neil and Buzz. After their spaceship touched down on the surface of the Moon and they stepped down onto the surface Steve, Neil and

Buzz looked around at the stars and Neil who was the tallest of the astronauts, turned to the other two spacemen and said. 'Well, here we are on the Moon what do you wanna do?'

Steve the second space-traveller said. "Well look at all those stars I bet it would be really cool if we took a photograph of us standing on the Moon with all the stars behind us, to show people when we get back to Earth otherwise nobody will believe that we were up here on the Moon at all."

"Then Neil who was the nearest said..." Gyro suddenly heard the familiar sound of time folding and found himself suddenly staring into the top of a cup of warm milch kaffee as he looked through the window of a cafe on Christburger Strazer. Outside the streets were aligned with the neat crisp uniforms of Nazis lined as far as his eyes could see. The cafe seemed to be totally empty and as Gyro looked down to see the folded cover of TIME magazine on a table lying nearby. He found himself surprised to read the date at the top. 1938. A large picture of Adolf Hitler depicted on the front with the words MAN OF THE YEAR printed across it. Outside the cheers and shouts of people echoed into the cafe as the barman wiped down the tables. Gyro caught his own reflection in the mirror and realised he still had his Ray-Bans on. As he looked down at the cover of TIME he quickly considered whether sunglasses had been invented. The only reference he had were Hollywood movies who had always depicted Nazi Generals as wearing them. Yet he knew that had been the movies and that what he was now experiencing was real life. He suddenly thought that with his bleached hair and blue eyes his appearance could be of benefit rather than a hindrance.

Gyro realised that the streets outside were aligned with uniforms standing prepared for his arrival. He looked in his hand for the bottle of G-WIZ and read the words that appeared across the label;

ANSWER. THAT YOU ARE HERE AND LIFE CONTINUES THAT THE POWERFUL PLAY GOES ON AND YOU MAY CONTRIBUTE A VERSE

As he looked over at the newspapers hanging from long wooden poles like towels on the wall of the cafe and listened to the cheers outside of children as they waved flags with swastikas on them. The red white and black of the swastika had been printed on flags that hung everywhere. Even in the cafe he was now sitting in. Draped across the bar.

The last thing he had expected to see in a cafe in Berlin during 1939 was hanging from one of the wooden poles with the other newspapers. He immediately recognised the words of English on the faint pink paper but could not believe what he read until he remembered the words of Britt on the plane. He walked over to the newspaper and forgot about his surroundings momentarily as his eyes fell across the words printed on the front. The conversion rate of the Euro is currently 1.53727901614. Read the headline of The Financial Times.

SATURDAY 8TH SEPTEMBER 2001
NIGHT / THE WAREHOUSE

THE SIZE OF THE UNIVERSE

What's the sense in ever thinking of about the tomb
When you're much too busy returning to the womb?
THEY MIGHT BE GIANTS

THE NUMBERS WERE swimming around his head as O.D. Darren stumbled into the second kitchen of the warehouse and discovered the video camera belonging to Valentina left on a pile of old magazines. He recognised the title of Empire written on the tops of the magazines and chuckled at the sight of someone having accidentally built yet another empire, which seemed as if it would collapse if it had reached any higher. The light of the kitchen light reflected onto the walls was warm orange and sepia brown and glowed with a soft blaze emitting from inside every brick. O.D. Darren placed the camera on the table and sat on a chair looking into the lens. Valentina had been recording parts of the party all night and had shown him earlier how easy technology had grown over the years. As the gorgeous Italian drank red wine in one of the small side rooms she had shown O.D. Darren some of the footage of the party and he had found himself in hysterics at the sight of Britt walking into the room with a group of twelve men all dressed in smart blue suits with dark glasses and neatly trimmed beards following her as if they were in a jazz band. O.D. Darren had been impressed. When he had asked Valentina who they were she had told him that one of them was John and kept referring to them all as The Time Disciples. He recalled thinking that was the coolest name for a jazz band he had ever heard.

Now as he sat in the kitchen all he had to do was push buttons on the side of the digital camera.

The hippy brushed his long hair back so his face could be partially seen instead of completely covered and rested the camera propped against a book for stability, then pushed the record button. He had approximately fifteen minutes of tape to explain what some people took a lifetime to express. He quickly did a test run, to check the machine was working and then rewound the tape so he could record over the test. Then clicked the silver record button again.

"Good morning. You know who this is yes?" He peered into the camera and waved. The distant sounds of the party in full swing could be heard all over the warehouse and were echoing behind him. *"I had to say goodbye one last time I guess and I have to also say that it was nice of you to all come to the funeral. My FUN-eral! There is an emphasis on fun at this one and if every detail has been carried out then it should be Tony's house that I am looking out onto and there should be a lot of people enjoying themselves at that wonderful place."* He burped and smiled his notorious wasted smile. *"I'm about to die, I should first say that I wanted to...die that is. Die is only a word that means THE in German after all. I have my reasons but don't get upset. I'll be back, you just won't recognise me next time. I worked out why we say goodbye a lot because one day you're here, the next maybe you're gone. Winmau has his money so I should be okay for another..."* He looked at his watch. *"Ooh three hours at least, but I'm going to speak to Gyro about the arrangements that you should now be enjoying. I will see you all in the Diner Holistic at some point, so don't be too worried. This is the end my friend...sorry, always wanted to say that. I just had an argument with Liz the woman I will now go off to meet in another time. When she is old, she's very cool. LIZ YOU'RE SO COOL! I'll see you after Tibet love. I've made some wrong moves in life and I know now that the best thing to do is come back fresh as a baby and if everything goes accordingly spiffing as I'm told by the good doctor then I'll simply see you all later for an amazing magic act. Meanwhile I'll say over to Gyro who will explain the rest of the stuff and David Copperfield...watch this!"*

He then reached out and clicked the button off.

From the perspective of O.D. Darren, the kitchen was almost exploding with light shining in every direction and he placed the camera down as he discovered it on the magazines. The intensity of the rush from the fifth or eighth ecstasy tablet was calling him to the dance floor and he could hear the most beautiful music he had ever heard cresting up from the staircase. He stumbled down from the upstairs kitchen and down the concrete steps. As O.D. Darren reached the last staircase, supporting himself against the cold blue walls he looked down at a small travel mirror that he thought someone must have dropped on the floor and stumbling to the floor of the stairwell. He picked it up and placed it in his chequered shirt pocket.

Hypnotically, the hippy followed the music like a drunken dog sniffing for raw meet and found himself in a room that he could not remember being in the warehouse even when he had lived there. To his right he could see the fading form of a man with a hat on and wearing a fifties style brown suit holding a cane and smoking. The smile seemed to be illuminated but the face was obscured. O.D. Darren could see the teeth, huge and broken.

"*Ahhh O.D. Darren me boy! You're almost ready to take my job yes?*" Said Mr. Bittre. "*Just for a short while...*"

"Which room is this?" Asked the hippy.

"*Never mind now. Take this pill. Have some wine.*" Said the voice of Mr. Bittre.

"*Cheers.*" Said O.D. Darren barely holding onto reality.

"*Splendid.*" Whispered the voice.

Suddenly O.D. Darren found himself walking across bodies treading on soft legs and he could hear complaining but could see nothing in the dark room. He remembered the travel mirror in his pocket and took it out. He attempted to ask if anyone had lost a mirror but words were not working. The hippy felt his legs buckle slightly and knew he needed to sit down quickly in the dark. He reached out to the only light coming from the window and placed the mirror on the ledge carefully above the sink and took one step back. He felt the weight of his whole body fall back into the comfort of a huge soft chair and smiled as the warm wave of energy swept over his entire body. Then O.D. Darren died.

The numbers were swimming around his head as O.D. Darren stumbled into the second kitchen of the warehouse and discovered the video camera belonging to Valentina left on a pile of old magazines.

SUNDAY 9TH SEPTEMBER 1933
PROBABILITY / TIME POCKET

EINSTEIN A GO-GO

You're a ghost on the highway and I love you forever
MAZZY STARR

THE SMALL BONFIRES of books were burning quietly in the cold morning air of Berlin as Albert walked hurriedly through the snow filled streets. He walked past his favourite bakery that sold cobbler-boy brown bread. Along Christburger Strazzer he stopped at the corner outside his shoe shop and looked down at the white snow on the ground. Two piles of books were neatly stacked in a tall pile by the window as if someone had constructed two tall towers. The heavy snow had already covered most of them. Albert felt obliged to wipe some of it away from the top and read the title of the title out of curiosity. Across the square the shoemaker could hear shouts from German soldiers nearby to move on. As he looked up Albert watched carefully as two Nazi Stormtroopers headed towards him. Albert counted at least twelve separate bonfires throughout the square, the black smoke curling up and floating into the white clouds above. He stood still in the cold morning as wind forced tears from his eyes. He knew the only thing he could do when spotted by the Nazis had been to be polite. He was merely a shoemaker after all. Albert looked up at the two tall guards on duty and greeted them both politely by raising his hat then reached into his pocket and withdrew his identification papers.

One of the Stormtroopers aimed his Baretter automatically at the dowdy German and asked him to raise his arms in the air. Albert held onto his ID papers with one hand and slowly turned to face the front window of his shop trying not to shake. As he turned he heard the definite crack of a rifle sound out and saw a lady at the end of the street fall to the ground, dead. Around seven o'clock in the morning and Albert had already witnessed one murder. He sighed.

The identification papers were pulled from his gloved hand and Albert closed his eyes and waited to be shot. He held the image of his wife in his mind and felt himself smile slightly just as the two soldiers instructed him to lower his hands. They were both satisfied for now that he was who he claimed to be. One of the soldiers gestured with his gun for Albert to pick up the books next to him and throw them onto the nearest bonfire. The shoemaker loved books and as he bent down to pick up the first pile he could hardly believe that half the stack contained some of his favourite titles. Books he could not even afford to buy and would never be able to read now were already decided as unfit for public consumption. At the age of fifty-five Albert had managed to remain quite agile and yet as he looked down at the titles from William Shakespeare as they fell onto the fire and burned. The thought crossed his mind that he would be shot once he completed moving the second pile. He looked up at the two German soldiers. They must have both been about twenty-six years old with blonde hair and blue eyes. Arrian features. Albert Einstein smiled as he looked up at the pair of them, quickly thinking of an offer. He pointed at his shoe shop and suggested perhaps they could both use some new Winter shoes as a gift. The offer of comfortable shoes was far too tempting for guards that had already spent three days and nights standing in the cold Winter of Berlin. The Stormtroopers agreed on condition that the second pile of books be burnt first. They both pointed the Barretters at Einstein again to reinforce the order. Albert Einstein reached down and picked up the second tower of books and carefully placed works by his friend Max Born and THE COSMIC CODE by H.R. Pagel into the crackling flames and watched them turn to ash and spiral upwards into the freezing cold Berlin sky. The German had always found physics fascinating and as Albert watched the books burn he briefly wondered if he had chosen the right career path by becoming a shoemaker.

Albert unlocked the front-door of the shoe shop and as the little bell rang out announcing the arrival of customers he welcomed the two Stormtroopers over to the counter and pulled out two pairs of comfortable black shoes made from the finest leather. The soldiers were both momentarily speechless as they received the gifts. They both saluted Albert. *"Hail Hitler,"* one of the guards exclaimed enthusiastically. Albert smiled and saluted back as both Stormtroopers left the shoe shop pleased with their new footware. The little bell rang out as the door closed. Albert sighed. He knew that incident had been the closest to death he wished to get for one day. The shoemaker checked his watch again as he placed the sign in the window that read CLOSED / GONE WRESTLING. He pulled down the venetian blind and locked up for the day. He had to go and talk with his friend Erwin Schrodinger the tailor over in Potsammer Platz.

As Albert walked away quickly from the square and headed across the icy wastelands of Berlin in the snow, he felt the reassurance of one of the books he had saved from the fire in his coat pocket. When he was certain the Nazis were not around Albert walked around a corner and stepped into a quiet cafe. He ordered a milchkaffee and stood away from the Nazi flags draped across the bar. When the coffee arrived Albert Einstein cupped the coffee in his hands still shaking from his ordeal. *"If I knew they were going to force me at gun point to burn books I would have become a Quantum Physicist."* Said the shoemaker to himself quietly as he left the cafe and headed to the house of Erwin Schrodinger. Patting the book by Lewis Carroll kept safely in his pocket.

The small bonfires of books were burning quietly in the cold morning air of Berlin as Albert walked hurriedly through the snow filled streets.

MONDAY 10TH SEPTEMBER 2001
PROBABILITY / THE HOUSE

THE LOVE FOR THREE ORANGES

Everybody's got their own kind of hope
Some people got dope
I've got a feeling for all the people in the world
MONIE MARKE

GYRO STEPPED BACK inside the warm security of the kitchen of the large manor house. Inside he could see a well-dressed man in a suit and a spectacular haircut smoking a Lucky Strike cigarette stood leaning against the large white Americana fridge in the corner. The man seemed placid as he listened to Liz talking of the funeral and something about the way he was dressed caused Gyro to think, that if he had seen this particular man arrive at the driveway of the house, Gyro would have expected him to have driven with the fridge already attached to the roof of the car. The figure gave the immediate impression of having worked in an art gallery. However his demeanour focused so intently at Liz that Gyro thought whatever they were both discussing, had reached the point that conversations can sometimes blossom into at parties. When the people having them, somehow have inversed the entire surrounding scene into being just another anecdote.

Tony Webb stepped through the doorway leading towards the lounge with a stack of compact discs in his huge hands. He was searching through a wine rack for another bottle of Oxford Landing.

"Ah Mister Scope. Are you on the move for the toilet?" He asked in his usual gentle tones.

"Yup! I've left the others under the tree but I think Charles Darwin is tripping on mushrooms." Said Gyro.

"Bless him. That sounds like Charles. Nice man." Tony found another bottle under the rack. *"More than can be said for your friend Ray!"* He exclaimed standing up.

"He's not my friend." Said Gyro helping him with the bottles. *"He's Liz's boss and after the way he was speaking to Laurie Anderson, I don't think he'll be hanging around here much longer!"*

"Do you want me to ask him to leave?" Asked Tony standing to full height.

"Well, was he rude?" Asked Gyro.

"It's a party. I don't think O.D. Darren would mind too much but then he is dead." Said Tony handing him a bottle.

"What instructions did you get from for all this?" O.D. Darren enquired Gyro.

"Darren called in the evening on Friday and said he wanted to borrow the place for a party and then all these caterers and stuff turned up about two hours later." Tony stood up as his voice dropped to a low hush. *"All this money turned up in my bank account the next day. Which is unfathomable. Usually it takes a week to clear a cheque. I have to check with the bank tomorrow. Great party though. All he said was 'make it fun' and 'you're in charge'. Then he hung-up."* Tony leaned against the door and sighed.

"Do you know what the time is?" Asked Gyro grabbing another of the bottles of wine.

"You could ask The Physicists but I don't think you'll get a straight answer. They're going through pints of eggnog and Icke's hitting the Beaujolais like a bastard. Mind you they're chilled out." He said thoughtfully.

"How much of the wine is there?" Asked Gyro.

"That's what I've been meaning to tell you, but I didn't want to say anything in front of your friend Laurie...I think David Copperfield's at work here. Whenever I check the supplies they're just back to where they were at the beginning. Like they've not been touched. But you've go to see this." He gestured with his hand.

Gyro followed Tony up the stairs where Kate Bush and Naomi Klein were still sitting drinking and laughing outside the bathroom. *"Excuse me ladies."* Said Tony winking at them both.

Opening the wooden door of the bathroom, Tony presented the bath to Gyro as they both stared down at the dark red contents of liquid within.

"Jesus Christ!" Yelled Gyro. *"Is it blood?"*

"No. Taste it." Said Tony grinning madly and turning one of the taps as more of the wine poured out.

"Holy..." Gyro began.

"Bingo!" Finished Tony for him. *"Something really strange is going on tonight. I've even looked in the attic for some sign of a break-in and its just water in the emersion tank. There's someone in the party and they're having an effect on the water supply. I'm just hoping it hasn't gotten into the radiators."*

"I think I know who it is." Said Gyro. *"And it isn't David Copperfield."*

"Can you have a word with them? It's great for a party but it's useless when we need a bath. Strange thing is all the other bathrooms are fine. It's just this one."

They both descended to the first floor, passing various dishevelled people on the way. The main body of guests were now dancing to The Doors in the lounge and Tony briefly nodded towards a large antique clock in the hallway.

"The other thing is the time. All the clocks in the house have stopped and anyone I ask has said their watches have done the same thing. I can't get a straight answer out of anyone about why it's happening."

"Have you seen Hawking anywhere?" Asked Gyro.

"In the dining-room with that weird advertising bloke last time I looked." Replied Tony.

"I think I better go and ask what's going on." Said Gyro.

In the dining room The Physicists seemed to have tactfully sidestepped from the question Ben had originally asked and become distracted by the appearance of Ray Connif who was sitting like a King at the end of the table. Gyro casually sat down and offered his bottle of wine around the table.

"*Don't be too worried gentlemen. The future is history anyway, so let's just make some money yar?*" Announced Mr. Bittre, his cigarette filter was still clenched between his teeth. "*They are offering a future of technological advancement so advanced that you are slowly slipping down the grade by comparison.*" Said Mr. Bittre

Gyro lifted the bottle from the table and offered it around. "*Would anyone care for some...*"

"*SHUT THE FUCK UP! Don't ever interrupt me you little weasel!*" Bellowed Mr. Bittre at Gyro as he stood up and slammed his hand onto the table. The room fell into a tense awkward silence.

"*Molecular Graphic Design. Genetic food crops are both advances in technology, which cannot be ignored. The planet Earth is running out of space and these solutions can only enforce the survival of the planet.*" Said Mr. Bittre.

"*Have you thought about asking anyone first?*" Suggested David Icke. "*Are these not the same ideas that caused the Holocaust fifty years ago? I don't recall anybody I've ever met on this planet asking for a War. These decisions that super-powers make always seem to be derived from an inability to communicate and live peacefully on a planet that all of us live on. A lot of people don't want any of these new inventions.*"

Everyone nodded in agreement and turned their attention back to the looming figure of Mr. Bittre who was gradually and accidentally revealing his horrible smile to everyone in the dining room. Saliva and blood were dripping down his suit until it ran from his mouth and dripped onto the table.

"*I don't care what people want. I am here to explain how things are going to be.*" He snarled at everyone in the room. "*You have few choices in the future and by tomorrow afternoon you will all be staring in shock and holding your heads with dismay as the start of a new day will bring forth yet more shit to worry about. The plans for molecular graphic design are already in operation throughout Big New Yorker. I have the contracts and the work all lined up. Thanks to my clones nobody will know what's going on.*" The room became horribly silent again as everyone became hypnotised by the sight of the intense and disturbing features of Mr. Bittre. Who had seemingly grown larger and more menacing by the second. His black thick hair just beginning to scrape the surface of the ceiling.

Just at that moment the wooden oak door of the room opened and Tony Webb stepped in with Laurie Anderson standing next to him on one side with his youngest daughter Ely standing on the other. Ely held a huge bunch of colourful flowers out towards Mr. Bittre smiling and performed a quick pirouette. Then she bowed gracefully and presented the bouquet to Mr. Bittre with outstretched arms. Everyone in the room applauded.

"Excuse me Mr. Bittre but I think there's a taxi outside with your name on it." Said Tony smiling cheerfully and offering him the door.

After Mr. Bittre had been escorted through the hallway and out into the front of the house with Liz and David Lynch still enquiring as to what her phone number was. Tony came back into the dining room and sat at the table with yet another bottle of wine and offered it around the various guests whereby some of the Physicists were now hurriedly discussing the paintings that were hanging on one of the far walls.

Albert Einstein turned and looked bashfully at everyone sitting around the table and his eyes scanned the room at the various assortments of scientists sitting and drinking. They all seemed to be suddenly paying attention to the paintings in the room as well and were all buzzing with excitement over the appearance of two other children who came running in asking Tony who everyone was. Kate Bush and Naomi Klein followed with a small box of Quality Street that they had both found in the kitchen and Charles Darwin tagged along, led by the hand of Ely, who was explaining to everyone how to play the chord of E on her acoustic guitar.

Tony smiled across at Juliet Binoche, the French actress and at all the faces in the small moderate dining room and poured out some more wine as Albert moved back to the compact disc player and pushed a silver disc marked with *Offenbach 'Barcerolle'* on it in bold blue type. Ely danced around the room gracefully. The distant sounds of rock and roll could be heard coming from the lounge and the sparkling blue eyes of Charles Darwin lit up with bright enthusiasm as he clenched his hands into fists of excitement just hearing the opening guitar notes of Muddy Waters playing Mannish Boy.

"Oh splendid!" Said Charles Darwin grinning happily. *"Let's go and dance! I love this track!"*

As everyone ran out into the lounge to dance, moving out of the rush of guests Gyro stepped back inside the warm security of the kitchen in the house.

FRIDAY 7TH SEPTEMBER 2001
PROBABILITY / FIFTY-FIVE CANCRI

WISH YOU WERE HERE

I'm sorry that I hurt you please don't ask me why
I want to see you happy I want to see you shine
GARBAGE

THE DINER HOLISISTIC had tarnished slightly around the edges and reminded Static of everything he had ever seen on Earth all at the same time. Where ever he looked there seemed to be something named or reflected which made up a memory from his life. Every molecule could be seen through his vision.

"We are getting blamed for too much these days." Said a voice seated next to him. "I wish at times we could keep in touch with the pilots sent there but the size of the Universe only comes out at night."

Earth has helped us in the past. Which is why we are now helping in return. To say thank you.

"You all have missions yet they have to come when you are each ready and like dolls of Russia each will be unfolded once you sit and listen. Please don't get angry with us." Said Benedicto Perky Eco.

"There is a plan."

                        "…….*with us.*"

"*There is always a plan…*"

                        "*Static*"

"*Static*"

                  "*You've been everywhere already.*"

"In Heaven everything is fine..."
"Static"
"You've been here before - don't you remember?"

"Why do you think you're on Earth? You chose to go there for a holiday?"

"Static"

"Earth needs help..."

"Earth in each one of you always needs help.... cannot die.... over.......
...................."

"Earth in each one of you....

cannot die.... over.........................."
"Static"

"Help Earth.......................
"..................................."Static"
"YOU MUST WAKE UP"

YOU MUST WAKE UP...

BOOK VII

sTAtic waaaakke up

YOU MUST WAKE UP...

THE DINER HOLISISTIC had tarnished slightly around the edges and reminded Static of everything he had ever seen on Earth all at the same time.

YOU MUST WAKE UP...

BOOK VII

MORNING / UNCERTAINTY

YOU MUST WAKE UP...

The act of observation

affects that which is

being observed

FRIDAY 7TH SEPTEMBER 2001
PROBABILITY / CARISBROOKE

YOU MUST WAKE UP

We'll always be together no matter how far it seems
We'll always be together forever in electric dreams
PHIL OAKLEY / GEORGEO MORONER

FLASHING PETROL BLUE digital numbers on black blinked on and off. Illuminating the lounge with a pale glow in the moderate semi-detached house in Carisbrooke. The video-recorder had been unsettled in a house as Static and Gyro walked past the window, in the direction of the worn stone strewn path they used to walk to school on over fifteen years before. They both arrived at the pond where they had discovered the cycle of life through the magic of nature and frogspawn. Then continued to walk on under the overhanging trees that seemed to have never been pruned in all that time.

"Man...do you remember walking down here with Gill your first girlfriend and Sid when we were at school?" Asked Gyro as he bent down to pick-up a stone and throw it into the pond. The ripples spread out across the water.

"Every day I think about that...time." Said Static.

"What happened to her?" Asked Gyro squinting his eyes in the light rain.

"Apparently, she went to Latin America where she now lives... with her husband. I met her Mother down here a while ago. Did you know her Father died?" Static asked as he walked under the dripping leaves of the overhanging tree.

They both continued along the path in silence, through the graveyard that Static had once asked if Gyro would walk through at night for a million pounds. Back in the days when they attended the nearby school of Saint Thomas of Canterbury. As they headed across the road and along the path which led towards Carisbrooke Castle. Gyro found himself becoming overwhelmed by nostalgia after travelling around the world and through time.

They both began the traditional ascent towards the lush green scenery of the castle. Through fields filled with sheep who were running under the large oak trees for shelter from the September rain. Crows flapped and squawked overhead and as they walked up the narrow path Gyro noticed that even though he appeared to be in the wrong year, his home village of Carisbrooke seemed to be permanently fixed somewhere in the middle ages. Nothing had changed around the castle since he first ran around the ancient stonewalls during freezing cold days of cross-country at school.

They finally both arrived in the car park at the top of the steep hill where they were able to look down upon the whole surrounding area of Carisbrooke. The grey clouds were beginning to rain down onto the cold stone. Static pulled his raincoat together tightly to keep in the warmth of the sudden downpour, as they stood in the car park and looked over the surrounding hedge down onto the rooftops.

"So they're just going to chuck it all in the Solent then?" Asked Static. Referring to the black case of G-WIZ.

"Well, what else can they do?" Replied Gyro peering through the rain at the small windows as various lights were switched on all over the village.

"What about Australia? What's it like?" Asked Static with his hands in his pockets.

"Hot! Not like here. Yet I must say, I've never been anywhere quite like it." Replied Gyro.

"Duurh...was it a good time there?" Asked Static.

" Well, I got married. So I must have been doing something good-ish..." Replied Gyro as the rain fell onto his face and rolled down the back of his coat.

"And now you're divorced. You wouldn't go back?" Asked Static.

"That is the plan. I'll see when I get to Tibet." He said preferring to change the subject.

They both began their traditional walk around the castle in the rain. The magnitude of what had occurred at the Gods Providence tea rooms was slowly dawning on them. Static could not resist his usual run down the grassy slopes of the moat of the castle. He had watched Copper the Springer Spaniel do this the week before and was amazed at how much fun it really was. He came running back up the moat impersonating his dog with his tongue hanging out and joined Gyro who was still on the higher level of the green grass. His hands dug deep into the pockets of his long black overcoat.

"You're really off again? Why don't you ever stay in one place man? The whole world comes to you if you stay in one place for a while..." Said Static as they walked around another corner of the high castle walls.

"Yeah, but the world constantly needs saving...that's why I left. Adventures and stuff...you know..." Replied Gyro.

"I really missed you Gyro, when are you back from Tibet?" Asked Static.

"I should be back in 2001 by the time I leave Tibet..." Said Gyro as he smiled at his younger friend.

"Do you want us to come with you this time?" He asked.

"I'll be back before you know it! In fact, if all goes accordingly then I should see you at your house in about three days ago." Said Gyro slightly bewildered that this actually made sense to him at the moment.

"Will I remember any of this moment?" Asked Static. "I mean, if we all head backwards in time?"

"Static do you remember anything anyway?" Smiled Gyro.

"I remember this moment now!" Said Static tilting his head back and trying to catch the rain in his mouth. "...and I remember cross-bloody-country in cold weather like this, when we were at school!" He smiled, spinning around.

"Then you'll probably remember this conversation." Whispered Gyro. "I've got to meet Liz, Max and Dr. Bostrom outside the front of the castle in one hour. They should be here in Max's new Mini."

"I guess it's time for the last joint then." Said Static pulling out the worst rolled joint of his life and attempting to light it in the rain. "I always thought it was unlucky when a joint blew out because of the wind." Said Gyro inhaling on the joint. "Now I think it's the angels trying to stop me smoking. I think its time to stop smoking you know."

"Well, technically speaking... we never smoked this!" Replied Static smiling.

They continued smoking the joint and walking along the top of the moat, in the September English rain as dogs occasionally walked past them, walking their owners. Gyro suddenly remembered one of the infamous theories of his friend about the weather.

"Static! What was that thing you used to say about the rain when we were doing cross-country up here?" He asked focusing his attention on his friend.

"Oh the Tectonic-Freighters." Recalled Static. *"That the rain is really water leaking down from huge cargo ships you mean?"* Gyro suddenly found himself laughing so hard that he had almost forgotten how to. He stood in the rain and looked at his friend. Unable for a moment to control himself.

"Oh man, that's hilarious! You came up with that fifteen years ago and these days I keep wondering if someone will prove it someday." Gyro shook his head with disbelief.

"Oh yeah right! But you're going time-travelling with a dead body and that's okay!" He exclaimed back at his friend, laughing in the rain. They stared at each other as the cold rain came down harder.

"I should get back and check on Copper, he'll probably be going mental. I left him with Jack and Gertie, the neighbours across the road." Said Static.

"I'll bring him back a bone from Tibet!" Exclaimed Gyro eagerly.

"Promise?" Asked Static

"Promise..." Replied Gyro.

As they rounded the last corner of the castle together they could see the green Mini parked in front of the castle with Max and Liz crammed into the back seat smiling. Dr. Bostrom was driving and yet Max Born was continued to give orders from the back seat on how to control the vehicle. The two wet friends walked over to join the car. The rain was coming down now even harder. The good doctor opened the front door for Gyro to get in as the artist handed the joint back to Static.

"Has all the G-WIZ been dumped?" He asked to all three of them inside the car. Liz reached out and handed him a small sealed orange cellophane bag. *"All except the last packet for you and Darren's journey to Tibet."* Said Liz.

"Okay then...er..." He turned to look at Static as he stood in the rain. *"I'm off to Tibet! I'll see you on the 7th of September 2001."* Gyro laughed at the surrealness of the statement and looked at his watch nervously.

"Right." Replied Static slightly unconvinced.

"What are you up to today then?" Asked Gyro.

"Oh...I've got a few weeks until the parents are back to fix the VCR. Eraserhead got stuck in it and it won't play anything else. I guess I'll be walking up here with Copper before it gets dark and I'll wait until the clocks go back...and see you getting off the ferry at Cowes. Give us a ring, I'll come meet you...er...last week!" He said smiling.

"Splendid!" Said Gyro as they shook hands and hugged. Static was already crying but with the rain it was hard to see if it had not been just the rain falling down his face. Gyro climbed into the warm interior of the Mini. Dr. Bostrom merrily beeped the horn as they reversed back and then sped off down the road towards Newport. Static watched until the car had disappeared into the distance, then began the walk back to Kitbridge Road in the rain, smoking the last of the joint and wondering how he could write down everything before the time shift occurred and it would all be lost.

As he walked along Hinton Road he thought about how himself and Static used to walk along the road to school every day for eight years and rounded the corner leading down onto Kitbridge Road, at the house marked number one he knocked on the door and could already here the yelps of excitement from Copper as his middle-aged neighbours Jack and Gertie Madden opened the front door. The Springer Spaniel leapt up all over him excited, his whole body wagging as if he was about to explode. He patted and stroked the dog attempting to calm him down.

"I hope he wasn't any trouble." Said Static as Copper bounced like a cartoon character.

"He was a pleasure to have in the house." Said Mr. Madden the tall friendly Irishman. *"Anytime!"* Said Mrs Madden standing next to him smiling.

Static thanked them both and walked back across the road with Copper leaping frantically up and down, his tongue hanging out of his mouth in the same style that Static had been mimicking up at the castle. He had not seen his owner for three days and had decided that it was about time to communicate his important mission details to him when they got back to the house. Regarding the location of Holly Grail.

Walking into the house of his parents Static fumbled around for the dog bowl in the corner of the kitchen and filled it with food for the dog to eat. On the table in the dining-room paper was scattered all over the place as Static attempted to tidy up the various manuscripts and film scripts he had been working on since his parents had left the house and headed over to Lymington.

Static thought about the film-script he had had sent to London and wondered why Ray Connif had not called back to say if he had received it or not. Maybe a book would work better instead of a film he thought. The Tectonic-Freighters would have to be definitely included in it somewhere. Static decided that after all that had been happening he could at least wait until Gyro turned up three days ago. He had been exhausted after the three breakfasts meeting in Gods Providence.

Then he walked into the lounge and attempted to eject the video of Eraserhead from the machine much to no avail. The moment Static switched the VCR on the tape automatically moved into play mode and he decided that it could easily wait until tomorrow. He sat down on the sofa and looked around the lounge as the Lynch masterpiece began its second screening. It felt fantastic to be back on the island after the experience of London. Fresh air and castles. He could hear the cold rain already lashing against the glass of the front window. Static noticed how dark the interior of the room had become thanks to the heavy dark clouds forming outside. Gradually he became hypnotised by the flashing of the blue numbers from the VCR. Static decided to have a quick nap before walking the dog. He lay down on the sofa and closed his eyes. Just for five minutes. Flashing petrol blue digital numbers on a black background blinked on and off. Illuminating the lounge with a pale glow in the moderate semi-detached house in Carisbrooke.

ONE PART OF THIS STORY IS NOT TRUE...

...BRITT'S DEAL WITH PARAMOUNT IS YET TO BE SIGNED

EMPEROR PENGUIN/1832

Aptenodytes Forsteri

The largest penguin, the Emperor stands waist high to a man, and weighs between 20 and 45 kg. Well adapted to an icy climate, these birds live along the coasts and neighbouring seas of Antarctica. They breed during the perpetual darkness of the Antarctic winter, gathering at rookeries during the months of April and May.

When they are courting they display brilliant orange ear patches. They do not build nests or establish territories. Within a few hours after the female lays a single egg, the male positions the egg on top of his feet and covers it with a warm fold of feathered abdominal skin. Shortly thereafter, the female travels over the ice to the open sea to feed, leaving the male to incubate the egg. About two months later she will return to feed and brood the newly hatched chick. They are also able to fold time from any point in the known Universe.

PENGUIN BISCUITS/1960

McVitius Snackius

Arrnot biscuits in Australia repackaged them as TIM-TAMS and I'm sorry but they are nowhere near as fine in taste or even packaging. Without Penguin biscuits the entire education system in the United Kingdom would grind to a halt along with the entire dentistry profession no doubt. There is of course the joke of marine information, which goes like this: Question: Why is it that polar bears do not eat penguins? Answer: Because they cannot get the wrappers off! Boom boom. Telling this joke in South America or even Antarctica is not a wise move but beats a slap around the face with a wet fish.

KING PENGUIN/1833

Benedicto Perky Eco

Despite the name, King penguins are not the giants of all penguins; those are the Emperor penguins. Their average population is 3.2 million and growing strong. King penguins are considered stable, but they do have predators. These animals are the usual suspects: leopard seals, skuas and petrels and Tax Inspectors.

King penguins feed upon crustaceans, small fish, squid and plankton and can be found in the Periantarctic and Subantarctic islands year round. Despite their scientific name, patagonica, there's no evidence that they ever lived in Patagonia. Earlier reports of their breeding on the South Sandwhich Islands, where they were recorded by the Eights (1833) in 1829-30, lie far south of their present range, and seem an improbable breeding ground for birds, which normally form colonies in the shelter of dense tussock grass.

Males and female penguins are monomorphic. Which means that they like to listen to the same music. Sorry, I meant it means that they look the same. Like politicians.

ACKNOWLEDGEMENTS

This project could never have even begun if not for the production assistance of Martin 'two sheds' Griffin, Nick and TINSTAR DESIGN. The New Forest. McColls foodstores. Housekeys to Medowlands by JMA. Originally typed on a Bridgitt manual typewriter in Berlin courtesy of Hilke 'please I'm trying to sleep' Schilling in 1999 then transffered over to a Computer in September 2002, using Microsoft Software WINDOWS on Fujitsu by Siemens & Euroline. (I prefer the typewriter myself) Transferred again through Quark Xpress (big cheer) via Adobe Photoshop (men on the Moon? You must be joking!) on Tinstar Design's new Apple Macs. Cover design by Liam J Madden / Hilke Schilling / Britt Johannes based on an original design by Liam J Madden. Cover Art Direction by Liam J Madden and Martin Griffin.

During the writing and production Liam J Madden consumed: Pure Cod Liver Oil capsules by Seven Seas. Good health - naturally! Vitamin B12 by Holland & Barrett and his family for food, patience, support and Axl the dog. McVities Biscuits. Plain, Milk Chocolate Digestives. 8 Penguin selection packet. Tetley Round Tea Bags - naturally rich in antitoxidants. Coffee by Kenco. Nouvelle toilet paper - soft on you, soft on nature. Pasta & a variety of fresh vedgetables. Johnsons Baby soap. Semi-skimmed milk. Liam was interrupted three times by a shrill telephone by British Telecom which was luckily intercepted by an answer-machine produced by Southwestern Bell Freedom Phone. Images of Nick Bostrom, Stephen Hawking and Sir Roger Penrose (A knight of mathmatics? Puuurlease!) are courtesy of Oxford University Press. Images of Max Born, Max Plank, Werner Heisenberg, Albert Einstein, Erwin Schrodinger courtesy of J. J. O'Connor and E. F. Robertson.

LONDON

Mrs. Fawcett. Steve Fawcett and Jo Fawcett of Maxim, Empire, MOJO and Loaded magazine for saving my life and everything else. Lonely Goat; Deborah Hogan & Andy Cronk and Mrs Cronk. Andrew Holmes at Mo Wax for DJ Shadow. Grant Fulton, Jo Hey and Sid. Bill Williamson a great Editor and the staff of Midweek / Ms London magazine. Bruce. Tom Chance. Juliet

Reiden. Cathy Howes for showing me how to pay a telephone bill. Wendy Copping. Diane Parker. Kirk Blows for football. Ben Thompson for the free music. Julian Cope for the inspiration. Gideon London. Gyles and Lennie Lee for the Channel Four documentary. The artists and musicians of Ellingfort Road Hackney, for taking me to places I nearly didn't see. American Mike and Jo. Alan Pike. Sam Dightam and The Eight-Track Cartridge Family for not being serious.

My surrogates in London; The Marshalls the nicest family in the world; Korda, Vanda, William and Molly & Rammi. Michael Limmer and Michelle Le Moigne. Tim the Rastafarian. Joss, his Italian girlfriend and his two baby daughters. French Egor. The artists Ben and Chris. Valentina. Thomas. David and John. Sue. Rob and Saron. INCHWORM; the greatest jazz band in the Western world were; Michael 'Sharky-Boy' Limmer. *Duke Garwood. *Paul May. Anyone who drank in the Samuel Pepys between 1997-1999. Tony. Lara./Alan Pike & Liz Broberg for cats, love & beer. London the first time with Vanda Peterson; Nancy, Coco, everyone at BMG music and publishing. Alex & The Orb; Alex Patterson and Slash, Martin from 808 State, Brix Smith, John Bonham's son, Robert Plant, Annie Lennox, All About Eve, David Bowie. Smash Hits. Talking Heads. Tom Waits. John Cleese & Monty Python. Prominent Features. Jack Docherty. Morwena Banks & ABSOLUTELY. The French people; Steffanie, the ex-prisoner of San Francisco, beauties of Paris. The Bon-Bons and Bon-Bon Kaotikai. The Box. LipstickBuddha. Ian with the missing front teeth. The princes and princesses of Germany; Hilke, Florentina, Steffanie, Jennifer, Jason and his brother, Pete, Toot, anyone who waited in Ellingfort Road and had a cup of tea; Critical Mass & Reclaim The Streets. The assorted crew of The Factory 2. The Eagle Factory and Broa Sams' The Grey Area. The assorted Communities of Hackney. Asian Dub Foundation. American Lynda, Emanuella Rossi, The people of Columbia Market and Brick Lane, the flowers of Columbia Market. Rob, Sarron and family. All the kings horses. Melissa. The Irish musicians who brought The Penguin Café Orchestras music to The Pub on The Park but NOT the landlord of Pub on the Park. Tina the cat. Grant Fulton, his daughter Sid and Mother Jo Hey. Christopher Morris for Blue Jam. Blue & Red, the cats. The woman from Greece who was known as John Travolta to me but Irene to Mike. Mike's Mother in Norwich & Glen. Anyone who drank beer on London Fields between 1997 and 1999. Especially in the Summer! Linda. Kevin of the piercings and articulate humour. The staff of every pub in the area of Hackney with the exception of the Landlord of The George. Liz Broberg and her laugh, Laurence Dodd, Anthony antpeople are the warriors and Laurence's sister, Danielle Holton-Picard, Alan Pike, Steve

Fawcett, Tamsin McNeil. Karl. American Mike. Jo Berry. Tom. Any music released on El Records, especially MOMUS. Evendine College 34 Oxford Street and 145 Oxford Street.

* Appear courtesy of Leo Records 2001 - Buy the CD of Carolyn Hume and Paul May - ZERO

AMERICA

New York; Sara Stemen, Simon Poulter, San Francisco; Dennis Mobley and Yumiko, Josh, Rob and Jill Toyoshiba, Corpus Christi; Jessica Dirkin for terrible jokes. Washington DC; George Bush and all the staff at the White House for making life on planet Earth so interesting. The guy in New York (not the bloke, but the guy) who replied 'Go buy a book buddy!' when I asked him for directions to St. Marks Place. Along with the assorted new stand vendors of New York who must be doing the most dangerous job in the entire world apart from being a miner. Also the crew of the Staten Island Ferry.

IRELAND

Cousins Colleen and Maria Madden. Uncle Eamon, Auntie Madge. Cousin Dermot and family, Cousin Brian, Cousin John Rogers and family and Cousin Margaret and family. Luke and Ivan. All families from Ireland especially The Gallaghers in Co. Leitrim. Uncle Danny Reagan, Cousin Brian and family in Fermoy, Cork. Chris De Burgh. Phil Lynott. Kimberly Biscuits. Guinness. The assorted teachers of Gaelic language and the Irish Salmon, although not the English salmon that sometimes intermingles.

THE BEAUTIFUL SOUTH

Cousin Ivor Kelly and his family. Cousin Al and family. Auntie Phil, Uncle Dinny. Uncle Billy, Nora and Siobhan.

Southampton Institute of Higher Education; Tony Hunt, John Willis and the graphic designers of 1985-1987. The entire population of Le Havre and the students of Le Havre Art College in France for one of the best Summers of my life.

ISLE OF WIGHT

My brother John Madden for an eventful life with apologies. Chunky, Roz, Paul, Maggie & the assorted dancers along The Mall including Debbie Pummel & her sisters. Grandfather Sean Madden and Grandmother and Michael Collins. Grandfather Reagan and Grandmother. Helen Hoey and Geoff Hoey. Ann Madden and John Angel and Enya. Sammy my God-daughter and Siobahn Hoey my niece and J. J. my nephew for not expecting too much from an Uncle. Bambi, Dawn and Rosie. Emma Rich and sister Michelle. Max Brennan & Alison. Amanda, Remi and Zoe. David Icke & family. Tony Webb and family in Shorwell for expanding my library and being a true hero as well as making me laugh. Julie and Lotti. Yvonne Carter and family. Anyone who worked in The Crispin, Newport between 1977 and 1979. Tracie Heal. St. Thomas of Canterbury Primary School. Stephen Webb, Karl Wherry, David Wilcox, Stephen Cross, Dario Cretella, Lee James, Gavin Long.

Liz Murphy for being there with slacks, Sam Dightam, Bernadette Tagart, Catherine Saunders. Mr Dimarco. Denis Jenkins. Peter Pontin and assorted brothers. Tim Dadswell and family. Mr. Greenwood. All the nuns of the Isle of Wight, thanks for your grace and guidance. Father Quinn for Holy Communion. Darren Steed. Cash and Carry. Mrs. Day Philip and Caroline. Julianne Molloy for my first erection. Mark Smith. Excalibur! Debbie Pummel and her gorgeous sisters. The original Damn Those Welders crew. Rod Gammon and his wife. Sister Bernard for French. Sister Dolores. Sister Gerard for Blackgang Chine. Heidhi Marke and family and The Bonzo Dog Doo Dah Band. Deborah Wavell and Martin Thearle. Joanne Kennedy and family. Karen 'no really, we'll be friends at 30 honest!' Sidwell and Jonathan Sidwell & parents, Lucy Adams & sister & family. The Kennedy clan. Gillian Attril & Mother. Linda Jolliffe, Martin Griffin, James and the Kit-Kat Club. Becki Fulton and Frazer Fulton. Everyone at Hospital Radio in St. Marys Hospital. Everyone in Parkhurst Prison and Saint Mary's Hospital. Cobwebs Nightclub. Bambi, Dawn and Rose. Copper the dog. Simon Richardson and his family for milk.

GERMANY

Everybody who works in a swimming pool in Berlin for the greatest swimming experience known to man. Hilke Schilling for teaching me to swim. Florentine Hoppe. Marion Schilling for the use of her VCR. Hilke's Muter for teaching me how to breathe again. The Johannes family, especially Britt the DJ. Balisto Biscuits. Fresh vedgtables without plastic wrapping that seem to have disappeared from England even though they won the War (yeah right). The snow of Berlin and the staircases. The man who came out of the pub in Berlin and trampled over a car over and over after his wife had been killed in a car accident and was not arrested by the police proving that justice does exist but only it seems in the least likely of places.

NEW ZEALAND

My class in Auckland at The Dominion School of English. Especially Kotaro. Along with the AOTEAROA International College of Studies. Although NOT Andrew Williamson who is a raving psychopath who should have biscuit crumbs poured into his bed on a regular basis. The staff of Starbucks Coffee shop and of course Borders book store for allowing me to read nearly every book in the shop without paying for it and for allowing me to teach conversational English in the cafe although I understand the cafe staff were not entirely happy with the way an American company established itself in Auckland.

AUSTRALIA

Allanah Wesson and Kurt, Chris, Gregg, Deb, Suzanne and Noah Taylor - a great actor. Jackie Holton-Picard. Paul and the enigmatic Grant Holton-Picard. Simon 'Woody' Woods. New Zealand Adrian, Thomathy, Katie Hoskins, assorted Andrews. Timothy, Suzanne the hippy, Vincent, Lisa, Debbie, Alanah Wesson, Kurt Wesson and Chris. Pete, Cathy and Rick. The coach-driver who joked all the way to Ulurah. Anyone I met in Australia between 1995 and 1999. Friends of Woody. Michael Hutchence RIP, Kylie Minogue Korda Marshall and all assorted Mushroom Record molecules. The aboriginal people of Australia and Alice. The disciples of Ulurah of New Years Eve 1997 in Ayers Rock, especially Ben. Johnny Morris for Animal Magic. The crew of The Magazine Group in Balmaine, especially Suzanne Hodge for cheering up the entire world and saying 'Oh my GodFather'. MACTEMPS in Sydney. Cafe Open. Round The Clock. All the cafes in the Newtown area including the people who smiled and sang and waved at me everyday as I walked to work reinforcing the idea that Australia is indeed the lucky country, unless of course you happen to be Aboriginal.

SERVICE IN PEACE AT THE DINER HOLISTIC

NOREEN GALLAGHER *for opening my mind up, see you later* JAMES' MOTHER MARY *at The Barnaby's Picture Library for being English* GRANDMOTHER REAGAN *Granny Reagan and Husband who was Yoda* SEAN MADDEN *and wife Grandfather and friend to Michael Collins* NOEL MADDEN *Uncle and brilliant story-teller* MAUREEN MADDEN *Auntie and biscuit enthusiast* MR.FAWCETT *Steve's Dad* MR.WELLS *The Most patient Art Teacher in the world* MR.CRONK *Andy's Dad* JEFFREY BERNARD *For ALWAYS getting his copy in on time, everyone else lied and The Coach and Horses* PETER COOK *For being the funniest earthling on the planet* DUDLEY MOORE *For being the shortest* MR.CARTER *Father of Yvonne, Gary and Sean* RUSTY *the mad-bastard dog* DOUGLAS ADAMS *A true visionary* QUENTIN CRISP *for inspiration and teaching me the importance of politeness* MICHAEL ENGLAND *friend* BRIAN DAY *the calmest neighbour* IAN KENNEDY *the other funniest man on the planet* MR.ATTRIL *Gills Father threeee double nine eight*

THE FIFTH DIMENSION

Britt Johannes as she journeys on towards Dagadoogoo and the clones to come. Thanks for helping a great number of people to have their minds gradually opened up by your unique perspective of the world and living up to the expression 'Tu bist cald zer ice' as written by Mahfred Krugg. Juliet Binoche for making films and not just staying in her room and fiddling with her hair or doing croche or something. Hilke Shilling for proving that it is possible to be reincarnated and teaching me how to swim. All aliens and pilots of UFOs throughout the known Universe for that fantastic display I witnessed over the Dominion Park in Auckland along with the display over Sydney in Australia which seemed to prove that yes indeed UFOs & aliens do exist but they're just very shy. The staff of McGraths.

CHAPTER TITLE / BAND

YOU MUST WAKE UP//KATE BUSH NO ALARMS AND NO SURPRISES PLEASE//RADIOHEAD THE HAIRSTYLE OF THE DEVIL//MOMUS VISITING TIME IS OVER//THE CURE SPIRITS IN THE MATERIAL WORLD//THE POLICE THE PLANET OF SOUND//THE PIXIES THE REVOLUTION WILL NOT BE TELEVISED//GILL SCOTT-HERON I WANT TO BE A PART OF IT//FRANK SINATRA I CAN FEEL ONE OF MY TURNS COMING ON//PINK FLOYD WHATEVER HAPPENED TO REAL LIFE?//MOSE ALLISON BRIGHTER LATER//NICK DRAKE I WAS LOOKING HANDSOME SHE WAS LOOKING LIKE AN EROTIC VULTURE//THE PIXIES THAT WAS THE RIVER AND THIS IS THE SEA//THE WATERBOYS A CHURCH NOT MADE BY HANDS//THE WATERBOYS HOW CAN THE ANGELS GET TO SLEEP WHEN THE DEVIL LEAVES THE PORCH LIGHT ON?//TOM WAITS THE ECSTACY OF DANCING FLEAS//PENGUIN CAFE ORCHESTRA WELCOME TO THE OCCUPATION//REM FEELING YOURSELF DISENTIGRATE//THE FLAMING LIPS DEATH IN VEGAS//FLYING DRUGS WON'T CHANGE YOU RELIGION WON'T CHANGE YOU//TALKING HEADS SIX GNOSSIENNES:NO.2 AVEC ETONNEMENT//ERIK SATIE:ANNE QUEFFELEC I LOVE EVERYBODY ESPECIALLY YOU//LYLE LOVETT THE OTHER SIDE OF MIDNIGHT//YARGO WHEN WILL I GROW OLD GRACEFULLY?//UNLABELLED/OUT OF MY MIND ON DOPE AND SPEED//JULIAN COPE THE NEW FRONTIER//DONALD FAGEN THINKING ABOUT SEX AGAIN//THE WAITRESSES SIMPLY EVERYONE IS ON COCAINE//THE ENGLISH POET SCARY MONSTERS AND SUPER CREEPS//DAVID BOWIE AT HOME WITH RAY CONNIF//RAY CONNIF & HIS ORCHESTRA LISTEN TO THE VOICE OF BUDDHA//THE HUMAN LEAGUE INCHWORM//INCHWORM ARTISTS ONLY//TALKING HEADS SCISSORS CUT PAPER BUT PAPER WRAPS ROCK//MOMUS DON'T YOU POINT THAT RAY-GUN AT ME//THOMAS DOLBY LOST WEEKEND//LLOYD COLE & THE COMMOTIONS FANFARE FOR THE COMMON MAN//MEXICO CITY ORCHESTRA/ENRIQUE BATIZ MOVING THE RIVER//PREFAB SPROUT THE CARPENTERS //CALLING OCCUPANTS OF INERPLANETARY CRAFT LISTEN TO THE VOICE OF BUDDHA//THE HUMAN LEAGUE TOMORROW WILL BE LIKE TODAY//MONIE MARKE EINSTEIN-A-GO-GO//LANDSCAPE THE LOVE FOR THREE ORANGES//LEIUTENANT KIJE//LONDON SYMPHONY ORCHESTRA/SIR NEVILLE MARRINER

THE LOW-TECH SOUNDTRACK

CHAPTER SUBTITLES / ARTISTS / TITLE / TRACK

EDIE BRICKEL/SHOOTING RUBBER BANDS AT THE MOON//WHAT I AM **THE CRUEL SEA**/THE HONEYMOON IS OVER//DELIVER MAN **TRIO**/TRIO//BROKEN HEARTS FOR YOU AND ME **LEE MARVIN**/PAINT YOUR WAGON **MOSE ALLISON**/THE BEST OF MOSE ALLISON//JUST LIKE LIVIN' **STEELY DAN**/KATY LIED//DADDY DON'T LIVE IN THAT NEW YORK CITY NO MORE **THE VIOLENT FEMMES**/WHY DO BIRDS SING?//I LIKE AMERICAN MUSIC **THE VELVET UNDERGROUND**/THE VELVET UNDERGROUND//VENUS IN FURS **THE SUGARCUBES**/HERE TODAY TOMORROW NEXT WEEK//PLANET **THE SUNDAYS**/CAN'T BE SURE//READING WRITING ARITHMETIC **JOHN LENNON**/MINDGAMES// INSTANT KARMA **DAVID BYRNE**/ FEELINGS//EVERYTHING IS FI-NITE **THE WAITRESSES**/BRUISEOLOGY//THEY'RE ALL OUT OF LIQUOR, LET'S FIND ANOTHER PARTY **THE CRANBERRIES**/EVERYBODY IS DOING IT SO WHY CAN'T WE//DREAMS **PINK FLOYD**/DARK SIDE OF THE MOON//DARK SIDE OF THE MOON **DAMON ALBAR**/BEST OF BLUR// SONG 1/ **GARY NUMAN**/THE PLEASURE PRINCIPLE/OBSERVER/ ONE **THE HADDOCK**/EP: DEAR GOD HELP ME/**BILLY BRAGG**/LIFE'S A RIOT// THE MILKMAN OF HUMAN KINDNESS//**JAH WOBBLE** & INVADERS OF THE HEART/**SINEAD O'CONNOR**//VISIONS OF YOU **THE THE**/DUSK// BECAUSE THE NIGHT **YARGO**/ BODYBEAT// GET THERE **CAMPER VAN BEETHOVEN**/CAMPER VAN BEETHOVEN//TAKE THE SKINHEADS BOWLING **LOU REED**/NEW YORK//ROMEO HAD JULIETTE **THOMAS DOLBY**/THE FLAT EARTH//THE FLAT EARTH **FLUKE**/ NEON//BULLET/ **SUZANNE VEGA**/SUSANNE VEGA//CRACKING **REM**/DOCUMENT// THERE'S SOMETHING STRANGE GOING ON TONIGHT **BJORK**/DEBUT// HUMAN BEHAVIOUR **LOOPER** /LOOPER//THE GIRL FROM AMONGST THE PILLARS **CROWDEDHOUSE**/CROWDEDHOUSE//TELL ME ALL THE THINGS/**GOMEZ**/BRING IT ON//FIFTY-FOOT WOBBLE **KATE BUSH**/ THE DREAMING//SAT IN YOUR LAP **JOE JACKSON**/NIGHT & DAY// CANCER **PJ HARVEY**/RID OF ME//PUT IT ON **AIMEE MAN**/MAGNOLIA //ATMOSPHERE **THE BREEDERS**/THE LAST SPLASH//DO YOU LOVE ME NOW? **LUSCIOUS JACKSON**/ ELECTRIC HONEY//ALIEN LOVER **MERCURY REV**/DESERTER'S SONGS//HOLES **RICKY NELSON**/THE HITS//DREAMTOWN **ANNIE LENNOX**/DAVID STEWART/SAVAGE/// NEED A MAN **PETER GABRIEL**/GENESIS //COUNTING OUT TIME **TOM**

PETTY & THE HEARTBREAKERS/WILDFLOWERS//*TIME TO GET GOING* **DONOVAN**/THE BEST OF DONOVAN//SUNSHINE SUPERMAN **LYLE LOVETT**/I LOVE EVERYBODY//*PENGUINS* **LAURIE ANDERSON**/BIG SCIENCE//*BIG SCIENCE* **MANU CHAO**/MANU CHAO//*BANGING ON A BONGO* **KAREN CARPENTER**/THE BEST OF THE CARPENTERS//*CALLING OCCUPANTS* **GRACE JONES**//*THE APPLE STRETCHING* **JONI MITCHELL**/ CLOUDS//*BIG YELLOW TAXI* **LLOYD COLE**/EASY PIECES//*LOST WEEKEND* **NEIL YOUNG**/ HARVEST//*ARE YOU READY FOR THE COUNTRY?* **THE WATERBOYS**/ROOM TO ROAM// *STARTING TO SEE A BIGGER PICTURE* **THEY MIGHT BE GIANTS**/LINCOLN//*SHOEHORN WITH TEETH* **FRANK BLANK**/TEENAGER OF THE YEAR//*HEADACHE* **GILL SCOTT-HERON**/GLORY//*CHANGE* **MONIE MARKE**/ PUSH THE BUTTON/*TEACH ME* **GARBAGE**/VERSION.2//*PUSH IT* **PHIL OAKLEY**/GEORGEO MORONA //*ELECTRIC DREAMS*

NOBEL PEACE PRIZE ACCEPTANCE SPEECH

Your Majesty, Member of the Nobel Committee, Brothers and Sisters:

I am very happy to be here with you today to receive the Nobel Prize for peace. I feel honoured, humbled, and deeply moved that you should give this important prize to a simple monk from Tibet. I am no one special. But I believe the prize is a recognition of the true value of altruism, love, compassion, and non-violence, which I try to practice, in accordance with the teachings of the Buddha and the sages of India and Tibet. I accept the prize with profound gratitude on behalf of all of the oppressed everywhere and for all those who struggle for freedom and work for world peace. I accept it as a tribute to the man who founded the modern tradition of non-violent action for change- Mahatma Gandhi-whose life taught and inspired me.

And, of course, I accept it on behalf of the six million Tibetan people, my brave countrymen and women inside Tibet, who have suffered and continue to suffer so much. They confront a calculated and systematic strategy aimed at the destruction of their national and cultural identities. The prize reaffirms our conviction that with truth, courage, and determination as our weapons, Tibet will be liberated.

No matter what part of the world we come from, we are all basically the same human beings.

We all seek happiness and try to avoid suffering. We have basically the same human needs and concerns. All of us human beings want freedom and the right to determine our own destiny as individuals and as peoples. That is human nature. The great changes that are taking place in the world, from Eastern Europe to Africa, is a clear indication of this. ...

As a Buddhist monk, my concern extends to all members of the human family and, indeed, to all the sentient beings who suffer. I believe all suffering is caused by ignorance. People inflict pain on others in the selfish pursuit of their happiness or satisfaction.

Yet true happiness comes from a sense of peace and contentment, which in turn must be achieved through the cultivation of altruism, of love and compassion, and elimination of ignorance, selfishness, and greed.

The problems we face today, violent conflicts, destruction of nature, poverty, hunger, and so on, are human created problems which can be resolved through human effort, understanding, and a development of a sense of brotherhood and sisterhood. We need to cultivate a universal responsibility for one another and the planet we share. Although I have found my own Buddhist religion helpful in generating love and compassion, even for those we consider our enemies, I am convinced that everyone can develop a good heart and a sense of universal responsibility with or without religion.

With the ever-growing impact of science in our lives, religion and spirituality have a greater role to play reminding us of our humanity. There is no contradiction between the two. Each gives us valuable insights into each other. Both science and the teaching of the Buddha tell us of the fundamental unity of all things. This understanding is crucial if we are to take positive and decisive action on the pressing global concern with the environment. I believe all religions pursue the same goals, that of cultivating human goodness and bringing happiness to all human beings. Though the means may appear different, the ends are the same. As we enter the final decade of this century, I am optimistic that the ancient values that have sustained mankind are today reaffirming themselves to prepare us for a kinder, happier twenty-first century.

I pray for all of us, oppressor and friend, that together we succeed in building a better world through human understanding and love, and that in doing so we may reduce the pain and suffering of all sentient beings.

Thankyou.

Tenzin Gyatso

14th Dalai Lama of Tibet December 10, 1989, Oslo, Norway, Earth

FROM THE AUTHOR

On September 3rd 2001 I travelled to New Zealand from the Isle of Wight as part of a one man show I was performing entitled *'10 Questions For God'*. Which is a series of interviews with members of the public all over the world answering the same ten questions. The project has so far covered around 20 countries including Australia, the United States and Russia. After arriving in New Zealand and spending an enjoyable time in Auckland, I decided to head onto New York. I was told by STA Travel in Auckland that I would have to wait two days for clearance on changing my ticket from a return to London to New York. I waited two days. On 11th September 2001 I walked down the high street of Auckland in the warm heat of the morning towards the travel agents and watched a scene from the movie Independence Day replayed for my benefit. People stopped their cars in the street and just stood still. They all stood on sidewalks and stared at televisions in the kind of way a person does when they know something important has happened. I'm a person who tends to ignore television as much as I can.

I walked into the travel agent looking forward to my trip to New York. STA Travel informed me that there was no news from London regarding the ticket exchange and to come back tomorrow. When I walked out onto the sunny streets of Auckland and looked up to see what it was that everybody standing in the streets was staring at I felt a huge wave of deja vu pass through me as I watched a Jumbo Jet crash into the World Trade Centre. A building I used to walk past on a daily basis on the way to work when I once lived in New York. After some investigating I understood from the travel agents that the plane I had been waiting to be booked onto had been the ill-fated *'hijacked'* plane. A few friends were waiting in America for my arrival and I spent the following weeks in a backpackers attempting to locate them and let them know I was fine. That day my life changed, as it did for a lot of people. Before I had left England for New Zealand I had a dream. A book on dreams in my hometown of Newport suggested that I should not go travelling for two weeks or else I would die. These days I listen to my dreams.

After such an event I decided to spend some time in Auckland. For 6 months I taught English at the Aotearoa College waiting for the airline to sort out my ticket. Although this book is dedicated to my long-term friend, the Irish writer Noreen Gallagher who died in a car crash I would like to also dedicate it to the various members of staff I worked with at the college and the various travellers I met living at the back packers there. Especially the teacher Hong Jin Wu who helped me to understand that not everyone Chinese hates Tibetans. Heading for a country for two weeks and staying 6 months I would recommend to anyone who enjoys time-travel. This book has not been an attempt to exploit the memory of what happened to those who died or suffered during this event but has been written from the hopeful perspective of myself and others who escaped with our lives in tact simply by the delay of waiting. Our lives were changed by the change of events. It seemed someone has to be used as a scapegoat when things go wrong in life and I believe that the world would sleep safer at night knowing that blame is never the answer. Hence the appearance of the Dalai Lama in this book and the introduction to Tibetan philosophy which I read thanks to my brother John Madden who helped me through the hardest part of my life after my friend was killed in a car crash by the simple act of giving me The Tibetan Book of Living and Dying by Sogyal Rinpoche to read. It is my belief that such memories as September 11th cannot be owned by any one person or government and I have used artistic licence on more than one occasion to write about an experience which I hope occurs on a regular basis that of escape and hope. The Earth is indeed an incredible planet.

It seemed for three days after the event, that the reality of World War III could easily become apparent. Nobody on Earth can claim ownership of history. Neither can they own the air that you breath or the land that is walked on by every living part of creation, but by jove, they are trying aren't they. Love them all. As we continue onto the next millenium the media machine has stepped up a gear into overdrive. You rarely hear on The News of the birth of a baby or the success of a marriage or how someone took out the garbage and walked back safely to the house. This does not sell newspapers. However it should also be remembered that there's no smoke without fire. My love is spread over the country of Germany like a big woolly blanket and with others across the entire planet who need forgiveness more than most others for the suffering of the last century. I agree with David Icke when he said, 'I have never met anyone in fifteen years of travelling this planet who wanted a War.' The lease of *'peace'* that we have known since 1945 needs to be extended. A person only has to travel across the world to see that War is a crap idea. Warm coffee with milk is a nice idea although Chinese people tend to inform me that tea is better for a person. Europe is fantastic and really does not need to be reminded of the horror, otherwise it cannot sleep at night. When I visited Berlin I met a city that filled me with hope for the future. It is necessary for a person's life to forgive people for the mistakes of the past and move on. No one is to blame.

Also love goes out to all the students who allowed me to teach them English and Art over the last fifteen years and to my parents who persuaded a foetus to turn into a baby and then love that child into turning into them. The process I watch occurring all around me everyday. Love kills the demons.

There is more than one side to every story.

History is written by the winners. In my opinion, it comes in waves.

Liam Joseph Madden
November 2002
Meadowlands
Earth

Liam Joseph Madden once attended the wedding of Stephen Hawking at Cambridge University by complete accident and he would like to apologise for getting in the way when the professor had his wedding photographs taken. SAVE CHANGES © Copyright of Liam J Madden 2003. Any two particles that are free will accelerate towards each other. Why not get on the electronic mailing list for the column Gyro Speaks please. savechanges@yahoo.co.uk or you can just buy the book. Oh please go on, I can't afford to stick a free chocolate bar on the front.

SAVE CHANGES AGAIN
THE TIME DISCIPLES SEARCH FOR GYRO & THE HOLY GRAIL

continues the adventures of The Gyro Chronicles

Lightning Source UK Ltd.
Milton Keynes UK
UKOW02f1238181116

287978UK00002B/445/P

9 781452 016887